Many dangers lurk in the deep.
The worst of them are human.

"*Deep Shadow* is a novel that begs to be read
in one sitting."—*The Clarion-Ledger*

"The story races to its conclusion."—*The Miami Herald*

"*Deep Shadow* might have you catching your breath next
time the shrubbery in your backyard starts to rustle."
—*St. Petersburg Times*

continued . . .

TITLES BY RANDY WAYNE WHITE

NONFICTION

FICTION AS RANDY STRIKER

DEEP SHADOW

RANDY WAYNE WHITE

BERKLEY BOOKS

NEW YORK

THE BERKLEY PUBLISHING GROUP
Published by the Penguin Group
Penguin Group (USA) Inc.
375 Hudson Street, New York, New York 10014, USA

Penguin Group (Canada), 90 Eglinton Avenue East, Suite 700, Toronto, Ontario M4P 2Y3, Canada
(a division of Pearson Penguin Canada Inc.)
Penguin Books Ltd., 80 Strand, London WC2R 0RL, England
Penguin Group Ireland, 25 St. Stephen's Green, Dublin 2, Ireland (a division of Penguin Books Ltd.)
Penguin Group (Australia), 250 Camberwell Road, Camberwell, Victoria 3124, Australia
(a division of Pearson Australia Group Pty. Ltd.)
Penguin Books India Pvt. Ltd., 11 Community Centre, Panchsheel Park, New Delhi—110 017, India
Penguin Group (NZ), 67 Apollo Drive, Rosedale, North Shore 0632, New Zealand
(a division of Pearson New Zealand Ltd.)
Penguin Books (South Africa) (Pty.) Ltd., 24 Sturdee Avenue, Rosebank, Johannesburg 2196,
South Africa

Penguin Books Ltd., Registered Offices: 80 Strand, London WC2R 0RL, England

Sanibel and Captiva Islands, and the area near Venus, Florida, are real places, faithfully described but used fictitiously in this novel. The same is true of certain businesses, marinas, bars, and other places frequented by Doc Ford, Tomlinson, and pals.

In all other respects, however, this novel is a work of fiction. Names, characters, places, and incidents either are the product of the author's imagination or are used fictitiously, and any resemblance to actual persons, living or dead, business establishments, events, or locales is entirely coincidental. The publisher does not have any control over and does not assume any responsibility for author or third-party websites or their content.

DEEP SHADOW

A Berkley Book / published by arrangement with the author

PRINTING HISTORY
G. P. Putnam's Sons hardcover edition / March 2010
Berkley premium edition / March 2011

ISBN: 978-0-425-24009-0

BERKLEY®
Berkley Books are published by The Berkley Publishing Group,
a division of Penguin Group (USA) Inc.,
375 Hudson Street, New York, New York 10014.
BERKLEY® is a registered trademark of Penguin Group (USA) Inc.
The "B" design is a trademark of Penguin Group (USA) Inc.

PRINTED IN THE UNITED STATES OF AMERICA

10   9   8   7   6   5   4   3   2

This book is for my pals
Mark Marinello and Coach Marty Harrity,
who lured me back to Dinkin's Bay.

AUTHOR'S NOTE

One of the joys of writing is doing research. Details regarding Florida geology and cave diving required and received particular attention. I would like to give special thanks to Florida geologist Jason Sheasley, and also William and Cameron Barton, for reading an early draft of the manuscript and offering their insights. Lee Florea of the Karst Research Group, Department of Geology, University of South Florida, and Dr. Bruce Flareau, M.D., provided valuable information on air bells and karst topography. Bob Alexander of NAVSYS Inc. was of great assistance in helping me select a first-rate underwater night vision system, which I used often as reference while writing this book. For assistance in research regarding Florida exotics, monitor lizards, neurological pain, cerebral diseases, the effects of blood-thinning poison on stroke victims and the luminosity of various dive watches, I want to thank the following people, in no particular order: Oklahoma authority Henry Baker; Ken Warren, public affairs officer, South Florida Ecological Services office, U.S. Fish and Wildlife Service; Jenny Edgar of the Mermaid Restaurant; Dr. Brian Hummel; Captain William Gutek; Dr. Donald

Slevin; Captain Russ Mattson; Marvin Metheny; Nitrox diver
Audrey Fischer; Dr. Chance Wunderlich; chronograph experts Eric Loth, David Camba and Alexandra Castro; mae-
stro O. J. Whatley; and marine biologist/watch entrepreneur
Dr. John Peterson. If there are factual errors in the narrative,
they are wholly the fault of the author.

The early chapters of this book were written in Cartagena,
Colombia, and Havana, Cuba, and I am indebted to friends
who helped me secure good places to live and write. My
thanks go to Giorgio and Carolina Arajuo for their help in
Cartagena, as well as Evelyn, Eliana and Elisa for their kind
attentions, and also to my pals Ron Iossi, Marlin, Javier and
José of the Hotel Centro. In Cuba, my Freemason brothers
Ernesto Batista and Sergio Rodriguez were particularly helpful, as were Roberto and Ela Giraudy, Raúl and Myra Corrales,
Alex Vicente and Mack Wiggins. Through the generosity of
the Robert Rauschenberg estate, much of this book was written on Captiva Island, in a fish house, thanks to Mark Pace,
Darryl Pottorf and Matt Hall.

Most of this novel, though, was written at a corner table,
before and after hours, at Doc Ford's Sanibel Rum Bar and
Grille on Sanibel Island, Florida, where staff were tolerant
beyond the call of duty.

Thanks to my friends and partners Brenda Harrity, Heidi
Marinello, master chef Greg Nelson, Dan Howes, Brian
Cunningham, my baseball pal Chad Cook; Reynauld Bentley,
Andrea Guerrero, Dawn Oliveri, Mojito Greg, Liz Harris,
Captain Bryce Randall Harris, Milita Kennedy, Kevin Fillio-
wich, Kevin Boyce, Eric Breland, Sam Khusan Ismatul, Olga
Guryanova, Rachel Songalewski of Michigan, Jean Crenshaw,

Lindsay Kuleza, Greg Barker, Roberto Cruz, Amanda Rodriguez, Juan Gomex, Mary McBeath, Kim McGonnell, Allyson
Parzero, Cindy Porter, Sean Scott, Big Matt Powell, Laurie
and Yak'yo Yukobov, Bette Roberts, as well as the wonderful
staff at Doc Ford's, Fort Myers Beach. At Timber's Sanibel
Grille, my pals Matt Asen, Mary Jo, Audrey, Becky, Debbie,
Favi, Bart and Bobby were, once again, stalwarts.

I would especially like to thank dear Iris Tanner, my helper
and appointed angel, for clearing the decks, gradually over
the last few years, so that writing, finally, has become my primary focus.

Last, I would like to thank my two sons, Rogan and Lee
White, for helping me finish, yet again, another book.

—Randy Wayne White
Casa de Chico's
Sanibel Island, Florida

He who fights too long against dragons
becomes a dragon himself;
and if you gaze too long into the abyss,
the abyss will gaze into you.

—FRIEDRICH NIETZSCHE

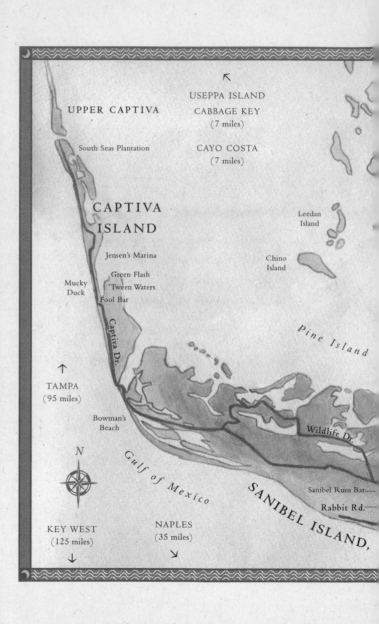

UPPER CAPTIVA

USEPPA ISLAND
CABBAGE KEY
(7 miles)

CAYO COSTA
(7 miles)

South Seas Plantation

CAPTIVA
ISLAND

Leedan
Island

Chino
Island

Jensen's Marina

Green Flash
Mucky   'Tween Waters
Duck
        Fool Bar

Pine Island

Captiva Dr.

↑
TAMPA
(95 miles)

Bowman's
Beach

Wildlife Dr.

N

Gulf of Mexico

Sanibel Rum Bar

Rabbit Rd.

SANIBEL ISLAND,

KEY WEST
(125 miles)

NAPLES
(35 miles)

↓   ↘

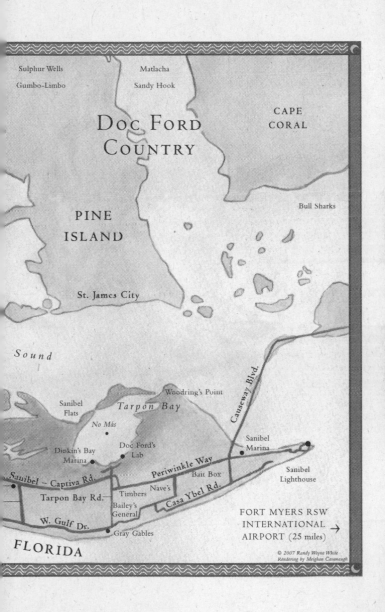

PROLOGUE

TUESDAY MORNING, KING WAS WATCHING THE sky, relieved there were no search helicopters plowing the horizon, like the day before, and he thought, *Good.*

Maybe Florida cops had arrested someone else for the murders.

King was about to tell Perry, "Let's get the bikes and head south," meaning Homestead or Key West. Anywhere but here, where they'd been hiding for two days, sleeping with ants and mosquitoes, near a teardrop-shaped lake, black water and cypress trees, in the boonies of central Florida, sixty miles south of Orlando.

Perry had shushed him, though, flapping his hands, saying, "Listen. You hear that? Someone's coming." A moment later, Perry had crouched lower, hissing, *"Listen!"*

Perry, a man with small hands and a small brain but good ears.

Shit. He was right.

Twenty minutes later, King and Perry were in the trees, south of the lake, watching four men with machetes hacking a path for a diesel pickup, a truck that made a whining sound when it accelerated. Three men plus a teenage boy, actually. Indian-looking kid in jeans, a red wind band around his head, black hair long, like an Apache in a TV western.

Miles from the nearest dirt road, but here they were. Perry's expression read *Can you believe this crap?*

The truck crept forward . . . stopped . . . bounced over palmetto stumps, then stopped again, while a crabby old redneck sitting behind the wheel yelled orders.

"Fifty more yards, Doc, we got her licked!"

Doc? King studied the men. Unlikely that it was the hippie-looking dude, skinny with ribs showing, or the Apache teenager, which left the man who was doing most of the work. He was a nerdy-looking guy with glasses tied around his neck, but he had a set of shoulders on him. Forearms, too. A doctor, maybe, but the teacher variety, not a real *doctor,* because, sometimes, when they spoke to the guy, they called him *Ford.*

Perry whispered, "You think they're cops? They don't look like cops."

No. Cops wouldn't be driving a truck loaded with scuba diving gear, a generator and a bunch of other stuff that Perry and King watched the men unload, half an hour later, interested now instead of worried.

Nice-looking Dodge with oversized tires, the tow-rig package. Easy to steal, once the men put on those wet suits and went into the lake, which it appeared they were going to do—as long as they left the keys in the damn truck.

It should have put Perry in a better mood. Instead, when King said, "Looks like the King was right. Our luck's changing," Perry stared at him, then spit in the direction of King's feet, before saying, "You haven't been right since we left Indiana."

Not something King would have admitted, but it was true.

From the bus station, downtown Bloomington, an Arctic low had followed the two men south like bad luck, blowing snow across parking lots from Nashville to Atlanta, then Macon, too, which caused Perry to finally say, "Maybe Florida's not such a hot idea. I feel like we're being chased into a corner."

To which King had replied, "What? You're blaming me for the shitty weather now?"

A little later, thinking about it, King added, "A corner has walls. That was a stupid thing to say about Florida."

Perry said, "What do you call an ocean? The damn state's surrounded on three sides."

It took King a moment. *Surrounded by water,* Perry meant.

King said, "You ever seen a wall that could take you to Mexico? Costa Rica, maybe. I hear that's sweet. Stick with the plan, Jock-a-mo. With enough money, a man can live like a king in those places. Personally, the King's ready for a change. Or maybe you're getting homesick for Joliet?"

It had irritated Perry, at first, the way the man spoke of himself, the King this or the King that, like he was speaking of a third person, but Perry was used to it now, and said, "How much, you think?"

Money, Perry meant.

King knew what Perry wanted to hear, so he went over it again, saying, "We each put a couple hundred grand in some Mexican bank, the word will get out. That's millions, when you convert dollars into pesos. How you think that would feel, to be a millionaire?

"Cops will protect *us,* for a change. No questions, no trouble. We do this right, you'll have yourself maids, a cook, hell, a driver, if you want. Be pretty nice, wouldn't it, wake up and have a pretty little Mexican maid standing there, ready to give you the big finish before your day even starts."

King smiled, his expression asking, *Is the King right?*

Perry liked that, no matter how many times he heard the story, but then he had to go and spoil it by looking around the truck stop, beyond the eighteen-wheelers parked in rows, and saying, "Snow's sticking on the damn palm trees! You believe this shit? The leaves are silver, like ice."

King told him, "Dude, that's not snow. It's neon light that does that, the way the wind hits the trees. An optical illusion."

King, the know-it-all, an expert on everything.

Perry had lit a cigarette, his expression saying, *Whatever,* as he shifted from foot to foot, the two of them standing near gas pumps, waiting for the Greyhound to load. Two a.m. Damn, it was *cold.*

"When you talked Florida, you never mentioned snow. I'm starting to wonder if you've really been here before."

King, who had never been south of St. Louis in his life, said, "Believe what you want. Backstage at a Buffett concert, maybe Jimmy will help me convince you. Besides, Macon's not Florida. Orlando, that's *Florida.*"

Perry was twenty-three, King, thirty-one or thirty-two, he wasn't sure. Both men skinny with Adam's apples showing, combs in their pockets, King carrying his belongings in an Army duffel, Perry with his in a backpack stolen from a playground. The men had been cell mates at Statesville Correctional, near Joliet, which worked out okay because neither of them was into the butt-buddy thing. At Statesville, sleeping on your belly could be interpreted as an invitation, so having a cell mate who dug only girls was worth a hell of a lot more than friendship. They had both worn their pants low, kept their mouths shut, and done their time kicking around ways to get rich when they finally made parole.

It was at Statesville that they met Julie, a black dude, who told them about a man he'd worked for in Winter Haven, which was near Orlando, doing lawn maintenance, picking oranges—an old man, he said, who had a coin collection worth a fortune and paid his help in cash, usually twenty-dollar bills. Older bills, Julie told them, the picture of Jackson small on the front, which suggested to King, the thinker, that the old man didn't use banks.

"How'd he make his money?" King had asked.

"Family owned a thousand acres of citrus," Julie had told them. "Then Disney came along. The old man still owns a hundred acres—six years ago, he still owned it, anyway. You'd need a calculator to count that much money."

Julie was doing life but wasn't a typical con, because the man he'd killed was a one-time thing, and he had it coming, from the way Julie told it.

"I wasn't drunk, never used a damn drug in my life, but when I heard what the son-bitch did to my wife, I sort of went nuts. I used a shotgun, four rounds of bird shot. It took a while. I wanted to give the son-bitch time to review the rules."

When King had asked, "Why didn't you go for the old man's money while you were at it?" the look of contempt on Julie's face said more than any parole board would ever know.

"I worked for that man. The man paid me on time, and he treated my family fair. What kinda punk-ass question is that?"

After that, Julie wouldn't give King or Perry the time of day, but they'd learned enough by then. They knew the old man's name, and that what was left of the citrus farm was set back off Green Pond Road and Route 27 on property north of Winter Haven, most of it probably golf courses and trailer parks by now, but the big white house still there, Julie guessed, hidden by trees.

It took a few weeks thinking about it before King really latched on to the idea of Florida, heading south, scoring big, then buying their way out of the United States and into foreign lives. It wasn't until then that King mentioned he'd once lived in Florida. He claimed he'd worked as a lifeguard in Palm Beach, hustling rich old women, wearing custom-sewn jackets—he'd even done some scuba diving, he said, when he wasn't sitting on the beach, eating mangoes and drinking orange juice, every morning.

Six months they'd been cell mates, and it was all news to Perry.

"You ever had fresh squeezed? Not the crap that comes out of a can, the real thing. Sun's hot, tan all year round, but with a nice cool breeze off the ocean—try to picture it. And the girls, they've got no reason to wear clothes. Before you even say hello, Jock-a-mo, you're halfway home."

King, a tropical expert all of a sudden, particularly on Florida. He'd been reading about Mexico and Central America, too.

Perry suspected King was full of shit, but the man had ideas, he was ten years older, always thinking, so maybe it was okay. Perry wasn't a thinker. Perry was a doer.

King processed out three months before Perry, but he was there in the visitors' parking lot, waiting, carrying a magazine, *Florida Travel & Life,* that was folded open to an article entitled "Winter Haven's Stubborn Son."

It was a story about the old man, whose name was Hostetler, refusing to sell the last fifty acres of his property, even though the county was pissed off because they were losing taxes that Disney or Comfort Suites were eager to pay. The picture showed a sour-looking old man with bitter, superior eyes, sitting next to a dog, some kind of pointer that looked more crippled up than the old man.

Damn, the guy was real. Just like Julie had said.

King had flipped to a page that showed another photo, the man inside his house, pointing at a painting. The magazine said it was the old man's grandfather, the property's original owner. There was something else, in the background, that was of more interest to King, who'd brought along a magnifying glass.

"A mint set of American gold eagles," he had told Perry, an authority on coins now, too.

"How you know they're mint? The picture's blurry."

Patiently, King had explained, "Because they're framed, for chrissake. The photographer was focusing on the painting of the dude in the old Army uniform, not the coins. A set like this is worth twenty grand, easy. How many more you guess he's got stashed away in that big old house?"

Twenty grand was more money than Perry had ever had in his life, but it was a figure he could get his mind around. Two hundred grand, or two million, those numbers came into his brain as blank pages. But if King said it was possible, maybe it was . . .

Perry, the doer, had said to King, "The dog looks too

old to cause trouble. But we can't just bust in there and expect Hostetler to fill a bag."

King had already thought of that, too. "I got my hands on a little Hi-Point three-eighty," he said.

When Perry asked, "You ever shoot a gun?" King snapped, "I was in the Army for a year, wasn't I?" but he wasn't convincing.

The men had taken a bus back to where King was rooming because Perry, who read gun magazines, wanted to see the little palm-sized pistol—black on silver; five rounds in the clip, one in the chamber—for himself.

The gun was a cheapie, it couldn't be very accurate, but it would do the job. Same with the two plastic-handled switchblade knives, all in a box.

"One old man, one old dog," King had said. "House-sitting out there all alone, full of gold coins and twenty-dollar bills. Hell, like the article said, we'd be doing Florida's taxpayers a favor to free up that shitty excuse for a farm. It's such an easy setup, I'm surprised some-one hasn't tried it before."

On the thirteen-hundred-mile trip, Bloomington to Orlando, Perry wondered about that. Three times they switched buses—Evansville, Nashville and Atlanta—and, at each stop, because there was still an opportunity to buy a ticket home, he'd brought up the subject with King, saying "Why you think that is?"

Why hadn't anyone tried to rob the man? Perry meant.

King and Perry arrived at the Orlando Greyhound ter-minal, North Magruder Avenue, an hour before mid-night on Saturday, only a few hours ahead of the Arctic low. They stepped off the bus into a balmy, orange-scented night that caused Perry to say, "Maybe this wasn't such a bad idea, after all."

By Sunday morning, though, at first light, the Arctic wind was silver in the palms. By midnight, it was so cold Perry could see King's breath pluming as he used a screwdriver to lever a window open, then stepped back so Perry could be the first to climb into the old man's house.

It wasn't as easy as they imagined because Perry was even drunker than King, plus he'd scored a bottle of Adderall behind the Greyhound station—20-milligram tablets, pure pharmaceutical speed.

Inside the house, when Perry finally found his balance, and his eyes had adjusted, he had his question answered—*"Why'd no one ever try to rob the guy before?"*

Alfred Hostetler was standing there, shouldering a shotgun, squinting with his bitter, superior eyes, ready to pull the trigger. Cowering behind him was what looked like a Mexican family, a woman and a couple of kids—no, three kids, two snot-nosed boys and a pretty little girl who was maybe thirteen.

It took Perry a moment to arrange it in his mind. He had climbed into the mother's bedroom, he realized, probably the maid.

"You better be carryin' more than a damn screwdriver, you expect to rob a man like me and walk out alive," the old man said to him, sounding pissed off, with no hint of fear, like he had more important things to do.

Even so, that struck Perry as an odd thing to say because it was King who had the screwdriver. Perry was carrying the gun. One of the switchblades, too.

Clack . . . clack-clack. It was the sound the shotgun made, both barrels misfiring on 12-gauge shells that might have been as old as old man Hostetler. Perry had thrown both arms over his head, terrified, but recovered fast enough to shoot Hostetler twice, in the stomach, as the Mexican maid and her brats screamed, then ran for their lives into the darkness of the big wooden house.

Perry sprinted after them, but shoved the gun into his pocket in favor of the switchblade he was carrying.

A knife would be quieter, he decided. More hands-on and personal, too.

That little pistol was *loud.*

Two hours later, riding in what was probably the maid's car—a beat-up old Subaru that smelled of diapers and Taco Bell—Perry was now getting pissed off himself because King, who was driving, kept saying to him, "Jesus Christ, I can't believe this is happening!"

Because of the Adderall, the man's voice was abrasive in Perry's brain, as penetrating as the orange caution lights flashing down MLK Drive at three a.m. on this morning, with a black wind scattering trash across the asphalt.

Perry said, "It *happened,* so get over it. What was I supposed to do? The guy was pointing a gun at me! The shithead tried to shoot me, goddamn it. I could be *dead* right now!" He had been scrubbing at his hands and jeans with a towel. Now he cranked down the window, let the wind take the towel, and couldn't help grinning as he yelled, "That was wild, man! Talk about a fuckin' high! I was *that* close to dying, dude!"

Perry had never experienced what he was feeling. It was an overwhelming rush, a screw-it-all freedom that was like soaring, a complete letting go. His brain was flashing postcard images of what he'd done: colors *bright*, dripping like fresh paint, startled faces, screaming wide eyes, five people, the old man, the woman, then the kids, finding them hidden in closets, under a bed, one by one, the girl last—settling into it then, taking some time to enjoy how her muscles responded to the point of the switchblade—but he hadn't touched the dog.

Nice dog.

In fact, Perry had said that as he left, walking out the front door, using the towel so they wouldn't leave prints.

"Nice dog. Good doggy . . . Yes you are!"

King had repeated what he'd said about not believing this was happening, then made a show of calming himself, before saying, "Okay, okay, here's what we do. You sober enough to at least listen?"

Perry was crashing from the speed, his nerves sparking, but he was sober enough.

What they did was park the Subaru near a pool hall, keys on the dash, and walked fast down MLK to where it became Lake Silver Drive, the wind pushing them along like leaves beneath streetlights. They kept right on walking, even when a cop slowed, cruising past, but the cop never stopped, so they did seven or eight miles before first light, finally buying coffee and doughnuts at the Perkins on Cypress Gardens Drive, both men spending some intense time in the washroom first.

Three miles later, they saw a dozen bicycles racked outside Candlelight Christian Academy off Highway 17. It was early Sunday—probably a soccer team or something doing an overnight, King decided, before saying, "Make sure you take a helmet, too."

Christ, a *bike helmet*? After murdering five people?

Perry responded, "Whatever," keeping watch as King chose a nice Trek, then grabbed a bike for himself.

The two men pedaled south, not too fast—"Like we're sightseeing," King kept reminding Perry—riding until noon, which was when they noticed two helicopters flying search patterns to the north, and King said, "We gotta find trees to hide under. A place to camp, maybe, for a few days, where there's cover—and water. I want to wash this shit off me."

King's slacks and shirtsleeves were stained, too. He was the one who had pulled the girl from beneath the bed, then held her so Perry could use the knife, but not before saying first, "Give the King about five minutes alone with this pretty little thing. Okay?"

Perry did it—but only because one of her brat brothers was making a wheezy, crying sound, still breathing.

Where?

It took Perry a while, maybe five full minutes, down on his hands and knees, crawling with the bloody knife in his hand, searching until he found the kid under a blanket.

Perry guessed the brat thought he would be safe there. But he wasn't.

For a couple of hours, the men hiked inland, ducking branches, until they found a lake so far from the road that there was no sound of cars, only wind blowing through the high trees where a hawk screeched, but not another living thing around.

Near the lake was a hunters' storage shed, padlocked, about the size of a Porta Potti. Inside were cans of food in Tupperware tubs, and military Meals Ready to Eat, dense as cheese blocks in their rubberized brown bags.

"No one will bother us here. You think?" King said to Perry, as he collapsed, cross-legged, in the shade.

Perry was walking toward the lake, where trees threw shadows along the southern perimeter. The water was black and clear in a way that reminded him of looking through smoked glass, like a black marble he'd had as a kid.

Perry answered, "I ain't going back to the joint." Meaning no one had better try to come after them. He had lost the switchblade during all the excitement, but he still had the pistol.

King had held on to his knife. He used it now to slit open an MRE, took a few bites of a fig bar, then decided to recount the gold coins that had come spinning onto the floor when the fancy frame busted.

Eleven gold eagles, and seven hundred dollars, cash, in twenty-dollar bills, that's all they'd found worth a

damn—but it wasn't like they'd spent much time searching the place after doing what they'd done.

Perry was staring at the lake—it was teardrop shaped,
sharp edged, like a bowl—seeing fish nosing among roots
that protruded, knee-high, from the water.

"Weird-looking trees," Perry said. "Sort of like in
comic books, the fantasy ones, you know—girls with big
boobs, carrying spears." He lit a cigarette, crumpled the
pack, then watched the wind sail it across the lake.

"They're cypress trees," King told him, looking at the
sky, before adding, "This cold front's moving south. By
tonight, it'll get warmer here, but cold as hell in Miami.
Probably the Sarasota area, too." An authority on the
weather now.

Perry was still staring at the lake, his eyes suddenly
wider, as he whispered, *"What the hell was that . . . ?"*

He had seen something so unexpected that it startled
him. A huge fish or something from beneath the surface,
something dark with a tail, had stirred a refrigerator-
sized swirl beneath the Marlboro pack. Like it had swum
up through the black water intending to eat the glittering wrapper but had changed its mind.

Goddamn, it was *big*. Seven or eight feet long, at
least.

Perry almost said something to King, but decided *no*,
there was a chance he had imagined it. *Could be*. He had
swallowed two more tabs of Adderall and could feel his
edges sharpening, the chemical sparkling through his
brain, brightening dark threads and creating halos around
trees where wind was blowing the waxy light.

There was another matter Perry had been waiting to
address. The topic was creating pressure inside his skull
and needed to get out. Perry was still fuming about the
way King had almost bolted, back there at the old man's
house, instead of joining in and doing what had to be
done. There was something else, too.

"The next time we steal bicycles," Perry said over his
shoulder to King, "I take first pick. I wanted that Trek,
but you took it. Didn't even ask."

He gave the man a hard look, adding, "Bikes or anything else. The King don't get first pick anymore. Understand?"

King swallowed without making eye contact, afraid of
his cell mate for the first time since Statesville.

"Sure," he said, "whatever." He was chewing the fig
bar, letting his attitude say, *No big deal,* settling himself
by turning his attention to practical matters. Thinking
was *his* job; Perry was a two-time loser, nothing but a
punk.

King took some time to review. How safe was this
place?

The hunters' shed was a quarter mile away, no path
cut to the lake—like the hunters didn't know the lake
existed. There was a swamp, remnants of a barbed-wire
fence cutting through—private property. Maybe that was
the reason.

Today was . . . Monday?

Yes, Monday. He and Perry had food, and they could
find a place to sleep beneath the cypress trees. Tomorrow,
regular people would be working, no hunters to worry

about. With any luck, a couple of Perry-dumb punks had spotted the Subaru on MLK, keys on the dash, and would give the cops something to do besides search the area again with helicopters.

King could picture it, the cops spotting the stolen car—*Smart*—and he let himself relax a little. Couple of days sleeping near the lake, then back on the bicycles and head south. Key West, just like regular tourists.

Safe. Yeah . . . And it got even better the next morning, Tuesday, when the men with the scuba gear and pickup truck appeared out of nowhere.

Perry and King watched the men from the distance. Watched the skinny hippie, with his ribs showing and his ponytail, and the Apache-looking teenager and the nerdy-looking guy with glasses and shoulders take their sweet damn time before suiting up in their scuba gear, wearing short-sleeved wet suits, then walking their fins into waist-deep water before submerging, one by one.

That left the old redneck man, the one who'd been driving the truck, alone onshore.

Perry looked at King, but King took his time acknowledging Perry—back in charge now, and he wanted the punk to know it.

"Dude," Perry whispered, "I wouldn't go in that water. No fucking way, dude. What you think they're after?" He still hadn't told King what he had seen yesterday afternoon, the large dark shadow swirling beneath the surface.

King didn't answer. An executive silence, that was the way to handle punks on speed.

"Maybe fishing, huh?" Perry said. "Or looking for something. How long you think they'll be down?"

King held his hand out until Perry finally figured out what it was he wanted.

"Long enough," King said, as Perry handed him the pistol. "You know what's funny? They're down there having fun, thinking nothing in the world can go wrong. But here we are."

King was smiling, picturing the divers' faces when they surfaced, finding their truck gone, and the old redneck dude shot or cut up—probably dead, knowing Perry.

ONE

ON A WINTER AFTERNOON, DIVING AN INLAND lake, south of Orlando, every small thing was going right, far better than I had anticipated, but then it all went suddenly wrong in ways I could not have imagined.

That's the way it happens, when it happens. People like me, the obsessive planners, the compulsive guardians, always say later—if they survive—"It's the one thing I didn't think about."

On the water, though, it's seldom just one thing that goes awry. A single miscalculation can catalyze a disastrous momentum that no amount of planning can interrupt. Much of life is random. It's as simple as that, although my spiritually devout friends wouldn't agree. Some people find the illusion of order comforting.

I don't. I prefer unencumbered facts even in an arbitrary universe. When plans unravel and the sky begins to fall, I'm all too aware that the tiniest bit of random luck can mean the difference between life and death.

On this winter afternoon, for example.

I was fifteen feet beneath the water's surface, in what should have been one of the safest little dive spots in Florida, when I heard a clatter of falling rock and looked up just in time to kick free as a ledge collapsed, burying my two dive partners beneath a ton of archaic limestone.

Fossilized bone atop living bone. Water is a relentless and dispassionate reorganizer.

We had been clustered near the ledge when it fell. One of my partners had found a handhold in a rock vent as we peered through masks, studying a yard-long chunk of ivory that was tannin-stained the color of obsidian. It was the tusk of a prehistoric animal, a mammoth. For one million years, the animal had rested here—its calcified scaffolding, anyway. A couple of rib bones lay nearby; possibly a splinter of femur, too.

Then the three of us came along. We disturbed the delicate balance of limestone, causing a million years of history to come tumbling down with inverse irony: the very, very old burying the new.

My partners included my boat-bum hipster pal, Tomlinson, and a troubled teenage Indian kid from Oklahoma via the juvenile court system, William J. Chaser. Will, for short, to the people he'd met around the marina, except for Tomlinson, who called him Will-Joseph—Joseph being the kid's middle name.

From the beginning, I'd argued against the boy com-

ing along. I'd finally consented, though, as a favor to a
high-powered woman—Will's temporary guardian—and
also because Tomlinson had fronted a convincing argument. The boy was a novice diver, true, but he was also
an athlete, a high school rodeo star, tough, and as quick
as a cat—when he wasn't stealing horses, selling pot or
running away from one detention center after another.

We had been underwater for half an hour. The kid was
doing okay—impressive, in fact. He was as confident
wearing fins as he was sitting a rodeo saddle. Tomlinson
was having fun, and so was I. Old man Arlis Futch—a
commercial fisherman and a friend—was miffed because
he wasn't in the water with us, but that was the way it
had to be. Someone had to stay topside and watch the
truck, right?

We were doing everything by the book—a book I
had personally modified to add additional layers of safety
net. Then the sky fell. Literally.

Tomlinson had found the spiral of fossilized ivory,
and he had waved us over to look. The tusk was, indeed,
an ancient and articulate relic to gaze upon. That's when
Will Chaser made a rookie mistake. I compounded the
mistake by allowing him to do it. The kid was having
trouble neutralizing his buoyancy. To steady himself, he
thrust his hand into a rock crater and pulled. The lake's
basin was honeycombed rock, a delicate latticework of
limestone. Will's not a big kid, but he's all muscle and
sinew, and the pressure he put on the latticework was
enough.

I didn't see it coming, nor did Tomlinson. The man

is relaxed and at ease in any situation—with the possible exception of an encounter with police—and he has great instincts. But he was in the wrong place at precisely the wrong time. A microsecond before I reacted, my pal's Buddha eyes narrowed, aware and thoughtful, then widened, alerted by sound and the changing water pressure from above. But too late.

In the slow explosion of silt, I was thinking, *This can't be happening,* as I kicked free of the landslide.

It happened.

For a panicked few seconds, I raced away from the murk, staying just ahead in clear water, as if I might suffocate if the silt engulfed me. The reaction was not befitting a marine biologist who has logged hundreds of dive hours.

Me, the so-called expert diver—but that's exactly what I did. It's the way our brains work. When darkness triggers the flight mechanism, we bolt for light because light means safety. It means freedom . . . and air.

Air, suddenly, was something that was in limited supply.

We had been exploring the lake's shallow perimeter for thirty-seven minutes. Because I'm obsessive when it comes to safety, and because I was the most experienced diver, I'd insisted that we not go deeper than thirty-three feet, which is the minimally more dangerous demarcation between two and three atmospheres.

The lake was a geological oddity—a teardrop-shaped

pool, central Florida, northwest of a crossroad village named Venus, three miles from the nearest dirt road. We'd had to bushwhack across plains of palmetto scrub and pasture, cutting a track for Arlis Futch's big-tired truck. It had taken all morning and part of the afternoon.

The lake sat between two ridges, a natural basin with cypress trees on the southern perimeter, then a pocket of cattails to the north where the lake narrowed. Beyond lay a marshy expanse of saw grass and cypress trees, a variety of Florida swamp where reptiles of every variety thrive, and so most people avoid such areas for a reason.

The lake consisted of an acre of water, which is about the size of a football field. It was manageable, I thought.

The water was clear and shallow in all but one dark area. There, the bottom funneled downward, vanishing into depths that were linked to the surface by pillars of silver light.

A "bottomless lake" is the colloquial term but inaccurate. A "cenote" is what similar sinkholes are called in Central America. A thousand years ago, Mayan priests dropped gold offerings into their depths—they gifted the heads of their enemies. Such places were considered holy. *Ojos de Dios.* The Eyes of God.

This lake was, in fact, the uppermost promontory of a water column that connected with the Floridan Aquifer. "Underground river"—another colloquial term. It was the safest of places to swim and dive, if you didn't stray too deep . . . and if there weren't man-sized gators in residence.

There were no gators. We'd made sure of that.

Alligators are, of course, a concern when diving the lakes and rivers of Florida. Because Arlis, a state-licensed hunter, had heard rumors that an oversized gator sometimes inhabited the lake, we took special precautions. I had done the research to confirm what I remembered and what Arlis swore was true: Alligators have a bottom time of two hours, max, usually much less. So we had watched, and waited, circling the lake several times. The precaution put us in the water later than we expected, with only an hour of good light left.

So what? It was the prudent thing to do.

I went in the water first. I did a lap across the lake and back, wearing a mask so I could have a look at the bottom. Tomlinson joined me on a quick bounce dive. Then we checked out Will's scuba skills before continuing. It was only the boy's second open-water dive, but he demonstrated more confidence than most hobbyists and more poise than at least a few so-called pros.

Even so, all the beginner protocols were in effect, plus the standard protocols employed when diving a remote inland area. We had brought the requisite emergency gear, in case we had bad luck, along with some basic salvage equipment—in case we had very good luck.

There was a reason we had brought salvage gear.

All divers enter the water in hope of finding something, *anything*, unexpected. Our hopes were more specific. We knew exactly what we were after—just as we knew how unlikely it was that we would find what we hoped to find.

We each carried a waterproof flashlight, as well as dive

slates for communicating, miniature emergency air canisters holstered to our tanks and one inflatable marker
buoy per diver. Will and I also carried knives. But Tomlinson, being Tomlinson, did not.

Once we were beneath the surface, we moved in a
pack of three, no swimming off alone. I had modified
the old rule of thirds to be doubly safe. When a pressure gauge indicated a tank was half empty, no matter
whose tank, we would surface as a unit. That was our
plan.

As an additional safeguard, Arlis remained topside,
equipped with a cell phone and a handheld VHF radio,
ready if needed. He had bristled at my decision that he
couldn't join us on the dive.

"Marion Ford," he had complained, "I've spent more
time on the water, and underwater, than you three boys
put together. Diving this sinkhole was my idea. Now
you're tellin' me I let you have all the fun? Ain't no safer
diving in the world than a puddle like this! And who the
hell's gonna mess with my truck way out here?"

Valid points—or so it had seemed at the time. What
could possibly go wrong on a calm, winter afternoon,
diving a parking lot–sized sinkhole in the remote pasturelands of central Florida?

"The buddy system just gives bad luck a bigger target." Tomlinson had said that before we entered the
water, rolling his eyes as I laid out the rules. It was a look
I've come to know too well. It summarized his amuse-
ment and impatience with my linear, logical efforts to
defuse destiny and to impose order on fate.

In this case, as it turned out, the man was right. He often is, although I seldom admit it.

Will's air tank was half empty when Tomlinson found the mammoth tusk. I know because I checked the kid's pressure gauge—*1490 psi,* it read—before gliding over to take a closer look. The tusk protruded from the ledge, curved and singular, as dark and dense as Chinese scrimshaw. It resembled an ivory question mark, broken at the base.

The elephant tusk was an unexpected find. It was not an uncommon find. The largest mammoth skeleton on record was recovered from the Aucilla River, to the north. At nearby Warm Mineral Springs, a lake only fifty miles to the west, archaeologist divers regularly found bones from mammoths, sloth and saber-toothed tigers. They have also found artifacts and human remains that date back twelve thousand years.

Human artifacts found at Warm Mineral Springs are so old, in fact, that they have challenged the theory that all *Homo sapiens* arrived in the Western Hemisphere via the Siberian land bridge.

Unexpected accessibility to the past—it's one of Florida's most compelling qualities. The state's history lies in delicate layers. The layers ascend by decades, and then aeons, from sea level downward. The peninsula is, in fact, little more than a sand wafer, rooted to skeletons of sea creatures that lived and died long before Africa's first primates dropped from the trees.

The geological term is "karst topography." The land-

scape appears flat and monotonous, but that's an illusion.
The Florida peninsula is, in fact, an emerging plateau,
honeycombed with voids and vents, caves and underground waterways. Travelers on Interstate Highway I-75
have no idea that, beneath them, are cave labyrinths still
being mapped by speleologists—"cavers," they prefer to
be called. These men and women ply their passion in
darkness, night or day, equipped like astronauts, using
battery-powered scooters—diver-propulsion vehicles—
to extend their range.

The invisible complexities of water and rock—another
aspect of Florida that I find compelling. Check the *Miami
Herald* or *St. Pete Times*. Several times a year, there's a
headline about a section of road, or an entire home, disappearing into a sinkhole. Without warning, the earth's
crust implodes, exposing a world of subterranean ridges
and valleys. Gradually, rain and underground springs fill
the hole. The geological latticework vanishes beneath the
surface. History appears briefly, then disappears. A new
lake is formed.

The formation of sinkholes is increasing because Florida's aquifer is overstressed by the water demands of Orlando and Tampa. Underground passages that were once
filled with water are now only partially filled, so the in-
terstices below cannot support the weight above.

Over aeons, Florida's sea level rises, recedes and rises.
It's true now. It was true a million years ago when the
tusk that Tomlinson found had been used to forage
and to fend off saber-toothed tigers. It was also true

twelve thousand years ago when, possibly, a prehistoric man had squatted beside the same limestone ridge, puzzling over the same ivory artifact.

Some anthropologists believe that man's fascination with dragons dates back to contact with survivors of the dinosaur era. Florida is a natural funnel, the historic conduit, of wandering predators. It has lured dragons of many varieties over the last twenty thousand years. Tomlinson had, indeed, stumbled upon one. Not the woolly mammoth—our dragon was the fragile limestone ledge.

After I'd gotten a good long look at the tusk, I backed away so Will could get closer. I didn't protest when he jammed his big teenage paw into a limestone vent to steady himself. I should have motioned him away. Instead, I held up five fingers, then gestured with my thumb. To make it plainer, I scribbled on my dive slate, *Surface in 5.*

Will had replied with a look of irritation, but then nodded as I made room. Tomlinson was grinning beneath his mask, ponytail drifting weightless, his expression saying, *Look what I found!*

The circumstances were about as benign as they get. We were only fifteen feet beneath the surface. We had safe reserves of air and an hour of daylight. The lake perimeter was so shallow, we could have searched it using snorkels instead of tanks. But it was good practice for the three of us as a team, I'd told myself, in the unlikely event that we actually found what we hoped to find. The prehistoric elephant tusk was interesting, but we didn't need three people to salvage it—if Tomlinson had chosen to disturb the thing, which would have been out of character.

That's another sport-diving protocol: Look but don't disturb. But we hadn't come to this lake as sport divers. We were on a mission, of sorts, although the kid was the last to know.

It wasn't until just before we entered that water that Arlis Futch gave us a nod, meaning it was okay to finally tell Will Chaser the truth about why we were here.

Tomlinson did the talking—not just because the man is talkative by nature, although he is. He served as our spokesman because he was one of the few adults that the teenager seemed to like and trust.

Tomlinson made it short and sweet. He told Will that we hadn't trucked forty miles inland, carrying scuba gear, a generator and a jet pump, plus sundry supplies, to search for fish, or fossils, or to catch specimens for my lab.

No, nothing that simple.

"We're looking for an airplane," Tomlinson had explained, enjoying himself, "but not just any airplane. Fifty years ago, a cargo plane left Havana. The plane was overloaded. It probably got caught in a storm, and it crashed south of Tampa. No one's ever found it. Arlis thinks it went into this lake."

"Overloaded with what?" Will had asked, interested, but with a teenage reticence to display enthusiasm.

I watched the boy's eyes change as Arlis fished a hand

into his pocket, extended his arm and said, "Maybe these."

The man was holding two gold coins. They were hundred-peso coins, struck in the 1920s. José Martí's profile was on the obverse side. REPUBLICA DE CUBA was stamped on the back. Even though we were outside, standing in the middle of nowhere, Arlis had shaded the coins and kept his voice low. Treasure hunters tend to be a noisy, talkative bunch until they think they've actually found something. It's only when they turn quiet that I take them seriously.

"I'll tell you the details later—if there's need for that," Arlis had said to Will. "Depends what we find. A few weeks back, I bought this chunk of land. About ten acres—lake included. It cost me more money than I have, but that don't mean lawyers and cops won't get involved down the road. Either way, you'll be cut in on the profit—today only, I'm talking about. And that depends on what we find, and how long you work, and how hard you work. That sound okay with you?"

I was still watching Will's expression. He and Arlis hadn't liked each other from the start. Arlis was quick to give orders, and the teen was slow to comply. Halfway to the lake, Will had bristled at something Arlis had said, and he had called him a "mouthy old redneck." Will had said it to the man's face—not something a man like Arlis Futch would normally tolerate. I had thought that was the end of the boy's afternoon dive.

To Arlis's credit, though, he ignored the insult, but the two hadn't spoken a word to each other until Arlis stuck out his big hand to display the coin. I could see that Will was surprised by Arlis's offer—but no more surprised than I.

"You're serious?" Will had said.

"About the lawyers trying to take it away from us?" Arlis replied. "Hell, yes, I'm serious."

"No, about offering to let me help. No one said anything about a sunken plane." Then the boy added, smiling, "But you don't have anything to worry about. Not from me. I'm used to dealing with lawyers and cops. They don't bother me a bit."

Tomlinson was nodding his approval. Arlis liked it, too.

After that, there were no more surly teenage looks from Will, no more grumbling complaints and no more calling Arlis names. He believed the man. Will expected to find more gold.

Personally, I'd grown incrementally more certain there was nothing to find. I'd believed it right up until Tomlinson discovered the ancient tusk. During our half-hour dive, we'd done a random search of the perimeter, circling farther and farther from shore.

No sign of a plane.

Nor did we find the human detritus—beer bottles, old tires, fishing line—typical of such places. One exception: a crumpled Marlboro pack, suspended in silt. Otherwise, the place was pristine. It was a pleasant discovery that confirmed the lake's inaccessibility.

It wasn't until I backed away to give Will room to inspect the tusk that I saw something else that was man-made. Something that changed my mind about the lake . . . and the plane wreck.

Maybe.

I had glanced down to make certain my fins were clear of the bottom. I didn't want to murk the water. And there it was—proof we weren't the first humans to breach the lake's surface.

It took me a moment to understand what I was seeing. On the bottom, lying in the sand, was another gold coin. Our fins had fanned the silt away. The coin was as yellow as molten brass. When I got a closer look, I saw that it was similar to the two coins Arlis had already found.

Diving to retrieve the coin is what saved me. It lured me away from the ledge. Bad luck, good luck—it's all random. Because the kid and Tomlinson were focused on the ivory artifact, they didn't follow me.

A moment later, I heard the ball-bearing clatter of rock on rock. One million years of limestone wall came cascading down.

As I raced ahead of the murk, I was already berating myself, thinking, *How stupid! How very damn stupid!*

It wasn't just because I had allowed Will to jam his hand into the delicate limestone. It was the whole situation that I regretted.

I, too, had made a basic mistake. Instead of following my instincts, I had allowed myself to fall under the influence of friends. One friend in particular: Arlis Futch.

TWO

THREE DAYS EARLIER, ON THE WARMEST, mangrove-sultry February afternoon in recent memory, Arlis had come clomping up my laboratory steps wearing boots, a coat, dressed for snow, and told me that, after years of searching, he'd finally found something very, very damn valuable. But it took us thirty minutes of verbal sparring before he finally told me what he'd found and where he had found it.

"It's in a sinkhole," he said. "A little bitty lake that's shaped like a drop of water. It's way the hell off the road, so nobody goes there. *Ever,* from the way it looks."

Typical of the man.

Arlis is a talker, but, when he has something important, he measures out the information at a speed proportionate to the worthiness of his audience. The audience doesn't have to be interested—and I wasn't. Arlis kept talking, anyway.

The fisherman began his story obliquely, saying, "There's a cold front coming. Feel it? If it weren't for this norther blowin' in tonight, we'd both be rich men by Tuesday. Friday, the latest." He tossed it out there and let it hang.

It was a Saturday, Sanibel Island, on the Gulf Coast of Florida. I replied, "Weather radio says the front arrives tomorrow, late. I was just listening."

"They're wrong—as usual," Arlis had snapped. After several seconds of silence, he returned to the subject of getting rich, saying, "You can't comprehend the amount of money I'm discussing, so I don't expect you to thank me now."

"Then I won't," I said. I was fine-tuning an aquarium, just beginning a new project. Sea horses. It wasn't research, really. The sea horses were a tangent inquiry. Animals of a more academic interest were in two large tanks nearby: electric eels from the Amazon, via some pet-shop hobbyist who had released them into a ditch east of Naples.

Arlis told me, "It's part of my nature to share with my friends when I come across a big chunk of luck. Most folks would expect something in return. Not me, it's just the way I am. But down the road, a man of character would want to return the favor."

Arlis has a knack for shading innocuous remarks with subtle criticism. We are all manipulators, sly in our methods, but the man uses guilt as weaponry—a device I find

particularly irritating. I didn't look up, and I took a measured interest in showing no interest as I peered into the
aquarium, watching four freshly netted sea horses adjust
to changes in salinity and the absence of tidal current.

"You act like I'm interruptin'. Like you're too busy
to listen."

I replied, "Acting's on a long list of things I'm not
good at."

"But you heard me. *Rich,* I'm telling you. Both of us.
Your hippie friend, too, if he's willin' to work for it. We
can all kick back and retire."

My hippie friend is Tomlinson, a middle-aged oddity,
part sinner, part saint, a Ph.D. brain coded with a sailor's
sensibilities, all hardwired inside a scarecrow's body.

I asked Arlis, "Which is it? A Spanish galleon or an
investment scheme? I'd guess the track, but I know how
you feel about horses and gambling."

"Only thing stupider than a horse," Arlis replied, "is
a man dumb enough to bet on something dumber than
he is."

I smiled, filing it away for later, and replied, "I'm out
of guesses," then returned my attention to the aquarium, noting the balanced mobility of sea horses as they
ascended and descended, erect as chess pieces. Four
weightless knights powered by a hummingbird blur of
fins.

Arlis baited me, saying, "You couldn't guess in a
month of Sundays."

I replied, "Then I won't waste my time."

I was fiddling with the aquarium pump, having trou-

ble with the flow valve. Wild sea horses are more fragile
than the pet-store variety. They require a tranquil environment and no surprises. The man watched me open a
yellow legal pad and calculate a stress-free rate of water
exchange: $50 \times 4 = 200 \times 1.75 = 350\ gph$. Then he endured several more minutes of silence as I began replacing the large pump with two smaller pumps. Finally, he
lost patience.

"Dang it, pay attention. This is big! I found something most men quit looking for years ago. But I finally
figured it out. You're the first I've told. How you figure
it'd feel to have a hundred million dollars in the bank?
Maybe five hundred million, depends on gold prices.
I'm talkin' about *bona fide rich*."

He pronounced it "bone-a-FI-DEE," a man with
enough swamp and saw grass in his ancestry to speak
with an authentic Florida Cracker accent.

"Gold," I said. "You think you found a Spanish wreck.
I was right."

"Nope. Not the pirate treasure variety, anyway. I ain't
no schoolboy dreamer and I ain't senile. I'm sure about
this one, Doc."

I stood, removed the glasses that were tied around
my neck on fishing line and used microscope tissue to
clean the lenses.

"Just like you're sure about the cold front? VHF
weather says it gets here tomorrow afternoon. You
say tonight. Usually, faith and fact don't have much in
common."

The man touched the zipper of his coat, then produced leather gloves from the pockets. "I'm right, you'll see. You're gonna need that new wood-burning stove of yours. By sunset, the wind will start to gust. Four hours from now, it'll feel like Canada's pissing on us with a cold hose. Nothing to slow that north wind but the Georgia border and a couple of parking lots at Disney World."

I turned to the windows above the dissecting table where chemicals and test tubes were lined on shelves. The sky was Caribbean blue. The bay was silver where clear water met mangroves along the shoreline. It was eighty degrees and calm. Pelicans crashed bait near an oyster bar where—bizarrely, but not unexpectedly—my boat-bum neighbor, Tomlinson, was sloshing in the shallows, wearing baggy Thai fishing pants, no shirt, a bucket hanging from the crook of his arm. He was as animated as a kid collecting Easter eggs.

Tomlinson was harvesting oysters for dinner, I decided. I made a mental note to pick a few fresh limes when I walked to the marina and buy a couple of more quarts of beer.

"Arlis," I said, "I'm working. If you want to tell me what you found, tell me. If not, there's one last beer in the fridge and plenty of books to read until I'm done. But take it outside."

"Doc, you're always in a hurry. You ain't changed a gnat's nut since you was a boy. You call this work? Now, mullet fishing's *real* work, not playing around with little bitty fish to be sold to some laboratory or Yankee college professor."

He was referring to my little company, Sanibel Biological Supply—purveyor of marine specimens and consultant for hire when a worthwhile project comes along.

I turned to him and saw that he was unzipping his coat, sweat beading on his forehead, as he came closer to the aquarium. "Man, it's warm in here," he added. "Don't your ceiling fans work?"

I gave him a closer look. "Are you feeling okay?"

His face was flushed, and I noticed that his hands vibrated with what may have been a neurological tremor. Arlis is seventy, but the man is fitter than most thirty-year-olds.

"I'm fine, just fine," he replied.

I told him, "Shed a few layers of that snowsuit—if you're willing to risk frostbite. But do it outside. Don't make me ask again."

In reply, I received a pointed look, his rheumy gray eyes huge behind thick glasses, a young man alive in his brain, still in command of the aging body.

"You tellin' me to leave?"

"I'm telling you I can't talk about getting rich until I'm done doing what I get paid to do."

"No need to get mouthy about it. A week from now, you'll be wondering how a man could be so generous—that is, if I don't get pissed off and march my ass right out of here."

I replied, "Unless you messed with the bolt, Arlis, the door's not locked. I wouldn't want to be the one to stand between you and happiness."

The man glared at me for a moment. "Well, if you did, it wouldn't be the first time, Dr. Marion D. Ford!"

I knew what the man was referring to. It was a woman whom we had both known and admired—and possibly loved, in our respective fashions—but then she had died. I sighed. I shook my head. I said, "Jesus, Arlis, let it go."

"I didn't bring her up—you did."

I replied by returning my attention to the sea horses, suddenly envious of a species that is blessed by the inability to speak.

Arlis is a variety of old-time fisherman seldom encountered these days, possibly because, on the Mangrove Coast, men as irritating and assertive as Arlis often died suddenly while being choked, or shot, or left behind to drown.

I like the man but in small doses. I appreciate the fact that he's among the last of a very few people whose toughness reflects the Florida biota by virtue of having been forged by its hardships.

Arlis continued staring at me for a long moment, before saying, "I found his treasure plane. Batista's treasure plane."

I said, *"What?"*

He said it again.

Suddenly, the man had my attention.

"This isn't the first time someone's told me that," I replied, trying to recover from my surprise.

"It's the first time *I* ever said it," Arlis replied. "I suppose now you're gonna tell me that don't make a difference. This is *me* talking, Doc. By God, I found it. I'm not going to beg you to listen."

Arlis was right. It was different coming from him. He

was talking about a plane commandeered by Fulgencio Batista, the man who had ruled Cuba before Castro seized power.

Arlis paused, taking his time as he gauged my interest. "You know the story. I can see it."

I said, "I've heard rumors."

"This ain't rumor. I know people who know people."

"Everyone does. And everyone has a treasure story. They print wreck sites on restaurant place mats. It's what boat salesmen talk about before they reach for the contract."

"Not men who've lived on this coast long as I have. I'm discussing fact, not faith."

The old man let that sink in, before adding, "Batista was a thief—just like the Castro brothers. I've heard he was an even worse killer. Nastier about it, anyway. When there was a man he particularly hated, I heard he'd march him to the zoo outside Miramar and toss him in a cage at feeding time."

Arlis was watching my face, disappointed possibly that I didn't react. So he added, "While the prisoner was still alive, of course."

"Waste not, want not," I said.

"You think I'm joking?"

"No. I'm thinking about the flow rate of this pump. I think the impeller's bad."

"It could be true," Arlis said.

"Yeah," I answered, "the impeller's usually the first thing to go."

"No! I'm talking about ol' Batista. He had a special

fondness for that zoo. That's what some of the marlin fishermen told me, anyway, down there in Cojimar, before the Castros took over. Batista grew up poor. Like a lot of poor kids, he liked bright, fancy things—including circuses. Some of the animals for that zoo, he picked out personally and had them flown back to Cuba. You know—when he was traveling around different parts of the world, a very important man all of a sudden after being nothing but a broke-poor cane cutter."

As I worked, I let my expression tell him, *I've never heard that one before.*

Arlis responded, "People forget what Batista was like. They forget that a lot of folks hated him."

"That's true," I said.

"He knew he'd lost control of Cuba. He knew the Castro brothers were coming and that he had to leave the island—or maybe they'd cart him down to the zoo, his own self, come feeding time. But Fulgencio Batista was as greedy as he was mean, and he wasn't about to leave that island empty-handed."

I knew more than Arlis realized about Cuban history, but I asked, "What did he take?"

"Before he ran, he robbed the fanciest museums in Havana. He robbed the national treasury, too. In December 1958, four cargo planes loaded with art and gold— mostly gold bars and coins—left Cuba for Tampa. Only three planes landed. The heaviest-loaded plane disappeared. That pilot's last radio transmission is in Coast Guard records, if you know where to look. The pilot called a few Maydays, then he said, 'We're goin' down.

We're goin' down in the water'—or something close to that—and that's the last anyone ever heard."

I crossed the room to the chemical cabinet, listening to him talk.

"For fifty years, the scuba-doo divers and treasure hunters searched for that plane. Some of 'em actual pros, like Mel Fisher's bunch outta Key West. No one ever found the first trace. Draw a rhumb line 'tween Tampa Bay and Cuba, and men have hunted every yard of that route. In all that time, you'd expect someone to find something, wouldn't you?"

I thought about it for a few seconds, before I said, "If the plane actually existed—maybe. Maybe not. Three hundred miles of water is a lot bigger than three hundred miles of land."

The man appeared pleased. "Ab-so-lutely by God right, Doc. Most people, they don't know the difference between water space and land space 'cause they ain't lived the difference. That's one reason I'm here talking to you now. We did okay a year ago, with that little salvage company we started."

Arlis, Tomlinson and our fishing-guide friend Jeth Nicholes had worked a World War II yacht that lies in seventy feet of water not far from my home on Sanibel Island. Finding the wreck was pure luck. What I'd said about water being more voluminous than land is true.

Salt water is a shield, occasionally a mirror, but seldom a lens—which is why sea bottom is among the last strongholds of human legend. Dreams are more safely housed in regions not despoiled by light.

The wreck we had salvaged was real, but so were the long hours we'd put in working below the surface and above. We'd all made a little money, but the profits were tiny in comparison to the time we had invested.

Arlis asked me, "You got a chart around here? It'd be easier to show you on some kinda map."

I said patiently, "It wouldn't mean anything. Point to a spot on a chart, the width of your finger is thirty miles of Gulf water. There's nothing to learn from that. I've got a business to run—this is the last time I'm going to say it."

The old man zipped his jacket as if slamming a door. "Thirty miles in the Gulf of Mexico, huh?"

"Depends. On a big chart, an inch equals sixty nautical miles. You know that."

"You just made the same mistake everyone makes who has ever searched for Batista's plane."

I let my expression communicate irritation. "Am I missing something?"

"The opportunity of a lifetime, Dr. Ford, that's what you're missing—if you don't start taking me serious. The pilot's last words were, 'We're going down in the water.' *Water,* that's what he said. The man never said nothing about the Gulf of Mexico."

I asked, "He ditched in the Atlantic?"

"I didn't say that. Didn't say the Pacific Ocean or the Arctic Ocean, neither. The weather was bad enough to blow the plane off course a little—probably as cold and windy as it'll be here in a few hours. She went into the water, but it *weren't* the Gulf of Mexico. Let your brain work on that while I go outside, like a good boy, and have myself a chew of tobacco."

I was picturing the Gulf basin, Cuba to the south, Key West dangling long into the Florida Straits, floating like a compass needle. Florida can be more accurately described as a land mosaic, not a landmass. The state is three hundred miles long, only a hundred miles wide and mostly water.

I thought about it for a moment, before saying, "There's only one other possible explanation," as the man pushed the screen door open. "If the plane didn't crash in the Gulf, it went into a lake. They ditched in a lake somewhere between Key West and Tampa."

Not looking over his shoulder, Arlis said, "Now, ain't you the smart one! When you're done playing with them fish, maybe I'll tell you how I happened to find that lake. If I'm still in the mood . . . and if I come back."

Arlis let the door slam behind him.

THREE

AN HOUR AFTER SUNSET, I LISTENED TO MY friend Tomlinson say, "The frost is hunting for pumpkins, Dr. Ford, but it will have to settle for coconuts. If this wind gets any stiffer, I'm going to make myself a hot toddy instead of having another cold beer. You have any socks I can borrow? Or maybe it's time to try out our new fireplace."

I had been trying to share Arlis's story with him but stopped long enough to say, "*Our* fireplace? I don't remember your name on the title to this place."

"I helped you install the damn thing, didn't I?"

"No," I said, "but you drank a six-pack of beer and ate my last pint of Queenie's vanilla while you watched me do all the work. Besides, it's a Franklin stove, not a fireplace."

The week before, I had installed an old wood-burning stove against the north wall, mounted on a platform of brick and sand for insulation. I'd found the thing while jogging the bike lane on nearby Captiva Island. There it was, sitting among junk outside a cottage that would soon be razed, then replaced by yet another oversized mansion—an ego-palace; a concrete grotesquerie as misplaced on that delicate island as a Walmart on the moon.

Among the wealthy, there are inveterate mimics. It is how some people compensate for their numbed instincts regarding style.

Because I was irrationally irked that Arlis Futch might be right about the cold front, I replied, "No fire. I want to give the chimney a few more days to seal. Besides, I was in the middle of telling you about the lake he found."

The aging fisherman had finally shared the details of how he had found what he believed to be the famous lost plane. I wanted to bounce his proposal off Tomlinson before guests arrived.

Tomlinson had dumped a bucket of oysters in the sink, shells and all. He was shucking the oysters, placing the spoon-sized shells on a tray where there was rock salt piled on a slab of stone and wedges of lime scattered. Looked good.

The hatch-cover table was set for four, the breakfast counter for one. I had invited two ladies for dinner, a current love interest, plus also my current workout buddy—a potentially dangerous mix, but what the hell. The fifth setting was for the sixteen-year-old juvenile delinquent, Will Chaser. The boy was another volatile unpredictable.

I said to Tomlinson, "This is Arlis talking, not me. Understand?" attempting to continue the story.

Tomlinson replied, "You've got two floor heaters in the lab. Couldn't I drag one in here? Just to sort of take the edge off."

He knew the answer. There were a dozen living aquaria in my lab, plus the new sea horses. Most of the aquariums have their own little heating systems, but the room needs to stay at a consistent temperature.

Tomlinson pressed, "Then what about those socks? You got some I can borrow?" The man was still wearing the Thai fishing pants, baggy around his waist, and a RED SOX hoodie. No shoes, of course.

I walked into my bedroom, opened a drawer and lobbed a pair to him, saying, "A month ago, a rancher hired Arlis to remove a nuisance alligator. That's how the whole thing started. A gator big enough to kill a steer and eat most of it—or so he claims. While he was looking for the gator, Arlis found a propeller from an old plane wreck. Not in the lake, but in a swampy area nearby. Arlis can be convincing. He believes it's the gold plane."

Tomlinson replied, "He convinced himself, so what? That doesn't mean anything."

I said, "He felt sure enough about it to buy the property. Ten acres, including the lake—plus a deeded ingress and egress. He closed on the property yesterday. He says that's why he waited to tell us."

Tomlinson was paying attention now. "That had to cost him a chunk of money."

"He had to mortgage his place on Gumbo Limbo. Something else," I said. "He says he found two gold pesos lying in a sand clearing. Just lying there, not far from the propeller."

"I'll be damned," Tomlinson said. "Sounds like it really could be the gold plane."

Batista's gold plane, that's the way it's referred to in Florida legend. No need to explain the backstory. The only thing typical about Tomlinson is that he has lived a boat bum's atypical life, gunk-holing the Caribbean, cruising from port to port, seeking a larger universe by simplifying his life within the cabin walls of an old Morgan sailboat named *No Más.* Like me, he has heard a thousand miles of treasure stories, including the legend of Batista's plane. Like me, he is seldom impressed.

"Did he show you the coins?"

I said, "He says he keeps them in his truck because it has a better security system than his house. Which I don't doubt is true."

Tomlinson said, "Hmm," before asking, "this thing killed a full-grown bull, huh?" He was more interested in a giant alligator than a massive fortune, I could tell—characteristic of the man.

"He claims something killed a yearling steer, not a bull. Even so, an animal that age would have to weigh seven or eight hundred pounds. And it wasn't the first time it happened. The rancher told Arlis his family had lost a lot of cattle in that area over the years."

"How many years?"

"Forty or fifty," I said, and couldn't help smiling.

Tomlinson was smiling, too. "Florida's version of the Loch Ness monster, huh? So the thing's become a family legend."

"The rancher doesn't actually work the land much anymore," I told him. "He inherited it. But back to the steer—"

"Bull or steer, what's the difference?" Tomlinson interrupted. "Half the males I know have lost their balls, one way or the other. That makes them malleable—and marriageable—not eatable. What's harder to believe is some rancher hired Arlis to kill a nuisance gator instead of doing it himself."

I said, "Yeah, I've got a problem with that, too."

Florida's interior is home to a sizable population of cowboys. Real cowboys, although historically they are known as cow hunters. The tourist brochures have no reason to mention that beef cattle are among the state's leading exports.

I added, "The way Arlis tells it, the rancher's afraid to go near that lake. The same with the men who work for him. Plus, the place is tough to access. There's no road, you've got to hike or cut a path."

Tomlinson continued shucking oysters, his expression dubious, as I said, "A more likely explanation is that the wildlife cops have cracked down on killing protected species. If you get caught killing a gator, there's a big fine, even some jail time. But Arlis has a state license, so it makes sense that the rancher called him."

"That's right," Tomlinson agreed, "he's licensed, which adds up, you're right. So he went to the lake, caught the gator and found the propeller, plus the two coins. So far, so good—not that I'm sold yet."

I shook my head. "He didn't find the gator—if there is one. There's more than one lake in the area, he says. The property I'm talking about is fifty miles inland, northeast, near a little crossroads named Venus. You know the place. It's in Highlands County—hilly country, by Florida standards."

Tomlinson nodded. It was mushroom country, too, although he didn't say it. Fanciers of psilocybin mushrooms tend to be closemouthed about their favorite hunting areas. Instead, he said, "There's a lot of cattle pasture and palmetto, elevation more than a hundred feet above sea level. Sure, I've spent a day or two in that area. But you wouldn't notice the elevation unless you're on a bicycle. I remember a Baptist church and a stand at a crossroads where they sell beef jerky and boiled peanuts. Really good peanuts."

I said, "It's probably still there—for now. It used to be ten thousand hectares of free-range cattle, but the strip malls are closing in. Now the rancher is ready to sell off a few hundred acres, and I guess he was afraid a cow-killing gator might ruin the realtor's sales pitch. That's why he accepted Arlis's offer and sold him a little chunk that included this lake."

"It was probably a panther," Tomlinson said. "Or wolves. I hear they're making a comeback."

"They found the steer—what was left of it—floating in the water. It could be anything."

Tomlinson was smiling. He liked that. "Something big lives in that lake."

I said, "The steer could have died of natural causes and fallen in. Or it could have waded in and drowned. Still . . . an oversized gator is easier to believe than a plane loaded with gold."

"Then how do you explain the two coins?"

I replied, "I don't doubt that Arlis found a plane wreck. But it's unlikely he found *the* plane wreck," as I crossed the room to make sure the windows were sealed tight.

I had been standing at the propane stove, making one of my specialties: pan-seared snapper with peanut gravy, which is sort of like satay sauce only easier. Fish renderings in a pan, then add a glob of peanut butter, a couple shots of chili oil, then simmer with flour and water until it thickens.

I was feeling the chill now, though, despite the propane burners on the stove. I live in what is known as a "fish house"—two small cottages built over water on stilts, under a single tin roof. In the early 1900s, fish were stored in one house, fishermen in the other. When I bought the place, I converted the larger cottage into a lab, the other into my home.

Dinkin's Bay Marina, just down the mangrove shore, is a neighbor. Same with the dozen or so people who live there aboard a mixed bag of million-dollar yachts and waterlogged junkers. Tomlinson, who keeps his sailboat, *No Más,* moored equidistant from the docks, is a local icon, a trusted friend and now my business partner, too. Not in the marine-specimen business. The man opened a rum bar only a mile from the marina, and I had recently bought a small interest.

It was cold when I'd started cooking, but now it was colder. Wind had shifted northwest, and a filament of winter moon floated in the corner window above my reading chair and shortwave radio. Next to the desk, my new telescope—an eight-inch Celestron—sat on its tripod, angled skyward, as if straining to have a look.

I was eager to get outside and take a peek myself. Saturn was suspended in the same small window, tethered to the lunar elliptic. The planet was brighter than the landing lights of a jetliner that was now arcing down over Sanibel Island.

February is tourist season. A few hundred souls on that plane, eager to de-ice in the tropic heat, were about to be disappointed upon landing. The temperature was descending more rapidly than the jet.

I didn't want to fire up the Franklin stove, but I had guests coming. Two women and a tough, judgmental kid. I could feel wind sieving up through the pine-slat floor, icy off the water. Concession was nipping at my toes.

Tomlinson said, "Looks like Arlis is right on about the weather," breaking into my thoughts.

"It's looking that way," I said. "I guess we'd better warm things up a little."

"I'll bring in wood," Tomlinson replied, still on target.

A few minutes later, he returned, his arms loaded with driftwood, muttering, "It's so cold that just to take a whiz, I had to goose myself and grab Zamboni when he jumped out. Temperature must have dropped twenty degrees in the last hour."

I was at the stove again, stirring a pot of milk, ready to add half a stick of butter, pink Caribbean sea salt and crushed pepper, as I replied, "Certain images don't mix with oyster stew—do you mind? And don't forget to wash your hands."

He dropped the wood onto a tarp near the Franklin stove, saying, "Doc, your lack of sensitivity used to worry me. Now I sort of miss the good old days—back when you were about as sensitive as this stove."

He busted a branch over his knee, pushed it into the fire and clanged the iron door shut.

A few minutes later, he said, "So what's the verdict? When do we dive the lake?"

He was doing it again. I had been picturing Arlis Futch as he idled away from my dock in his mullet boat. The last thing he had said was, "I'm right about the cold front, and I'm right about Batista's gold plane, too. Tomorrow's no good. Monday, either. But it should be warm enough by Tuesday. Have all your gear rigged and ready."

To Tomlinson, I said, "Maybe we'll give it a try Tuesday morning. I think the weather will be okay by then."

"Is that what Arlis said?"

I replied, "He's not the only one who listens to marine radio."

Now my mind was on Jeth Nicholes, the fishing guide, who had already told me that he had trips booked solid until the end of February. He needed the money and couldn't break away on something so risky as hunting for lost treasure. I'd had to admit to Jeth that the chances of finding anything valuable were slim, so that had settled the matter.

I listened to Tomlinson tell me, "Jeth's booked solid, so no point in even asking. Same with all the fishing guides." He let me think about that for a few seconds, before saying, "What about Will-Joseph? We'll need at least four people, and he's certified."

It was Tomlinson's pet name for the troubled teenager. The boy was spending the week in Florida, the guest of a woman I had been seeing, Barbara Hayes. Twice the boy had run away from a halfway house near his Oklahoma reservation. Barbara had finally stepped in and offered to help. Temporarily.

The woman had her reasons for feeling indebted to Will.

I was thinking, *No way in hell is that boy going with us.* I had my reasons, too.

The boy carried a lot of baggage, and, when it comes to travel or diving, I prefer partners who pack light.

Will Chaser had survived something that would have driven most people to the brink of insanity. Only a few weeks earlier, extortionists had buried him in a box, a copycat crime modeled on the Barbara Jane Mackle kidnapping of the late 1960s. Mackle had survived seventy-two hours in her grave; Will had escaped after less than a day, but only after killing one of his abductors.

Unless one is a sociopath, there is no such thing as guiltless homicide. No matter how good the reason, if you kill a man, he lives with you the remainder of your days. I had never discussed it with the boy, although Tomlinson had been nudging me to do so. Emotional scar tissue, like religion, is a private matter. As I told Tomlinson, from what I'd observed the boy appeared nonplussed by what he'd endured and done.

"Precisely why someone like you should talk to him," Tomlinson had countered.

The man was probably right, but dealing with young males, at the peak of hormonal flux, can be a gigantic pain in the ass. I wanted nothing to do with it.

"Will's too young," I told Tomlinson, as I scanned a list of alternatives, narrowing it down to people I hadn't yet contacted.

I could hear driftwood crackling. The fire was filling the room with a bouncing, ascending light as Tomlinson replied, "Shallow-up, Doc. Will's a good kid. Full of testosterone and anger, that's all. Besides, it's just a scout dive. If we find anything interesting, we'll have to replace the boy, anyway. He goes back to Oklahoma on Friday."

I said, "I doubt if he's even done an open-water dive. It's a bad idea."

Tomlinson was chuckling. "You know better than

that. Why do you think Barbara took him to Key Largo before coming here?"

It was true, I knew it, but I said, "He didn't mention anything to me about *liking* it."

"That's because you and the boy haven't said two words to each other since he got here. Or maybe you didn't notice that, either."

Yes, I had noticed. It had created tension between Barbara and me—not entirely Will's fault, because our relationship, I suspected, was coming to an end, anyway.

I said it again. "He's too young, and not enough experience. Truth is, we don't really need a fourth diver. You, me and Arlis. That's enough."

When he gets serious, Tomlinson has a way of lowering his voice to ensure attention. "As a personal favor, let the kid come along, okay? I'll take full responsibility. What could be safer than a freshwater pond in the middle of Florida? A nice, safe, shallow-water dive. The kid's a rodeo rider, for God's sake. He'll be fine, Doc."

I was thinking of an obvious objection, as Tomlinson added, "As long as that monster gator's not around, of course."

FOUR

TWO DAYS LATER, A MONDAY, I FINISHED CHECK-
ing and packing enough dive gear for an expedition instead of what I had expected to be a pleasant one-day
trip, then tiptoed to my bedroom. I wanted to check on
a Saturday dinner guest who had left with the others, but
then returned in the cold wee hours of the morning,
saying, "I pictured you sleeping up here all alone and
wondered if you might need a little extra heat."

It wasn't Barbara Hayes. She had left in a huff because
of some imagined slight. My bedroom guest was Marlissa Kay Engle, my workout pal and surprising new lover.
She was spending Monday night at my place, too.

Marlissa is a beautiful woman, all curves and flowing
hair, and I stood in the doorway until I had confirmed

that she was safe and asleep. Startled by something—a dream, perhaps—Marlissa stirred. Her rhythmic snoring was interrupted by a low moan.

I closed the curtains and went outside, through the shadows of mangroves, toward the marina. As I walked past the marina office, I could hear a television babbling from the upstairs apartment, a newscaster saying something about multiple homicides near Winter Haven.

I stopped long enough to listen. Five people had been murdered by two or more robbers at a secluded property north of Winter Haven, not far from Haines City. The owner of the house, his maid and her three children had all been killed. Shot or stabbed or both. Yesterday, cops had spotted the maid's car on I-75, heading toward Atlanta. Three suspects had been arrested, all illegals from Haiti.

Even Dinkin's Bay can't insulate itself from the outrages of the outside world.

I turned right at the bait tank, onto the docks, walking past the dozing cruisers and trawlers—*Tiger Lilly, Das Stasi, Playmaker*—and was about to knock to see if my friend Mike Westhoff was aboard when I noticed a lone figure in the shadows by the boat ramp dragging a canoe out of the water. I watched for a second, then called out a name, because there was no mistaking the jeans, the western shirt and the headband.

It was Will Chaser.

————————

As I helped Will drain the canoe, then flip it onto the rental rack, I asked him, "Were you fishing? Or visiting Tomlinson?"

No Más, moored a hundred yards from the yacht basin, blended with mangrove shadows, its mast a frail exclamation point that was tipped with stars. The portholes were dark, but there was a bead of yellow light strobing on the stern—a candle. The candle told me that Tomlinson was meditating—it was his morning and nightly ritual—but maybe the boy had just left. It was a risky combination: two delinquents with more than enough common interests to bridge the age gap.

"He was telling me about that lake you're diving," Will replied, "but he wouldn't say why. Why a lake instead of the Gulf, I mean?"

I was tempted to ask the boy if he had Barbara's permission to be out paddling a canoe so late, but it would have only put him on the defensive.

I asked, "How'd you get here? Rental bike?"

"Yeah, but I usually walk. It's only a mile to our beach condo, and I like this side of the island better. When I was paddling back from the creek, Tomlinson saw me, so I pulled alongside for a few minutes. He gets nervous around me. I think it's because he's stopped smoking weed until I leave the island."

It was true, I had insisted upon it, but it surprised me that Will knew. I said, "Uhh . . . are you saying you think Tomlinson smokes marijuana?"

"Unless he uses a bong for asthma, that would be my

guess. Have you ever been on his boat?" The teenager lifted his head and sniffed. "Hell, I can smell the stuff from here. But I've got a better nose than most."

"I don't know," I said. "Illegal drugs, that's a pretty silly risk for a man his age to take. You could be wrong."

There was a sarcastic pause, and I pictured the boy rolling his eyes before he ignored the lie, saying, "Mostly, though, I was canoeing. I paddled way back in the sanctuary."

I asked, "See anything interesting?"

The boy shrugged.

"Next time, I can loan you a flashlight."

Will had racked the two paddles and was now trying to force the rusty latch on the lifejacket locker. "Got one," he said.

"I have a bunch of really good small LEDs. It's sort of a hobby of mine. I could loan you one to try."

From his pocket, he took out a cheap rubber-coated flashlight to show me. "That's okay. I use my own stuff."

I said, "Ah," and became even more determined to have a conversation. "Did you see any alligators? You've got to watch yourself in the mangroves, even in a canoe. There are some big ones."

He replied, "Yeah," then punctuated the long silence by kicking the latch with the heel of his shoe—he wasn't wearing cowboy boots, I noticed. He usually did. Will kicked the latch twice more, hissing, "You stubborn son of a bitch," before the thing finally opened.

It was an aggressive display that had as much to do with my presence as the rusted locker. A full minute later, though, the boy sounded almost friendly when he added, "The same's true of coyotes out west."

I replied, "Huh?"

"Coyotes are dangerous when they're in a pack. People think animals act the way they see them on TV or in the zoo. Not me. Animals are always on a feed—the ones in the wild, anyway."

I was taken aback. The kid suddenly sounded well grounded and reasonable. And he wasn't done talking.

"I saw five gators tonight. Their eyes glowed kind of a dull red when I hit them with the light. On the way back, though, I saw one that had eyes more orange than red. It went under before I got a good look. Do some gators have orange eyes?"

I said, "Orange? You're sure?"

"That's what I said, isn't it?"

"Then you saw a saltwater crocodile."

The boy was impressed. "No kidding? I've seen them on television—shows on Australia and Africa. I didn't know crocs lived around here."

"They're a different species," I said, "but similar animals. There's at least one big female that hangs out in the sanctuary. It could have been her. How big?"

"Not that big, but definitely orange eyes."

The kid closed the locker and began walking toward the parking lot, where I could see a bike leaning against the ficus tree next to the Red Pelican Gift Shop. I fell in beside him, inexplicably pleased that he considered me worthy of conversation.

Will asked me, "Are they exotics?"

In my mind, the kid's stock was rising. "Nope, crocs are native. Florida's home to about every form of exotic animal you can imagine. But saltwater crocs were here long before people arrived."

"Like the electric eels in your lab." He offered it as an example of a feral species.

"That's right. Plus a hundred thousand boa constrictors and pythons, between Orlando and Key West, all gone wild. Monitor lizards, iguanas, Amazon parrots and monkeys, too—you name it."

"That's kind of cool," Will said, but his tone was cooling. "Is that why you're diving a lake instead of the Gulf? To check it out and see if there are any exotics?"

I shrugged, a perverse streak in me wanting the boy to know what it was like to be answered with silence.

"You're not going to tell me why you're diving the lake, either, huh?"

I said, "It's not my trip. A friend of ours planned it. Any questions, he'd have to answer."

"Do I know the guy?"

"His name's Arlis Futch. Captain Futch. He'll be here in the morning."

"Tomlinson said there was a chance you might let me go."

"That's up to Captain Futch, too."

The windows of the Red Pelican produced enough light for me to read the boy's reaction. He didn't believe me.

"What're you going to tell the guy when he asks about me?"

I said, "Knowing Arlis, he won't. But he might ask you about your first open-water dive. How'd you like Key Largo?"

Will ignored the question and skipped to my reason for asking. "It doesn't bother me a bit, being in closed spaces. Being kidnapped—that's what you're wondering about, isn't it? Underwater, same thing—I *liked* it. You sound just like the shrinks now. If you've got something to say, why not just come out and say it?"

I smiled. Smart kid. "Okay, I will. Even in a lake, a diver has to be able to count on his partners. There's nothing simple about recreational diving. I don't know why they use that term."

I expected the adolescent shields to drop a notch. Instead, he replied, "I count on myself all the time. Always have, so I guess you can, too. If I do something wrong, all you have to do is tell me. I'll fix it. That sound fair?"

Yes, I had to admit it. It was reasonable and fair.

Before I could respond, he added, "Or maybe there's something else you're worried about. The shrinks don't come right out and ask me about that one, either."

I started to pretend I didn't know what he was talking about but decided that lying was the worst way to deal with William Joseph Chaser. He was talking about the man he'd killed, one of his abductors. I said, "It doesn't worry me. You had a choice and you made it. It was the right thing to do. If anything, it tells me you can handle yourself in a tight spot."

Will said, "What's the problem, then? I'd like to go.

I've never been underwater in a lake before. Maybe you can tell the guy in charge—Captain Futch, you said? Maybe you could convince him that I'd do okay."

There was something in the boy's tone that bothered me. It was the airy way he had asked, *What's the problem, then?* Tomlinson had been pushing me to discuss the subject, so I decided I would never have a better opportunity. I said, "How do you feel about it? You killed a man. Does it bother you?"

"I thought we were talking about diving a lake."

"You said if there was something I wanted to say, say it. So there it is. I've heard that you won't discuss it with your doctors. That you don't talk with anyone about what happened."

We were beneath the ficus tree now. Will took his bike by the handlebars and swung his leg over the seat as if mounting a horse. "Sometimes I know things about people," he said. "It's always been that way. So I know enough to keep my mouth shut because there are things I don't want people to know about me."

"Intuition?" I said.

"Maybe. Or instincts—the kind animals have. I'm not sure how I know things, but I do."

I listened carefully, inspecting his tone and his words for arrogance, but there was none. He had said it matter-of-factly, more like a confession than boasting.

"Tomlinson asked me to bring up the subject. Do your instincts tell you why?"

I expected the question to unsettle the kid, but instead he looked at me until my eyes had found his. In the winter light, his eyes were as black as his Apache hair. "I feel just like you must feel after getting rid of something that needs to be killed. Does that answer your question?"

I said, "You mean how I would *probably* feel—*if* I'd ever done something like that."

Maybe the teen smiled, I couldn't be certain, but he allowed his intensity to dissipate, then looked away. He shrugged. "Yeah. That's what I meant. I wish it hadn't happened. It comes into my mind every day. I don't feel bad about it, but I don't feel good about it, either. No, wait—" He was reviewing what he'd just said. "Can I tell you something? Confidentially, I mean."

I said, "Maybe. But maybe not. If you tell me something Barbara should know—for your own good, I'm saying—then don't risk it. Otherwise, you can trust me."

"Most people would've said sure right off the bat."

I said, "I'll keep that in mind the next time you think about sharing a secret. What did you want to tell me?"

"The truth, I guess," he said slowly. "The truth is, I feel *good* about what happened. I was lying about that. The man tried to kill me, so I killed him. I'd do it again. My guess is, you know what I mean."

I straightened my glasses, then put my hands in my pockets, giving it some time, before saying, "Tomorrow morning, have your gear checked and ready to go. Be here at eight sharp—just in case Captain Futch says yes."

FIVE

IF I DO SOMETHING WRONG, JUST TELL ME, I'LL fix it . . .

Will had meant what he'd said, yet I was the one who had screwed up. I had allowed him to jam his hand into the rocks and topple the delicate scaffolding of underwater limestone.

Will had told me, *I count on myself all the time, so I guess you can, too . . .*

What did it matter, if I couldn't count on myself?

When the ledge collapsed, burying Will and Tomlinson, I compounded the mistake by panicking. I bolted from the scene, swimming ahead of the murk, until my intellect finally subdued my instincts. It took only seconds, yet I was already berating myself, as I drew my knees up and thrust out my hands to stop my momentum.

I did an about-face and swam into the cloud of silt, kicking hard toward where I'd last seen Tomlinson and the boy. Because visibility had gone from bad to impossible, I extended my left hand as a bumper.

First, though, I paused long enough to check my watch. I had to mark the precise time of the landslide. If Will and Tomlinson had not already wormed themselves free, they had a finite amount of air remaining in their tanks. If they were trapped, I needed to know how long I had to get them out.

We had been underwater thirty-eight minutes, according to the chronograph on my new dive watch. That wasn't a large or forgiving window.

Will, the novice, would have consumed more air than we had. That was predictable. He might have as much as twenty-five minutes remaining or as little as ten, depending on how he now handled the shock of being caught under the rocks.

Tomlinson would deal with it more calmly. The man is benignly neurotic, as high-strung as a poodle during the normal course of his abnormal life, but when events turn sour, and the sky begins to fall, the man changes.

I've seen it often enough to know.

When the pressure's on, Tomlinson withdraws into some ancient retreat inside his head. His voice softens, his mannerisms slow. He exudes an unaffected calm—a serene acceptance that is sometimes comforting but occasionally maddening.

What I hoped was that the guys had already dug their way out of the pile. I hoped they were now kicking their way toward the surface with nothing more than a few bruises and cuts to deal with. If true, the landslide was something we could laugh about later.

After a full minute of kicking through the murk, though, I began to have my doubts. With each stroke, I expected to collide with remnants of the fallen ledge.

I did not.

I changed direction, certain I would hit bottom. Wrong about that, too. So I recalculated, and made another attempt to find the ledge, both hands extended, feeling my way.

Nothing.

I was disoriented. The sediment was so thick there was the illusion that I was descending, not traveling on a level course. The silt, as it boiled around me, appeared to be siphoning downward, too.

Or was it illusion?

I swam blindly for another few seconds before I stopped, and told myself to calm down, to *think*. I checked the depth gauge attached to my buoyancy compensator vest—a BC. The gauge was a simple recreational-dive computer, with a needle and precise green numerals. Even so, visibility was so poor I had to hold the thing against my mask to read it.

48 ft.

Damn it!

It wasn't an illusion. I had been descending. Without landmarks to guide me, I'd been following the lake's rim downward toward the mouth of the underground river.

My brain analyzed the inference. If silt was being

drawn downward, there was a reason. It meant there was a subtle, siphoning current. I had been swimming with the same current, following the path of least resistance.

I took two slow, measured breaths. Because I no longer knew up from down, I cupped my regulator and watched the bubbles. Next I jetted a burst of air into my BC, then followed the bubbles slowly toward the surface, exhaling as I ascended, left hand extended above my head, right hand holding the pressure gauge near my mask.

When I got to twenty feet, visibility had not improved. I purged my BC until buoyancy was neutral, then hung suspended for a few seconds. Where the hell had the lake's bottom gone?

I spun around, searching . . . and was instantly disoriented again.

Granules of sand swirling before my eyes assumed the pattern of distant stars . . . then zoomed closer, thick as a soup of protoplasm. I knew I had to surface to get my bearings. When I burped more air into my BC, it reacted with a thrusting space-shuttle jolt and began to transport me upward.

At ten feet, I stopped again, surprised by another thunderous rumble. Water conducts sound more efficiently than air. The rumble came from beneath me, vibrating through flesh, resonating in bone.

Another landslide?

No. The sound was different, an abrupt thud of weight, then a mushrooming silence. If a massive slab of limestone had collapsed, it might make a similar sound.

I waited, dreading confirmation. The confirmation arrived via an upward surge of displaced water and a blooming cloud of darker sediment.

The landslide had caused a section of the lake's bottom to collapse. I knew there was a chance that Will and Tomlinson had been swept deeper by the implosion.

I surfaced in a rush. When I'd broken free of the murk and pushed the mask back on my head, I used fins to do a fast pirouette, examining the lake's surface. I hoped to see Tomlinson and Will floating nearby, laughing in the winter sunlight, already recounting their brush with death.

Instead, the lake was a solitary disk, wind-rippled, empty.

I checked the time. Forty minutes, I'd been down. At the max, Will had twenty minutes of air left, Tomlinson thirty . . . if they were still alive.

I faced the lake's southern shore, searching for our vehicle. It was a four-wheel-drive Dodge Ram truck, parked on a cypress ridge, fifty yards away across the water. I began calling for Arlis Futch and expected to see him exit the vehicle, hands on hips, still in a foul mood because I'd made him stay ashore.

The truck's door was open, but there was no sign of the old man. There was no sign of life, period, save for a pair of loons V-ing toward the lake's far rim and the ascending whistle of an osprey that wheeled overhead.

I cupped my hands and yelled, "Arlis? *Arlis!* Call nine-one-one!"

I waited before adding, "Tell them we need an emergency response team. *Arlis!* Rig the jet pump and start the generator!"

Silence.

Above, the osprey tucked its wings and dropped like a boulder. The hawk crashed the water's surface, splashed wildly for a moment, then struggled to get airborne, gaining speed, its claws dripping . . . but empty.

"Arlis! Do you hear me? Goddamn it . . . *Arlis Futch!*"

Near the vehicle, a rabble of crows scattered above the cypress canopy, black scars animated on a blue sky. Something beneath the trees had spooked the birds. If Arlis was somewhere back there in the cypress grove, he wasn't answering.

Tomlinson and Will had to be beneath me. Some where. There is no such thing as a bottomless lake, so I would find them. Somehow.

I cleared my mask, purged my BC, then piked downward. I let the weight of my legs push me toward the bottom.

Years ago, diving a sinkhole in the Bahamas, I swam down through a pea-soup murk only to suddenly bust through into a globe of glacier-clear water. It was like entering a crystal vault from above. The light was muted because of the gloom, but visibility was flawless.

On that occasion, I had pierced the aqueous lens of an underground spring. Fed by ocean currents, the outflow of water created a bubble of clarity. It was like discovering a secret world.

Something similar happened now, as I descended, although the change in clarity wasn't as abrupt. Sediment was dissipating, visibility improving. It was surprising because there hadn't been enough time for the murk to settle. It suggested that clear water was now flowing into the area from below. Perhaps the landslide had uncovered a spring.

At ten feet, I observed a vague, stationary darkness take form. It was the lake's shallow perimeter. The ledge that held the prehistoric tusk had stood fifteen yards from the rim of a drop-off. The sandy rim remained—a relief to see a familiar landmark—but the bottom had changed. The rim soon assumed color in patterns of gray and white. I was peripherally aware of varieties of fish— bream and immature bass—that had been drawn to the disturbance.

As I drew closer, I could also see that the bottom hadn't just changed, some of it had vanished. A section of ridge the size of a car had imploded, taking the ledge with it. From the appearance of the crater, the area beneath it had dropped about ten feet. The elevated wall had collapsed atop it and was now a mound of oolite and sand. The area was littered with fossilized oysters. The oyster shells were the size of footballs.

Then I saw something else I recognized: the prehistoric tusk. It lay bare on the sand. The thing was twice as long as I'd supposed. It was six feet of black ivory, spiraled like a corkscrew.

I swam downward, spooking fish as I approached,

and lifted the tusk—it was *heavy*. I waited a moment, ears adjusting to the pressure, then let the artifact drop. It made a satisfyingly hollow thud. The vague percussive sound told me that the bottom was porous, not solid.

Good.

It gave me hope.

First things first, I had to mark the spot. I pulled a dive marker from my vest and secured the nylon cord to a rock near the tusk. I inflated the marker, then watched it rocket to the surface.

From a calf scabbard, I removed my dive knife. Normally, I would have been carrying something cheap—more than one diver has died because he dropped an expensive knife and chased it into the depths. But this was to have been a shallow-water dive, so I was carrying a treasured possession. It was one of the last survival knives made personally by the late Bo Randall of Orlando. The handle was capped with a machined brass knob. I used the handle now to tap on the tusk, then straightened myself to listen, hoping to hear a response.

Nothing.

I tapped again, a measured series, then gave it a few silent seconds before leaving the tusk and swimming down into the crater.

A vein work of fissures thatched the crater's limestone floor. Tendrils of gray silt vented upward from the cracks, as symmetrical as smoke on a windless day.

A volcanic effect.

It told me yes, water was flowing out through the

latticework of stone. It also told me that the area beneath me was porous, not solid—possibly not heavy enough to crush two men.

Using the knife, I began tapping on the limestone, traveling along the bottom in an orderly way. *Tap-tap-tap.* I waited. *Tap-tap-tap.* I listened.

After several attempts, I abandoned the crater and followed its outer wall downward. At the edge of the wall, the bottom angled deeper. It dropped toward a funneling darkness: the mouth of an underground river.

Again, I went through the ceremony with the knife. *Tap-tap-tap.* Wait. *Tap-tap-tap.* Listen.

Twice, I worked my way around the wall, tapping, then waiting. When I finally heard a dull *Tap-a-tappa-tap* in reply, I thought I might be imagining it. I wasn't convinced until Tomlinson added a vaudeville rhythm: *Shave-and-a-haircut . . . two bits.*

The sound was muffled but the source familiar. Rap an air tank with a knife—it was the same bell-like sound. It told me at least one man was alive. No . . . they were both alive, I realized. I was now hearing a duo of bell sounds: Tomlinson and Will both banging on their tanks.

Tomlinson didn't carry a knife—it was irrational, but he never did—so he must have been using a flashlight or a D ring from his vest.

The clanging was steady, not frantic, which I found reassuring. My partners were trapped somewhere under the crater floor, beneath a plateau of rock and sand, but obviously they had room enough to move their arms. It suggested that they were in a crevice or in an underground chamber that had been covered by rubble.

I unsheathed my knife and began to dig methodically, pulling away rock, digging at the bottom. It was mostly sand. Frustrating. Digging a hole underwater is an exercise in futility. If I scooped out two handfuls of sand, twice that amount sieved downward and filled the temporary hole. Thinking it might be more efficient, I grabbed a pan-sized oyster shell and used it like a shovel.

It wasn't much better. Until I returned with the jet dredge, though, a shovel was my best option. I continued digging, burning my dwindling air supply, until the clanging signal from beneath the crater changed. It caused me to pause.

I heard an articulate *TAP. Tap-tap-tap* . . . *TAP* . . . *tappa-tap*. Over and over, with the same careful spacing. Some sounds were intentionally louder, it seemed.

I banged the oyster shell against my own tank, parroting the signal . . . then received a different signal in reply.

Tap . . . *TAP* . . . *tap*.

It was Tomlinson. Had to be. Tomlinson, the bluewater sailor, the maritime minimalist. He was attempting Morse code. The man had been studying code for nearly a year, inspired by a late, great friend who had railed against our growing dependence on technology.

I've been a devoted user of shortwave radios since childhood, but I'm not a student of Morse code. I know a few basic shorthand signals, but now was not the time to test my skills. We had less than twenty minutes of air left. Subtleties of communication would have to wait.

I returned to my digging, bulling chunks of limestone to the side, then using the oyster shovel to scoop a dent in the sand. I kept at it until a sound within the wall caused me to pause once again.

It was an alarm sound, the rapid *clang-clang-clang* of a fire bell. Tomlinson was telling me to stop digging.

Why?

I could think of only one possibility: My digging was somehow threatening the stability of the space that was providing them refuge.

Maddening! If I couldn't dig, how did Tomlinson expect me to free them? After several seconds of silence, he tried Morse code again.

Tap . . . TAP . . . tap.

I forced myself to concentrate. The louder clanks, I decided, were *dah*s in Morse. The faster, lighter raps were *dit*s.

Tap . . . TAP . . . tap.

Was it the letter *R*? Yes, an *R*. *R* is the most common Morse abbreviation. Even I recognized it. *R* stands for "roger"—"signal understood."

It was Tomlinson's way of beginning a dialogue.

I attempted a *dit-dah-dit* reply, then waited.

Once again, he tried to signal, but the letters wouldn't take shape in my head. Because I didn't understand, I let silence communicate my confusion.

Tomlinson tried a different pattern. I heard: *Dit-dit . . . DAH . . . dit. DAH . . . dit-dit-dit*.

Three times, he sent it, before I recognized another common Morse abbreviation. *F-B*. It was short for "fine business"—the equivalent of "everything's okay."

Everything was certainly not okay. He was telling me they weren't hurt—not seriously, anyway. So why had he sounded an alarm?

I tapped out the letter *R* in reply—"understood"— then listened to a string of louder, methodical bell notes. Instead of attempting to translate, I counted . . . counted four distinctive clangs, but the fifth—if there was to have been a fifth—was interrupted by a cascading clatter of rock and then a thunderous thud.

Another section of lake bottom, or possibly the interior wall of the crater, had collapsed—loosened by our clanging sound waves, more than likely.

I was blinded by another silt explosion, but this time I held my ground. I hung tight to a wedge of rock as the murk enveloped me. For a full minute, I waited for the unstable limestone to settle before I attempted to signal Tomlinson again.

This time, when he replied, the sound was much fainter. Either more sand and rock separated us or his location had changed.

I didn't want to risk another exchange in Morse code. Sound waves are corrosive, and the lake bottom was too unstable. I needed the jet dredge.

A dredge is the underwater equivalent of a pressure washer. The one we had brought consisted of a generator, a heavy coil of hose that floated on a tractor-sized inner tube and a brass nozzle fitted into a three-foot length of PVC pipe. The thing shot a laser stream of water that would cut through rock and sand and was commonly used for setting pilings—or for treasure hunting. That's why we'd brought it.

I had to get the generator going, prime the pump and return with the hose. I needed Arlis Futch's help.

On the chance that Tomlinson and Will had, in fact, found refuge in an underground chamber, I located a crevice below the crater. It took a while to find one that looked to be about the right size. Without removing my BC, I popped a latch on the backpack, freed my air bottle and pulled it over my head. After I had inhaled a couple of deep breaths, I closed the valve, then purged my regulator before removing the pressure gauge and regulator hoses.

Full air bottles sink. Empty tanks float. Mine was half full, so it was easy to maneuver. I wedged the bottle into the crevice, valve up, and braced it with a chunk of rock. When I was convinced the tank was secure, I opened the valve a quarter turn.

A silver chain of air bubbles ascended from the tank. They began to disperse along the underside of the crater. The bubbles became as animated as ants as they probed the rock face, seeking vents and passages to continue their ascent. If there was a chamber above, the bubbles would find the open space and burst free.

I am not a cave diver, although I had explored a couple of caves years ago beneath an island off Borneo. But

I've spoken with, and read about, Florida's cave divers—an exacting, dedicated group that has lost more than one comrade to their collective passion for mapping subterranean labyrinths.

From these people, I had acquired a sense, at least, of the complex geology that defines the underwater karst catacombs that exist beneath the flatlands of central Florida. A small rock vent can lead to an ever-narrowing dead end, but it might also open up into a cavern. Caverns have been discovered beneath Florida's flatlands that are the size of airplane hangars, vaulted cathedrals of limestone. Some were formed during the Pleistocene and had once been home to wandering families, human and animal, before the rising sea level flooded them.

I had heard that such caves might contain air bells—pockets of air—although I doubted the truth of it. Not in Florida, anyway. An airtight vault in rock as porous as limestone? It was unlikely.

Even so, wedging a bottle beneath the collapsed ledge was worth a try. Maybe, just maybe, Will and Tomlinson had been lucky enough to find an air pocket. Maybe, just maybe, I had provided my friends with additional air.

I started up with a few kicks of my old Rocket Fins. When I broke through the surface, I was already yelling for Arlis Futch.

This time, Arlis was waiting. He was standing at the edge of the lake, next to his truck, but his posture was oddly stiff. He was standing as if he were at attention. There were two men with him.

Where the hell had *they* come from? We hadn't told

anyone about the lake—Arlis had demanded secrecy—
and the nearest road was miles away.

I had to clear my prescription mask and square it on
my face again before I could be sure of details. Only
then did I understand why Arlis was standing oddly. One
of the men was holding a pistol to the back of his head.

The second man was also armed. He had a rifle
pointed at me.

With his trigger hand, the man was waving me out of
the water, calling, "Come up out of there, Jock-a-mo,
and meet your new playmates. We got lots to talk
about."

SIX

TOMLINSON'S FIRST LUCID THOUGHT, WHEN he realized he was pinned under a pile of rock and sand, was an automatic attempt at humor, a comforting cliché: *Looks like I picked a bad week to quit smoking.*

Not cigarettes, marijuana.

He had promised Ford that he would quit because Will Chaser was on Sanibel for a week, and the biologist was worried the kid would sniff out Tomlinson's love for the bud.

Apparently, Will had an interest in the subject that went beyond that of a hobbyist. He didn't need any more bad influences in his life.

Ford didn't particularly like the teenager, that was obvious. But the man still felt some responsibility because Will was traveling with Ford's on-again, off-again squeeze, the high-powered Iron Maiden, Barbara Hayes.

Barbara was not always iron, as Tomlinson had discovered only three nights before, and she was certainly no unschooled maiden.

I'm a sinner, God knows it, so let the games begin!

More than a tad ripped on rum, Tomlinson had said exactly that to Barbara an hour after she'd left Doc Ford's lab, where they'd eaten dinner. Really excellent snapper, with peanut gravy, but the lady was pissed off about something, no telling what. Tomlinson had said the words just before unsnapping the Iron Maiden's bra free, the first ceremonial, no-going-back gesture in the betrayal of his best friend.

Later that evening, the betrayal had caused Tomlinson much angst. He was a sensitive man with morals— although Tomlinson seldom allowed morality to interfere with his personal life. But the betrayal had at least one positive result. It had steeled his determination to honor his promise to Ford that he wouldn't smoke the entire week, for the sake of the kid.

Tobacco was never mentioned in the agreement, however, so at midnight on Sunday Tomlinson had ridden his bike to the 7-Eleven, where he'd bought a pack of Spirits, organic cigarettes in a yellow pack. He hoped the smokes would mitigate the withdrawal symptoms he had suffered during the previous few days. He had been having weird dreams, he couldn't eat and a restless gray depression had descended upon him with a weight that— although more subtle—was no less distressing than the weight of the mound of limestone and sand that now covered him.

That night, pedaling home to Dinkin's Bay, Tomlinson had lit the first cigarette he had smoked in . . . how long?

Ninth grade? No . . . the last cigarette he had smoked was in tenth. He'd had a brief fling with tobacco during that period, smoking Camels, in an effort to add to his James Dean mystique. Another reason he'd chosen Camels was that unfiltered cigarettes made his hands look bigger, and Tomlinson's primary obsession had from earliest memory been women, and women were perceptive and impressed by such things.

Tomlinson had been weaned by a wet nurse   his family was wealthy. She was a Scandinavian dream with translucent melon breasts, so alluringly traced with veins that even as a child Tomlinson had loved maps, with their blue rivers that tracked true to the sea.

The Spirit cigarette, though, tasted like crap and had left his breath smelling worse than bong water. Adding to his displeasure was the awareness that smoking an organic cigarette was the way trendy tobacco slaves rationalized their addiction while also feeding it.

Tomlinson had an aversion to endorsing trendy behavior via his own behavior. He felt he was above such silliness. It struck him as common.

As he lay beneath the rocks, he thought, *One last joint. If I'd smoked a number last night, this bullshit would be easier to deal with now.*

He'd almost done it. After leaving Barbara's beach

rental for the second time in three nights, he'd come *this* close to breaking his promise about getting high on weed. Tomlinson had hidden aboard *No Más* a baggie full of jays, beautifully rolled, all sprinkled with resin crystals from his kef box. The jays had glittered like éclairs when he held them near the candle he had lighted before sitting in meditation, as he did every day twice a day.

Meditation stilled the chaos of stars inside Tomlinson's head. That's why he did it. Smoking, though, sometimes added colors to the stillness. After a few ghost hits from really good shit, meditating also brightened the swirling stars and warmed the black chill of inner space.

Tomlinson hadn't broken his promise, though. There was a reason. Just as he was about to light up, the kid had paddled past *No Más* in a canoe.

Damn kid. I should've ignored him. I could've pretended like I'd passed out or something, how would he know?

Talk about divine intervention! God had a wicked sense of humor for someone who had carved out so many prissy rules about behavior, but a reminder of the promise to stop smoking weed was exactly what he deserved after two-timing a close pal.

Tomlinson thought, *I've got to deepen up here. I've got to take stock.*

Yes, he did.

The regulator had been knocked from Tomlinson's mouth when the first rocks fell, but he had managed to fit it in place before the second wave of limestone covered him. It was a pounding weight that had compressed him, in a fetal position, in darkness against the lake's rocky bottom.

That was the way he lay now, as he tested the weight of the rocks that covered him. He moved his elbows, his feet, his fingers, relieved that his nervous system seemed to be okay and also that the rock and sand that covered him seemed to be malleable.

Will Chaser was beside him, still alive and conscious. Tomlinson knew because the boy's fins were in his face. Every time the kid tried to struggle free, he came close to knocking off Tomlinson's mask or kicking the regulator from his mouth.

But where was Ford? Had he been caught in the landslide, too?

Tomlinson let his mind settle, and then he pinged the area around him for information. As he did, his memory reviewed the moments prior to the wall's collapse. He recalled Ford turning away from the mammoth tusk and then looking downward. In his peripheral vision, Tomlinson had seen Ford jettison air from his BC, before jackknifing toward the bottom. The man had one arm extended as if to pluck something from the sand.

And then . . . what had happened? Rocks had begun raining down, and Tomlinson couldn't remember anything else but trying to fend off the crushing weight.

Now, beside him, Will Chaser rallied and tried to battle his way free once again. One of his fins knocked Tomlinson's mask askew before the boy stopped struggling.

Tomlinson thought, *First time in my life I've been kicked in the face, and I'm happy about it.*

He felt good, but only for a moment. The feeling was soon replaced by the memory of what he had said to Ford: "I'll assume full responsibility for the kid's safety."

Gad! What a ridiculous thing to say.

Why did he make such stupid promises? There was no controlling destiny—few people knew that better than Tomlinson. Guaranteeing some future reality was as futile as attempting to change the past. But he had done exactly that—flipped God and destiny the finger, in effect—and now here they were.

Ford's gonna kill me for this one! I don't blame him, either.

That was almost funny, thinking about how pissed off Ford would be, but not for long, because the shock of what had happened was beginning to solidify in Tomlinson's brain. His was a big brain, with banks of active synapses few other people possessed, but it was not an orderly brain. The cerebral segments were complexly wired, but they were also interrupted by filaments of scar tissue—not unlike the trunk rings of a tree that had been struck by lightning many times.

Tomlinson had, in fact, suffered several electrical shocks in his life, most as medical therapy, but some not. Plus there were also scars related to his experimentation with drugs, which, as Tomlinson viewed it, was part of his job description.

As a social scientist, it was one's duty to explore the inner universe.

Ford had once told him, "The way your brain works,

the shortest distance between two points is a circle."
The man had been frustrated by some debate they were
having, something to do with philosophy or possibly
baseball, which were pretty much the same thing in
Tomlinson's estimation.

Baseball? Why the hell had his brain leaped to that?

Maybe he had suffered a concussion when the rocks
fell. It was possible, so Tomlinson's focus turned inward.
He inspected the inner workings of his skull, but there
was no pain, and his memory was definitely in the pink.

*You don't have time for this, dumb-ass. Hunker down
and concentrate—or the boy's going to die.*

Tomlinson knew it was true.

The fact that he, too, would die was a secondary consideration. Tomlinson believed—believed to the core—
that he had already died, and not just once. He had died
at least three times, he felt sure, and possibly more. He
was a walking ghost and he was comfortable with that
fact. But Will Chaser's life mattered. The kid was only
sixteen. He had never driven a car, as far as Tomlinson
knew, and had probably never been with a woman—or
possibly even kissed a girl.

Tomlinson thought, *I've got to save this kid. I've got to
save him or go down trying.*

That thought came into his mind with a force that
was as violent as anything he had ever experienced in his
existence, dead or alive. It was then that Tomlinson
asked himself, *How would Ford deal with the situation?*

It came into his mind formulated like a weird chemical equation. It was another semihumorous cliché that would have irritated the hell out of the ever-pragmatic Dr. Ford: *W2D2*.

What would Doc do?

Marion Ford was, in Tomlinson's experience, the most competent man he had ever met. Ford had a dark side, true. The man danced with demons, but at least Doc kept the contents of his dance card to himself.

Ford had a first-rate intellect, but it was not a dazzling intellect. He possessed no stellar gifts, mental or physical—something Tomlinson wouldn't have said to the man's face, but it was also true.

What Marion Ford did possess, though, was a genius for getting whatever needed to be done *done*. He was steady and relentless, and so by God dependable that Tomlinson actually admired the man for their polar differences, and he was a little jealous, too.

As Tomlinson lay beneath the rocks, a sensory impression came into his brain. It had to do with Ford, something current, not a memory from the past. It wasn't just a feeling, it was a defined presentiment that was more like data being fed to him by a scanner, a mechanism of sorts, that existed outside himself. He waited, and soon the data took the form of an intuitive voice telling him, *Ford's okay. He's alive . . .*

Tomlinson inspected the impression until he felt certain it was true. His sensory probing—along with his

recollection of Ford jackknifing away from the wall—
were additional proof that the man was still out there,
swimming free. The confirmation created such a jolt of
optimism in Tomlinson that he could have wept, had he
allowed himself.

Instead, he tried to manipulate his brain into making
an orderly assessment of the situation, which is precisely
what Doc would have done.

First things first: How much air did he and the boy
have left?

After a moment spent trying to organize the figures,
Tomlinson gave up, thinking, *Oh . . . shit-oh-dear!* because he realized he didn't have a clue how much air
they had left. He had been so focused on the dive, on
what he was seeing, sailing over the pristine lake bottom,
then finding the beautiful mammoth tusk, that he had
lost all track of time.

His dive-gauge console would have the information,
but he couldn't reach it. The console, which was attached by a hose to his BC, was somewhere pinned beneath him. Without it, all he could do was guess at how
long they'd been down.

No, wait! That wasn't true. Moments before the wall
collapsed, Ford had scribbled something on his dive slate
and showed it to Will. Ford had written, *Surface in 5.*

The man wouldn't have written it unless he'd checked
Will's pressure gauge and knew that the boy was down
to half a tank. That had been only a few minutes ago.

Tomlinson thought, *The kid's got between twenty and*

*twenty-five minutes left . . . if he doesn't start panicking
and suck the bottle dry.*

Twenty-five minutes was a sad excuse for a lifetime.
Unless . . . unless one happened to be meditating, or
zone-locked, soaring on some horizonless high, a feeling
of euphoria that Tomlinson had experienced plenty of
times but the kid probably had not. Sex came close . . .
But only twenty-five minutes? Tomlinson reminded himself it was unlikely that Will Chaser, age sixteen, had
touched that particular base.

*Twenty-five minutes . . . Jesus, what a rotten hand to be
dealt!*

Or . . . maybe not. Could be that twenty-five minutes
was time enough. Right now, Ford was probably hovering above the rubble, bulling rocks, clawing at the sand,
digging like a cadaver dog to free them.

But what if he wasn't?

Tomlinson closed his eyes in the blackness and listened. He could hear the metallic exhalations of Will's
rapid breathing. He could hear the percussive croaking
of distant fish and the grandfather-clock ticking of limestone as it settled. But he didn't hear anything that
sounded like digging. Where the hell was Ford?

Tomlinson gave it some thought, then decided, *We
can't wait here, expecting Doc to find us. I've got to do
something now.*

He took three long drags on his demand regulator.
The hiss of compressed gas jetting into his lungs was
louder than the percolating bubbles that he exhaled.
Next, he pushed the face mask tight to his face, levered

an elbow under his ribs, then bucked hard against the weight of rubble that covered him.

The rubble moved.

The rocks didn't budge much, but the weight above him shifted, and he gained enough space to use both hands.

Tomlinson tried it again and managed to fight his way to his knees. As he rested, he wondered why the limestone continued to move and grind next to him. Will Chaser, he realized, was struggling to create his own space. There was a danger, of course, that by struggling they would damage their tank fittings or crush a regulator hose, but there was no other option. Just lie there and die?

Nope, we've gotta ride, Clyde.

Tomlinson bucked his hips upward, but this time the rocks didn't move. Twice more he tried, then attempted to think of a better method as he rested. His fins were making it difficult to find purchase with his toes, that was the problem. He couldn't reach his feet with his hands, so he used his heels to pry one fin off, then the other.

When he felt ready, he got his knees under him, dug his toes into the sand and used his back to lift mightily, straining against the suffocating weight as if lifting a piano. The weight shifted as rocks grated overhead, but there was little gain.

Damn it.

He tried again. He lifted until his muscles trembled and his ligaments popped . . . and then something very strange happened. The limestone above him didn't move, but a plate of rock beneath him made a bone-cracking sound, then splintered beneath him like a trapdoor. Tomlinson felt his body fall several feet. It was like falling through a rotten floor.

He winced, expecting the limestone above to come crashing down, but it didn't. There was a brief clattering of rock, then silence. He had thrown his arms over his head to protect himself, but now he opened his eyes and stared up into a blackness that was like looking into an abyss.

The discomfort of crushing weight was gone, and now . . . now he could sense space around him. Not much space, but he could move his arms and legs. Tomlinson got his knees under him and very slowly sat up. When he did, he felt limestone hard against the back of his head, but there was a foot of clearance above his head.

He realized that they had dropped into a karst chamber or vent—a chamber that had been sealed by one or more large slabs of limestone as they fell.

Like a blind man, Tomlinson extended his hands, with his fingers wide, to explore the space around him, only to be suddenly blinded when Will Chaser switched on the little rubber-coated flashlight that he was carrying. The kid was pointing the beam directly at Tomlinson's face.

Damn . . . the thing was bright!

It wasn't as powerful, though, thank God, as the little light that Ford had loaned Tomlinson. Of course not. Ford was a flashlight snob. An aficionado of high-tech

LEDs and all instruments that manufactured light—understandable in a man who had spent so much of his life in dark places.

Fortunately, or maybe not, Will had insisted on carrying what equipment he had, which included the cheap little vulcanized flashlight. The thing was bright enough, though, to be blinding after so many minutes of total darkness.

Tomlinson made an *awwggg–shittt* sound through his regulator. He covered his eyes with one hand as he used the other to find the boy's arm and then he pushed the light away.

Before the rock slide, he and the boy had gotten pretty good at verbal communication despite clinching regulators between their teeth. In Tomlinson's experience as a diver, not many people could do it. Communication with a chunk of rubber in one's mouth required mental skills that bordered on the telepathic. Ford refused to attempt it, but Will Chaser was a natural.

The boy spoke to Tomlinson now, saying, "Ooh . . . oou . . . UHH-aye?" Will might have been asking, *Are you okay?*

Tomlinson responded, "'Ucking . . . linded . . . meee!"

Will apologized, saying, "Aww-reee," as the beam of light angled downward into blackness. Then Tomlinson heard the teen reprimand himself. "'Ucking id-ot! 'Uck-meee!"

The kid was mad at himself, no doubt, but Tomlinson was heartened by this reaffirmation of Will's ability to translate vocal rhythms into words. The teen obviously possessed heightened powers of perception. From the moment of their first meeting, Tomlinson had sensed that boy was different—*very* different—plus it was also good to know that a concussion hadn't damaged the kid's brain or his abilities.

Tomlinson found Will's arm again, then squeezed the boy's hand, communicating, *Don't worry about it*. He sensed that the kid wasn't panicky. Will was afraid, yes, but the boy hadn't lost his cool. The information was all right there for Tomlinson to inspect, flowing between their two hands—and still plenty of strength in the kid's grip, too.

Tomlinson found his own flashlight and spoke three gurgled words—*Cover your eyes*—before pointing the light at his fins and turning it on.

Visibility was zero. All Tomlinson could see was a universe of swirling silt, the granules colliding against his face mask. Plus, his eyeballs were still throbbing from the recent light explosion.

He closed his eyes, giving himself time to recover, as he traced a hose to his console, then held the console close to his mask. Its two small instruments—a dive computer with depth gauge and a pressure gauge—were luminous green, but he still had trouble seeing the numbers because the silt was so thick.

Finally, though, he read:

1520 psi.

18 ft.

Now he was sure of what had happened. The limestone floor had collapsed beneath them, but not far. The good news was, he had more than half a bottle of air remaining. For Tomlinson, that meant more than thirty minutes of bottom time. And only eighteen feet beneath the surface! He felt the irrational urge to launch his body upward, through the rock. He yearned for sunlight. The sky was so damn close!

Stay cool! Pin your damn butterfly brain to the track.

Visibility seemed to be improving, but too slowly for his mood, so he switched off the light and used his hands to explore the rock chamber. His fingers touched plates of limestone and oversized oyster shells that he knew were fossilized—he'd seen a bunch of prehistoric oyster remnants earlier on the bottom of the lake.

A massive rock seemed to cover the chamber, which explained why they hadn't been crushed by rubble. The walls were composed of rock and loose sand, which wasn't a comforting thing to discover. The whole damn place could come crashing down at any moment. Overall, the space wasn't much larger than a shipping crate, but it was an improvement over where they'd been.

Tomlinson squeezed the boy's shoulder to reassure him, then sat back, resting one shoulder against the rocks. They weren't free, but they were in a better position to dig themselves out—as long as they didn't disturb some weight-bearing slab and get themselves killed when the ceiling collapsed.

Tomlinson calmed himself by reviewing the facts. He and Will both had miniature emergency canisters holstered next to their primary tanks. Redundancy air systems—or "bailout bottles," as they were called. Tomlinson's canister, which had SPARE AIR stenciled on the side, was good for only a couple of minutes. But Will's pony bottle was twice as big—thirteen cubic feet of additional air. That was Ford's idea, of course, the obsessive safety freak.

Tomlinson remembered rolling his eyes at the man as he had listened, impatiently, to the predive checklist. Later, if Ford gave him a ration of crap about the way he had behaved, no problem. Well deserved—if they survived.

Tomlinson guessed that Will's spare bottle was probably good for ten minutes of additional bottom time. Question was, how much air did Will have remaining in his primary tank?

Tomlinson reached until he found the boy's shoulder. He felt around until he located the hoses, then the dual gauges on Will's BC. He pulled the gauges close to his face. The numbers were encouraging.

1380 psi.

Most novice divers were air gluttons. Not Will. The kid had steel woven into his heart—not surprising, after what he had survived only a few weeks before.

Tomlinson decided to try his flashlight again, so he turned it on, and shined it toward his feet.

Visibility had improved. He could see his own toes, long and thin, and he could discern the vague shape of Will's legs next to him. A slow current was siphoning the silt downward, clearing the water.

An underground river, Tomlinson guessed, flowed beneath them. It was pulling water toward the sea.

It was still too murky to use his dive slate to communicate with the boy, but it would soon be an option. He patted Will's arm, switched off his light and considered a few other reassuring facts as he rested.

Arlis Futch's truck was loaded with gear. Some of it was safety backup stuff—Ford again—but Arlis had also packed equipment they would need to begin salvage work, if they actually found Batista's plane.

There were three or four extra bottles of air and at least two spare regulators. There was an inflatable lift for muling heavy objects to the surface and there was a generator rigged with a compressor pump and hose, used to jet-wash through sand and rocks. It was a sort of reverse-suction dredge. Arlis had built it in his shop—useful for setting pilings at marinas or blasting sand away to expose gold coins.

That's what they needed, the jet dredge. The hose was banded to a length of half-inch PVC pipe. It wouldn't be easy for one man to use alone, but Ford could manage. Arlis would have to stay onshore to monitor the generator and the pump intake.

Would Ford think of the dredge?

Of course he would.

Tomlinson's thoughts were interrupted by a distinctive sound.

Tink . . . tink . . . tink . . . tink.

Tomlinson held his breath, listening. He heard it again: *Tink . . . tink . . . tink . . . tink.*

It was Ford, signaling them. He was using his knife to tap on something—a rock, possibly—Tomlinson could picture it. The sound seemed to come from beneath them.

Without prompting, Will began banging on his air tank in reply, using something metallic, and Tomlinson joined him, using his flashlight. So Ford would know they were both responding, Tomlinson added a signature rhythm—*Shave-and-a-haircut . . . two bits.*

It was the knock he sometimes used before entering the lab.

Ford responded, sounding closer.

Tomlinson was grinning. He decided to try some basic Morse code abbreviations before using code to remind Ford about the jet dredge. He also wanted to communicate that they had only about twenty minutes of air left.

Banging the flashlight against his tank, Tomlinson signaled several times, but Ford's silence told him he didn't understand, which was frustrating. He tried again. Same result.

Tomlinson thought, *Concentrate, Ford.* It was a rare night when the man didn't sit in his reading chair, fiddling with the dial of his shortwave radio. But did he spend his time learning ham chatter? No—the guy preferred overseas programming, the traditional news source for American State Department types.

Damn spooks . . .

Morse code wasn't working, and the sound of Will's breathing was as steady and insistent as a ticking clock. Tomlinson tried once again to communicate that they now had only nineteen minutes of air left and clanged much harder, aluminum flashlight against aluminum tank. He rang the bell notes in a methodical way, hoping Ford would count them.

As his impatience grew, he clanged the tank harder and harder—a mistake. Sound waves have a potent physical energy. It was something that Tomlinson knew, of course, but he didn't pause to consider.

As he banged away at the tank, the corrosive sound loosened the limestone. Tomlinson was thinking, *Hurry up, Ford—hurry!* when, for the second time, he heard limestone beneath him splinter and he felt the sickening sensation of falling into darkness.

Beside him, Will Chaser yelled, "'Ummm assss!" as the floor beneath them collapsed and the vacuum sucked them deeper.

Tomlinson wrapped his arms over his head, anticipating the crushing weight, as the world went black again.

SEVEN

AS I WADED ASHORE, THE MAN WITH THE PIS-
tol was grinning but sounded jittery as he called, "You
need some help, Jock-o? We heard you yelling. Drag
your ass up here, tell us all about it. Me and Perry, we're
full of ideas."

Perry, an intense man, was leaning toward me, his
cheek pressed to the rifle. I felt my abdominal muscles constrict. Any second, his finger could slip . . . or he
could pull the trigger intentionally.

I recognized the weapon. It was a battered Winchester
30-30, a classic carbine favored by cowboys and at least
one alligator hunter. It was Arlis Futch's rifle. Arlis being
Arlis, I knew the weapon was loaded.

Obviously, the two men had already been inside the
man's pickup truck. It was parked behind them, beneath

cypress trees, the driver's-side door still open. I wondered what they had done with our cell phones and the handheld VHF.

The edge of the lake was moss coated and slippery. I was carrying fins but kept my hands at chest level. As I walked, my eyes shifted from Arlis to the man with the rifle—Perry—then to his partner, who held the little silver automatic. "Pistol"—it became his designation, a way to differentiate between the two because they looked so much alike. They were of similar height, one a decade older than the other, but both men skinny in slacks. Perry wore a short-sleeved shirt, Pistol wore a jacket so wrinkled that it looked like he'd slept in the thing. Maybe he had. The men might have been brothers were it not for differences in facial structure.

So far, Pistol had done all the talking, and I now listened to him ask, "Why were you yelling for Gramps to call nine-one-one? One of your buddies get eaten by a shark?"

Gramps—he meant Arlis.

I said, "There's no need for guns. I've got two friends in trouble. If you help us, maybe we can help you."

Pistol replied with a mocking grin, and said, "Of course we'll help you. But, Jock-a-mo, we need you to do us a favor first. We want the keys to that cowboy Cadillac. The old man says he doesn't know where they are."

The man nodded toward Arlis's black diesel truck: twin cab, four-wheel drive, tow-rigged with mud flaps, a bumper sticker that read EAT MORE MULLET.

I didn't respond.

As I drew closer, the man pressed, "Maybe you didn't understand. I'm trying to be friendly. It can be dangerous out here in the sticks, you know."

I was looking at Arlis, seeing his left eye swollen purple, his mouth busted, lips the color of grapes. Normally, Arlis is a talker. He'd been badly beaten. It explained his silence.

Pistol was getting mad, which broadened the vowels of his Midwestern accent. "You got a hearing problem, mister? I want those goddamn truck keys!"

When Arlis signaled me with a slight shake of his head—*Don't cooperate*—the man with the rifle, Perry, decided to demonstrate that his partner was serious. He crow-hopped toward Futch and used the rifle butt to spear him behind the ear. The sound of wood on bone was sickening.

Arlis buckled forward and fell. Because his hands were taped behind him, he couldn't break his fall. He landed hard, face-first, on limestone.

I tossed my fins onto shore and slogged faster toward Arlis, ignoring shouts—"Stop right there, Jock-o!"—as I used my peripheral vision to process details about the gunmen. I had to read the situation fast and accurately or we would all die, Tomlinson and Will included.

Both men had the bony, wasted look of hitchhikers. The type you see at intersections, holding signs, their displaced expressions as masked as their egos. They had feral, gaunt faces. Long Elvis hair matted from sleeping on cardboard; clothes from some Salvation Army box or maybe pilfered from a trailer-park laundry.

Look into their faces, and I suspected that I would see interstate highways. I would see random crimes.

Random. That was my quick read. Stray dogs in primate bodies. It insinuated a pointless wandering, a string of indifferent outrages. They struck me as loners who had lived their lives in corners but who lacked some basic human component that drives others to seek bottom in an attempt to change.

My mind shifted to the recent murders in Winter Haven, remembering details I'd heard at the marina. Winter Haven was forty miles north. The newscaster, though, had reported that police had caught the killers near Atlanta, driving the maid's car.

Suddenly, I was unconvinced.

What were the odds of running into the killers? The astrology crowd does not believe in chance intersectings and random meetings. But here, in these two men, was an illustration of randomness incarnate.

They were cons, or ex-cons, I decided. And desperate. They were on the run from prison or from the Winter Haven killings and had bushwhacked to this remote area to hide. Why else were they willing to shoot two men for the keys to a truck?

More than willing. They were eager, in fact. That was evident, too. I perceived it in Perry's brittle movements, his twitching impatience. He had used the rifle butt on Arlis's head with an explosive, joyous abandon. I would be next, if I gave him a reason.

Pistol was the mouthpiece, I decided. Perry was the killer.

When I got to Arlis, I knelt beside him. He was trying to roll onto his back. The skin on his forearms felt loose, paper-thin, as I lifted him to his knees, then helped steady him on his feet. The rifle butt had dented the bone below his ear, blood was flowing.

Arlis is seventy, but he had never showed—or acted—his age. Until now. The man moved with a weary, testing fragility. But the fire inside him was still burning. It was in his expression, visible in his eyes. His eyes were pale, smoldering and resolute. They communicated more than an apology when I looked into his face. Arlis Futch was furious—furious at his captors and at himself.

It gave me a little boost.

Arlis spit, then spit again, hacking sand from his ruined mouth. "That son of a bitch," he said, his voice hoarse. "Cut me loose, Doc. I'd trade ten years at Raiford for ten minutes alone with this Yankee spawn." He stared at the men, talking loud enough for them to hear.

It earned Arlis a burst of jittery laughter. "Whoa, listen to Grandpa! Still talking like a hard-ass!"

Perry, with the rifle, wasn't feeling playful. "What do I care how he talks? He keeps yapping, I'll do it again!"

Perry couldn't stand still. His eyes were moving, checking the horizon, scanning the sky. He reminded me of a rodent watching for hawks.

Pistol wouldn't let it go. "Grandpa, maybe I should make you drop your pants. You get sassy again, I'll spank your ass good. How'd you like that?"

More laughter.

I caught Arlis when he lunged toward Pistol. There

wasn't time to let him calm down, so I gave him a little shake, and said into his ear, "Listen to me. We've got other problems. Tomlinson and Will are stuck down there. They're alive, but they're under a ton of rock."

It stunned him. Because the information required Arlis to think, it displaced his anger.

"They're trapped?"

"Maybe in a crevice. That's what I'm hoping, anyway. I tried digging, but we need to rig the jet pump."

"How deep?" Arlis was favoring his left shoulder, I noticed. Maybe he'd busted a collarbone when he fell.

I said, "Fifteen, twenty feet maybe. Definitely less than thirty."

He understood the significance. "They got a chance, then."

"Yeah."

Pistol didn't like us whispering. He was shouting at us, telling me to get away from Arlis. He told me to stop with the talking and do what I was told.

I ignored him. Kill us now, kill us later—it was Pistol's choice. I had to make things happen fast or there was no hope of freeing Will and Tomlinson.

Arlis whispered, "How much air?"

"Twenty minutes, a little more. Depends. There's a chance they found an air pocket. It's unlikely that deep, but I guess it's possible."

"Jesus Christ."

"How bad are you hurt? That eye looks bad." I tried to cup the man's face in my hands and check his pupils. He pulled away as I said, "You might have a concussion,

too. You need to lay down and get your legs elevated."
I glanced at the men, thinking, *Give me one opening. Just
one.*

Arlis ignored me as he returned his attention to the
gunmen. He said softly, "Did you read about the five
people murdered up near Orlando? A grove owner,
the television said. Plus the maid and her three kids.
They were shot and stabbed, I read. I think these are the
birds."

I didn't want him to see how worried I was. "Good,"
I said. "Then that means the cops are already looking for
them. Choppers will be flying over. We might need a
chopper to transport our guys to the hospital, once we
get them out."

"If that's good," Arlis replied, "I don't know the
meaning of bad."

Arlis's hands and his injuries told a story. His wrists
weren't taped or tied, as I'd assumed. They were tie-
wrapped. Earlier, I'd seen a bag of industrial-sized
tie wraps in the back of his truck. I thought about it as I
let the two men watch me take my knife from its scabbard and cut Arlis free.

While I was underwater, Pistol and Perry had sur-
prised Futch—possibly spooking crows from the trees as
I'd surfaced earlier. They had a gun. The cheap little Hi-
Point pistol, black on silver. They'd used it to overpower
Arlis before trying to steal his vehicle. The Winchester
had been inside. Probably a couple of boxes of cartridges

under the seat, too, knowing Arlis. Plus our phones and the radio.

Arlis had put up a fight, obviously. So the men had tie-wrapped his wrists before continuing their search for the keys. I wondered what else they'd found in the vehicle.

"Jock-a-mo, I'm tempted to shoot you in the ass right now, just for shits and grins. You don't follow orders very well, do you?"

The men had been yelling at me, telling me to leave Arlis tied. I had continued to ignore them, but now I wondered if maybe I'd pushed the envelope too far. As I sheathed the knife, I gave Pistol my full attention. He was edging toward the lake, probably to change his line of fire. I guessed he was thinking about pulling the trigger, giving it serious consideration. Perry had upstaged him, clubbing Arlis, then I had to add to the insult by ignoring Pistol's orders. Maybe Pistol wanted to prove he was a tough guy, too.

I called, "What the hell's wrong with you two? Why beat up an old man?"

Arlis made an indignant guttural noise as Pistol replied, "The keys, Jock-a-mo. How many times I gotta say it? You find us the keys, we'll stop beating on Grandpa."

I straightened and looked at them both. "My name's Ford. This is Captain Arlis Futch. We don't have the truck keys. You want them?" I motioned to the lake. "They're down there."

"You gotta be shittin' me."

I said, "I can get them. Ten or fifteen minutes underwater, that's all I need. One of my friends has them in a pouch."

It was a lie. I had no idea where Futch had hidden the keys, but I knew they weren't in the lake—not with Tomlinson and Will, anyway.

I'd told the two that I could retrieve the keys because I wanted them to believe that we had something of value to trade. I also wanted to establish our identities as individuals. Armies depersonalize the opposition for a reason. Criminals do the same. It bypasses the genetic restraints that make killing taboo.

If Arlis had guessed correctly about these two, however, it was wasted effort. If they'd already murdered five people, two more wouldn't bother them a bit.

Pistol had stopped moving. He was staring at me as he evaluated what I'd said about the keys. The man with the rifle, Perry, was thinking about it, too. "Shit, King. You believe him?"

"Shut up. Give me a minute."

King.

So they were Perry and King, a pack of two. King, with the pistol, was the alpha male. Perry, the tagalong, had been gifted with the stolen Winchester, but he wasn't beyond thinking for himself or doubting his partner's judgment. Perry had his own agenda, and a brittle impatience. King irritated him, I could tell.

The two men had somehow stumbled onto us . . . or possibly they had been watching us from the beginning, hiding in the trees. It was risky for the two of them, armed with only a pistol, to attempt to overpower the four of us. So they had waited, trying to time it right.

Once three of us were underwater, King and Perry had moved in fast and hard to steal the truck, intending to make their escape before the scuba divers surfaced—and possibly after killing Arlis.

But there had been a snag. Arlis had somehow managed to hide the keys before they got to him. And he had refused to talk—so they had beaten him. Now the men were stuck with another crime on their hands and nothing to show for it but a Winchester and whatever they had pilfered from the truck.

The truck was parked in the shade of a cypress tree but still visible to a low-flying police chopper. If this became a crime scene, and if King and Perry couldn't get away from the area in a hurry, they were screwed.

But we were in a jam, too, and they knew it. They had heard me calling to Arlis, telling him we needed help. The men had seen the extra air bottles and the truck filled with gear. They had probably already robbed our duffel bags, containing wallets, glasses and cell phones.

Three divers had gone into the water but only one had returned. They knew I had to cooperate or my pals were goners.

King said to me, "You're in no position to get tricky, Jock-a-mo."

I looked from King to the truck, then at the sky, as if there might be a helicopter approaching. I allowed my expression to tell him, *Neither are you*.

Pointing the rifle at me, Perry said, "I got a bad feeling about this dude. He's trouble. Look at how he's acting. Why waste time talking to the asshole?"

King didn't answer immediately, and Perry lowered the rifle as he patted his breast pocket, then his pants. "Shit," he added, eyes shifting to the sky. "I'm out of cigarettes.

I stepped away from Arlis, creating some distance between targets. "If I had the keys," I said, "don't you think I'd tell you? I've got two friends down there, trapped under some rocks. There was a landslide, and I need to get them out before their air runs out. Let us rig the equipment we need and I'll bring you the keys. You can have the truck. We'll find our own way home."

King said, "*That* simple . . ."

"No," I said, "but it's possible."

"How stupid you think I am?"

I said, "Not stupid enough to kill two people, then try and hike out of a place like this. Or kill four people—that's the way a judge will see it if my friends die down there."

In the hush of twittering birds and wind, I nodded toward miles of palmetto scrub, seeing a blue ridge of trees on the horizon and a couple of miniature radio towers. "It took us more than two hours to cut our way in here," I said, "and we were riding in a truck."

King said, "Listen to this guy!" and tried to laugh.

Perry said, "Maybe we should. We need those damn truck keys, man. He's right about that."

King was looking at me, holding the pistol at his side. "I heard someone call you Doc. You're no doctor.

Maybe a cop. Or—you know what you look like? A teacher I had in middle school." It was spooky the way the man was staring at me.

"Does it matter? I'm trying to be reasonable."

"Reasonable, huh . . ."

It took some effort not to check my watch. I could feel the minutes ticking away. "I'm not a cop or a teacher. I'm a marine biologist, that's why we're here."

Perry surprised me by asking, "You went diving in that lake to look at fish and bugs and stuff, huh?"

"Fish, yes."

"Did you see anything big when you were underwater? Really big, I mean. A shark, maybe, like the one in the movies? Only not as long." It was an odd question, but the man had asked for a reason, I felt certain. His intensity told me that he'd seen something in the lake. What?

I said, "Nothing bigger than a three-foot gar." I was watching his reaction. He'd probably seen one of us—Tomlinson, Will or me—beneath the surface and imagined he was seeing something else.

Perry was shaking his head, his expression saying *No, what he'd seen wasn't a yard-long fish.*

For King's benefit, I added, "In sinkholes like this, there are a lot of bass, sunfish, bream—all the typical species. But I might have seen a couple of crystal darters, too. They're rare. Nothing bigger than the gar, though." I wanted to convince the alpha male that I was a biologist, not a cop.

It made me uncomfortable the way King was look-

ing at me. The man was squinting, not smiling, seeing me
but seeing something else, too. Something in his brain
maybe.

Turns out the possibility of me being a cop wasn't
what bothered him.

King said, "This teacher I'm talking about, he was the
world's biggest prick."

Back on the teacher again. The teacher had done
something to insult King or humiliate him, apparently,
and I resembled the man.

I thought, *Damn it,* and peeked at my watch. Tomlinson and Will had now been underwater for forty-six
minutes. They had thirteen or fourteen minutes of air
remaining, plus another couple of minutes for Tomlinson if he was able to use his spare emergency reserve
bottle and maybe ten minutes for Will because I'd rigged
his tank with a larger bottle.

I tried to appear unconcerned as I listened to King
say, "A couple of days ago, I was telling Perry about this
teacher I'm talking about. I told Perry, 'Man, I'd love to
get my hands on that ass-wipe teacher.' Isn't that what I
said?"

Perry was busy shouldering the rifle, checking the horizon, still scanning the sky. He replied, "Whatever."

"Seriously. I don't want Jock-o to think I'm lying.
Trust is so damn important in a partnership. That's what
he's offering us: a chance to be partners."

The man's sarcasm implied intelligence, and I began
to hate him for his plodding indifference. King was

smart enough to know that my friends were running out of time. He was enjoying it, making me squirm.

Perry said, "Make up your mind. If you want to do these guys, fine. Let's finish it and get moving. But this standing-around-doing-nothing bullshit is driving me nuts." His hand moved to his pockets again, seeking cigarettes.

Ten seconds, fifteen seconds, King stared at me without blinking. I hoped he was thinking about my proposition, working it through to an obvious option. He could wait until I returned with the other two divers, plus the truck keys, then kill us all and escape in the vehicle.

I didn't want him to push the scenario any further, though. Because of that, I took a chance and said, "What do you have to lose? A few minutes underwater, that's all I need. Let me change bottles. You can take off in the truck when I get back."

King said, "Why the hell would anyone take keys underwater? The damn truck's got electric windows, it's all tricked out. And Grandpa was driving. That doesn't make any sense, Jock-o."

So they had been in the trees, watching us when we arrived.

I said, "Captain Futch was driving, but he doesn't own it. It's my buddy's truck. He's got the keys in a waterproof pocket"—I opened a Velcro pocket on my BC to validate the lie—"they're built into the vests. That's better than surfacing and finding your truck gone."

Perry muttered, "Goddamn it!" as I continued, say-ing, "Half an hour at the most—any longer, my friends will be dead, anyway."

As the words left my mouth, I realized it was a stupid thing to tell them, but I kept going, adding, "One of the guys trapped down there is a teenage boy. The other's the laid-back hippie type—he's the one who owns the truck. They're no threat to you. Give me half an hour, you'll get your keys. It would take you half a day to hike out of here. There's no cover, nothing but palmetto scrub."

Because I didn't get an immediate reaction, I added, "Give me thirty minutes. It's a no-brainer—for anyone with half a brain, that is."

That hit a nerve. King took a couple of quick steps toward me, pistol raised, as if imitating Perry, the way he had clubbed Arlis. But then he changed his mind. My knife was still strapped to my calf, and he didn't want to put himself at risk by getting too close to someone my age, my size, whose hands were free. King was also a coward. No surprise there.

The man was four paces away when he stopped—a safe distance. He motioned with the pistol. "Take off that vest and throw it over here. I want to see what you got in the pockets. Maybe you're the one with the keys."

I ripped open the Velcro straps, slipped the harness off and tossed the BC toward his feet.

"Now the knife. Unbuckle it, but don't take it out of that damn rubber case. Pull that knife, it'll be the last thing you ever do."

He was pointing the pistol at me, both hands steadying it like maybe he'd seen tough guys in movies do. He kept his finger on the trigger, not parallel to the barrel like an experienced shooter.

Before King knelt to retrieve my vest, he stuffed the pistol into his back pocket, saying to Perry, "Forget Grandpa. Keep the rifle on Jock-o. If he moves, shoot him in the belly. Hear me?"

Perry positioned himself so he could do it.

I had been so focused on Tomlinson and Will that I'd forgotten about the gold coin I'd found until I saw King grin, drop my BC on the ground and turn to Perry. He was holding the coin so it caught the sunlight. "Goddamn, ace, look what we got here!"

When the rocks started falling, I must have stuffed the coin into a pocket.

Perry leaned close to look, saying, "Another one? How much you figure these things are worth?" Now he was taking a similar coin from his pocket to compare.

I had begun unbuckling the knife scabbard but stopped.

Another one?

It took me a moment to understand. Commercial fishermen are superstitious. For luck—and maybe so he could show Will—Arlis had brought along the coins he'd found earlier. Perry and King had found them in the truck or on Arlis, apparently.

Gold. I could see the greed in their faces.

Suddenly, I knew that I had all the leverage I needed—

if I worked it right. Diving to look for Cuban coins was a more attractive gambit than looking for nonexistent truck keys.

What's the smartest way to play this?

I had to get it right the first time, there was no room for error. Push too hard, Perry and King would sense it—they would have survivor instincts, if they had spent time in prison. Go too slow, Will and Tomlinson would run out of air and die.

I remained on one knee, a nonthreatening posture, and stole another look at my watch.

Fourteen minutes of air remaining, give or take. Sixteen, maybe twenty, counting their emergency bailout bottles.

EIGHT

KING'S EYES WERE MOVING FROM ME TO THE lake to the coin in his hand, putting it together, as he exchanged coins with Perry. He said to me, "You came clear out here to the middle of Fumbuck, Florida, to study the fish, huh?"

I said, "That's right." The knife was still strapped to my calf, but King no longer seemed interested. The third coin had hooked him, I could see it.

"You gentlemen show up with a truckload of gear just to swim around and look at fish because you're some kind of scientist, huh?"

"A *biologist*. It's what I do."

King's expression read *Bullshit*. "Then where'd this coin come from? It's just like the two we found in Grandpa's pockets."

I shrugged but didn't give it much.

King said, "You're a smart guy, Jock-o. What do you figure a coin like this is worth? Couple grand each? Just for the gold, I'm saying."

I didn't want to sound too eager. I said, "If the coins are real, maybe. For all I know, they're fakes."

"You're full of shit. They're real. Feel the weight." King was holding his palm out like a scale, judging the density of the coin. Perry did the same.

"Feels about the same as the gold eagles, that's what I think," Perry said.

Gold eagles? I wondered what that meant.

King was nodding as he held a coin close to his face, lips pursed as he deciphered details. Perry did the same, reading aloud, "Re-pub-lick-A dee-Cuba."

King corrected him, saying, "Re-pub-lic-uh DAY-Cuba," showing off, I realized, wanting to impress me for some reason or to prove something maybe. Then he asked, "How many more of these things are down there, Professor Jock-a-mo?"

Back on the teacher thing again.

I said, "Three, that's all we found. For all I know, they could be brass. Some kids could've thrown them in the lake, screwing around. We didn't expect to find them, they were just there."

Arlis picked up fast on what I was doing, and managed to say, "What we found is none of your damn business," giving it just the right touch of guarded indignation. "I own this property and I want you the hell off my land."

Perry was still studying a coin, obviously impressed,

as King looked from me to Arlis, letting his imagination put himself in our shoes. "What I think is, there's a bunch more of these things down there. That's closer to the truth, isn't it?"

I gave Arlis a nasty look, as if he'd said too much.

When King smiled, he had an odd way of tilting his head back, as if focusing through bifocals. He said, "Perry, I think we're onto something here. But I think Gramps and the professor don't want to share. Isn't that right, Jock-o? If you're smart, though, you'll play nice and tell me the truth. What'd you dudes find down there on the bottom?"

Arlis and I exchanged looks but remained silent.

Perry spoke. "These coins are from Cuba. What they doing out here in the middle of this shithole?"

King told him, "Miami's loaded with Cubans. You don't watch TV?" After several seconds, he added, "It's the dates that don't make sense. The coins are dated"— King reached to take Perry's coin, then compared the two—"one says nineteen twenty, the other nineteen eighteen. That's too old to be from Miami and too new to be found on what you'd call a 'sunken galleon.' Back in those days, they cut the silver and gold from bars, so the coins were sorta square, not round."

The man paused but wasn't done with his history lesson.

"Do you know what a twenty-dollar American gold eagle sells for? Mint condition, uncirculated?"

He was showing off again.

"No reason for me to know," I said.

"You probably don't even know what an ounce of gold sells for, either. And you being such a smart guy! You must have a hell of a lot of education, but you don't even know something so simple as the price of an ounce of gold."

I said, "When you make what a marine biologist makes, there's no reason to keep tabs on world gold prices."

King grinned. "See there? A real smart dude."

I was still on one knee, my knife hanging by a strap, and now I was calculating the distance to Perry's legs. If I could get in under the rifle, all I had to worry about was King, with his pistol . . . or the possibility that Perry would ignore me and shoot Arlis.

My eyes must have given me away. Both men took a step back, their feral instincts on full alert.

King said, "No reason for you to care about what an ounce of gold is worth, huh? You just came out here to check on the fish and got lucky? Perry, would you listen to this guy? He's such a shitty liar, how long you figure he'd last in the joint?"

Perry said to me, "Meat, if you keep lying to us, I'll put a bullet in your head. Tell us what you found down there."

I looked at Arlis again. I could see that blood was soaking into his shirt. He stared at the ground as if embarrassed. I was afraid he was going to pass out.

King said, "Know what I think? These dudes have found themselves some kind of sunken treasure. They don't give a damn about their two butt buddies. That's all show. They're more worried about protecting what they found. Otherwise, Professor Jock-o wouldn't be blowing smoke, promising us the truck keys, if we let him go back in the water."

I said, "Do you want the keys or not? I need extra tanks, I need to rig a piece of equipment and get down there." I caught my own left wrist before raising it to check my watch.

King acted as if he didn't hear me. He was stalling. He said, "Maybe it wasn't an accident, Jock-o, your two little girlfriends getting trapped. Split the take two ways instead of four ways, just you and Grandpa. Or maybe knock Grandpa in the head and leave him in the lake, too. That would make the math a whole lot better."

Arlis turned to give me a nasty look as if he'd already considered the possibility. He was hanging in there, playing his role.

Perry was bouncing the coin in his hand, looking at King, his expression saying *How many more do you think's down there?*

King was smiling now. "By coincidence, me and Perry have us a situation. The sort of situation where a bag full of gold coins could buy us a change of scenery and a whole bunch of good luck. But guess what, Jock-o?"

I waited.

"Perry and me, we're in no real rush. So I say let's all four of us stroll over to those trees, sit ourselves in the shade, and maybe you'll decide to stop lying—in, say, half an hour or so."

The smile vanished as the man raised the pistol toward me. He took a step closer so he wouldn't miss, and yelled, "You take that goddamn knife off your leg like I told you. Hear me? *Now.*"

As I unbuckled the scabbard, I said to Arlis, "I don't have a choice—you heard the man. They'll kill us. I've got to tell them the truth."

Arlis looked sick and shaken—which he was—but the expression of disgust he gave me was pure Hollywood. He turned away as if he wanted no part of it.

I said to King, "Okay, here it is. There's a plane down there. That's why our truck's loaded with extra gear for salvage work."

King said, "A plane," watching me closely. "What would a plane carrying Cuban coins be doing in the middle of Florida?"

I said, "It happened. Just *listen*—okay? In nineteen fifty-eight, a cargo plane from Havana, on its way to Tampa, crashed. It was a stormy night, the plane was slightly off course and no one ever found it. It was on its way to Tampa because this guy—he was the Cuban dictator before Castro—had robbed the treasury and was on the run. It's in the history books, if you don't believe me."

Looking at the two men, I could see their expressions. They believed me.

I nodded toward Arlis. "A couple of weeks ago, Captain Futch found the wreckage by luck. It's on the bottom of the lake—we're the first to find it—and the thing's untouched. We don't know for sure how much the plane was carrying in coins and gold bars, but figure it out for yourself. This guy robbed the national treasury of an entire *nation*."

When Perry said, "But Cuba's an island, right, not a nation," King told him, "Shut up and listen," giving me his full attention.

I said, "I was down there. I saw what the plane was carrying—some of it, anyway. But the wreckage is lodged under a big limestone ledge and it collapsed after my friends and I finally managed to pry open the cargo door. That's how my friends got trapped. They're down there now. With the gold."

Perry's breathing had changed.

Softly, King asked, "How much in all, you think?"

Arlis said, "Don't tell them any more. Shut your damn mouth! I'd rather die right here than let this spawn in on the deal!"

Perry snapped, "Shut up, Gramps, or you just might get your wish. Let the man talk." He focused on me. "A guy like you would'a done a lot of research and stuff. What's it say in the books you read? How much did the Cuban dude steal?"

I pretended to ignore Arlis and looked toward the trees. "He and his men loaded four cargo planes in Havana, but only one crashed. It's impossible to say how much the plane was carrying because no one knows for sure. They didn't keep a list."

"You know what I'm asking you," Perry said. "Answer the goddamn question. How much gold's down there?"

I let the men watch me think about it before I nodded toward the truck. "There's too much to carry it all in the bed of one pickup—that's how much. It would take three or four loads."

King said, "You're shitting me. That can't be true," but the tone of his voice said he wanted to believe it.

I shrugged, my expression telling him *Believe what you want,* before saying, "I'd guess there's at least half a ton in bars alone—they're stacked in what were probably wooden cases. I didn't see them all, but there's got to be more."

"You saw the stuff?"

"The wood's rotted away. The coins are scattered all over the bottom, but the bars—the stacks I saw, anyway—mostly settled in one place. It looked like the bars were stacked two high, probably eight to a box, and I saw at least eight boxes of the things. What used to be boxes, anyway. So that's at least sixty-four bars, but there's bound to be more. And there's definitely a lot more coins."

Perry said to King, "How much is a bar of gold worth?"

King was blinking his eyes, possibly staggered by the fortune I had just described. He said to me, "Why didn't you bring up a bar instead of just one shitty little coin?"

"I'm not going to stand here and argue with you. I saw what I saw."

"You're kinda touchy, aren't you, Jock-o? What do you figure one of those bars weighs?"

"Standard mint is one kilogram, isn't it? That's what I would guess."

Perry said, "How much is that? I hate that European bullshit. In pounds—talk English, goddamn it."

"A kilogram's a little over two pounds," King told him. "Sixteen ounces per pound, thirty-two ounces per bar, plus a little extra—say, forty ounces even, just to keep it simple. And you say there's at least sixty-four bars?" King was calculating it in his head but still giving me his full attention.

"More probably, but that's what I saw. You're the expert. How much does gold sell for by the ounce?"

King was smiling as he looked at Perry. "Those bars would sell for about sixty grand each. Sixty-four bars, that's . . ." He had to think about it. "That's three or four million bucks. Plus the coins."

"Jesus Christ," Perry said, his voice soft, "And it's just sitting down there. Waiting."

I was wondering why King knew so much about gold prices, putting it together with the American gold eagles they'd mentioned and the five dead people in Winter Haven, as King asked me, "How many coins, you think? Coins'd be easier to carry. Easier to sell, too."

"There's more than enough to split six ways, that's the point I'm making," I replied. "You guys are on the run for some reason—that's obvious. I don't care why and I don't want to know. But it kind of works out, you showing up. You need help, we need help. Look at it as purely business."

Perry said to King, "How many pounds are in a ton? Just in case he's telling the truth. I used to know, but—"

"Two thousand pounds," King said. "Half a ton is a thousand. And that cowboy Cadillac over there is big enough"—he was measuring the truck's bed with his eyes—"Jock-a-mo could be wrong about not being able to haul it all out of here in one load. But good coins are worth more. That's what we want, Jock-a-mo, the coins. But a couple dozen bars of gold, that'd be okay, too. We could walk out of here with a few million each, easy." The man's smile hardened as he stared at me. "Drive out, I mean."

He was lying about splitting the take, of course. King wanted it all, I could see it.

I said, "The gold's one thing, but my friends are part of the deal. You don't get the keys until we get my friends."

"You keep saying that."

"They're down there with the gold. A ledge collapsed and covered everything. I can't do it by myself. We brought a jet dredge. I need it to blast the sand and rocks away. But the pump takes at least three men to run. Two in the water and one man on land to tend the generator and keep the intake filter clear."

Perry asked, "What's an intake filter?" but King wasn't interested in the details. He said, "If that's what you've got to do, then get to work! You and Grandpa do the water part. We'll stay on land and run the machine, or watch the filter—whatever it is you want us to do. But we're also gonna keep the rifle handy in case you try something cute."

I was shaking my head. "Captain Futch is in no condition to do anything. Look at him."

Arlis's face had gone pale. Sweat on his forehead was streaking the coagulating blood, but he was still willing. He snapped, "I can work, don't you worry about that."

Even if he'd been able, I didn't want Arlis's help. My brain had been assembling a workable scenario, and I knew how I wanted it to go—how it *had* to go—if Will, Tomlinson, Arlis and I were to get out of this mess alive.

I ignored Arlis and spoke to the men. "It was stupid what you did to him, but now we're stuck with it. If you want the truck keys and a share of the gold, you two have to help me, not him."

"A share," King said, sarcastic. "Sure, we'll be happy with a share. What do you want us to do?"

I was getting to my feet, already reaching for my BC. "First thing for you to do is push the truck closer to the water while I get ready. There's a hundred feet of hose, and I'm going to need it all."

The men were looking at the truck thirty yards down a grade parked beneath trees, their expressions reading *You've got to be shitting me.*

Talking fast, I continued, "I need one of you in the water—on the surface, in an inner tube, not with tanks. Not at first, anyway. We don't have an extra wet suit, and there isn't time for that, anyway. Which one of you is the best swimmer?"

Instantly, Perry said, "He's the best swimmer. He'll do it."

King's expression read *Huh?*

"King worked as a lifeguard someplace in Florida. That's what he claims, anyway. Where'd you say it was?"

The way King stood fidgeting, not answering, reminded me of a child who's been caught in a lie.

"It was in Palm Beach," Perry added, "that's where he worked. He was the head lifeguard on some rich beach, weren't you, King?" Perry was skeptical, though. It was in his tone.

King answered, "Sure . . . I lifeguarded for a while, but—"

"He said he did scuba diving, speared fish, the whole works." Perry was talking to me, now.

"Well . . . sure. Yeah. Goddamn right, I did, but the thing is—"

Perry interrupted, saying, "You ain't backpedaling now. He's a big shot—all the time, he's got to be the big shot. Now's his chance to prove it, for once."

King started to say, "Without a wet suit? When I was lifeguarding, we had decent equipment—"

Perry interrupted. "Go naked, for all I care. I want some of that gold and I want those truck keys. I'll help push the damn truck, but there ain't no damn way I'm going in that water."

Perry was an angry man, but it wasn't just anger I was hearing. He had seen something in the lake that scared him. I was sure of it now.

Arlis, I remembered, had said the rancher who sold him the property had behaved the same way. He had refused to come near the place.

"Even the roustabouts who work for the man," Arlis had told me, "are afraid to go near that lake."

NINE

THE THING THE PROFESSOR-LOOKING DUDE,
Ford, called a "jet dredge" reminded King of a pressure
washer he'd used to clean aluminum siding at a motel
where he'd worked for a few months outside Kirkland,
Illinois.

It was the same motel where King had robbed guests'
rooms half a dozen times, but then pushed what was a
sweet setup a little too far. He had surprised one of the
guests showering—a decent-looking brunette, although
a little chunky—then exposed himself to the woman,
who turned out to be a librarian from Moline who
didn't take shit off anybody, particularly a skinny maintenance man wearing a soiled blue uniform that smelled
of wine and Pine-Sol.

When King had tried to calm her down, telling her he

was on leave from the Air Force, that he didn't know a soul in town—he was just lonely, that's all—she had thrown an ashtray at him, and that's when things had really gone to hell. A military man deserved respect, after all, and King had tried to force the issue by forcing the woman, naked, onto the bed.

Next stop, Statesville Correctional. King had been sentenced to seven years but got out in three. At Statesville, the work coveralls were orange, not Air Force blue.

The pressure-washer gizmo that the old man and Ford had brought—the dredge pump—was the size of a bread box but heavy. It floated on an oversized inner tube, connected by a waterproof cord to the generator onshore. Coiled beside the pump was a hundred feet of commercial garden hose, the end clamped to PVC pipe and fitted with a nozzle. Hit the trigger, and water jetted out in a stream finer and harder than any pressure washer King had ever used—Ford had tested it, even though he was in a hurry.

The rig was homemade, with redundancy kill switches in case water breached the power contacts. Ingenious, King had to admit. The old man and the professor dude were smart, he had to admit, too.

So what?

He had met a ton of men like these two. Superior acting. Always so sure of themselves. Smart, yes, but all of them born with a sort of governor inside their heads that stopped them from crossing certain lines of behavior. They were like dogs chained to a wall, which made them easy to tease. Self-important suits, too good to sink to the King's level.

King hated them for it. He always had, he always would.

Early on, King had learned that he would never be accepted by these superior asshole types. He would always be considered an inferior. It was pointless to challenge their tight-ass behavior one-on-one, so King had learned how to choose his shots. He had learned how to erode their authority, and how to get even, by picking away at their weaknesses like a crow picks at garbage.

Sabotage and slick tricks. Bosses, his asshole sister's friends who had dissed him, his teachers—especially his pompous eighth-grade science teacher—King had become expert at disrupting their plans, at screwing up their work, at inflicting small, sly wounds without them even knowing.

Common examples: Spitting in drinks, when no one was looking. Robbing wallets, a few bucks at a time. Dragging his feet when someone was in a hurry or making excuses when an important job needed to be done.

Like now, pretending to help Ford.

It was best when the superior assholes suspected that he was doing it but couldn't prove it. It gave King a tight, glowing feeling of victory in his belly. If they failed, the King won.

That feeling was in his belly now, as King held on to the inner tube, floating neck-deep in the chilly water, following the professor dude toward the orange buoy that the man claimed marked the wrecked airplane.

King wasn't totally convinced there was a plane full of gold down there, but he sure as hell wanted it to be true. He was desperate to believe. Five counts of first-degree murder in a state that still strapped killers in the electric chair? Man, King needed all the help he could get.

That goddamn Perry and his goddamn knife!

Shit! Loading that shiny diesel truck with gold bars and coins was their only hope. If they actually got the stuff, if the asshole, Ford, wasn't lying—man, what a *break*. First, they would fence enough to buy passage on a boat to Mexico. After that, they'd be in the clear, living rich, kicking back with enough wine and young girls and cash to finally tell the world, *Screw you!*

What had convinced King was the way Ford had rattled off his story, detail after detail, never once hesitating. No way he could have made up a tale like that. King was sure because *he* couldn't have done it, and he had spent his life making up stories about himself.

No, Ford was the straight type. Just another dog chained to the wall—a tight-ass suit with boundaries— which only made the man easier to tease. It also made it more unlikely that the guy could invent some wild lie about a plane crashing, loaded with Cuban gold.

"Hurry up, come on! What's your problem?"

Ford was yelling at him again. King looked over the inner tube, seeing the man's dive mask tilted up on his forehead, seeing the man's assholish superior expression of contempt as they swam the jet pump toward the orange buoy.

Truth was, Ford was doing all the work, pulling the

heavy load, kicking with his fins. King was making it harder for him, mostly by just hanging on, but also by letting the fins he was wearing create drag. Sometimes King even backstroked to slow things down.

No way Ford could prove it, although the man knew. King let him read the truth in his innocent *Who? Me?* smile as he replied, "Take it easy, Jock-a-mo. We're almost there."

"No thanks to you. Look over there—see that?" Ford motioned to a yellow scuba tank that had just popped to the surface near the buoy. The tank was floating away.

"What about it? It belongs to your friends?"

The expression on Ford's face said *Dumb-ass.*

"It's my tank. I left it down there for them and it means we're almost out of time. Quit fighting me. I'm not stupid, I know what you're doing!"

No, Ford wasn't stupid. But there wasn't a goddamn thing in the world he could do to change the fact that King didn't give a damn about the man's two friends who were running out of air beneath them. Ford's friends had screwed up. So what? It was their problem, not the King's. Besides, why help save the assholes when it was easier to deal with only two people—Ford and the old man, who Perry would soon kill, anyway.

Perry had whispered that to him as King stripped down to his Fruit of the Looms.

"I'm thinking a knife in the throat is the only thing that will make the old bastard shut his mouth," Perry had said. That was true, but it was more than that. Perry *wanted* to do it. He had a thing for knives now after using the switchblade on the brats and the Mexican girl back in Winter Haven.

Perry had said to him as they'd pedaled the bikes south, "You ought to try it—using a knife, I mean. It's kinda cool the way they just lay there when they know it's happening. Like, they *want* me to finish—you know? Get it over with, so they lay real still all of a sudden, wanting me to end it for them."

His former cell mate wasn't asking for permission to use the knife on the old man. Perry was asking to borrow King's switchblade because he'd lost his during all the excitement—this was before he'd snagged the professor's big stainless dive knife, of course.

Perry wasn't like Ford. Perry had no boundaries. Not anymore. Perry hadn't even realized he was no better than a dog on a chain until two nights ago at old man Hostetler's house. But Perry had a taste for it now. King had seen the same sort of change in cons back in Statesville, two- or three-time losers who had discovered themselves when they finally tasted blood.

Not King, though. He'd never killed anyone, ever. Not even at the Hostetler place, although he had helped in certain ways. What choice had he had? Perry, who had been speed crazed and drunk, was nuts enough at the time to use the knife on King if he hadn't pretended to join in the fun.

No doubt about it, Perry got off on killing people, and there was no going back. Perry had found himself.

Question now was, how would King deal with that? He would have to come up with a way, he knew it, and he would—later.

Ford was bitching at him again. "Okay . . . *enough*. Take off your damn fins and lay them on the inner tube beside the pump. I know what you're doing and I don't have time for your crap!"

King had been letting his fins drag, but now subtly began kicking in reverse, as he said, "I'm doing the best I can. If I take off my fins, I might drown. Then who's gonna help you with this hose?"

The expression on Ford's face, pure frustration—and King *loved* it.

"I thought you said you could swim. You never spent one day as a lifeguard. Have you ever told the truth about anything in your life?"

King used that smile again—*Who? Me?*—teasing the man with the truth. "You think I'm lying? Well . . . maybe you're right. But don't tell Perry, he's just a kid. You wouldn't want to disillusion a kid, would you?"

As he grinned at Ford, the King was thinking, *Now who's the dumb-ass?*

The hell he couldn't swim. Swimming was one of the few things King was pretty good at. He'd done a lot of it at the municipal pool, growing up. Of course, he had never actually been a lifeguard like he'd told Perry. But he could have been. Maybe. So what was the difference?

King was enjoying it, teasing the professor-looking guy because the guy was such a damn tight-assed nerd.

"Maybe my technique's wrong," King said. "Let me

try something different. Don't think you're the only one worried about your pals trapped down there under all that rock."

When Ford replied, "Sure you are," King told him, "Seriously. I believed it when you said we need four men to salvage the stuff 'cause it's so heavy. I'm looking at this as a business deal—you're the one who got us into this, so don't blame me!"

As Ford started to say something else, King floated his legs out behind him, then kicked hard with his fins. The sudden thrust caused the inner tube to shoot forward and almost run over the man.

When Ford surfaced, spitting water, King said, "Now look who's slowing us down. You expect me to push this heavy bastard all by myself?" He couldn't help laughing—Christ, the expression on the dude's face!

It didn't matter whether he cooperated or not now. They were already at the orange buoy.

King watched Ford check his watch, his eyes cold, then look around until he said he could see two sets of air bubbles not far from the buoy. The bubbles weren't well defined because the wind was coming up, raking the pond's surface into rows of moving water.

"How much time do your girlfriends have left?" King asked.

Rinsing his mask, then positioning it on his face, Ford replied, "Just shut up and make sure the hose doesn't kink. Think you can handle that?"

King was grinning as the professor dude disappeared beneath the surface.

Perry was standing next to the truck, with its tailgate open, scuba gear scattered on the ground near the little Honda generator. The guy, Ford, had gotten ready in a hurry, yelling orders, throwing things around. That's why the area was such a mess.

Perry was watching Ford now as King helped him swim the inner tube, loaded with gear, toward the orange buoy, where the color of the water changed from silver-blue to black.

Water was deeper out there, Perry guessed.

It gave Perry the creeps, wondering about what might be living deep in the black water below the two of them, looking up from the bottom at their shapes and bare legs.

Man . . . it was *scary* just thinking about it.

Perry wouldn't have admitted that, though, even to King. Not after what he done two nights ago, the way he'd felt, chasing the woman and those kids through the dark house. Perry believed he would never have to show fear again.

After feeling that kind of power? The night had changed him in an unexpected way, made him feel larger, more knowing—treetop tall—a man who could look down and choose his targets instead of living in fear, as Perry had lived all his life.

People died so *easily* beneath his hands.

It was the most surprising truth he had ever experienced. It had created a power in him, a soaring feeling that connected his brain and his heart, and a strange hunger, too, that was ready and waiting, close beneath the surface, eager for the next time.

There would be a *next time*. It would happen. The power was there, a bottomless hunger, like jonesing for a cigarette. So what did he have to fear?

Black water, that's what. That was true, too. He couldn't admit it, but there it was.

Perry let his eyes move to the trees, then to the curving shoreline. Automatically, his hands went to his pockets, seeking a pack of Marlboros that wasn't there.

It brought the memory back to him, Sunday afternoon, lighting his last cigarette, crumpling the pack and lobbing it into the lake. Wind had pushed the silver-cellophaned Marlboro 100s toward the black water, not far from where the orange buoy was now anchored.

That's when something . . . *something* had ascended beneath the pack, a long black shape that was blacker than the black water, with a tail that looked to be almost as long and wide as a man.

Perry hadn't imagined it. He'd been jazzed on Adderall, sure, but he wasn't drunk. He had seen it.

The thing—whatever it was—had appeared suddenly, as if it had rocketed up from the depths to swallow the cigarette pack. At the last second, though, it had slowed itself, large and dark beneath the surface, and the big tail had swirled a whirlpool of water that was half the size of the truck that Perry now leaned against, trying to freeze that image in his mind. . . .

"Your idiot friend swims like a damn anchor. Look at him, holding Ford back."

Goddamn old man. He never stopped talking.

Perry said to him, "The only reason you talk so tough is 'cause you're too old to fight. Shut your mouth for a change."

Arlis snapped back, "I might be too old to fight you, but I ain't too old to kill you. If you had any brains, you'd know how dangerous it is to mess with a man too old to fight."

Perry muttered, "Fucking old dudes . . . *man*."

"You hear what I said?" Arlis pressed. "Or maybe you're whacked out on some kind of drug—marijuana and crack cocaine, maybe. Where'd you scum come from? Wherever it is, I wish you'd go back and climb under your rock."

Damn it. Arlis Futch had just ruined the way Perry's mind had been replaying the scene. Even with a busted mouth, the man couldn't stay quiet.

Perry's mind blanked, and the dark creature vanished. That quick, he was standing next to the truck again, where the generator was running smoothly and not too loud for him to hear the old man yammering away, bitching and criticizing, despite the blood seeping from the back of his head.

"Our friends are down there dying and your hotshot pal is dragging his ass. Look at him! He's doing it on purpose."

The old man had gotten to his feet and walked away from the blanket that Ford had spread for him in the grass beneath a tree thirty yards from the truck. Now he was standing knee-deep in the lake, filling a water bottle, then pouring it over his head, after having just been sick, kneeling behind a tree for privacy, coughing until there was nothing left in his belly.

Perry had felt good, hearing the old man be sick. He had caused it.

As the old man washed, Perry watched King and the professor-looking dude as they approached the orange buoy. The buoy was bouncing like a punching bag as waves passed beneath it, but the thing stopped when Ford got a hand on it.

"Ten minutes, maybe, that's all the air our guys have left. You two Yankee scumbags don't care what happens to them. All you want is our damn gold! And you're trespassing on private property, which I'm gonna keep reminding you until you two turds go off and leave us alone."

There was something about a redneck accent that was grating, and Perry tried to ignore the man. Later, after he had loaded his backpack full of Cuban coins, he knew how he would handle it. Perry would march Futch into the trees—the old man's hands would be tie-wrapped, of course—then he would use Ford's big steel knife with the serrated blade, not the switchblade he had borrowed from King. Right in the throat, that's how he would start, just like he'd described it to King.

Knives. Perry liked them. In Mexico, after they put money in the bank and found a big house with maids— a "hacienda," King called such places—maybe he would buy himself a nice knife. Good steel that didn't rust, and a genuine bone handle, not plastic, like the one in his pocket.

And, of course, he would keep Ford's knife. The man soon wouldn't have any use for it, anyway.

Until then, though, Perry knew that he had to tolerate the old bastard. Kill him now, they would have no way to leverage Ford, the expert diver. Ford might try to drown King, then sneak off into the swamp without sharing a penny, if the old man wasn't there to give Ford a reason to come back.

"You're not going to get one ounce of that gold if you let our friends die. You know that, don't you? One of them's just a boy, a teenage Indian kid off the Oklahoma reservation, and now this happens to him!"

Perry, who was holding the rifle in the crook of his arm, said to Arlis Futch, "Shut up and keep your opinions to yourself. You want some more of me?" He swiveled just enough to point the rifle toward the lake where Gramps was standing.

The old man stopped pouring water over his head and looked at Perry long enough for his expression to be read *Anytime*. Of course, the man didn't make a move to do anything about it. All talk, just like King.

Perry said, "That's what I thought," and returned his attention to the orange buoy, which marked the site of the plane wreck. It was too late to re-create the details about Sunday afternoon, the big creature surfacing, but he could see what was happening now.

He watched Ford say something to King, a pissed-off

expression on his face, then pull the mask down and disappear underwater, hauling two extra tanks and the PVC nozzle with him. He watched King handling the coiled hose, feeding it out but not too fast.

That was to be expected. King had whispered to Perry before wading into the lake, "There's no reason for us to be in a hurry, is there? Watch how I deal with that tight-assed prick."

Nope, there was no reason to hurry, but Perry had added, "Unless the cops come looking in their helicopters again. If that happens, I'm outta here, dude. So don't waste too much time, that wouldn't be smart."

No shit, Sherlock. That was King's know-it-all response.

The orange buoy and the inner tube were less than halfway across the lake but only about forty yards away, which was close enough for King to know he had an audience now that Ford was underwater. King was a show-off, and Perry wasn't surprised when his partner suddenly pretended to be fighting a fish, pulling on the hose as if it were a fishing line. Perry wondered how Ford was dealing with that, the man now swimming somewhere beneath the water's surface. The hose went taut at first, but then it went slack. Perry guessed that King had pulled the damn thing right out of Ford's hands.

Funny.

The old man didn't think so.

"What is that useless son of a bitch doing out there now? Jesus Christ! Doesn't he know men's lives are on the line?"

Perry told him, "Shut your damn mouth or I'll hit you with this rifle again. I'd rather listen to you spitting teeth than your goddamn yammering."

That quieted the old fool. Perry stopped giving him his hard-ass stare long enough to check the sky. It had been calm, but now wind was starting to move through the trees. The wind was pushing vultures high overhead, in a whirlpool circle, but there was no sign of helicopters searching the horizon. All he saw was blue sky and sunlight, black birds and wind. But it was getting late now, the sun hanging low in the sky.

Good. Maybe the cops had given up.

Perry hoped it wouldn't get cold again. For the first time since Saturday night, it felt like he was in Florida, the way the air felt grassy warm like summer, and he didn't want it to change.

The old man interrupted his thoughts again, saying, "I'll be damned. I didn't notice these before."

Now what was the old bastard doing? Futch was wading around in the shallows, looking at the bottom. He had a towel—the thing was black with blood—draped over his head as if to keep the sun out.

Perry stepped away from the truck toward the water. "What are you looking for? You old son-bitch, if you tossed those truck keys in the water, I'll—"

"The keys to the truck are with our friends, just like we told you," the old man shot back. "You wouldn't understand what it is I'm looking at—since you're nothing but Yankee white trash."

Perry's hands went to his pockets, feeling for cigarettes but finding the switchblade instead.

Walking toward Futch, Perry listened to the old man say, "Gator tracks, that's what I'm looking at. A damn big gator, too. And the tracks are fresh. First time I noticed them. You ever seen a big bull gator? Not in some zoo—a real live predator, out here in the wild."

That caused Perry to stop. "How big? Are you serious?"

"Boy," the old man said to him, "you're talking to one of Florida's foremost leading experts on alligators. It's what I do for a living. What you think brought me out here to this lake to begin with? I was hired to catch a big-ass gator that was killing cows on this property. But, damn, if this isn't the first sign I've seen of the thing."

Perry said, "Show me," and walked to the edge of the lake as the old man reached down into the water, picked up a rock or something, while pointing with his free hand.

"Right there," Futch said. "You got to be blind not to know what made that track."

Perry stayed a safe distance away from the man and leaned to look, saying, "Sunday afternoon, I was standing over there by the trees and I saw something big come close to the surface. But then it disappeared. I've been wondering what it was."

The old man straightened as if surprised. "Sunday?" he said.

"It looked black. Are alligators black?"

The old man asked, "Are you sure?" suddenly sounding concerned for some reason.

Perry was trying to see down into the water, waiting for the murk to clear. Every time the old man moved his feet, a cloud of silt exploded around them.

Perry replied, "I just said it, didn't I? Of course I'm sure." Then he said, "Where? I don't see any tracks. Wait—is this what you're talking about? This isn't an animal track . . . you made this with your hand."

It was true, Arlis had made the track, wanting to scare the skinny Yankee idiot and also to divert his attention, but he didn't reply. He was looking at the lake now, studying the surface, his expression worried.

Perry said, "Tell the truth, you lying old bastard. These aren't claw marks. You used your fingers to make some bullshit fake track, trying to scare me. I got eyes, dumb-ass. I can see."

Something Perry didn't see was Arlis slipping the keys to the truck, dripping wet, into his pocket.

TEN

I WAS UNDERWATER NEAR THE EDGE OF THE drop-off when I felt the hose go taut, as if King, his fins still visible above me, were a fisherman setting the hook and I was a fish.

The strike was so unexpected that it yanked the PVC nozzle out of my hand. It also caused me to drop the air bottles I was carrying, two aluminum tanks plus regulators, all roped together. Because the tanks were full, they sank as if they were made of solid steel.

I had been looking for the crevice where earlier I'd wedged the yellow air bottle. I wanted to plant another tank in its place. Instead, I watched the tanks clank against the lip of the drop-off, tumble briefly down the side, then accelerate, stems first, toward the lake bottom, regulator hoses flailing, where they hit another ledge, plowing up twin clouds of silt, then continued rolling downward into an unseen crevice.

What appeared to be the lake's bottom, fifty feet below, was not the deepest part of the lake. I guessed there would be a maze of vents and crevices down there, inclining gradually toward a water vein that siphoned into a river two or three hundred feet below the earth's crust.

King had intentionally yanked the hose from my hand, and I thought, *That's one more reason the man won't leave here alive.*

If I hadn't been so desperate for time, I would have been tempted to surface, snatch King from behind and drag him down, down, down into the mouth of that underground river. In my imagination, I could picture a man-sized fissure, a perfect spot to wedge King's body.

Maybe later.

Yes, later . . . And later I would have to decide what to do with King—and Perry, too. For now, though, I had to play by their rules while I focused on rescuing Tomlinson and the boy.

"If you try anything stupid," King had told me as I got ready for the dive, "Perry will start carving up Grandpa."

Arlis, too far away to hear, hadn't seen Perry grinning as he pulled my Randall knife from his belt and flashed it around like a movie swordsman.

I knew that failing to return with a sack full of gold would catalyze the same reaction. I would have to deal with that, too. But later.

For a moment, I considered leaving the bottles where they lay. A scattered blossoming of bubbles, leaking from the limestone, told me that Will and Tomlinson were somewhere beneath me still breathing. They couldn't have much air remaining.

No way of knowing exactly how much time they had left.

Objectively, though, I understood that it would take me several minutes at the very least to carve enough sand and rock away with the jet dredge to free them. Excavating required too much time, and there was too little air unless I recovered the tanks.

In my mind, I inspected a rapid-fire chain of scenarios. By spending a minute or two now retrieving the tanks, I might well provide Will and Tomlinson with an hour or more of air later when I found them. It could mean the difference between life and death. Maybe one or both of the guys were injured. Maybe their legs had been pinned beneath boulders. What good would it do to find them only to have them die after sharing the last of my air?

I checked the time. Tomlinson and Will had been underwater for fifty-six minutes. Nine or ten minutes left, counting their spare air bottles. That gave me all the more reason to go after the tanks.

I purged air from my BC and angled downward, swallowing to clear my ears as I descended. Visibility was good now. I could see largemouth bass nesting in shallow sand craters, a school of bream butterflying among the branches of a waterlogged tree limb. I also saw a big

alligator gar fish hanging in the depths as dark and motionless as a barracuda—the biggest I had seen so far,
maybe five feet long.

Maybe that's what Perry had seen. Magnified by the
lake's surface, the fish would have looked man-sized to
someone like him.

As I descended beyond the ledge, the lake basin
bulged wider like the bowl of a brandy snifter. It was the
typical geology of a sinkhole, or what is sometimes called
a "karst window": a small, watery mouth atop a globular
basin that then narrowed beneath a protruding ledge.
The ledges were probably remnants of a karst bridge
that had once crossed the subterranean river.

As I traveled deeper, though, I realized that I was
wrong about the shape of the lake. If the basin had been
surveyed and plotted on graph paper, a vertical slice
would have resembled an irregular hourglass more than
a brandy snifter. Because the karst bridge had collapsed
at the center, it projected twin limestone wings toward
the middle of the lake and created an hourglasslike
stricture.

The bottles had tumbled down a ravine, their resting
place screened from my vision by depth and also because
the protruding limestone shielded the bottom from
sunlight. The twin wings, or overhangs, were fifteen to
twenty feet thick. They were jagged at the ends and
similar in most ways, although the northernmost wing
where Tomlinson and Will were trapped was the thicker
of the two. I found that reassuring because the overhang was sufficiently thick to contain karst chambers—

possibly even a vent—that the two could have followed to an air bell.

An air bell—I still wanted to believe that such things existed.

I checked my depth gauge as I kicked downward.

68 ft.

Under the northernmost overhang, the lake bottom narrowed and then bellied wider—wider than the actual circumference of the lake. It was like an opening into a gymnasium-sized hollow that extended beneath the cypress trees where we'd first parked the truck and possibly under the swamp beyond. There, the bottom of the lake appeared to flatten—I had to guess—at a hundred and fifty feet.

I still couldn't spot the damn bottles, so once again I considered returning to where we'd found the mammoth tusk and getting to work.

No . . . I had read too many accounts of cave divers, trapped or lost, who had died because their rescuers had panicked and made fatal miscalculations. The rescuers had rushed to help instead of methodically hurrying to help. There was a difference.

I knew that decompression wasn't a concern for me because recovering the bottles amounted to a fast bounce dive—although there were inherent dangers with any bounce dive that exceeded a hundred feet. I would risk narcosis if I descended too fast, and, in the resulting confusion, there was also a chance of overbreathing my regulator. I had to pay attention. Under any other circumstances, it would have been a foolhardy thing to

attempt. But I had to do it. I needed those tanks. My
dive computer would automatically compute the short
amount of decompression time required—close to zero,
I guessed—and I would spend that time using the dredge,
cutting my friends out of the rocks.

At one hundred and thirty feet, I saw the tanks. Both
had come to rest among a pile of rubble created by falling rock and surface debris—roots of a long-dead cypress tree, silt detritus . . . and two cow skulls, too, amid
scattered rib bones . . . and what looked at first like the
crushed remains of an automobile.

Someone had dumped a car here? That struck me as
unlikely. It had taken us two hours to hack a trail wide
enough for Arlis's four-wheel-drive truck. Why would
someone come clear out here to ditch a clunker?

Descending toward the tanks, I didn't slow as I
pulled out a palm-sized LED flashlight and painted the
bottom with light.

It wasn't a car, I realized. It was the fuselage of an
airplane. And I thought, *My God—Arlis was right.*

As I drew closer, details revealed themselves, frozen in white wafers of visibility. I saw twin twisted
propellers . . . then twin windowless sockets that opened
into the plane's cockpit. Soon, I could make out the
shape of a broken wing that was mud coated and angu-
lar. In the gray depths, the wing appeared as symmetrical
as a gigantic bird feather.

I was looking at a cargo plane. An old DC-3 possibly.

Under any other circumstances, it would have been

cause to celebrate—even if it wasn't Batista's gold plane, it was an extraordinary find.

But not now.

I looked at my watch, feeling the weight of water on me. As my chest worked harder to suck air, I could hear the muted pinging of my own air exhaust, the sound compressed by five atmospheres of pressure.

143 ft.

It was no place to linger—and not only because of the depth. Tomlinson and Will had been underwater for fifty-seven minutes now. Logic and experience told me that soon—*very* soon—Will would attempt to draw a breath, but his regulator would not respond. If the teen was in a place where he could move his arms, he would have his emergency bottle ready. The same was true of Tomlinson—he, too, was almost out of air. When trapped underwater, the demarcation between a lifetime and a spent life is one long, terrifying minute. Because of King's antics, I was cutting it way too damn fine.

When I got to the bottles, I grabbed the line hitched to the valve stems and kicked toward the surface, forcing myself to ascend no faster than my own chromium-bright bubbles.

I couldn't hurry. It was suicide to hurry. To pass the time, I allowed my eyes to assess the unexpected geology of the sinkhole, as viewed from below. Unexpected because, for the first time, I could see that the plane, when it crashed, had compromised the integrity of the limestone hourglass. It had cleaved a massive wedge from the overhang above me. As a result, the stone stricture into which Tomlinson and Will Chaser had disappeared, although thick at both ends, was perilously thin at midpoint.

If I made a mistake with the jet dredge, if I cut too deep or in the wrong place, the lake basin's entire limestone scaffolding could collapse.

Tink . . . tinka . . . tink-tink.

I had returned to the place where we'd found the mammoth tusk, and Tomlinson was signaling me again.

Shave-and-a-haircut . . . two bits.

It had become his audio signature. He was still alive, but his tapping sounded more urgent now. It wasn't my imagination.

Ninety seconds—that's how long it had taken me to retrieve the tanks and return to the rubble that marked where the limestone ledge had once been.

I didn't waste time responding.

He was signaling, I knew, because he'd heard me as I wedged one of the bottles into the crevice below the rubble and then opened the air valve a half turn. There was no need for me to answer the man. Soon enough, he would hear the jet dredge cutting through the sand above him. He would know that I was doing everything I could to get him and Will back to the surface.

The decision I now had to make was an important one: Where should I start digging?

After anchoring the second spare tank nearby, I lo-

cated the hose to the dredge. It hung in a limp coil beneath the inner tube, where I could see King's legs
dangling. I swam to the PVC tube, checked the brass
nozzle to make sure it was clear, then touched my finger
to the makeshift trigger and tested the thing.

The sudden pressure caused the handle to kick in my
hand as water jetted out the nozzle, an expanding swirl
of bubbles that had the velocity of a dentist's drill.

I removed my finger from the trigger and began to
search for the best area to begin excavating. I wanted to
locate the exact spot where Will and Tomlinson's bubbles sparkled up through the limestone base . . . But
there was no single exit point that I could find. The air
ascended from several areas of rock.

That was okay. I told myself it didn't matter. Even if
I had found a precise exhaust point, it was no guarantee
that it marked the location of my friends. Like water
through a leaky roof, air bubbles traveled the path of
least resistance, following angles and curves, until they
found an opening. The guys might have been directly
beneath their bubbles, but just as likely their bubbles
had traveled many yards before finding a porous area
through which to ascend.

It was also possible that Will and Tomlinson had
moved from the spot where the ledge had collapsed.
They could have burrowed into some unseen crevice or
followed a karst vent, seeking an exit, leaving a trail of
trapped air bubbles behind them.

I swam to the drop-off to get one last overview of the
limestone overhang. If I excavated too close to the frag-

ile midpoint, the whole slab might shear away. I chose an area slightly inland from where the ledge had collapsed and decided that it was safer to dig from the side of the overhang instead of directly downward.

I bled every bit of air from my BC to ensure negative buoyancy, then pulled on the hose, telling King that I needed slack. I dreaded the man's response, but I was prepared when he attempted to yank the thing from my hands again.

I tugged twice more, battling my temper and still wrestling with the temptation to surprise the man from behind and break his neck. There is a type of person who teases and taunts but always with an exacting sense of boundaries. King was one of those, and he must have sensed he had pushed me to the limit because suddenly coils of hose dropped down from the inner tube as he provided me with enough slack to work.

I raced to the edge of the overhang and used my left hand to anchor myself to a slab of limestone before squeezing the jet dredge's trigger. The PVC pipe jolted; the hose began to snake, writhing with pressure. When I touched the brass nozzle above the rock, sand exploded around me. The laser jet of water plowed a furrow that smoked like a lighted fuse.

I began cutting at a slight upward angle, attacking the overhang as if peeling an orange. Rock and sand appeared to melt away, creating a slow landslide that dropped beneath me as I progressed. Because it was important that I knew how my work was affecting Tomlinson and Will, I stopped after only thirty seconds. After a long pause, I tapped the nozzle of the dredge against my air bottle. Eight taps—probably not timed correctly, but Tomlinson would know what I meant.

The letters *E-R*. *Everything okay?*

Tomlinson's response was barely audible, but I received eight taps in response.

Weird. It sounded as if he was now farther away . . . or deeper into the overhang. Maybe they had found a widening interstice—a keyhole passage. It suggested to me that they had moved from the site of the initial collapse. Perhaps they were following a tunnel—a tunnel that led to the surface—or even a cave that contained an air pocket. It was *possible,* and I hoped it was true.

More likely, though, if they had actually found a vent large enough for them both to negotiate, the tunnel would angle downward toward the subterranean river, not upward toward the surface.

As I began cutting again, I glanced at the murk below my fins, thinking about that possibility. At its narrowest point, the remnants of the limestone bridge were no more than twenty feet thick. Maybe I had been wrong to try excavating from the side. Would it have been wiser to attack the overhang from beneath? I imagined myself cutting through rock and sand until my friends literally fell to safety.

My eyes moved back and forth, monitoring the trench I was digging while also considering the geology of the lake.

No . . . I couldn't risk excavating from beneath. It was smarter to stay where I was. I had seen the ledge from the vantage point of the wrecked plane. The lake's hourglass scaffolding was too fragile, already compromised by the plane crash. Cutting from below would be like sawing through the load-bearing beam of a house. The entire structure could come crashing down.

For what seemed a long time, I worked hard, cutting deeper and deeper with the dredge, afraid to risk a glance at my watch. Internally, I was battling a welling panic. I vented energy by attacking the overhang, clawing away boulders and fossilized shell, ripping my way into the earth.

Finally, though, I knew I had to stop and assess. I looped the hose over my shoulder and banged the nozzle against my tank. Eight taps or nine—I wasn't certain. My hands were shaking as I listened.

Nothing.

I signaled again. Then *again*. As I gripped the pipe, ready to continue dredging, I heard a very faint *tink-tink-tink . . . TAP-TAP-TAP . . . tink-tink-tink.*

It was Tomlinson, but only Tomlinson, and there was no mistaking the meaning of those nine distinct bell notes. He was now sending me an SOS. *Emergency. Need help immediately.*

Perhaps the pilot of the wrecked plane had sent out the same signal before crashing into this lake. It was a three-letter cry for help.

I checked my watch. The orange numerals seemed inordinately bright and stabbed at my eyes. Sixty-three minutes since we had begun what should have been an uncommonly safe dive on an uncommonly warm and calm February afternoon. The watch confirmed what I feared.

Tomlinson and I had been friends for so long, we had shared so many experiences, good and bad, that I knew he would not resort to an SOS unless he was at his end. Maybe Will was dying . . . or maybe the kid was already dead. Tomlinson would soon follow.

I shouted a pointless refusal through my regulator mouthpiece. *"No!"*

No—I wasn't going to let it happen. Sometimes, the most dangerous option is the only option. I had made progress digging into the side of the overhang, but it was time for a more extreme approach. I had to risk cutting into the overhang from beneath. We were out of time, and it was my last best hope. Bringing the limestone bridge crashing down atop me was preferable to what I knew was the inevitable alternative. If I didn't free them within the next minute or two, later, much later, I would have to wait while a recovery team retrieved the bodies of my closest friend and a sixteen-year-old boy who had already suffered too much trauma in his life.

I yanked hard on the hose, demanding slack, and realized as I waited that I was at risk of biting through my rubber mouthpiece. King's instincts were still good, however. More coils of hose descended above me. Without pausing, I sprinted downward, kicking hard with my fins, towing the hose behind.

I knew that the thinnest section of the overhang was shoreward, midway. There, the composite of limestone and sand was only twenty feet thick. As I swam, I traced the contour beneath the wide ledge. Gradually, bands of sunlight that pierced the surface disappeared behind me. Ancillary light, mixed with water and shadows, created a turquoise gloom that soon enveloped me, but there was still enough visibility to make out details.

The underside of the overhang consisted of hardened marl and limestone. The facing was pocked like the surface of the moon. The formation suggested the slow-motion cataclysm that had formed our planet, the geological grinding of water, rock and wind over aeons.

When the plane had crashed, it must have been nose-diving, because it had sheared off a pie-shaped wedge of the horizontal strata. Where the plane had made contact, the rock facing veered sharply upward, where the overhang had nearly been severed—a fault line.

I positioned myself beneath the fault line and jetted a few bursts of air into my BC—enough to create positive buoyancy. The vest lifted and anchored me against the rocks above. The hose was stretched so tight, however, that I couldn't get a good working angle on the fault.

Once again, I tugged on the hose, demanding slack. Once again, I was prepared when King yanked hard in response. Instead of just a single, testing jolt, though, King continued pulling the hose, but now he was also kicking hard with his fins—he had to be, because I couldn't stop his momentum. He began hauling me toward the edge of the overhang as if hauling in a fish.

I gripped the PVC pipe in both hands as he continued to drag me along the underside of the bridge. It went that way for several seconds, my aluminum bottle clanking as it banged against rocks. Finally, I managed to turn so that my fins were in front of me and I began kicking, fighting to reposition myself.

Above me, King was in an untethered inner tube. He had no leverage, only the swim fins I had loaned him, yet it wasn't until I had freed one hand and jammed my arm deep into a rock vent that I finally stopped myself. As I battled, the strain on the hose was so great that I feared it would snap.

A rock vent . . .

In that instant, an image flashed into my mind: Will Chaser sticking his big teenage hand into a similar rock vent, then applying pressure as he tried to steady himself.

The image was detailed and luminous in my brain as I heard a sapwood-cracking sound, then a rumbling billiard-ball percussion.

I was still holding tight, one arm in the vent, one hand on the hose, when the ledge above me broke free. Then the entire overhang fell with the weight of a marble ceiling . . .

ELEVEN

WHEN WILL HAD RECOVERED FROM THE SHOCK of being buried under a ton of rubble, his first thought was *Not this again . . .*

But it wasn't the same. Not at all like a few weeks ago, his first moments sealed in a wooden crate, listening to the men who had kidnapped him shovel dirt onto the crate. He had never experienced such a sickening panic, which perhaps had numbed his threshold for fear. Because now, lying curled beneath the crushing weight of rock, Will felt in control. He was spooked and shaken, but he wasn't crazy scared.

Or was he . . . ?

Will let his brain take stock, testing his appendages for pain or wounds, as he assessed his immediate state of mind. Nope, he was a little stunned, true, but he was not feeling the magnitude of fear that could be accurately defined as "scared shitless."

Will would have been startled by his self-control had he spent more than a few seconds thinking about it, but he didn't because he was too mad to waste time analyzing his emotions. Not just mad, he was furious—furious at the random, shitty bad luck and at his own uncertainty. He didn't know what had caused the ledge to collapse on him or how deeply he was buried. All Will Chaser knew was that he had survived worse and he was going to survive this, by God!

At least he could move a little, and he did. Slowly, foot by foot, Will wormed and muscled his way into what might have been a rock crevice, where there was enough space around him to move his hands and find the little flashlight clipped to his BC. The flashlight was rubber coated, waterproof to thirty-three feet—or so the box had claimed—and he'd brought it on this trip even though he didn't expect to get a chance to use it. Not underwater, anyway.

Will preferred using his own gear. It's just the way he was, which is why he'd refused when Doc, the biologist, had offered to loan him two additional flashlights that looked expensive, with their flared lenses and dense metal tubes. Doc had tried to force him to carry the things, which at the time seemed stupid. Why the hell carry extra flashlights on a sunny winter afternoon? The lake didn't look that deep, and they would be out of the water, packing to leave, long before sunset.

Well . . . turned out the biologist wasn't so stupid,

although there was now no doubt in Will's mind that a weird, wild streak of bad luck stalked Doc Ford. Twice, Will had been with the guy, and both times the shit had really hit the fan.

Bey-HO-ayh. Back in Oklahoma, on the reservation, that was the word that the elder Skins used when referring to some pain-in-the-ass white guy who radiated bad luck. The word sure fit the man . . . And just when Will was starting to like the guy. Sort of.

*When I get out of this mess, I'll call Ford that—*Bey-HO-ayh—*and let him figure it out. Tell the man right to his face and watch how he reacts. Asshole!*

Ford wasn't an asshole, and Will didn't really believe it. In fact, there was something solid and comforting about being around the guy. They'd had a pretty good talk the night before. The man had tried bullshitting him, telling the typical adult lies, but didn't seem to mind at all when Will had called him on it.

Now, though, Will was mad and frustrated. Picturing himself confronting the big biologist gave him an immediate objective, one more reason to get himself free of this mess. He would dig his way from under the rocks, swim to the surface, and call to the man, "Hey, you—*Bey-HO-ayh*! Take a guess at what that means, dipshit!"

It could happen. No, it *would* happen. Will felt certain of it when he found the hippie, Tomlinson, unhurt and alive curled next to him. Only a minute or two later, they heard Ford somewhere above them, signaling. If Ford wasn't beside them or below them, he had to be free, out there, swimming around. Ford would help dig them out. If he didn't, Will would manage by himself.

I've been in worse fixes than this.

No one could argue that.

Ten minutes later, though, Will had lost some of his confidence. The lake's rock floor wasn't solid as rock should be. It was as fragile as rotten ice. The floor kept breaking beneath them, first dropping him and the hippie into a small crevice, then a slightly bigger crevice, sort of like falling through the floors of an old house into progressively larger closets. As the water cleared, Will could see details when he or the hippie shined their lights, but the water was never clear for long.

The third implosion had dropped them in a limestone chamber, where the floor was littered with what looked like giant fossilized oyster shells. There were shells and rock packed tight all around them, with barely room to move, and the rocks overhead were too unstable to touch.

Will had tried digging upward, as had the old hippie. Remove a single chunk of limestone, though, and a barrel of sand and rock fell with it, pouring into the crater like water down a funnel. It destroyed visibility and gave Will a choking feeling, even though his regulator continued jetting air into his lungs when he inhaled through his rubber mouthpiece.

How much air did he have left? That was the question. And how long would the batteries of his flashlight last? That was another important one.

Will didn't doubt that he could endure just about any

damn thing bad luck threw at him, but his scuba tank lacked his heart. The thing was made of aluminum and had limits—the amount of air it could hold, for instance. Will knew it had to be getting low.

Using his flashlight, Will kept an eye on the pressure gauge that was attached to his vest. First time he checked, the needle pointed just below the *1400 psi* mark. Moments later, though, he had sucked down a lot of air when, for the second time, the floor gave way. It was a shocking thing to experience, the earth collapsing beneath him. But that was several minutes ago, and Will decided to have another look at his gauges. He used his flashlight, careful not to blind Tomlinson, who had sensitive eyes apparently.

The needle on the pressure gauge pointed just above the *900 psi* mark. The needle of the depth gauge pointed at *20 ft*.

Damn. Not good. He was a novice diver, but the written exam was still fresh in Will's mind and he knew that *1000 psi* was dangerously low. Even if he had forgotten, that portion of the pressure gauge was colored red to remind him. When the needle touched red, it meant it was time to surface, no dawdling.

The fact that they were now twenty feet underwater, instead of at fifteen feet, also told Will that the lake floor had indeed been dropping them into progressively deeper pockets. Thirty-three feet was another important boundary, the entry into three atmospheres of pressure, which required the use of decompression tables and also caused a faster drain on the air supply.

Depthwise, at least, he and the hippie were in safe territory. They might drown, but there was no chance of them dying from the bends, which was almost funny if it wasn't so damn true.

Will had confidence in what he had learned. He had aced the NAUI Open Water written test, much to the surprise of everyone but himself. A scuba class wasn't like school. Learning something useful, information that could save his life—or even lure a pretty girl into bed if a willing female scuba enthusiast appeared—was worth the effort.

Getting Will scuba certified was the idea of his court-appointed therapist, a woman who wore loud, clanking Indian jewelry and was a closet smoker—Will could smell it on her clothes and in her hair. She had discussed the subject with his probation officer, then the Minnesota couple that was trying to adopt him and, finally, with Barbara Hayes before offering Will a choice. He could take a dive course at the Seminole County Rec Center—Oklahoma, not Florida—or he could agree to more therapy sessions specially designed by her to deal with patients who had unusual gifts—Will being among the few who qualified, she said.

It was the therapist's secret hope that Will would finally be forced to admit his claustrophobic anxieties and decline the dive course.

Fat chance.

"I'm immune," Will had told the shrink, referring to claustrophobia. "Being buried alive in a box has cured me for life."

The scuba course lasted three weeks, which had left Will's hair stinking of chlorine and also delayed his plans to run away from the court-appointed "boarding school," which is what they called reform schools in Oklahoma. It was worth it, though, because Will enjoyed diving.

He liked being underwater, in the silence of his own skull, even in an indoor swimming pool. Diving a coral reef, though, was a hundred times better, as he had discovered the day they had spent on Key Largo. Will had never experienced anything like it in his life, and it was something good to think about just before going to sleep.

That first dive was as clear in his mind as the water of the Florida Keys. He could picture himself dropping down through a luminous blue gel, all those waxen coral shapes assuming definition as he descended, colors brightening in his brain even as they were dulled by filtered light. Fish, as they moved among coral canyons, were as animated as wildflowers, whole schools of fish that appeared wind-tumbled by tidal current yet were as symmetrical as geese in flight.

Take a look.

Tomlinson had just now written that on his dive slate, then surprised Will by nudging him before putting the slate in Will's face and using his flashlight.

Will had to lean closer to see the words, then he asked, *Look at what?* speaking through his regulator, so it sounded like "Ook uh-hh utt?"

His eyes were already following Tomlinson's flashlight to the narrowest part of the chamber, where there was a bowling ball–sized hole into which silt and sand created a small whirlpool as they were drawn downward by current.

Will had already seen the hole. In the last four minutes, he and Tomlinson had probed every inch of the chamber with their lights.

Tomlinson rubbed the dive slate clean and wrote, *We have to move. Agree?*

Will nodded. No doubt about it, they had to do something before their air ran out. It had been nine minutes since they had last heard Ford above them, once digging so frantically that Tomlinson had had to bang a warning on his tank—the biologist was causing more rock to collapse on them.

Next, Tomlinson wrote, *Can't go up. Agree?*

Will shook his head. The idea of being crushed by the unstable ceiling scared the hell out of him. "Nooo 'uckin 'ay," he responded.

Once again, Tomlinson used the flashlight to point at the bowling ball–sized hole. He wrote, *You stay. Conserve air!* then banged a fist against his own chest, the gesture communicating *Leave it to me.*

The light went out. It was like being immersed in a barrel of oil—that kind of blackness. Aside from an occasional flicker of firefly green—Tomlinson's dive watch, as Will had already figured out—the only respite from the darkness were the thought patterns flowing behind Will's eyes. They created pulsing yellow blossoms, and a linear red thatching that streamed and throbbed in his brain.

The colors signaled frustration. Impatience, too. Will was getting angry again.

He spent a full minute listening in darkness as Tomlinson worked at the hole. He could hear the random clank of the hippie's air bottle against rock; a digging sound, then a grunt followed by more digging. Finally, Will had to look. He pointed his flashlight at his fins before touching the switch, then shined the light toward the hole.

He saw that Tomlinson had removed his BC and air bottle. The man was on his knees, pulling away chunks of rock, widening the hole, but the regulator was still in his mouth. He had made a startling amount of progress in a short time. The hole was a couple of feet wide now but still too narrow to enter, Will decided. Tomlinson was scarecrow thin, but he had a wide bony rack of shoulders.

Will grunted to get Tomlinson's attention and wrote on his dive slate, *U—R—2 big. Me first.*

Tomlinson responded with an emphatic shake of his head. "Nohh 'ay, Ohhh-zay."

No way, José?

Maybe so, because seconds later Will watched Tomlinson wiggle his head and shoulders down into the hole, pushing his bottle and BC ahead of him. He had to scrabble hard with his toes to force his body through, but he did it. A moment later, the man disappeared into a blooming cloud of silt that was suggestive of a magic trick.

Will gave it a few seconds before crawling over and pointing his flashlight into the darkness. There wasn't much to see: boiling silt and blackness. But the hole did appear to widen as it angled downward, about the same steep angle as a slide at a playground.

Crap! Weird-ass hippie! Why doesn't he shine his light and let me know he's okay?

After a scary several seconds, though, Tomlinson did signal, and the three dull flashes seemed to originate from someplace far below. The light echoed in the darkness, illuminating the murk, but there was no single beam to mark the man's location. Will flashed his light three times in reply, his heart pounding.

He expects me to follow?

Apparently so. Silt was clearing, siphoning down the hole as if a plug had been pulled, sucking water into a space beneath him. The hole, jagged-edged, looked smaller now for some reason.

It's because I've got to crawl down into that son of a bitch, that's why.

Will was getting angry again, pissed off at what he was now forced to do. What he'd told his therapist about being immune to claustrophobia wasn't exactly true. Since what had happened to him, being packed tight in a crate and buried, Will sometimes awoke at night in a choking, sweaty fever. He felt like darkness was suffocating him, seeping in through his pores.

Even so, Will had never admitted the truth to anyone or even risked providing some sign that he was afraid, such as sleeping with a light on. Leaving a light on at night was tempting, but Will refused to indulge in that sort of weakness. Make even a small concession to what had happened and there was no telling where it might lead to. He could end up a drunk, passed out in a ditch like too many other Skins he'd seen on the Rez.

Besides, being scared was his business, nobody else's.

As Will studied the hole, he realized that he was breathing faster, burning up air. He waited until he had flipped his BC and tank over his head and pushed them halfway down into the hole before checking his pressure gauge one final time.

The needle pointed close to *700 psi,* although it was hard to be sure because the needle wasn't as exact as a digital gauge.

Christ, I've been sucking air like a drunk guzzling whiskey.

How did *700 psi* translate timewise? He might have ten minutes of air left, fifteen at most, plus he had the reserve bottle. Will didn't own a dive watch and now he was almost glad. It was better not to know how long they'd been down.

What Will was sure of, though, was this: He wasn't going to die, boxed in by rocks, without doing whatever he could to escape—not alone in darkness, no goddamn way!

Will switched off his light and secured it under the sleeve of his wet suit, aware that his entire body was shaking. *Goddamn, it's dark!* After thinking about it for a moment, Will looped the flashlight's lanyard over his wrist so it would be right there when he needed it. Just the thought of losing the little flashlight gave him a sick feeling in his abdomen.

I'll never go near the freaking water again without carrying an extra light. A swimming pool, to take a piss, doesn't matter. Lose this, I've had it. Why the hell didn't I take those flashlights that Doc offered me?

Tomlinson had removed his fins to get better footing, and now Will did the same. It was easier without the fins. Tomlinson's fins were sinkers, but Will's were floaters, and they had made it difficult to neutralize buoyancy. When he took the fins off, they floated past his ears and attached themselves like magnets to the limestone overhead.

Once again, Will shined his light down into the hole and flashed it three times. Tomlinson responded by swinging his flashlight back and forth, an invitation.

Come on!

Will forced his head, then his shoulders, down into blackness, pushing his tank ahead of him. He dug his toes into the limestone and used the tank to bulldoze a path.

He thought, *I'm in a cave. I knew this was going to happen. A week ago, I knew it. Now here I am, goddamn it!*

Sometimes, Will knew things. He didn't know how and he'd never really wondered why, but now here he was. It was happening just as he'd known it would.

A week before, on his way to Sanibel, riding in the
rear seat of a Lincoln Town Car, Will hadn't paid much
attention to the woman beside him until she got on the
subject of Florida's underwater caves.

"We might be driving over a cave system right now,"
Barbara Hayes had told Will, then nodded, studying a
map as a road sign blurred past.

ORLANDO/DISNEY WORLD 146 MILES.

"There are miles of caves in this area, according to
this," the woman continued. "Natural tunnels with chambers big enough to drive a truck. This is the right area"—
she had glanced at the map for confirmation—"caves with
branches that run beneath shopping malls, highways,
even this interstate. There could be scuba divers under
our car right now. *Seriously.* It doesn't matter that the
sun's setting. What does sunlight matter to a cave diver?
They dress like astronauts—you know what I mean, they
wear helmets with built-in lights and breathing hoses.
They use battery-powered scooters so they can travel
faster. Wouldn't that be fun?"

A moment later, Hayes didn't appear too sure but
sounded hopeful as she had added, "I thought you'd
find that interesting."

Will did. He had leaned his face near the window, picturing a semi they were passing, its lights on, far beneath
the road in an underwater cave that was more like a city
in outer space, scuba divers soaring through the darkness,
their helmets shooting laser beams, milky white.

It was weird to hear the woman talking about caves because the countryside along the interstate was so flat. But she was right. There was a cave beneath them—no scuba divers, but the cave was there. Will could feel it. He had a sense for such things. Images came into his head less like pictures than as overlapping impressions that communicated colors, spatial volume, odors. He wasn't always right, but he was right often enough.

"Synesthesia," the shrinks back in Oklahoma called it. Synesthesia was a special gift, according to his government-appointed counselor. She had told him it was a complex neurological condition that caused a heightened sensitivity to all sorts of things.

The boy had touched his nose to the car window and allowed his mind to fill with the scent of algae, salted rock, empty space, and he also sensed a conduit of flowing water beneath them. It was down there, a cave, far below the six lanes of asphalt where billboards were frozen, solitary and bright, among palm trees that caught the windy sunset light.

Beside him, Hayes had interrupted, saying, "It's hard to picture, I know."

Will had replied, "Yeah."

"Wait . . . I just realized maybe the idea of cave diving doesn't appeal to you. Or does it?" Her tone asked *Did I say something wrong?*

Will said, "Naw, it does. I'd like to try it if I ever get the chance. I think it would be fun."

Barbara said, "I forget sometimes. Not about what happened to you. God knows, I could never forget that.

But that you might be sensitive . . . that it might make you uncomfortable, the thought of being in a cave. Good Lord!—now I don't even know why I brought it up."

The sophisticated woman wasn't sounding so sophisticated now, which was typical of childless women who tried too hard to relate to him. Will had experienced it often enough to know.

Because he liked her, though, Will had made eye contact and let her see him smile, but only for a second. "What happened doesn't bother me a bit," he said. "I don't know why people keep asking. It really doesn't."

Will was sick of talking about what everyone in the world had seen on TV and in newspapers, all those stories about him being buried in a box by extortionists who had intended to bury the woman instead. It had happened more than a month ago, but the woman still felt indebted. It was the reason he was in a limo with her now, driving south to Disney World—Will already knew he would hate the place—then on to Key Largo and, finally, Sanibel Island.

Mrs. Barbara Hayes, a widow—also a United States senator—had the hots for a man who lived there, a marine biologist named Marion Ford, but everyone called him "Doc." He was a big, nerdy, friendly-looking guy who didn't say much and who Will sensed wasn't as nerdy or as friendly as he appeared.

Will had wondered how he and Doc would get along, not that it mattered much.

Well . . . we'll see.

Sounding relieved, the senator had said to Will, "I'm so glad to hear you feel like you're recovering. I wonder sometimes—at night when I'm alone, you know?—how I would have reacted. If they'd done to me what they did to you."

Will wanted to get back to the images in his head, the scent and feel of rock tunnels below. He said, "Don't worry about it," and leaned his face closer to the window. End of conversation—he hoped.

No such luck.

The woman began laughing, sounding girlish, as she told him, "I stayed up past midnight, trying to find information about Florida I thought you'd like. That's how I know about the caves. I even marked it on a map. Here, look—I have a whole folder of things. Scuba diving, horses—there are a lot of ranches down here, cattle and horses. People don't realize."

As Barbara leaned to open her briefcase, Will had sat straighter, suddenly paying attention, but not because of the articles. The lady was old—in her forties—but she was still good looking, with a body that she liked to show off but not in any obvious way, which was usually the way with classy, good-looking women.

Like now, for instance, dressed for their long drive to Sanibel. Barbara was wearing a cashmere business jacket with a lavender blouse stretched tight over her breasts. The way the buttons strained allowed Will to peek at her beige mesh bra where white flesh bulged when she moved just right or, if Will dropped something, then made room so she could retrieve it.

Twice during the hour drive—Jacksonville to I-75, then south—Will had dropped his bottle of water, but the thing was finally empty so this was his first chance in a while to sneak a peek, and he leaned in closer to watch her lean down to flip through papers, separating files.

Barbara had said, "I brought some articles for you to read—but maybe you don't feel like reading."

"I do," Will had answered quickly, wanting the lady to stay right where she was. Then he'd asked, "Are you sure that's everything?" when she sat up and squared the papers on her lap.

She had told him, "I even brought an article on post-traumatic stress syndrome. You're old enough for me to speak frankly about it. Even if you feel fine now, William, it might be helpful to do some reading. It's important for you to get your feelings out. The therapist at the boarding school that you . . . that you left"—she hesitated, wanting to get the phrasing right—"the therapist says you don't talk much. Not to her, anyway."

The woman had faltered because Will hadn't left the facility, exactly. He had broken a window, jumped the fence and hitchhiked halfway to the home of his former foster grandparents, in Minneapolis, before the cops found him.

Will had replied, "It's easier talking to you," giving it just the right touch, a confession that laid his vulnerability out there for the good-looking older woman to act upon if she ever wanted to. Even if Hayes wasn't naïve enough to believe it, Will knew he could work it to his advantage.

It didn't take long.

A moment later, the woman freed the top button on her blouse, wanting to give herself space to move, after Will had asked, "Anything else in your briefcase for me to read?"

Will liked Barbara Hayes, but he wasn't going to tell her what he was feeling. Not really. Telling adults the truth had caused him nothing but trouble. It spooked foster parents. It invited more questions from disbelieving government shrinks, back on the shithole reservation where he lived when agencies weren't shuttling him from home to home.

Oklahoma Reform School was next in the cards if Will ran away just one more time. His parole officer had told him that before signing papers that allowed him to travel to Florida under Hayes's supervision.

Mentioning underwater caves was the first interesting thing the woman had said since the limo met him at Jacksonville International, the driver smiling, saying, "Welcome to Florida," as he placed Will's backpack in the trunk, then gave a fake salute.

Hayes was a billboard reader, which was irritating. The woman didn't think he could read for himself? It was a habit that she resumed after discussing the caves, looking out the window and saying, "Lake City, High Springs . . . they've got a knife outlet store. Oh! Boiled peanuts—you ever try those?"

Twenty miles down the road, she had said, "Gainesville, next four exits. University of Florida, Santa Fe Ju-
nior College. You should think about it. It's smart to
start the application process early."

Will was thinking, *With my grades and no money?*

Five miles later, she caused Will to bury his iPod ear-
buds deep, saying, "Ocala, Silver Springs. The Cracker
Barrel looks busy—but I hear there's a cold front coming. Frost in Orlando, possibly snow in Gainesville.
Don't worry, we'll be on Sanibel by then—but I wonder
how it will affect this area. Snow, I mean."

Will had pretended to adjust the volume on his iPod,
but it was silence that he wanted. His mind was still
probing the road for a dark space beneath them, sensing
it was important, the word *cave* having touched a chord
that produced colors and odors in his brain, all characteristic of a synesthete who had uncanny instincts for
intuiting future events.

Why?

On this Tuesday afternoon in February, diving a remote lake in central Florida, Will Chaser got his answer.

Tomlinson's flashlight was on, and he was doing
something—possibly writing another note on his dive
slate—as Will wiggled his body free of the passageway
and let the weights in his BC vest pull him face-first onto
the floor of what appeared to be a cavern filled with clear
water, a room the size of a garage.

Excited by exiting into an open space after twenty

yards of darkness, Will hurried to get his feet under him, which was a mistake, because it caused a cloud of silt to explode around him. He took his time putting on his BC, using the Velcro straps to pull it tight around his chest, while reminding himself, *Breathe slow, dipshit. You don't have enough air to be in a hurry.*

As he waited for visibility to improve, Will considered risking a look at his pressure gauge but decided against it. No matter how many times he checked the damn thing, it wasn't going to change the amount of air he had left.

Tomlinson didn't agree. When the water was clear enough, the man used his flashlight to look at Will's gauges before showing him what he'd already written on the dive slate.

Get reserve bottle ready.

That scared Will, so he checked the gauge himself. The needle was midway into the red zone, close to *500 psi*. He wondered what it was like when a tank ran short of air. That was something they hadn't covered in class. Did it become gradually harder to inhale a breath? Or did the regulator shut down abruptly due to lack of pressure?

The pounding of his heart had slowed since he had exited the passageway, but there was no controlling how his body responded to fear, and Will could now feel his chest thumping, blood pulsing in his temples.

Tomlinson pointed to his own air bottle. Attached to it was a canister about the size of a small fire extinguisher. The canister was yellow with a manufacturer's name, SPARE AIR, stenciled on the side. A single silicon mouthpiece was already fitted at the top.

Will had a similar reserve system attached to his tank, only the canister was bigger, but he hadn't paid much attention when Ford had explained how to use the thing because the system appeared self-explanatory. Bite down on the mouthpiece, turn the knob and breathe. Nothing hard about that.

Will remembered Ford saying that Tomlinson's bottle was only good for a couple of minutes. But how many minutes of air did *his* bottle contain? Ford had gone into detail but Will hadn't listened.

Crap! Next time, I'll carry extra lights, and I'll by God pay attention.

Will reached to find his own dive slate and began writing out the question *How much air in my . . .* but Tomlinson grabbed his elbow and stopped him. The man was shaking his head, his eyes large and emphatic behind the glass of his face mask, as he grunted, "Ohooo 'ime."

No time.

Tomlinson used his flashlight to rap on his dive slate, reminding Will to *Get reserve bottle ready,* then wiped the slate clean before helping Will free the bottle and position it inside his BC beneath his chin, ready to go when he needed it. Next, Tomlinson surprised him by giving Will his bailout bottle, too. Because he had no choice, Will held still while the man clipped the little tank to his BC.

Tomlinson wrote, *Stop breathing, watch bubbles.*

Will shook his head, letting his expression answer. *Huh?*

Tomlinson rapped his flashlight on the dive slate, telling Will, *Do it!* then panned the light along the ceiling of the cavern, maybe ten feet above them, where icicle-looking spears of limestone were hanging down—stalagmites or stalactites, Will could never keep the terminology straight.

He stopped breathing, as he'd been told, and watched Tomlinson use the flashlight to explain. The light threw a circle of white that moved from the ceiling to the floor . . . from the ceiling to the floor . . . then to the ceiling again, but more slowly.

It took Will a moment to understand. Air bubbles, that's what Tomlinson wanted him to see. Air bubbles were seeping out of the rocks beneath them, ascending until they collided with the top of the cavern. There, the bubbles congregated briefly, but then continued moving, tracing silver tracks toward what might have been a tiny opening in the highest part of the cave.

What did it mean? Was Ford somewhere beneath them? That had to be it. Where else could air be coming from?

As if on cue, Will heard a grinding, clanking noise from outside—faint, but it was the unmistakable sound of the biologist doing something, digging again possibly. Tomlinson held a palm up—*Stop*—and then attempted to signal Ford, but there was no response.

Seconds later, though, Will was startled by a muted

roaring, a mechanized sound, like a cross between a leaf blower and heavy rain. It seemed to be coming from above them but far away.

Tomlinson explained the noise by scribbling *Jet dredge* on his slate.

Will nodded.

Less than a minute later, though, the thing stopped, and they heard Ford signaling. The hippie responded, banging his flashlight against his tank in a deliberate three-beat rhythm. An SOS maybe?

Possibly so, or maybe it meant nothing, but Will suspected it did because when the jet dredge started again Tomlinson grabbed his dive slate and wrote, *Got to move now!*

Move? There was nowhere to go!

Tomlinson made his case by shining the light on the ceiling, reminding Will about the stalagmites or the stalactites hanging down, their points sharpened by a couple thousand years of dripping water.

Crap!

If the ceiling collapsed on them, getting crushed was the least of their worries. Those stone stilettos could skewer them both.

Will nodded his head rapidly, saying, "Esss eely 'ucks."

Yes, it did really suck. The cavern ceiling was covered with stone daggers. Where the hell could they go?

Up, as it turned out. Stay close to the ceiling, the stalactites couldn't build up speed if they fell. Which was smart, Will had to admit.

Tomlinson was writing again and then held the slate up for him to read. *Do what I do!*

Will nodded.

Holding the flashlight in his left hand, Tomlinson let the dive slate swing to his side, then exaggerated his movements as he opened the weight pockets on his BC vest. He removed four rubber-covered chunks of lead and dropped them, one by one, at his feet, then pantomimed how to inflate his vest manually instead of using the valve connected to his tank.

Conserving air. That made sense, too. And they sure as hell didn't need a bunch of lead to keep them on the bottom now.

Up. That's where they wanted to go. Damn right, that's where they wanted to go. The vibration of the jet dredge could cause those stone daggers to fall at any moment.

After Will had jettisoned his weights, Tomlinson used his thumb to signal toward the ceiling, then began inflating his own vest for real. The man became weightless, drifting upward as if levitating, and Will followed, allowing the image of astronauts to come into his head, lights piercing the blackness. It was the same tableau that had filled his mind while traveling I-75 with Hayes, in the backseat of the Lincoln.

Will remembered wondering, *Why?* It was a sensation so powerful that he had lost himself in the fantasy of being in a submerged cave, darkness all around. Now here he was, and it was all too real.

Outside, the leaf-blower sound of the dredge stopped once again. By then, though, Tomlinson was using one hand to fend off the rocky ceiling of the cavern while using the light to follow the path of their own bubbles.

Will gave the man room to work, first trying to steady himself by clinging to a spike of limestone—the thing broke off in his hand—then by purging air from his vest until he was less buoyant. He hovered below and behind the hippie, eight feet above the cavern floor, reminding himself, *Stay calm, breathe slo-o-owly,* as he watched Tomlinson move to the highest part of the cave.

Will was thinking *Where the hell is Ford?* when the sound of the jet dredge began again, then stopped seconds later. From beneath them came a random clanking noise, as if something was being dragged along the rocks under them, followed by a momentary silence.

Will thought, *Why is Ford under us now?*

Jesus Christ, what was the man doing? Didn't he realize that they were almost out of air?

Tomlinson was tapping on his tank to get Will's attention, waving for him to move closer, when they both heard a shuddering rumble that sounded like distant thunder. The sound grew progressively louder, vibrating through the cave walls. Soon, stalactites began dropping to the floor, the sharp stones clanking hard when they hit. The rumbling sound peaked, then faded, as if a train were passing. Then the rumbling stopped.

Scary.

A minute later, it got scarier. Tomlinson was using his flashlight to show Will what appeared to be a vent in the highest section of the cavern when a chunk of ceiling above them collapsed, brushing past Tomlinson's shoulder as it fell. In that same instant, Will ran out of air.

It wasn't gradual, as Will had expected. One second, he was breathing normally. The next second, the mouthpiece of his regulator felt as if it had been abruptly sealed shut. Will continued trying to suck air from the thing as his hands found the pony canister inside his BC. Use the largest bottle first, that seemed like the smart thing to do—and, besides, Tomlinson's Spare Air bottle was clipped to a D ring, which would require more time to free.

Will was thinking, *Stay calm . . . don't rush . . . that's how people screw up.*

As he tried to remove the little tank, though, the knob caught inside his vest. Fumbling in the darkness, Will tried to free the thing, but he yanked too hard. The tank went spinning out of his hands before he could take a breath . . .

TWELVE

WHEN THE LIMESTONE OVERHANG COLLAPSED, I let go of the jet dredge hose and tried to swim free of the chaos, but there was no escaping what followed.

Water, displaced by tons of rock, pushed a descending ridge of pressure that was stronger than any squall I had ever experienced. I felt like a seed being ejected from a grape. The shock wave hit me, tumbled me, then jettisoned me downward but also toward the concave wall of the lake and out of the path of the largest limestone slabs.

Smaller rocks caught me as I descended. I covered my head with my arms and kicked hard, riding the expanding pressure away from the worst of it, surfing the shock wave toward what I hoped was safety. The hiss of my regulator added a rhythmic counterbeat to the random clatter of rock colliding with rock and clanking off my air bottle. I continued swimming hard until the noise had ceased.

When I was safe within the great hollowed convexity of the lake's northern wall, I stopped and turned, straining to see through the silt. I hadn't intended to bring the entire overhang crashing down, only the midsection, but maybe the strategy had worked. Will and Tomlinson had been trapped somewhere inside the porous outcrop. It seemed likely that now, for better or worse, they were free. But where?

I checked my gauges. I was at forty-five feet and still had three-quarters of a tank of air. I had plenty of time to wait for visibility to improve, but my partners did not. They had now been underwater for one hour and seven minutes. If the collapse hadn't freed them, and if they were not already swimming toward the surface, it seemed probable that Will was dead. And Tomlinson . . . ?

The possibility of Tomlinson being dead—actually *dead*—was beyond my grasp. It refused to take root in my brain. The man had the sensibilities and instincts of a cat—the morals, too—which added credibility, however perverse, to the expectation that he was entitled to more than just one life. Even our history argued against the inevitability that Tomlinson would in fact one day die.

"There are ghosts at this marina," he was fond of saying, particularly after blending some illegal stew of weed and fungi, then chasing it with state-licensed rum.

Ghosts—ghosts at the marina, ghosts at home in Dinkin's Bay. He spoke of the things fondly as if they actually existed. I didn't believe it, of course, but at least the setting was acceptable. The marina was home. His boat and my lab were simply extensions of Dinkin's Bay, familiar outposts that would be suitable places for our haunted specters to reside, if such things were real.

Not here at the bottom of a lake, though. Not in a place so far from the sea—and not linked to a random series of events that had been catalyzed by two equally random losers, King and Perry.

I began kicking toward the surface, left hand extended as a bumper, the silt so thick that my mind had nothing to process but internal data as I calculated my friend's chances.

Tomlinson is never easy to assess or predict, and it was no different now, particularly after this chain of disasters. Tomlinson's idea of a tough workout was swimming a case of beer out to his boat. To him, hangovers were the only variety of endurance sport worthy of his participation. And, up until the last week, he'd been a habitual ganja smoker.

Could he still be alive?

Possibly, I told myself, because it was also true that the man was a meditation guru, a master of breathing techniques. Living aboard a sailboat kept him fit, all leather and sinew, despite his devotion to excess and debauchery. Because of this, he might have another five or ten minutes of air left.

Tomlinson *dead*? No, it couldn't happen. Bad enough was the probability that Will Chaser was gone, a tough teenage kid who, for no rational reason, seemed targeted by bad luck and fated to die young.

At twenty-eight feet, the water began to clear, although debris was still raining down—kept in suspension by the aftershock possibly or the result of miniature landslides from the last remaining truncated section of the overhang.

Beneath me, I could see a jumbled darkness that was a small mountain of rock. I decided that I would do another bounce dive if I didn't find Will and Tomlinson somewhere above me, but it would be the last place I looked because if they were on the bottom they were dead. There was no way they could have survived a collapse so massive. It was possible that even the plane wreckage was now buried. Not that it mattered. The plane, the prospect of finding more gold, were meaningless to me now.

I continued swimming toward the surface.

Above me, striations of light showed that the northern section of limestone bridge was gone. All that remained was a cavernous space from which silt boiled—the same dark silt that earlier had reminded me of volcanic ash.

Fluttering down through the ash, I noticed, were several glittering objects. They were bright as fireflies. The particles formed a sparkling, descending pointillism that spun through the silt, raining down on me. Still swimming, I held out a hand and caught one.

It was a gold coin.

I looked at it for a moment, then caught another.

There were dozens of the things. They appeared to gain speed as they fell.

I pocketed two of the coins but ignored the others. I didn't need the flashlight to identify them. I knew what they were. They were more hundred-peso coins, stolen from the Cuban treasury.

Arlis had been right. He had found Batista's gold plane.

Looking up, rays of late sunlight pierced the murk. I could make out the silhouette of the tractor-sized inner tube and King's idle swim fins. The man was still up there, waiting to see if I was alive or dead and if I had found more gold.

But his were the only fins visible, which told me that Will and Tomlinson hadn't made it to the surface. It gave me a sickening feeling seeing only King, and I slowed my ascent as I reassessed. If Tomlinson and the boy weren't above me, then they were somewhere below me. Either that or they had disappeared into the porous limestone wall of the lake.

Thinking that gave me hope—but not much.

A jagged indentation marked where the overhang had broken free. It was a vertical crater the size of a closet. It looked as if a giant molar had been extracted from a limestone jaw. I knew I was in the right area because, surprisingly, the coiled ivory mammoth tusk appeared through the swirl of silt. It rested only a few yards from the crater, undisturbed, on a platform of rock that now constituted the edge of the lake's shallow rim. The extra tank was gone, though, freed by the tremor, and had to be somewhere on the bottom.

There was no need to go looking for it now.

Probing ahead with my flashlight, I swam through black detritus, my hand extended. Visibility was so bad I had to find the inside wall of the crater by touch. If I pressed my face mask within a foot of the wall, I could make out coral patterns on gray limestone and dinosaur-sized oyster shells.

High on an inside corner, I discovered an opening. It was a karst vent less than two feet wide. I poked my head inside, feeling the limestone hard against the back of my neck. It took me several seconds to figure out that the vent angled downward, an incline as steep as a child's slide.

I considered pulling myself into the hole to see where it led, but an act so risky demanded some thought. Entering an overhead environment underwater is almost always a bad idea and often fatal. I knew from reading, and from friends, that more than a hundred divers had been killed in Florida's caves in recent years and an unsettling percentage of the victims had been cave trained and well equipped. I was neither, so the decision wasn't an easy one.

Unless the bodies of Will and Tomlinson lay under a ton of rubble on the bottom, there was still a chance that they had been trapped in and protected by a similar vent. Even though visibility was poor, I could see that the area was a catacomb of holes and crevices.

With so many conduits available, it was possible that they had clawed and dug their way into adjoining chambers and were now far from the site of the first landslide. If so, those chambers might be linked to the vent I had just discovered. In fact, considering the location, it could have been the very place where they had been trapped to begin with.

I made a low pass over the sandy plateau. There were now no bubbles to be seen. That should have been enough to convince me, but I couldn't let go of the hope that Tomlinson and the boy had followed one of the limestone corridors to safety.

The opening to the vent I had found, though, was so damn small. Would they have risked it? I tried to squeeze my shoulders into the hole, but the pillar valve on my tank stopped me, clanking against the rocks. Even if I had removed my tank, the space would have been too tight. But Tomlinson and the boy were both smaller than me. If they were desperate—and they *were* desperate— they could have forced their way into the thing and followed it.

I backed out of the hole and tapped my flashlight on my tank, hoping for a response. Several times I signaled, but there was no reply.

It was as telling as the absence of exhaust bubbles, but I refused to accept that silence as proof, either.

If they had followed the tunnel, I reasoned, they might be too far away to hear me. It was possible. If the vent actually did connect to a series of other tunnels and adjoining chambers, they could be a hundred yards or more from where they'd originally been trapped. In this part of Florida, there were underground labyrinths that traveled for miles before they dead-ended.

Intellectually, I knew it was unlikely. But I wanted to believe it, so I became even more determined to search the tunnel.

If I'd had my knife, it would have been easier to widen the opening, but Perry had grabbed it soon after I'd taken the thing off. Instead, I clipped the flashlight to my BC, light on, and used my hands to rip away chunks of limestone. It wasn't easy work, and I knew too well that I was inviting another landslide.

After a couple of minutes, I tried signaling again, then used the silence as additional proof that I was making the right decision. My partners weren't dead, they had traveled too far to hear me. I had to get closer before signaling again.

The human mind is at its inventive best when misinterpreting data to support a specific hope.

I flipped the air bottle over my head, pushed it into the hole and followed, feeling the jagged limestone tear at my skin and wet suit. The vent widened, briefly, then narrowed as I traveled downward, walking on my fingers and not using my fins, which was the best way to avoid disturbing the silt.

The vent wasn't much wider than a drainpipe. With the flashlight on, the rock walls were orange, encrusted with oxidized sediment. Exhaust bubbles, percolating around my faceplate, loosened the sediment, staining the water with a bloody tint. With the light off, the walls seemed to expand around me as if the shock of illumination had caused them to spasm tight around my body. I preferred the illusion of space so progressed in darkness.

Ten yards into the vent, though, I stopped, finally admitting to myself, *This is pointless.*

I didn't want to believe that, either. Intellectually, I knew it was true, but my brain had latched on to a fanciful thread. It was the irrational conviction that Will Chaser had indeed recently been here in this same dark space. It was an intangible sensation . . . a feeling, not a thought. Tomlinson had been here, too, presumably, but it was the image of the boy that was strongest in my mind.

I told myself, *That's ridiculous. Absurd—you're imagining things, Ford.*

I knew that was true, too. Tomlinson was my closest friend. I barely knew the boy—why would I feel some sensory connection with him? Plus, there is no validity to a perception that has been catalyzed by hope alone— or by fear. That variety of skewed thinking was the source of all superstition.

After another ten yards, I stopped again and tried the flashlight. Its beam created a milky tunnel through the silt. Was there an opening ahead? I couldn't be sure. I pressed ahead a few more feet before deciding that I was wrong. It was another illusion spawned by wishful thinking.

The vent was so cramped, I couldn't move my elbows, but I could move my right wrist. Eight times, I tapped the flashlight against my tank. Not hard—I didn't want to risk disturbing the rocks overhead. The possibility of being crushed was too real and the thought of being trapped here unable to move, biding my time until I ran out of air, was terrifying.

Three more times I signaled, but there was no reply.

It brought me back to my senses. Intellect displaced imagination, and I began to back out of the vent. As I did, I felt a sickening, visceral dread. It was an out-of-body sense of unreality. My movements became robotic as I paused to signal one last time, then waited in a roaring silence—a silence that became hypnotic, pounding inside my head. It communicated a single, throbbing reality: *They're gone . . . both dead. You can't help them by killing yourself.*

It was an unavoidable truth. I backed out of the hole, expecting the tunnel to collapse each time my elbow collided with a rock or when I had to brace a knee and apply force to lever myself backward another few inches.

When I was finally free, my mind functioned by rote as I continued exploring the area. I saw a few more coins, bright and solitary in the shallows. The sight catalyzed an irrational anger in me. Yes, Arlis had found Batista's gold plane—so what? I had no idea if there was a ton of gold beneath me or if the treasure included only the handful of coins I had seen fluttering into the depths. It no longer mattered. The plane wreck had cost two more lives. Nothing was worth that.

I kicked toward the shallows, my eyes moving from the bottom to the surface still hoping for a miracle. Once again, I searched the surface, hoping to see two pairs of legs dangling, but there was nothing.

Now even King was gone. I could see the underside of the inner tube still tied to my marker buoy, the hose floating in a loose coil, but the jet dredge was unattended.

I nursed a momentary hope that the son of a bitch had drowned, but only because I was still in shock. As I began to recover, though, my focus switched from the death of my friends to how I would now deal with the skinny drifter, with his slicked-back hair and his smirking contempt.

King had intentionally sabotaged my rescue attempt, slowing me as we'd positioned the jet dredge. He had caused me to lose a precious ninety seconds when I'd dropped the spare tanks. It was King who was responsible for the final cataclysmic collapse that had taken Tomlinson and Will, probably crushing them both.

King. He had taunted and manipulated me, confident that I, like most people, would not stray beyond the boundaries of normal behavior. But the man had no idea who he was dealing with. King and Perry were both about to find out.

I realized that I was hyperventilating. The realization produced a reaction that I found perversely comforting. A cold flooding calm moved through me that was familiar. It leached color from the glowing orange numerals of my dive watch. It dulled the undulate sky above. The reaction gave me focus.

King was up there. Maybe the sound of the ledge collapsing had spooked him. Maybe he had simply attempted further sabotage by abandoning me.

It didn't matter. The man was somewhere onshore,

and I would find him. There was no rush now. King and Perry wouldn't murder Arlis. Arlis was key to controlling me. They wouldn't kill me, either—not right away, at least—because they needed me to recover the gold.

Gold. They had Arlis as leverage. But I had leverage, now, too. I had two additional coins in my vest and there were more coins on the bottom of the lake. Play it right and their collective greed would give me the opening I needed.

I'll kill them both.

That's what I was thinking.

My gauges told me that I had burned another quarter bottle of air while worming my way in and out of the vent. It was additional evidence that Will and Tomlinson had perished if they had jammed themselves into a tunnel.

Comparing open-space diving to cave diving is like comparing a game of paintball to actual combat. The same is true of wreck penetration. It's not recreational sport, it's an unforgiving craft.

An overhead environment sparks involuntary physiological responses. Pulse and respiration increase proportionally as visibility and space decrease. The fight-or-flight sensors become the brain's primary supplier of data, and both the hypothalamus and the medulla begin a chemical dialogue with the spinal cord, releasing epinephrine to fuel a blooming panic.

If you're human, you react, and there is no ignoring

it. The responses can be mitigated only by a hell of a lot of training, preparation and experience.

If Will and Tomlinson had attempted to escape through a vent, their air consumption would have doubled, even at twenty feet. In all probability, they'd run out of air long before I had returned to the water.

Even so, I was reluctant to surface. I couldn't give up without at least checking the rubble below. I dreaded the thought of finding the bodies of my friends, but the idea of leaving Tomlinson and Will Chaser here, alone, on the bottom of this remote sinkhole, was even more repugnant.

I checked my dive computer to confirm that I hadn't accumulated a decompression obligation. I still had almost half my air remaining, and I needed time to think about how I would handle King and Perry when I surfaced.

No rush, I reminded myself as I kicked downward, descending headfirst into the blue. It had taken me less than two minutes to bounce-dive to the bottom and recover the spare tanks. Because of the depth, I couldn't risk lingering. But neither did I have to hurry.

At a hundred feet, visibility began to deteriorate, but I could still decipher the shape of limestone blocks and shell rubble that comprised a new underwater hillock— the term *mogote* came into my mind. Silt spiraled downward into the hillside, the flow line defined by a sumping whirlpool vortex.

It would have been interesting to introduce the chemical fluorescein into the lake, then trace that brilliant green dye to its emergence points. No telling where this underground river flowed, and there were probably many exit points—adjoining sinkholes, flowing surface rivers, the Gulf of Mexico sixty miles west or even Florida Bay a hundred and fifty miles to the south. It was not only possible, it was a probability that had been well documented by Florida hydrogeologists.

At the top of the hillock, I paused and used my flashlight. The beam penetrated the murk below, a solitary white laser in which silt became animated, boiling like smoke from a subterranean fire.

After checking my gauges—*105 ft*—I followed the beam down the hillside, kicking slowly. I told myself that I was looking for more coins. They would be useful for convincing King I had discovered a great treasure. But I was, in fact, on a reluctant search for two bodies.

As I descended, a peripheral awareness confirmed that the landslide had covered much of the plane wreckage. Only the nose of the plane was visible now. The vague geometrics of the cockpit windows were as bleak and unresponsive as the eye sockets of a skull. Atop the fuselage, I saw what may have been several more coins. Ironic, if they had come to rest here.

I wanted to swoop down and grab the things. It was pleasant to imagine myself showing King a fistful of gold while I searched his face for the greed that soon, I hoped, would allow me to lure him into the water, just the two of us alone, King and me.

No, I decided. Retrieving the coins was a bad idea. The desire to collect the things was an emotional response, I realized—a red flag at any depth below sixty feet. I was now at a hundred and ten feet, deep into nitrogen narcosis territory, where spontaneity can be a methodical killer. A few more coins, I decided, were not worth the risk of going even a few meters deeper.

Still using the flashlight, I started up, ascending more slowly than my bubbles, as I continued to search the rubble. I saw several more cattle skulls and another mastodon tusk—this one was a broken brown chunk of ivory, possibly the mate of the tusk that Tomlinson had found. I was tempted to take a closer look, but that, too, was irrational under the circumstances. It was another red flag, and I knew it was time to surface.

A few seconds later, though, I saw something that brought me to a stop. Protruding from beneath a slab of limestone was a lone black swim fin. I recognized it immediately. It was an old-style Jet Fin, similar to the Rocket Fins I wore. They were made of dense black rubber, open-heeled, heavy, wide and functional. I prefer fins that aren't buoyant, and the same was true with Tomlinson. He had joked that wearing dated old fins was a style statement—our lone similarity when it came to such things.

It was Tomlinson's fin.

I approached the thing slowly until I saw to my relief that the fin wasn't attached to a foot. I lifted it, inspected it, then pried away a few layers of rock from beneath it, searching for the remains of my friend. I even banged out a signal on my tank before positioning the fin beneath my arm, then continued my ascent, my mind trying to fix the details of this lake, this moment, in memory.

Underground rivers are also referred to as "lost rivers." I could think of no better description for this place.

According to my dive computer, I had accumulated a brief decompression stop at twenty feet. The obligation was only two minutes, but I would double that just to be safe. My gauges also told me that my air was low now, redlining at 1000 psi. I had very little time remaining.

As I kicked toward the surface, I looked for a comfortable place to wait while I decompressed. Water was clearer now where the overhang had broken away and that's where I chose to stop, backing into the crater as if it were a cocoon.

I neutralized my buoyancy and carefully—very carefully—locked my arm into the vent to anchor myself. From that vantage point, I could see the jet dredge above, still unattended, and the mountain of rock below where a good, good man and a very tough kid had ended their lives.

Because I had only one free hand, I decided to store Tomlinson's fin inside the vent until it was time to surface. I am not an emotional person, but there was something funereal and final about placing my pal's fin, alone, in a space so dark. I couldn't make myself do it and I stared at the thing as I battled an overwhelming flood of emotion that I suspected was normal dissemination. Grief, sorrow, guilt and regret. They are all variations on a common theme, and that very human theme is loss. Inexorable, inescapable loss.

The buddy system just gives bad luck a bigger target, Tomlinson had joked—but it was far more profound than a joke because this time he was right.

The man often was.

Three minutes into my decompression, just for the hell of it, I tapped my flashlight on my tank, eight slow bell notes, before clipping the light to my shoulder harness. It was the Morse abbreviation for F-B. *Fine business. Everything's okay.* It wasn't intended as a signal. It was offered as my farewell salute.

A moment later, though, I was shocked to hear— at least, I *believed* I heard—*TAP . . . TAP . . . TAP* in response. I was so startled that I dropped Tomlinson's fin. As I lunged to grab the thing, I heard yet another clanging series of sounds. Much louder, it seemed.

Impossible.

No, the sound was easily explained because the source of the noise was me. I had clipped the flashlight too close to my tank so that metal clanked against metal whenever I moved.

By the time I figured it out, I had been decompressing for nearly five minutes and I was too low on air to waste more time. There would be no more futile signaling, no more imagined replies.

It was time to surface. King and Perry were waiting.

THIRTEEN

KING KEPT HIS DISTANCE AS I SLOGGED TO shore, but he couldn't resist looking at the fin I carried beneath my arm and saying, "Looks like you found your girlfriend. Rescuing her one piece at a time, are you?"

The man's attempts at humor always had a vile edge.

I shrugged, my expression blank. I said, "Where's Captain Futch?" as I stopped to place the fin at the base of a cypress tree, then removed my BC and empty bottle.

From the truck, I heard Arlis call, "Is that you, Doc? Did you find 'em?"

I answered, "How are you feeling, Arlis?"

He hollered back, "The Yankee scum's got me tied up again. Damn cowards didn't want to risk two against one!" Once again, he asked, "Where's Tomlinson and the kid? Are they with you?"

I looked from the truck to King, then toward the edge of the clearing where Perry was preoccupied pissing in the bushes. The rifle, I noted, was leaning against a nearby palmetto. It meant that King was carrying the pistol. He had dried off and dressed, leaving his sodden underwear to dry on a wax myrtle tree. The pistol was probably hidden in the back of his pants.

No . . . the fool had put it in his pocket. I watched him wrestle it from his pants as I walked toward the truck. I was hoping the thing would go off accidentally and maybe sever his femoral artery, but no such luck.

"So what's the word, Jock-a-mo? Are we rich yet? You'd better by God have those truck keys!"

I ignored him as I went to the driver's-side window and looked in, seeing Arlis lying on his back, hands tie-wrapped behind him, his face now so swollen that I wouldn't have recognized him under other circumstances. The skin between his left ear and jaw was stretched bright in demarcations of purple, green and jaundiced yellow. On the towel next to him, blood was starting to cake.

King was calling to me, "Stay the hell away from that old man! You still don't seem to understand who's in charge here."

I said to Arlis, my voice low, "They're both dead. It's just you and me now."

I watched the man wince, his eyes closed tight. "Are you sure? Did you find them?"

I said, "They've been down there for more than an hour and fifteen minutes. There's no way they could still be alive. And there was another landslide—a whole wing of the lake fell. King caused it."

Arlis raised his head to look at me through his one good eye. "Fix it so I've got ten minutes alone with those bastards, Doc. I don't care if they kill me, I'll find a way to get a few shots in of my own first."

I said, "We will. We both will, trust me. But now it's time to move on to other things." I gave it a second, waiting until I was sure Arlis was still looking at me, before I mouthed a question, *Where are the keys?*

The man took a deep breath, shaking his head, as if trying to erase this nightmare from memory. Then with his chin he motioned toward what might have been the ashtray or the center console as he said something that sounded like "Cut me loose and let's get going."

"You've got them?"

He replied, "Yeah."

"Where?"

Arlis was trying to sit up. "Cut me loose and you'll see. I'm going to kill those two for doing this to us. Run them over with the truck. You just watch me."

I shook my head as I whispered, "No. You're getting out of here the first chance you get—and without me. Understand?"

I leaned in to get a closer look at the man's eyes, saying, "Do you know what they did with our cell phones and the VHF?"

"In their pockets, I guess," Arlis whispered as he lay back. His pupils appeared okay, his breathing was steady and the bleeding had stopped.

I told him, "You're going to be okay. If I talk them into cutting you loose, take off. Don't wait. You've got to go for help."

"Not without you," he replied.

"It's not your decision to make. When you get the chance, start the damn truck and go. Hear me?"

I turned away from the window because Perry was jogging toward us, yelling to King, "You dumb shit, don't let him near that truck. If the dude's got the keys, he'll drive off and leave us!"

Behind me, King was pointing the pistol at me, his voice oddly calm as he said, "Problem with you, Jock-o, is it's so damn hard to get your attention."

There was a pause before I heard *Whap-WHAP!* and realized that the man had pulled the trigger. I ducked reflexively, trying to shield my head with my arms. It sounded like two rapid-fire pistol shots, but, in fact, I'd heard only one shot, plus the simultaneous impact of a slug puckering the truck's front door close to my knee.

As I ducked, I spun toward King, who was still pointing the pistol. He stood between me and the lake, ten long yards away, a bizarre grin fixed on his face like some kid who had just made a great discovery.

The power of pulling a trigger, that's what he had discovered. A tiny little chunk of metal could make a big man jump.

"There!" he yelled. "Now I have your attention." King took a step toward me but decided no, he was close enough. "If you have the keys, you better toss 'em my way. How about it?"

He leveled the weapon, enjoying himself as he thought about pulling the trigger again, letting the idea move through his brain. *This time, put a slug closer . . . Maybe even wound me.* He was sighting down the barrel, thinking about it.

I said, "In my BC, there's something I want to show you."

"The keys?"

"You'll see."

Perry was next to King now, rifle held at waist level. He said, "What are you talking about? *BC*—what's that mean?"

Still grinning, King said, "Partner, haven't you been paying attention? It's the life-vest sort of thing divers wear. Pull a cord, the thing inflates and floats them to the top. But I guess Jock-o's girlfriends sorta missed that lesson." His attention returned to me. "Are they both dead?"

I said, "That's right."

"You don't look too broken up about it."

That's what I wanted him to think.

He said, "If you found the bodies, you've got the keys. Hand them over."

I made a gesture of impatience, and told him, "Put down that goddamn gun if you want answers. I can't talk with a gun in my face."

King began sidestepping toward my vest, not taking his eyes off me. "Not 'til I have those keys, Jock-o. Seems to me we've got us some serious trust issues."

It was another one of those moments. King could

shoot me or not shoot me—it was up to him. I waved the gun away and walked toward my vest, hoping his feral sense of boundaries would stop him in his tracks. It did.

I knelt, popped the air bottle free of the vest, then ripped open a Velcro pocket. I flipped one gold coin toward King's feet but kept the other.

Perry said, "No shit! How many did you find down there?" as he scrambled to get to the coin while King stared at me.

I stared back. "Not nearly as many as I could have. Some idiot screwed up the jet dredge when he yanked it out of my hands. Guess who?"

Perry's eyes moved to King as King told me, "I was getting bored. What can I tell you?" Then he said, "If there's so much of the stuff, why'd you come back with just two of these little beauties? And no gold bars."

I said, "You. You're the reason. You caused another landslide with your screwing around, playing games with the dredge. Now the whole bottom's changed. Most of the coins are under a bunch of rock. Same with the bodies of my friends—including the one who has the keys to the truck."

"Bullshit!"

I said, "I couldn't agree more—but it's your bullshit, King, and I'm sick of it. You want to leave here with a share of what's down there? You want to take the truck and drive out? Then you'd better stop screwing around. All I want is you two assholes out of my life."

As King smiled and said, "Assholes, huh?" Perry snapped at him, "Shut up and let the dude talk."

I said, "Why bother? He's not going to listen. I want to finish what we're doing and go our separate ways. No more of your partner's asinine stunts, okay?"

Perry was paying attention. He gave King a look as he said, "The dude's right. I saw your bullshit fisherman act. You need a job in the circus, numbnuts. Nothing but hicks in the audience because who else would want to watch?"

King attempted to laugh it off, but his face showed a childish irritation, eager to engage, but he was also unsettled by Perry's assertiveness. The guy was afraid of his jittery partner, I could see it—a recent development, I guessed, in what had been a one-sided partnership.

There had to be a reason. The murders in Winter Haven maybe. Or maybe King had learned something about Perry while they'd killed five innocent people. More likely Perry had learned something about King.

Perry said, "Goddamn it, I want the money that's down there and I want the truck. So shut your mouth and listen to what the man has to say."

I had turned my back to them, rearranging my gear, pretending to be very busy and in a hurry. But I wasn't. Not now. Sunset was a little after six—only half an hour away.

After a long silence, Perry said, "You got more air tanks, right? Fix yourself up another tank of air or whatever it is you need. This time, when you go down, you won't have no problems. I promise. Deal?"

I stood and turned. "Cut Captain Futch loose and we'll take it from there. That's the only deal I'll make."

King said, "Tough guy like you, what's it matter? You already screwed up and got two of your girlfriends killed. Third time's a charm, haven't you heard?"

I behaved as if King was invisible and spoke only to Perry, "The old man's hurt too badly to be a threat to you. With a head injury like that, he could aspirate and die. There's no way for him to move, or even roll over, because his hands are tied behind him."

Perry said, "*Aspirate?* . . . Well, yeah, I guess he could," not sure what the word meant, as King cut in, "How about I just shoot you in the goddamn knee unless you hand over those keys! I'll give you exactly one minute."

I continued speaking to Perry. "Your pal's not very bright. Haven't you figured that out yet? You could drive out of here a wealthy man. But instead you're letting him do your thinking for you." I shrugged, my expression saying *It's your choice, not mine.*

"He's a fucking genius, just ask him," Perry replied, and I noted the subtle way Perry had turned, the rifle now pointing in King's direction.

I found a mesh dive bag and held it up for Perry to see before tossing it toward him. "Because of the second landslide, most of the plane wreckage is covered up. That fisherman stunt cost us all a lot of time."

King made a whining groan of protest as I continued, "The cargo's scattered all over the bottom of the lake now. But if we do this right, and if your buddy stops clowning around, I'll fill that bag with whatever I can find and surface with the keys. But it's going to take me at least an hour—and I can't do it by myself. Not now."

King started to say something but Perry silenced him with a look. "What do you want us to do?"

I said, "Start by cutting the captain loose. I think he's dying. At least let him die with his hands free. He needs water, too. There's a bunch in the cooler—and I'm going to make a place for him to lie down. Under one of those trees would be good."

"If we do that, then what?"

I said, "One of the guys on the bottom—the guy who has the keys—his body's under about a ton of limestone. It would be better if I had a second diver with me. I could use the jet dredge while he moves rocks and keeps the hose from kinking."

Perry said immediately, "Numbnuts here—he'll do it."

"The hell I will!" King snapped. His expression read *Are you crazy?* He was looking westward where light was congregating in a late-winter sky, the sun transitioning from silver to bronze.

I said, "I wouldn't trust him with me underwater even if he was willing to do it. But I've got to have someone on the inner tube to feed me hose when I need it. Your partner's already proven he can't handle the job. Without someone helping me from the surface, I can't get the keys. And you can forget about more gold."

"It'll be different, this time," Perry replied, staring at King as he raised the barrel of the Winchester. "This time, there'll be no more of his stupid tricks."

King said, "Jesus Christ, it'll be dark in a few minutes—I froze my ass off in there last time! Jock-a-mo's lying, you can't tell? Let's send his ass back in there for the keys, then get the hell out of here. A hundred grand, maybe—that's how much we got already, counting the extra coins. Let's move!"

King, the invisible man, that's how he had to feel now because Perry wouldn't look at him, either.

"Go cut the old man loose," Perry ordered. "Just his hands, not his feet. No, wait—" I watched the man pat his pockets, not looking for cigarettes this time. "I'll do it, I've got the knife. You keep an eye on Ford."

King raised his voice, saying, "Who the hell died and pinned a crown to your ass?"

Perry, with his nervous eyes, didn't answer, something else now on his mind. "Jesus Christ," he whispered, looking above my shoulder at the horizon. Then he said, "Son of a bitch! That's a helicopter! A helicopter coming this way!"

King stood straighter. He could see it, too.

I had heard a wisp of a chopper's thumping minutes before, but now I could see the aircraft flying toward us, low and fast, from the northeast. If it stayed on course, the crew couldn't miss seeing the truck, and us.

King was already striding toward the trees to take cover, but Perry appeared frozen, angling his rifle toward the chopper as if thinking about trying to shoot the thing out of the sky.

I said, "Don't pull that trigger or you're screwed."

"What?"

I said, "They won't bother us. Just do what I say."

Perry's eyes were locked on the helicopter. "Those are cops. I can tell by the color. We're already screwed! Goddamn you, King, this is all because of you!"

Now he was shouldering the rifle, only four long strides away from me. Instinct told me I could get to Perry before he swung the rifle in my direction, but that's not what I wanted—not with the chopper crew soon close enough to make out details. In my mind, a chopper was no longer a rescue vehicle, it was a liability. The helicopter carried potential witnesses. With witnesses around, I would be denied my time alone with Perry and King.

Talking louder, I said to Perry, "Do what I tell you to do and they'll leave us alone. Goddamn it, listen to me!"

Perry snapped out of his trance and turned, his face showing confusion.

I told him, "Hide that rifle. Slide it under the truck or toss it into the bushes."

King, who had pocketed the pistol, called, "Don't be a dope, Perry. Jock-a-mo's setting us up." He was talking over his shoulder, moving faster toward the trees. *Leave Perry to confront police,* that's what he was thinking. King was out of here.

I picked up the BC and the spent air bottle and walked toward Perry, saying, "Take your shirt off and start walking this stuff toward the lake. Do it now."

"Huh?"

"Take your shirt off."

"You're crazy, dude. Let them see me? You don't know what they're gonna charge us with, man. You got no idea of the kinda shit that's about to go down. If you knew, you wouldn't—"

"Convicts on the run don't take time out to go scuba diving," I told him. "Listen to what I'm saying! They won't find out who you are unless you give them a reason to land."

The chopper had spotted us. I watched the craft veer two degrees, drop its nose and accelerate directly at us. Perry looked at the rifle, then lowered it before looking at me. "Okay, okay. Like I'm a tourist or something," he said. "Is that what you mean?"

"If you don't run," I said, "they've got no reason to be suspicious."

He replied, "I get it. Yeah . . . maybe . . . Maybe that's smart."

Perry hid the rifle by holding it parallel to his right leg until he was close enough, then slid it under the truck. I left the BC with the bottle standing upright as Perry removed his shirt—maybe a mistake because of his prison-white skin, tattoos showing, but there was no going back now.

As Perry carried my tank and BC toward the lake, I removed another bottle from the back of the truck and the canvas bag I usually carry on my boat, the one loaded with emergency gear. King and Perry had already pawed through the stuff, but it looked like everything I had packed was still there.

When the chopper was high above us, the pilot hovered, taking his time descending just in case we were armed and dangerous. The craft was painted govern-

ment green on white with a big golden sheriff's star aft
of the cabin. Inside, I could see the pilot plus two cops—
maybe wearing tactical gear, maybe not—but one of
them was using binoculars from beneath his flight helmet. I waved at the helicopter as I said to Perry, "Put on
that vest. Pretend you're adjusting it."

The man's tattoos were garish red and green on his
mushroom skin, a dragon covering his back, a snake
crawling across his shoulders.

Not looking at me, Perry called back, "I'm wearing
pants, for chrissake. They're not gonna believe I'm
going for a swim wearing pants and shoes."

The chopper was dipping lower, and I was smiling
up at the cops as I said to him, "You want them to ID
that ink on your back? Put on that damn vest before they
see it."

I was making sense—I could see the man's brain
working it through. He picked up the BC, saying, "Why
the hell are you trying to help us? Dude, that's what I
don't understand."

I didn't reply. By the time the chopper was close
enough for us to feel the wind wake, Perry had the BC
on and was fiddling with the straps.

"Look at them and wave," I told Perry, suddenly not
so sure this act was going to work, mostly because of
King, who, I now noticed, was crouched down beneath
trees, hiding near the truck. Behave as if you're guilty,
no matter what the crime, and cops will react as if they
are dealing with killers.

In this case, they were.

Because of the thick palmettos, there wasn't a clean LZ that would allow an easy landing, but if they saw King they would call for backup, then stand watch until help arrived.

I returned my attention to the gear bag I was holding as if getting ready for another dive, but I used peripheral vision to watch as the helicopter dropped low enough that cypress trees began thrashing. King was on his belly now, hands protecting his head from debris. Look straight down, the pilot might be able to see him.

Idiot.

The chopper looked like an executive Bell, two big windows on the port and starboard sides. I wasn't surprised that it was equipped with a PA system. I watched one of the cops lift a microphone to his lips before his voice boomed, "Orange County Sheriff's Department. Are you men okay?"

I let the cop with the binoculars see me nod. I held a fist in the air, a big thumbs-up.

The voice asked, "Do you have permission to be on this property?"

I doubted if they cared. There was no way the cops could check without landing, and I knew they weren't hunting for trespassers. It wasn't a question, it was a test. The man was fishing for a reaction as one of his partners studied us with the binoculars.

I nodded an emphatic *Yes* and added another thumbs-up.

"We're looking for two male suspects—two men traveling on bicycles. Or maybe on foot by now. They're both about the same height and build. About six-three, a hundred and seventy-five pounds. Have you seen anyone in the area who matches that description?"

As if asking Perry a question, I said to him, "Act like you're thinking about it, then shake your head no."

I noted that Perry's hands were shaking as he knelt over the air bottle and then reached for the regulator hose. He didn't look up as he replied, "We're fucked. I should've kept the goddamn rifle!"

I said in a pleasant voice, "Shut up and don't panic. You're okay," then looked up at the chopper. I shrugged and shook my head, *No,* my expression telling the crew *Sorry, we can't help you.*

"If you see two males who fit that description—if you see *anyone* suspicious—please call nine-one-one. Don't try to confront them, don't attempt to follow. Do you understand? These men are armed and extremely dangerous."

I nodded another emphatic yes as I watched the cop with the microphone listen to something the man behind him was saying. Again, the voice echoed down through the chopper wash. "Are you *sure* everything's okay?"

I nodded.

The two men conversed again before the PA boomed, "It's late in the day to be diving. Is there some kind of trouble?"

As I shook my head no I touched my watch, then I pointed to the sun. Next, I pointed at the lake. I punctuated the response by flashing an *OK* with thumb and forefinger, then another thumbs-up.

They could interpret that any way they wanted. The cops were trained in air recovery, which meant they knew something about diving. Novice divers often do their first night dive in the safe confines of a quarry. Maybe they would make the connection.

They did.

The PA system boomed, "Have a good day, gentlemen, but stay on your toes. The guys we're after could be somewhere in this area."

I offered a final thumbs-up, feeling the binoculars fixed on us, seeing the pilot inspect our scuba gear strewn around the truck, as the chopper tilted, then lifted slowly. The noise of the rotor blade rumbled louder as the aircraft spun sharply to port, then accelerated away.

Not moving, I said to Perry, "Keep doing exactly what you're doing. Do it until they're out of sight."

I gave it a few beats before I stood, turned and yelled to King, "Stay where you are, you dumb-ass. Don't move! This is the second time you've screwed up—and it had better be the last!"

When the chopper was gone, I walked toward the truck to check on Arlis. King emerged from the trees. He held the pistol in his right hand, not smiling. His face was different—a blanched, wide-eyed look that told me I'd finally gotten to him. The manipulator had been manipulated.

King hollered, "No more of your smart-ass remarks—

you hear me, you piece of shit? Mister high-and-mighty! Don't think the King won't shoot you 'cause I will." His voice had a different quality, too. All the smirking subtleties were gone.

I was thinking, *The King, huh?* and ignored him as he screamed, "Look at me when I'm talking to you!"

The real King had finally made an appearance—a fragile ego masked by bluster and all the machinations of a vicious child.

I didn't look at him. I continued walking. I thought he might pull the trigger again, but felt confident that he would intentionally miss. Cuban gold pesos and a vehicle—without me, King had no venue of escape.

From behind, I heard Perry gliding up beside me, walking fast, saying, "Hey—you gotta answer my question, dude. I want to know. Why'd you do that? You got rid of the cops—*why?*"

King heard him as he intercepted us. He was nodding his head, his face was mottled with anger. "There's something weird going on here, Perry. I don't like it, man. I don't trust this dweeb. What he just did makes no sense. Jock-o, what is your story?"

I said, "I don't have a story. You're too dumb to understand it if I did."

In the back of the truck was an Igloo cooler. I opened it, took out two bottles of water and turned to Perry. "Captain Futch needs his hands free. Cut him loose. Let me give him some water. I'm not discussing our next move until his hands are free."

"You're not going near the old man," King snapped. "For all I know, you've got the truck keys stashed in your wet suit."

I pushed the bottles toward King. "Then you do it, but I'm watching every move you make."

I stood near the window as Perry helped Arlis sit, then used my big survival knife to cut the plastic that bound his wrists. The knife was sharp and it took only a swipe. From Arlis, I expected threats and insults, but the man had been paying attention. For an instant, his eyes locked onto mine, and I understood. He was playing a new role now, the role of the injured old cripple. Let them think he was beaten. Arlis was still in the game.

I said, "Cut his ankles free, too. If he vomits again, he's got to be able to climb out of the truck."

Perry was in charge and he let me know it, saying, "Shut your mouth. Grandpa can puke all he wants, I don't give a shit. I'm not watching the old bastard every second. His feet stay tied."

Arlis was gulping water. I had never seen him so quiet and meek. "I ain't going anywhere," he mumbled through the window. "Just leave me alone, let me be." Without risking eye contact, he pulled the passenger door closed, then flopped his head on his chest as if he wanted to sleep.

I knew that Arlis had the keys. His hands were free. All he needed now was an opportunity to start the truck and go.

I took two bottles of water for myself and walked toward the lake, expecting Perry and King to follow.

They did. I was calculating Arlis's chances, picturing
how it would shake out. With his ankles bound, it would
be tough for him to manage the clutch and accelerator
without stalling the engine. But that wasn't the worst of
it. Once he got the truck started, he would have to
bounce through fifty yards of palmettos and bushes
before the tree line offered him any cover. Until then,
Perry would be able to plink away with the Winchester.
A 30-30 slug would pierce the thin metal of the cab, no
problem.

Now I wished I had told Arlis to wait until dark. As
King and Perry followed me to the lake, I tried to con-
trive a reason for returning to the truck so I could pass
along the message, but Perry wouldn't let me near the
thing.

"You're staying right here with me until you explain
what the hell's going on. You could have ratted us to the
cops but you didn't. Why?"

King couldn't keep his mouth shut. "Maybe he's
flush out of friends. He probably wants to spend some
quality time with his new playmates. Just the three of us,
alone. Isn't that right, Jock-o?"

I almost smiled. That was exactly what I wanted—me
alone with Perry and King, just the three of us. Instead
I said, "I lied to the cops because I had to."

"That answer doesn't cut it, man. Lied to the cops
because you had to?" Perry found that funny. "Jesus
Christ, who doesn't?"

"We don't have permission to dive this lake," I told
him. "But that's only part of it. The old man doesn't

really own the property. If the real owner finds out about the plane wreck, who do you think owns the salvage rights? Even if we do all the work, he can still claim everything we recover. That's why I didn't want the cops to land."

Perry thought about that until he decided it made sense, but King wasn't buying. Maybe it was because he didn't believe me, but more likely it was because he was pissed off and looking for an excuse to shoot me. It was all there in his face and his body language. Trouble was, King couldn't piece together an alternative motive. Why would I refuse help from the police?

King didn't understand because he knew nothing about me. He soon would.

King said, "Even with his two buddies dead and the old man bad hurt, he still didn't want the cops to land? This is weird, Perry, very weird." The man was shaking his head as he studied me. "Your pals are down there— we saw all three of you go in the water. The cops would've called in help. Other divers would've showed up to retrieve their bodies."

I said, "So what? There's no rush now."

"That's cold, Jock-o. One look at you, I can tell you never spent day one in the joint. But, man"—he allowed himself to smile—"you got all the qualifications. You don't give a damn about anybody but yourself. A marine biologist, huh?"

I said, "Nothing's going to change the fact that my friends are dead. When I get back, I'll call the police.

They'll have to notify the property owner. Do you see where I'm headed with this?"

King rolled his eyes as Perry took a step closer to hear, but not too close.

I said, "Police divers are going to see what's down there. They'll see the wreck. They're bound to see a few coins even after the rockslide. Or maybe a gold bar."

Perry whispered, "I get it now. Jesus Christ."

I said, "At least one of you has some brains."

"And they'll tell the property owner," Perry finished.

"They're required by law to inform the owner," I said. I didn't know if that was true, but it sounded plausible.

I had been busy rigging a tank and regulator. Now I looked from the lake to the Gulf horizon, where the sky was orchid streaked. I couldn't remember ever being so eager for nightfall. "What's a few hours matter?" I said. "It's not going to bring my friends back."

That was true, and I felt a dizzying vertigo as I spoke the words. I felt as if I was viewing the area from above, descending so fast into the reality of what had happened, my belly felt hollow, like falling through a trapdoor.

Perry believed me. He wanted King to believe, too. After all, King had to go in the water, not him.

"We got what's called a window of opportunity," Perry told him. "It's the damn chance of a lifetime! But shit, dude, it's gonna be too dark to see anything." He had followed my gaze to the horizon, watching the sun inflate, molten orange, as it absorbed light from an invading darkness. "But the dude's got underwater lights, right? See there, King"—Perry knelt by the canvas bag—"he's got three . . . four flashlights. Plenty of lights, plus this thing."

Perry stood. In one hand he held a broad-plated dive mask made of aluminum, black rubber and tempered glass. The front of the mask was fitted with a mounting rail. In the other hand Perry held a night vision monocular that was capped on both ends to protect the lenses.

It was an underwater night vision system made for me in Arizona by NAVSYS Inc., a manufacturer that specializes in tactical equipment.

Perry picked up the rifle, and gave me ten yards of clearance, as he carried the mask and monocular close enough for King to see.

King was in the middle of saying, "I'm not going into that goddamn water this late. You can forget about it!" but he stopped talking when he got a look at Perry's outstretched hand. The monocular was palm sized, tubular and precisely milled. The mask was as solid and well constructed as a copper diving helmet. It was a rare and expensive piece of equipage.

Instead of convincing King, though, the dive mask only made him more suspicious of me. I could read it in his expression. Maybe he had read about underwater night vision systems in some pseudomercenary magazine. Magazines like that would be popular in prison libraries.

Staring at me, King said, "Where the hell did you get something like this? If you wear this thing, you don't even need a flashlight. Does it work?"

For the first time in a long while, I smiled. "It works."

"You're shitting me! How'd you get it? You'd need a special license to own something like this. *Jesus*." King's expression now read *Who the hell are you?*

But he didn't get a chance to press the issue. That's when Arlis decided to start the truck. We all heard the roar of the revving diesel, then the sound of tires throwing mud as Arlis shifted the truck into reverse.

King and Perry stood frozen for a long second as we watched the truck lurch backward. The vehicle stopped, and there was the sound of Arlis shifting gears again. Because his feet were bound, though, he was having trouble using the clutch and the accelerator. The truck lurched forward, bucking like a horse. For a moment, I thought he was going to make it . . . But then the engine stalled.

By the time Arlis got the truck started again and into first gear, Perry had the Winchester up.

I was midstride, lunging toward the man, when he fired the first of three fast rounds.

FOURTEEN

WHEN THE TEENAGER, WILL CHASER, DROPPED his emergency air bottle, it was several seconds before Tomlinson noticed that the boy was in trouble.

Tomlinson was at the top of the chamber, using his flashlight to peer through a hole into a small room that reminded him of a snow globe—one of those little glass balls with a snowman inside or a Christmas tree next to a cake-icing chalet.

Instead of a miniature Swiss house, though, the room contained what even from a distance Tomlinson could see were man-made artifacts. There was pottery. Lots of broken shards, but a whole bowl, too. The pottery possessed an ancient Mayan curvature.

Was that a flint spear point?

Yes. There were several Indian points, plus what

looked like carved fishhooks. And . . . he saw splinters of bone. There were bones scattered everywhere, and what might have been the carapace from a long-dead turtle.

That's how clear the water was above them.

Into Tomlinson's mind came an image. Shake the rock room and snow—or silt, in this case—would swirl in an enclosed universe that was as round and rough as a geode, forever insulated from the outside world. Added to the image were the flint artifacts. People had lived in this room, but then time had stopped when the earth had changed, causing the sea level to rise.

Tomlinson liked the thought of that. It redirected his attention from the horror of their predicament. The hole he was looking through was small, no wider than his own thigh. By wedging the flashlight close to his ear, though, he could fit his faceplate into the opening and see the far side of the room, where flint and bones and pottery were scattered and where small stalactites dripped from the ceiling.

Strange. Otherworldly. The room suggested a safe haven, even though it refused Tomlinson entrance. Thousands of years ago, people—a small tribe, perhaps—had flourished in this space, only to vanish into a refuge of time and silence and darkness.

That darkness would soon claim him, Tomlinson suspected. Probably within a very few minutes unless Ford pulled off a miracle. The man was capable of doing just that, although Ford would have been the last to believe it. But even if the darkness didn't claim Tomlinson now, it soon would . . . So why did the timing matter?

As Tomlinson exhaled, he noted the sound and shape of his own exhaust bubbles. The bubbles expanded into silver oblong vessels, then burst into a star scape of smaller bubbles that scattered along the rock ceiling seeking corridors of ascent.

Watching the bubbles, Tomlinson felt a welling, peaceful euphoria. Transition . . . transformation . . . reformation. It was all right there, the whole human enchilada, inches from his own eyes.

It was kinda nice. Yeah, nice. No . . . it was *perfect*.

The feeling wasn't anything like some of the more familiar sensations that Tomlinson treasured. For instance, the warming kick of a rum shooter after sex on a rainy summer night. Yet what he was now experiencing, this strange sense of perfection, was in its way more comforting. His end was near—this portion of the journey, anyway. Indeed, what did the timing matter?

Tomlinson reminded himself, *Because of the boy, butterfly brain. That's why the timing matters.*

Which is when Tomlinson turned and shined the flashlight to check on Will and saw the kid fighting like a madman trying to swim toward the bottom of the chamber. Tomlinson noted that the kid was also trying to free the little Spare Air bottle from the D ring on his vest. Will's regulator was flailing behind him as he battled toward the bottom, and Tomlinson thought, *Christ, the kid's out of air!*

Tomlinson pivoted to swim after the boy as Will finally got the Spare Air bottle loose. But the thing somehow went tumbling from his hand and spiraled toward the sand below, where Tomlinson could see the larger reserve canister lying eight feet beneath them.

How the hell had Will managed to drop them both? It was a pointless question, and Tomlinson swam harder to intercept the boy. As he did, he understood why Will was having to fight so hard to get to the bottom. He and the boy had not only abandoned their fins, they had dumped all of their lead weight. Even with their BCs deflated, their bodies were ultrabuoyant now.

Tomlinson screamed through his regulator as he waved the flashlight to get the kid's attention. Then he pointed the beam at his own body, hoping Will would swim toward him instead of the air bottles. At that same time, Tomlinson ascended briefly to get a better start, then somersaulted downward.

He got both feet against the ceiling, the buoyancy of his body pressing him solidly against the rocks. He pushed off hard toward the boy only to feel the ceiling crumble as he thrust away. It killed his momentum, and Tomlinson began drifting upward again no matter how hard he stroked and kicked, and he soon banged hard against what was left of the limestone ceiling.

By God! He wasn't going to let it end like this!

Tomlinson jammed the flashlight into his vest, pushed off harder and tried to swim downward in the sudden gloom, but he couldn't fight his own buoyancy. He soared upward, and his tank, then his head, banged off the ceiling. An instant later, something kicked Tomlinson hard in the jaw, knocking off his mask.

It was Will's foot!

Without clearing his mask, Tomlinson felt around until he got a grip on the top of the kid's air bottle. He pulled Will toward him while simultaneously thrusting his own regulator toward what he hoped was Will's face. Hands found Tomlinson's hands, yanking the regulator away, as the two of them floated along the ceiling like zeppelins, then thudded hard against the rocks.

Holding his breath, Tomlinson cleared his mask, then found his flashlight. He pressed the button and was relieved to see Will's face inches from his own. The kid was sucking air, his eyes wide but not wild. Will was still in control, his attention focused inward until he'd taken enough breaths for his brain to function.

As Will passed the regulator back to Tomlinson, the kid's expression read *Man, that was close!*

Buddy-breathing, Will handled the exchange as if he had been doing it all his life. Talk about grace under fire! Tomlinson wanted to hug the kid. Maybe . . . just maybe . . . he would in a few minutes, as a final gesture of respect and farewell, because, after passing the regulator back to Will, Tomlinson checked his own gauges.

200 psi.

His tank was redlining, almost no air left. They might have five minutes tops, but probably far less with the way the boy was now drinking down the gas.

When Will pushed the regulator toward Tomlinson, Tomlinson refused it by holding up a hand. He steered the mouthpiece back toward the boy, as he allowed his body to relax, feeling his heart decelerate as his brain nibbled at the air within him.

Very slowly, Tomlinson shined the light toward the bottom. Because of the rocks he had kicked free, the water was murky, but he could see the two miniature tanks. He could also see that they were now partially covered by rocks that had fallen from the ceiling.

Tomlinson reached for his dive slate and wrote: *Spares empty?*

As the boy shook his head no, Tomlinson realized that it was a stupid question. Both Spare Air bottles had to be full or they wouldn't have sunk.

Tomlinson swung the light toward the roof of the chamber. What he saw gave him hope. The hole into the snow globe, where he had seen bones and artifacts, was now as wide as a drainpipe. When he'd pushed off from the ceiling, he had kicked some of the limestone free.

Tomlinson took another look at his gauges. The depth gauge was inexact at this depth, but it read *9 ft.*

My God, the sky was so damn close! Their own familiar world, rich with air, was only a few feet away.

Tomlinson accepted the regulator from Will. He took two long, slow breaths, thinking about what they should do next. Obviously, they should follow the passage upward—but should he go after the extra air bottles first?

Yes. He had to.

After Tomlinson had passed the regulator back to Will, he held up an index finger, then used the flashlight to illuminate the opening above them. It was close, only a few yards away. He let the kid see him smile, wanting to communicate *We still have a chance,* then handed the flashlight to Will before he ripped open the Velcro straps and slipped out of his BC.

Man, it felt good to be free of that damn cumbersome vest!

Taking his time, Tomlinson put the flashlight in his teeth and breaststroked to the bottom. In slow motion, he anchored one hand to a slab of limestone, gathered both bottles, then allowed his body to drift upward. As he ascended, he twisted open a valve on one of the bottles and took an experimental breath.

Air!

The spare bottles didn't contain much. A couple minutes of breathing time in the small bottle and maybe five or ten minutes in the larger bottle. They were for emergencies only—like now, for instance.

When Tomlinson was beside Will again, he exchanged the bottle for his own regulator. Tomlinson waited to be sure the kid was comfortable breathing from the miniature tank, then motioned for him to follow.

Using his hands to pull himself along the top of the chamber, Tomlinson returned to the opening into the snow globe. Once again, he peered up into the geode-round room, where the water wasn't so clear now but still clear enough. He could see the broken chunks of pottery, the turtle carapace, the elegant vase that had been resting on its side half buried in white coral sand for who knew how many thousands of years.

The hole into the chamber was wide enough to wiggle through, yet he hesitated. Tomlinson understood why he was reluctant without having to explore his own irrational response.

Or . . . maybe it wasn't so irrational. If the karst vent they were following dead-ended here, then they, too, were dead. Tomlinson much preferred the inexplicable to the inexorable. The unknown offered hope at least.

There was no avoiding the reality of what lay beyond, though. It was their only option, so he pushed himself through into the room, using a minimum of movement not only to conserve what little air he had remaining but also because he hated the idea of corrupting this idyllic pure space with silt—the murk of his own presence.

Tomlinson kept his legs together as if they were tied. He kept his arms at his sides. He used only his fingers to propel and guide his body as he floated into the room.

Will Chaser didn't hesitate, but he'd spent enough time by now to know that even the smallest movement in an underwater cave destroyed visibility. Kick too hard with a fin, stir the water with a free hand, and a cloud would form instantly and suck the light from his eyes.

Darkness. It was something else Will Chaser knew about.

Will mimicked Tomlinson's spare movements. He used his left hand to hold the air bottle to his mouth and he used the fingers of his right hand to propel himself crablike into a space that was illuminated in corridors of white by Tomlinson's flashlight.

Two corpses floating to the surface . . .

That was the image that came into Tomlinson's mind as his hand reached upward toward the ceiling of the snow globe. If this was to be their end, this was a fitting place. It was an ancient room where a people had vanished into time and space before them. When he was close enough, Tomlinson touched the rock barrier gently, *gently,* allowing his fingers to explore the rough surface.

The limestone felt solid—but that didn't mean much as Tomlinson knew too well. Using his flashlight, he moved along the top of the chamber hoping to find another opening. The room was small, the ceiling uniform. There was no opening that he could see.

This isn't what Tomlinson had expected. Until this instant, Tomlinson had believed, in some deep, private space, that they would find a way out. Not that he knew a lot about the topography of caves—he didn't. It was more of an intuitive belief that, once again, good luck and good karma would steer him to safety.

Tomlinson was an enthusiastic skin diver but a reluctant scuba diver. He preferred the simplicity of minimal gear—mask, snorkel and fins only. He disliked the straitjacket constraints of scuba. An aluminum tank whacking him in the back of the head whenever he attempted a bit of spontaneous underwater ballet was irritating.

However, he had logged many hours diving wrecks—usually with Ford. It was through Ford that Tomlinson had been introduced to the small community of scuba loonies—tech-freak athletes, he thought of them—who lived to explore Florida's underwater caves. His information on the subject had come from this small, devoted group of people.

It was from cave divers that Tomlinson had heard rumors of subterranean air bells that sometimes existed below the water table. He knew the story of the female cave diver who had failed to surface, was presumed dead but found alive three hours later, her face pressed tight to a rock ceiling where there was a three-inch layer of air. The woman had supplemented the air supply by emptying her BC into the space.

Tomlinson knew that such air bells were rare—if they did indeed exist. Especially in Florida, where limestone was too permeable to create the pressure-tight enclosure required. Physics also required that the cavern exist prior to the sea level's rise. Only then could air pressure, locked in such a rock chamber, exert sufficient force to find equilibrium with the pressure of rising water.

It was an unlikely combination. When Tomlinson found the snow globe, though, with its artifacts and prehistoric silence, he believed that his secret hope—the hope of finding an air bell—had been realized. It would have been yet another example of his precognitive abilities meshing with his paranormal powers. Once again, good luck and karma were destined to save his ass.

Not this time. Tomlinson had found his prehistoric cave. But it did not contain a prehistoric air bell.

When Tomlinson glanced at his depth gauge, though, he felt another spark of hope. According to it, they were now only five feet beneath the surface. *Five feet!*

The spark soon faded as he thought it through. What the hell difference did it make if they were within arm's reach of the surface or a hundred feet beneath it when they ran out of air?

The answer was zero difference. They would still drown.

Tomlinson's attention shifted from the room's construction to Will. The boy was ascending from below. Once again, Tomlinson was impressed. The teen remained almost motionless as he entered the globe. There were isolated explosions of silt around Will's finger as he maneuvered his body, but the eruptions were small and brief. The water in the little room remained clear.

With the flashlight, Tomlinson got the kid's attention, then pointed out the artifacts one by one. He thought Will would find them interesting while also encouraging him to continue his slow ascent. The artifacts might even comfort the boy during his last breathing minutes on earth. Tomlinson was now convinced that that was the case.

This is a good spot to wait for the Big Guy to finally pull the plug. Karmic, even. Sort of peaceful.

It was as if they had reached a chosen terminus. The pre-Columbian artifacts were reminders that Will was the progeny of an ancient race, and so the symmetry was plain enough. Will Chaser was a mix of·Indian descent: Sioux, Seminole and Apache. He was a full-blooded

"Skin," in the vernacular of western reservations, as Tomlinson knew through his association with members of AIM, the American Indian Movement.

Something else Tomlinson knew, however, was that Will didn't like discussing his own Indianness. Maybe that's why destiny had brought them here to die. One night, at the marina, Tomlinson had brought up the subject of Pan-Indianism. When he had suggested that Will consider embarking on a vision quest, the kid had actually flipped him the bird. It was a spunky response that Tomlinson admired, but it was also telling.

No need to discuss the boy's reaction. Tomlinson understood. Will had grown up living in reservation slums, attending Oklahoma boarding schools—a euphemism for "reform school." He had seen too much fakery in the made-in-China tourist shops and in the nearby towns where blue-eyed shamans dressed themselves in feathers and vinyl, then charged for sweat-lodge revelations.

Tomlinson had visited similar places. He had watched eager Buckeyes and moon-eyed intellectuals wait patiently in line for a nine-minute mystical experience that was followed by a post–sweat lodge buffet, cash bar only.

"That Indian stuff's all bullshit and you know it," the boy had told Tomlinson that same night at the marina. Ford, who happened to be close enough to hear, had nodded in agreement.

Ironic now, considering where they were. It had been impossible to argue about the power of spiritual synergy—until this moment—and neither he nor the boy had enough air to argue.

Tomlinson used the flashlight and let the contents of the snow globe make his point. He took his time, spotlighting one artifact after another. The snow globe became a life-sized diorama of pre-Columbian life. There was the spear point. It was six inches long, waxen silver like crystal. The fishhooks might have been made of bone, not flint. The vase looked as if it had been abandoned only days ago instead of several thousand years ago. The turtle carapace, wide as a suitcase, was pocked with barnacle scars from an ancient ocean.

As Tomlinson lighted the artifacts, he became aware of something else: His flashlight was getting dim. It reminded him of yet another error in judgment that he had recently made. Ford had loaned him the light and was looking for fresh batteries when Tomlinson had waved him away impatiently, as if Ford's prissy concern for details would mar yet another gorgeous Florida day. Yes, the beam of the light was dimming. Not good— even worse because the boy's cheap little flashlight was already out of juice.

Which would give out first? Their batteries or their air?

Air first, Tomlinson decided. That was better. Their end would be easier to deal with in light rather than darkness, so he left the light on as Will moved close beside him, then found his shoulder for stability.

Tomlinson gave the boy a moment to collect himself, then shined the light on the ceiling so they could decipher each other's facial expressions. Eyes only inches apart, Tomlinson attempted communication.

"Ah oohh ohhh-ayyy?"

Tomlinson had asked, *Are you okay?*

Will replied, "Eee-utt! Ellll oooh! 'Uttt-ooh—eeenk?"

Idiot! Hell no! What do you—think?

Tomlinson held a palm up, telling the kid to calm himself. They had come to a juncture so painful that he felt like bawling. How do you tell a sixteen-year-old boy that this is the end? Tomlinson considered writing something comforting and profound on his dive slate, but what? There was no way a few words could convince Will Chaser that the best thing to do now was relax, let his consciousness float into God's own flow, that he should *accept* what was coming.

Tomlinson decided to try. On his dive slate he wrote, *Sorry, brother! We're fucked.*

The boy studied the slate for a second before staring into Tomlinson's eyes, then the teenager flipped him yet another bird.

"'Uuuuck oohhhh!"

Will was still spunky, no doubt about it. It was a heartening response—and there was no mistaking the kid's fiery reaction. Will was also impatient, and he grabbed Tomlinson by the shoulder, then shook him hard, saying, "Auhh-uhh 'ut ayyyy. 'Eh oh!"

Almost out of air. Let's go!

Go where? Tomlinson didn't waste gas by replying because the answer was all around them. There was no escape. The room was round and solid. There were no shadowed vents, no rock creases to dig away at in the hope of continuing onward.

As the kid moved away, exploring the ceiling on his

own, Tomlinson followed him with the flashlight. As he did, he felt an overwhelming flood of remorse.

Don't worry about Will, Tomlinson had told Ford. *I assume all responsibility.*

Now here they were. Another day, yet another dumb-ass decision on his part. Marion Ford, as an accessory to the boy's death, would no doubt process a variety of emotions, but surprise that Tomlinson had screwed up once again would not be among them.

Tomlinson thought, *I'm a menace to myself and to everyone who's ever known me.*

It wasn't the first time he had thought those words. In his lowest moments, alone aboard his sailboat, he sometimes punished himself with what he alone knew was the truth about himself. Truth was, he was a fraud. He was a self-constructed caricature. He was an elaborate spiderweb of pretense who, at day's end, counted success only by his own selfish excesses.

Even in his lowest moments, though, Tomlinson knew that he was also a devoted admirer of his fellow human beings. He *valued* people. He admired them for their failings as well as their strengths. But Tomlinson sometimes also believed that he had perverted his own kindness into an effective trap. His affection for others had earned him many free drinks and forgiving friends, and it had won him an eager bedroom willingness from women who believed in his goodness—despite their own good sense, and their own moral obligations.

Tomlinson had *many* female friends. For him, women were neither a quest nor an obsession. Loving and ador-

ing and pleasing women was more a way of life—a fact
that he seldom discussed, even with Ford, and never,
ever bragged about.

Tomlinson delighted in the perfumed tribe. It was his
nature. He lusted for their confidences and their whispered secrets and their trust even more eagerly than he
lusted after their bodies. It didn't matter if the women
were engaged or even married. He loved the ceremony
of undressing a lady as much as a kid enjoyed unwrap-
ping presents on Christmas Day. Snapping a woman's
bra free, then leaning to behold her breasts—those sa-
cred, weighty icons of earthen femininity—ranked right
up there with the very best God had to offer.

For Tomlinson, the actual sex act wasn't as important
as sharing the profound intimacy that women offered,
although getting a woman into bed was one of the consistent perks, as he now had to admit to himself.

I'm a good-for-nothing dog, Tomlinson thought as he
watched the teenager explore the chamber. *I don't deserve the air I'm breathing.*

Convinced it was true, he began to move along the
ceiling in slow pursuit of Will. As he did, he pulled open
the Velcro straps of his BC and began to remove his vest
and tank. He would give the boy the last of his air.

I'm not going to die wearing a damn straitjacket!

It was something Tomlinson had vowed long ago
under circumstances that in fact were more stressful than
being trapped underwater in a cave.

He thought, *I'm dying a whole man. Free. Not stoned,
unfortunately—but who could ask for more?*

Tomlinson felt himself smile. In that instant, he perceived an unexpected truth. A final act of kindness was an invitation to absolution—and absolution was available in no other form.

When Will sensed Tomlinson behind him, he turned. The beam of the flashlight was flickering now. He watched Tomlinson take a long, slow breath—the man was smiling for some reason—before he removed his regulator and offered it to Will.

Will spoke through the Spare Air mouthpiece, saying, "Eeer-duho 'ippie. Auuk eet uff!"

Weirdo hippie. Knock it off!

Will refused the regulator. Instead, he took the light from Tomlinson's hand and used it to point to something embedded in the ceiling of the cave. Tomlinson had been so lost in introspection that it took a moment to swivel his attention from death to what he was seeing only inches from his eyes.

What the hell had the kid found now?

Holding his breath, Tomlinson pressed his faceplate close to the ceiling in the failing light. Will had discovered tree roots, he realized. A network of roots. Cypress trees probably were growing overhead only a few feet above them.

Tomlinson reached for his dive slate intending to write, *Use your knife!*

Before he finished, though, the flashlight flickered, then went out.

FIFTEEN

PERRY FIRED THREE SHOTS AT ARLIS, EACH slug banging through the truck as loud as a sledgehammer, then he swung the rifle toward me. I was several strides away. It was too late for me to duck beneath the barrel, so I threw up my hands—in protest, not surrender—and yelled, "Stop shooting! Use your brain!"

My attention was on the truck as I continued running. I juked past Perry, seeing the black Dodge still accelerating as it lurched sharply, then appeared to buck when its right fender clipped a cypress tree. The impact levered the vehicle up on two wheels for an instant and stalled the engine. Arlis was attempting to restart the truck as it coasted into the swamp, losing speed, then banged to a stop.

"Get your goddamn hand off that ignition!" Perry yelled at Arlis, shucking another shell.

I tried to throw off his aim by jumping into the line of fire but too late. The truck's rear window exploded. In the shock wave of silence that followed, birds spooked from the trees, dropping a detritus of leaves onto the Dodge, the vehicle's sudden stillness exaggerated by wind and shadows.

I called, "Arlis? Are you okay? *Arlis?*"

Silence.

I began walking, then running, toward the cypress grove. I looked back at Perry, who was now pointing the gun at me. "If you killed him, the deal's off. Understand me? You might as well shoot us both."

King called, "Love to!" and started after me.

I heard Perry tell him, "Stay here! Don't go after him, you idiot!"

"But if they get that truck started—"

"Dude, stop arguing and do what I tell you!"

I was hoping Perry would lose his temper and pull the trigger. Shoot King once, end of King. Shoot King twice, end of Perry, because the Winchester held only six rounds.

Instead, I heard King say, "So you're the boss man now, huh? Okay, boss man, just remember something. I warned you about that old fool. I told you not to let him in the truck, but you didn't listen. See what happens when you don't listen?"

"Shut up," Perry hollered. He waved the rifle at King before starting after me, walking fast toward the trees.

"I'm not going to shut up, Per, because my nuts are

in the wringer just like yours. Hear what I'm saying? One more time, I'm gonna warn you about Professor Jock-a-mo. He's conning us, partner. I'm not sure how he's doing it, but he's setting us up. Let's take the coins we got, grab the truck and get the hell out of here. Keep kissing his ass and we're screwed!"

Behind me, I heard Perry say to me, not King, "Is he right? He better not be right, dude, 'cause I'll use your own knife on you. Not a bullet."

Perry had been carrying my Randall knife in his belt ever since I'd dropped the thing. I ignored him as I approached the truck, seeing the driver's door open and Arlis slouched over the steering wheel.

The fourth shot had pierced the rear window, then exited through the windshield. Fragments of glass were on the old fisherman's arms and stuck in his hair. To the west, the sun was low. It projected shafts of light beneath tree limbs and through the broken windows of the Dodge, causing the glass to glitter like jewels. There was blood everywhere.

I touched Arlis's arm as I said his name, then my fingers moved to his neck feeling for a pulse. I was surprised. The man's heart was still beating, his pulse fast but strong. The right side of his face had been peppered by glass—that was the source of the blood, I realized. He didn't appear to be seriously wounded.

"Arlis, can you hear me?"

Futch's head moved only slightly, but he opened his good eye wide, focused on me for a moment, then replied with an exaggerated wink.

He whispered, "Those assholes can't shoot. Take the keys."

I whispered, "Did you get hit?"

"Glass, that's all." He said it again. "Them dumb-asses can't shoot."

I squeezed his shoulder. "Quiet. They're here."

I turned toward Perry, who was approaching cautiously, his rifle pointed at me from the waist. "Did I get him? Is he dead?"

I said, "It looks bad, I'm not sure." I pretended to check Arlis's pulse again. "No . . . he's still alive. But just barely."

To Arlis I said loud enough for Perry to hear, "Where are you hit? I need to get you out of the truck and onto the ground. Think you can stand?"

Arlis moaned and cussed, feigning a concussion or worse.

I told Perry, "This man needs to be treated for shock. He needs water and the first-aid kit." I turned away, adding, "There's a first-aid kit in my bag, the one by the lake. Go get it."

In the bed of the truck was a toolbox. I rummaged around until I found blunt-nosed pliers. From the back of the cab, I also took a blanket. Perry watched as he returned carrying my canvas bag. Neither he nor King protested when I clipped the tie wraps binding Arlis's ankles and helped him out of the truck.

I got the fisherman's arm over my shoulder, and the two of us staggered several paces to dry ground. When Arlis was on his back, he gave me another private wink.

In a normal voice I said, "Arlis, can you hear me? You need fluids. Rest a bit, then try to get some water down."

The man groaned but didn't reply.

I knelt to spread the blanket, then placed bottles of water within reach. I returned to the truck, pretending to palm the pliers. I opened the toolbox, thrust my hand in and then slammed the thing, but in fact I had left the pliers and a small flashlight wedged under Arlis's shoulder when I'd placed the water next to him.

Perry didn't notice. His attention was scattered. Maybe he was crashing from whatever drugs he was using. I didn't know, I didn't care. He and King were sloppy. If things went my way, their sloppiness would kill them.

King had remained near the lake—obeying orders, for once— and now he hollered to Perry, "Get those keys out of the ignition before they try it again. Hear me? Stick them in your pocket, someplace safe. You can kiss and make up with your new playmates later."

Perry was watching me as I knelt beside Arlis and opened the first-aid kit. He reached through the truck window, pocketed the keys, then surprised me after a moment by circling the truck and kicking the passenger's-side fender. Then he yelled, "Shit! I can't believe this. Why does shit like this always happen to me?"

It took me a moment to understand why he was mad. Perry was on the opposite side of the vehicle where he could now see the damage close up. It was worse than he'd thought, apparently. I left the first-aid kit open and walked over to take a look.

The impact with the tree had crushed the front fender and jammed the bumper into the right tire. The tire was shredded, but it appeared that the metal wheel was okay.

Furious, Perry looked through the passenger window and saw Arlis on the blanket thirty yards beyond, groaning in the shade. He screamed, "You lying old son of a bitch, I'll kill you for this!"

I didn't hurry, but I got to the door as Perry raised the rifle. I stepped in front of the open window, shielding Arlis. "What good will that do?" I said. "He's probably going to die, anyway, so why risk a murder charge?"

Perry yelled, "As if it makes any difference now!" He shouldered the rifle for another second before spinning away in frustration. "Shit! Now we've got no way out of here. We're totally screwed."

If I didn't keep Perry under control and on my side, Arlis and I were screwed, too. I had to do something, so I said, "You worry too much. You can still use the truck. Think it through."

Perry backed away as I moved closer and knelt beside the damaged fender. "There's a spare tire under the bed and plenty of tools. All we have to do is hammer the fender out, create some clearance, then we change the tire. It's no big deal."

Perry snapped, "*Everything's* easy, the way you talk."

I said, "We've got to move the truck to solid ground first. Closer to the lake. It's too soft here for a jack."

"That damn old man! I should've listened to King."

I stood and faced Perry, aware that everything hinged on what transpired during the next few seconds. If Perry sided with King, he would shoot me—or use my own knife—then make sure Arlis was dead, too, before the two of them tried to escape on foot. Perry would do the dirty work while King supervised. It was that kind of partnership.

Perry took a step closer, the sunlight harsh on his face. The man's history was there and it was not encouraging. Among the topography of long-gone acne were playground and battle scars and the unsound genetics of too many generations of dropouts, trailer parks and booze. The way his eyes glittered reminded me of glass from the shattered windshield. The sockets of his eyes were bright and empty.

Perry said to me, "Goddamn it, you knew he had those keys. *Didn't* you?"

Before I answered, I reminded myself of a Tomlinson maxim: People will believe a dozen outlandish lies if the lies are prefaced by a single self-incriminating truth.

I replied, "That's right. I knew he had the keys. Not at first, but I knew it before I went back in the water."

"It was all bullshit, that business about the keys being underwater with your dead buddies. *Wasn't* it?"

I said, "I just told you it was."

"You're a lying sack of shit, you know that?"

I said, "I wanted at least one of my friends to get out of here alive. I'd lie to you again if I thought it would bring any one of them back. But it's too late for that now."

King, who had moved close enough to hear, chided, ".I don't want to say I told you so, Perry, but I goddamn well told you so!"

Perry took a step toward me, but not close enough for me to make a move. He said, "Then you were lying about the gold, too. About what the cops would do and that bullshit about property rights—it was all lies. You didn't care if the old man took off in the truck and got help 'cause there's nothing down there to salvage!"

I watched him pull my heavy survival knife from his belt as his brain built a case against me, the veins in his neck showing, his face a bloated crimson.

I shrugged, my expression telling him *Believe what you want,* before I asked, "Then why didn't I tip off the police?"

It set him back and he listened to me say, "If I hadn't told you to put on that vest, they would have seen your tattoos and would have known. Or I could have waved them in. If there's no gold, why didn't I?"

I waited in silence as the two men exchanged looks. In their faces I read frustration and irritation, but they didn't have an answer.

After a few seconds, I said, "I'm not lying about the plane or what's down there on the bottom. It would have been harder for me if Captain Futch had taken off in the truck, sure. But I could've hidden my share and come back later. The guy who owns this land will get most of it once the police see what's down there, but I could've stashed away enough to last me a long time."

Perry was shaking his head, confused. "Jesus Christ," he muttered, "why does this sort of shit always happen to me?"

"Give me half an hour," I said, "and I'll prove it to you. I'll come back with a significant amount of coins, you'll see."

"*Significant?* What the hell's that supposed to mean?"

I said, "Enough to split three ways. A half million each, maybe more—all I can do is guess. You've got to help, though. I need a man in the water and one of you by the generator to keep the intake clear. That was our deal."

King yelled, "He's lying. What are you waiting for, Perry? *Do it!*"

Perry snapped, "Why does it always have to be me! If your balls were as big as your mouth, you might be worth a damn."

I said, "Perry, he's the problem and you know it. King knows I'm telling the truth. The gold's down there. There was no other reason for me not to signal the cops." I looked toward the lake as I added, "Isn't that right, King?"

"You got all the answers, Jock-o. Why bother asking questions?"

To Perry I said, "Your partner's afraid. You just nailed it. He's manipulating you—probably always has. He doesn't want to go in the water because it's getting dark. Whenever I mention it, watch his reaction—he's scared.

You could leave here rich. Instead, your partner would rather run."

King said, "You think you know so much."

I said, "I know what I see."

"I don't hear Perry volunteering to go in the water, wise-ass."

"You're the expert scuba diver," Perry countered. "An expert on everything! Hell, I can barely swim a stroke or I'd go in myself. Damn right I would. If it meant getting rich? Hell, I'd do it in a second."

I relaxed a little when I heard Perry say that. It was an obvious lie that told me that he had been reeled back into the fantasy I had created.

I should have stopped there. Instead, I pressed too hard, saying, "It's up to you. If King doesn't have the balls, there's nothing I can do to force him."

I looked at the Winchester for a moment, reminding Perry that he *could* force King into the water, before adding, "But if you pull the plug now, we all leave here empty-handed. Only difference is, I might get the chance to come back. You two won't."

Once again the two men traded looks, but it was a different sort of exchange. I could see in their faces that I had screwed up. I had been a little too smooth, too eager. I had talked too much—a manipulator's red flag on both sides of a prison wall.

King said, "Real-l-ly," in a sarcastic way. I watched him take his time as he walked down the embankment from the lake, his eyes moving from Perry to me, then to Arlis as he approached the old fisherman on the blanket.

For a few seconds he stood over Arlis, who was on his back pretending to be unconscious. King nudged Arlis with his foot, then looked at me, smiling. He maintained eye contact as he suddenly bounce-stepped and kicked Arlis hard in the thigh.

How Arlis managed not to respond, I don't know. His only reaction was a soft, sleepy moan.

I yelled, "Knock it off!" and started toward King. The man palmed the pistol, waiting for me, his face registering an exaggerated indifference until I got within ten yards.

"You can stop right there, Jock-o," King said, lifting the gun to chest level. "Perry? Am I allowed to offer you another little piece of advice? With your permission, of course."

Perry said, "Goddamn it, King, all I want is a chunk of that money and to get the hell out of here. I don't want any trouble between us."

"We don't have any trouble, partner." King smiled. "Everyone pisses on their own boots occasionally. Mr. Smart-ass here, he's the one to blame."

Perry said, "But why not at least give it a try, man? Let this asshole go down and swim around on the bottom while we fix the truck. Those cops ain't gonna give up looking for us and you know it. We need money, man!"

King nodded, thinking about it. He said, "That's right, we do. I can't argue with that one."

"He says it'll take half an hour? What's a half hour matter? It'll give us time to change that tire."

King leaned his head back, squinting as he smiled at me, and said, "Okay—Jock-o, looks like you win," but his expression said just the opposite. King was back in charge now and he stared at me until he was sure I knew it.

"So how about we handle it like this," King said to Perry. He backed away from me until he was next to Arlis, then swung the pistol toward Arlis's head. "How about we make Professor Smart-ass get down on his belly so we can tie him up nice and tight? Just until we get the truck working. How's that sound to you, Per?"

Perry replied, "Wait, you mean? I don't know."

"The darker it is, the better it is for us. Unless you'd rather listen to Dr. Wise-ass here."

"I don't give a shit about him. Whatever you say, man."

"Good," King said. "I wouldn't feel comfortable with Jock-a-mo swimming around in that lake all by himself while we fix a tire."

The last thing I wanted was to be tie-wrapped. Those flexible plastic-and-metal straps were what police used in lieu of handcuffs. Impossible to break, tough to cut.

I said, "There's no need for that. I have to rig fresh bottles. I'm not going anywhere."

"Jock-o, we're not asking you, we're telling you. Get down on your belly."

When I hesitated, King leaned the gun toward Arlis

and yelled, "I didn't stutter! Do it now—but not here, dumb-ass! Over there by the lake!" He motioned toward the water, a safe distance from Arlis and the truck.

As Perry bound my wrists, then my ankles, pulling the straps tight, King said to me, "After we get that tire changed, you're going for a swim. Not me, just you. And you're coming back with a bunch more of those coins or I'll put a bullet in the old man's head."

I said, "I already told you, I need help with the hose."

"Sorry, Jock-o. That's the way it is."

"But the hose on the jet dredge busted when you—"

"No more of your damn excuses!" he shouted. "If you don't come out of that lake with a sackful of coins, you're better off not coming back at all." King looked at Perry, his tone confident, as he offered, "Sound fair to you, Per?"

Perry was pacing, eyes wary as he studied the darkening sky. "Whatever," he replied.

SIXTEEN

IN FEBRUARY, IN FLORIDA, BECAUSE OF DAY-
light savings time, it's already dark by the time most
people get home from work. It was dark now as I listened to something large in the distance, crushing its
way through bushes, moving toward the lake. It was an
animal of some type, I guessed—maybe the gator Arlis
had been hunting. The sound came from the cypress
swamp, beyond the cattails at the water's edge, several
hundred yards away.

It had to be big for the sound to carry that far.

I had plenty of other things to worry about, but I was
tied, lying immobile on the ground. There was no way
to run if I needed to run, so maybe that's why the noise
captured my attention.

Initially, the first thing that flashed into my mind was

an image of Tomlinson and Will slogging their way back through the swamp from . . . *somewhere*. But the rhythms didn't mesh. Plus, it was an absurd hope. I couldn't see my watch, but the sun had set, it was now full dark, so I knew that at least two hours had passed since Tomlinson, Will and I had gone into the water. It would have required a miracle for them still to be alive, and I don't believe in miracles.

A gator? I strained to listen. Maybe . . . but maybe not. I couldn't be sure of what I was hearing. I've spent more time than most people in Florida's wetlands at night, but the methodical crackle of breaking tree limbs and the strange plodding continuity of movement were unfamiliar.

Arlis would have known. The man was a master bush-whacker, a pro when it came to tracking and hunting, but Arlis was thirty yards away, lying in silence. I had seen him stir only three times—twice to gulp down water, and once to give me a brief, private thumbs-up.

I managed to roll onto my stomach and lift my head off the ground. My hands and feet were numb because I was tied so tight. The strictures caused my pulse to thud in my ears. The auditory senses are easily confused when there is interference from within, so I gave the animal my full attention.

Whatever the thing was, it moved slowly, which implied bulk, and with a grinding familiarity with the area. Then abruptly the thing stopped and produced a new sound—a rhythmic, ratcheting noise, like metal claws scraping on rock.

Strange. What I was hearing wasn't human, that was for sure. Sane people don't hike around Florida's swamps at night. It had to be an animal. The list of possibilities was long, though, so I finally decided yes, it was probably an alligator—and a very, very large one.

In a way, having something new to think about was a relief.

Prior to focusing on the strange noise, I had spent thirty miserable minutes unable to move my arms or legs because King, with Perry's help, had strapped my hands to the band around my ankles. They'd pulled the wraps so taut that my back was bowed, as I rolled from one shoulder to the other in an attempt to keep blood circulating.

"Hog-tied," King had termed it, taking obvious pleasure in my pain. He'd also given me a private elbow to the kidneys or my ear whenever I winced or grunted in protest. As a final gesture of contempt, he had tossed a couple of packs of MRE crackers close enough for me to get to—if I was willing to chew open the wrappers with my teeth and eat off the ground.

I was willing. I needed fuel and I knew it.

When the two men left to work on the truck, I had inchwormed closer to the lake, trying to find a more comfortable spot, a place where limestone didn't jab my bare legs and arms. Such a place didn't exist, however, so I had willed myself to relax as best I could and then comforted myself by devising violent strategies.

Sooner or later, Perry and King would have to cut me loose. Sooner or later, I would look into King's eyes. I would remind him of the games he'd played while my best friend and a teenage boy died. Ideally, it would happen after I had dealt with Perry. Perry was the killer. But it was King who controlled Perry's trigger finger.

After a while, as I lay there, my mind shifted to my laboratory on Sanibel Island and to the little community of Dinkin's Bay. If I survived, I would have to return and share the news that Tomlinson and Will weren't coming home. It was among the most painful obligations I'd ever had to consider.

Death is difficult only for the living, and news about Tomlinson would shake the island. It would reverberate up and down the coastline, casting a wide gray wake. The news would, I believed, cause many of our friends to inspect their own frail realities. Even the strongest of them would question the inevitable losses, the pointless tragedies, that we all endure. The saddest of human refrains is also an imminently rational question: What is the *point* of it all?

Tomlinson was one of those rare people who, by virtue of his own contradictions, made peace with that question even though he was unable to provide a sensible answer. Tomlinson had bridged absurdity and reason. He was a neurotic oddball, brilliantly naïve, a spiritual beacon and a respected teacher, even though he possessed the morals of a rabbit and the sensibilities of a blue-water bum. The man was blissfully independent yet a hopeless addict—addicted less to recreational chemicals than to a relentless hunger for life, and to friends, parties, women, salt water and all things that floated.

Our marina, like all families, has weathered its share of tough times. There had been murder and miscarriages. There had been loves won only to be lost, bullies endured, bullets dodged and too many near tragedies at sea. But life at Dinkin's Bay *without* Tomlinson? It was only because of the man's absurd existence that it made sense for the rest of us to live on an island at a marina *in* the mangroves.

And Will Chaser? He was sixteen years old—what else was there to say? Allowing Will to join us on this dive was among the most irresponsible things I had ever done. Some mistakes you never stop paying for, and this was one.

As I lay there, watching the sky orbit into darkness, the winter stars emphasized the finality of this day's events. There is no peace in a night sky; only the indifferent physics of astronomy. Space and motion both refuse definition if there are no reference points, yet our planet does not wobble after the death of one man or after the deaths of ten million.

Inversely, nothing would change if I killed King and Perry. The balance of the universe had not been compromised, so there was nothing to set right. But I would do it. I would kill both men if I got the chance. In the astronomy of human consciousness, all points of reference are subjective. They are the inventions of our own brief orbit. Righteousness does not exist in an atmosphere of pure reason, so it was not a question of justice or morality or revenge. I wanted Perry and King gone from the space I inhabited. I wanted them dead.

It was that simple, and reason enough for me.

It was while sorting through these dark thoughts that I first heard the sound of the creature plodding through the swamp toward the lake. Instantly, my survival instincts took charge. Was it a predator? A meat eater? What I had told Will the night before about the number of escaped exotics in Florida was, in fact, an understatement. Out there in the darkness could be almost any variety of creature from anywhere in the world: reptile, feline, canine or primate.

It is a reality that Floridians don't take seriously when we are safely behind closed doors in the comfort of our own homes. Even those of us who venture into the backcountry at night don't give it much thought because we have been conditioned to believe that we sit rightfully atop the food chain.

It's not true, as I understood better than most.

My legs and hands were tied. There was no escape. Even so, I wasn't panicky. There were two men nearby whom I feared far more than any foraging animal.

Even so, I was interested.

What the hell was it?

Whatever was coming toward me, the animal had my full attention, and I wasn't the only one who heard it.

I lay back and closed my eyes—an attempt to spare my night vision—when King switched on one of my good flashlights and called, "That better not be you trying to sneak off, Professor Jock-o!"

The man probed the edge of the lake with the light until he found me, then said, "Good! For a second, I thought you were trying to crawl out of here on your belly—like a snake." He laughed.

A snake. King was joking, but he had made an atavistic association that I found interesting.

Because King and Perry were closer to the cypress grove than to the lake, I raised my voice to be heard. "You're not making much progress with that truck. Why don't you let me help?"

I was even more eager for them to untie me now. It was ridiculous, but at that moment I would have preferred their company to being staked out like a sacrificial lamb.

King switched off the light and said, "When I want something from you, Jock-o, I'll rattle my zipper." His phlegmy laughter was as repugnant as his sense of humor.

For the last hour, the two men had been hammering and bickering as they worked at bending out the fender before changing the tire. Because they didn't want to risk damaging the rim, they hadn't babied the truck far enough to find solid ground so the jack kept slipping.

Sloppy. It was typical of those two.

It had taken them twice the time it should have to get the tire on, but they obviously weren't in any rush. Sunrise was their only deadline, so they had ten hours to waste. I was the only person in a hurry, which gave King all the more reason to delay.

Once, when the two men had stopped to share an MRE, their careful whispering told me they were discussing what to do with me after I had returned from my dive, with or without more gold coins.

There was no mystery about their decision. Arlis and I were liabilities. Even if I returned with what they wanted, they would kill us. They'd probably try to sink our bodies in the lake or drag us into the swamp.

No . . . they wouldn't risk venturing into the swamp now. Not after what we were now hearing.

I knew it for certain when their bickering stopped long enough for Perry to say, "What the hell is that thing? It sounds like"—he had to think it through—"sounds like the sort of hissing a subway train makes when it stops. Like steam brakes—you know?" He paused for several seconds. "Hear it? Christ Aw-mighty!"

The creature was making yet another unfamiliar noise. It was a distant *Hawww*ing hiss that echoed through the trees. It reminded me of a kid with a microphone trying to imitate a crowd's roar in a baseball stadium. The call was brief, and then the thing began to move again.

"Hey, you . . . *Ford*. What do you think that is?"

I didn't know, but I didn't want to give King yet another excuse not to swim out in the inner tube when I went back into the lake.

I said, "Wild hogs, probably. They're harmless. They root and snort. They're common around here."

"Like wild boars, you mean?" Perry asked. He didn't believe the "harmless" part.

"No," I said. "I'm talking about farm pigs that escaped and turned wild. They're not native. And they're afraid of people. I'm surprised they've come this close."

From the swamp came another rumbling exhalation, then the ratcheting of metallic claws on stone. The animal was getting closer.

Now King was getting spooked, too. The flashlight came on again. It blinded me for a moment, then King began to search the edge of the lake. Water vaporized in gray tendrils, and cattails stood as erect and orderly as scarecrows in a field. I had to roll onto my side to follow the light as he panned along the far shoreline.

"What's that? See it? The bushes are moving! Right *there*." It was Perry's voice. Maybe he'd taken the light from King. The beam settled on a thicket of wax myrtles and cattails that were backdropped by a lone cypress tree.

Movement in the bushes, along with the noise, stopped instantly as if stilled by the unexpected light. A moment later, I watched an owl the size of a pelican drop from the cypress canopy, its eyes luminous and huge. It made a screeching hiss as it swooped low across the water, then ascended into darkness. The bird was silhouetted briefly by stars, then was gone.

In the fresh silence, I heard King laugh. "You dumbass," he said. "It wasn't nothing but a big bird. Jesus Christ, Perry, you'd be scared of your own shadow." He was still laughing, but it was the laughter of nervous relief.

Perry said, "Shut up and tighten them nuts. Let's see if this old wreck will move."

I was still looking at the sky, my brain working. An owl wasn't the source of the distant crashing we'd heard in the swamp. If the two cons believed it, good. But I knew better.

A few minutes later, I listened to a door slam. The truck's engine started. Lights came on, and the vehicle began to move. Once again, though, King or Perry had made a sloppy decision. I heard the tires hit a marshy area and then I heard them begin to spin. Whoever was driving shifted into reverse, spun the tires faster, then shifted into first gear and accelerated, as if attempting to escape a snowdrift. Back and forth the truck rocked as the tires dug themselves in deeper.

"Stop, you idiot! Stop or you'll bury her up to the rims!" It was King's voice, so I knew that Perry was at the wheel.

I heard the door open. There was a long pause of inspection before Perry's voice whined, "Son of a bitch, why does shit like this always have to happen to me? How bad is it?"

King snapped, "Worse than it would've been if you'd taken your damn foot off the gas when I told you. You're an idiot, you know that?"

As the men argued, my thoughts turned to Arlis. He wasn't unconscious and he certainly wasn't asleep. I knew that they had bound his hands and legs again, but they had tied his hands in front of him this time so he could drink when he needed water.

I had hidden the wire cutters and a flashlight under

the blanket. If King and Perry left him alone long enough, he could clip the tie wraps and run for it. Or he could even take the truck if Perry was dumb enough to leave the keys in the ignition. It didn't matter if the truck was stuck. Not with Arlis at the wheel. King and Perry didn't realize the vehicle had four-wheel drive or the tires wouldn't be spinning now.

I thought about that for a moment. I wanted Arlis out of harm's way, but I couldn't risk him taking the truck. Not now. Without the truck, King and Perry's plan to drive to freedom with a load of gold would collapse. They would kill me where I lay, then leave on foot.

I raised my voice and said, "Cut me loose and I'll show you what the problem is."

"The problem with what, Jock-o? You keep your mouth buttoned until I tell you to speak."

I said, "The truck has four-wheel drive. You've got to shift into low and lock the hubs. It's not that hard, but you've got to know how to do it."

Perry said, "Shit, that's right. It's got four-wheel drive, it says it right on the side."

King didn't sound convincing when he told Perry, "I knew that! That's what I was trying to tell you, numb-nuts. If you'd listened to me, you wouldn't have gotten stuck in the first place. Use the four-wheel drive, she'll climb right out of there."

I started to tell Perry that King was lying as usual but stopped in midsentence because I heard yet another un-expected sound.

This time, though, it wasn't an animal.

The sound came from the far, far distance, in the direction of the swamp, but it was more muffled, barely audible. It was a shrill, two-fingered whistle, a series of piercing notes that were absorbed by the dense tree canopy.

The notes had a familiar rhythm. Or was I imagining it?

I had been facing the truck and so I rolled onto my other side. I moved my head, ears searching, hoping to hear the whistle once again. As I lay there, I sorted through alternative explanations. Screech owls are common in Florida swamps, but what I'd heard was not the mellow trill of the eastern screech owl. No, someone was out there—a person, definitely a person this time. I'd never learned to whistle through my fingers, but I knew a lot of people who could—Tomlinson among them.

Was it possible that Tomlinson was signaling me from the swamp? It made no sense. If he and Will had somehow escaped from the lake, they would have hiked back to the truck. Unless . . . *unless* . . .

I came up with only two explanations: If it *was* Tomlinson, he was either injured and unable to move or he was trapped somewhere beneath the ground.

It was a startling possibility. If he and the boy were somewhere beneath the surface, even a shrill whistle would be almost inaudible. Water conducts sound more efficiently than air, but that didn't apply if Will and Tomlinson were beneath ten or fifteen feet of sand and limestone.

Suddenly, the impossible seemed plausible . . . even reasonable. I had read of at least one account of a similar incident. A female cave diver had survived underwater for several hours, only occasionally screaming for help, because she didn't want to deplete the few inches of air she'd found at the top of the cave where she was trapped.

I continued to listen, hoping for confirmation. The wind had shifted. It was freshening now, a chill breeze from the northeast. The wind seemed to brighten the stars as it moved across the lake and through the cypress canopy. After several minutes of silence, the wind carried once again a distinctive staccato series of notes.

Shave-and-a-haircut . . . two bits.

I didn't imagine it. As faint as the call was—and it was very faint—I was now sure. It was Tomlinson calling for help.

Struck numb, I listened to Perry say something to King and then I heard the truck start. There was a brief grinding of gears. Lights came on, illuminating the lake.

As the truck began to creep toward me, carrying the extra scuba gear I would need, I rolled onto my back.

I was thinking, *My God, they're still alive.*

SEVENTEEN

WHEN HIS FLASHLIGHT FAILED, TOMLINSON
closed his eyes to soften the darkness. He began to concentrate on channeling his core energy—and what he
hoped was comforting wisdom—into Will Chaser, who
was now breathing from the last emergency air bottle
while he stubbornly hacked at the ceiling of the snow
globe where he had found tree roots.

There were only a few minutes of air left in Tomlinson's primary tank—which is why he was now holding
his breath—and he knew the end was near.

The boy's knife made a steady metal-on-rock clink-
ing as Tomlinson focused, feeling energy move through
his arm, through his fingers, which were pressed against
Will's back, holding the boy in place as he dug. Channeling energy was something Tomlinson had done many

times—often gifting strangers who never suspected that
the strange, scarecrow-looking man next to them was
their benefactor. But he had never given so wholly as he
gave now.

Meditation was such an integral part of his life that he
could continue channeling even as his brain processed
unimportant details such as the glowing numerals of his
watch, which he saw whenever his eyes blinked open. It
was the only light in the blackness that engulfed them
and so was of peripheral interest at first, but then it became more than that.

It was a new watch, and the glowing face gave him
unexpected pleasure. The numerals were large and luminous, a swollen molten green.

As Tomlinson moved the watch closer to his eyes, the
numerals blurred like fireflies in flight. The next image
that came into his mind was that of an owl, its round
eyes ablaze. Envisioning an owl—an ancient symbol of
death—was an unexpected interruption and caused him
to analyze what was going on in his own brain.

*I'm buzzed because I'm holding my breath. Must be the
carbon dioxide. CO_2 is definitely not a marketable gas.*

It was 4:57 p.m. He and Will had been underwater
for nearly an hour, and they had been burrowing through
karst vents and chambers for at least fifteen minutes.

Tomlinson thought, *It'll be dark soon. The sun goes
down in an hour.*

Not that it mattered. He was now resigned to the fact
that this was one marina sunset he would definitely have

to miss. Sunset was always a fun and sociable time at Dinkin's Bay—there were lots of beach-weary, languid women around, usually—and it pained him to think that he would never enjoy another marina party.

Tomlinson moved his wrist closer to his eyes and focused on the sweep hand of his new watch. As he did, he wondered how long he could hold his breath. Two minutes maybe? Possibly longer—he hadn't smoked weed in almost a week, after all. His regulator was right there, somewhere in the darkness, if he wanted it, but he was determined not to use the thing. The air belonged to Will Chaser. It would be his parting gift to the boy, a final act of kindness.

Into Tomlinson's mind came a sentence he had written long ago: *The only light visible to us is that which we create for others.*

Light. The watch's sweep hand was hypnotic. It was as thin as a hypodermic yet bright in the cavernous blackness—a sight that produced another surge of pleasure in him—and it shifted his focus from the boy to his friend Doc Ford.

The watch Tomlinson was wearing was a big one with a big name—a Graham Chronofighter Scarab. It was similar to the watch the guys at the marina had given Ford for his birthday.

Well . . . actually, it *was* the watch the marina had purchased for the biologist. Tomlinson had intercepted the thing and kept it for himself—a fact that was yet another painful reminder that he had lived an imperfect life.

What an ass I am to steal Doc's new watch after all he's done for me. My God!

Marion Ford wasn't a complainer, but he had mentioned more than once that his Rolex Submariner was an undependable timepiece and impossible to read in low light. He had also mentioned what at the time was an esoteric wrist chronograph—the Graham.

Ford liked the watch, that was obvious from the accumulation of catalogs and literature that Tomlinson had found scattered around the lab. But he wasn't a man to rush into anything.

Because the Graham had a distinctive lever on the left side of the casing, Doc believed that it would be perfect for timing procedures in the lab. British pilots had used the same thumb trigger to time bombing runs during World War II because the human thumb is better than a trigger finger when it comes to starting and stopping a watch.

Doc had said it, so no one at the marina doubted it was true.

Chipping in to buy the Chronofighter for Doc was Tomlinson's idea. He then proceeded to do his own extensive research, a tangent that had turned into a full-blown binge—an Internet-and-retail frenzy—that had after a week or so caused Ford to become suspicious. Tomlinson had never owned a wristwatch—not that anyone could remember, anyway—so why the sudden interest? The brass chronograph aboard *No Más*, that was as close as he'd ever come.

When the dust had settled, Tomlinson finally chose

the Chronofighter from a short list of also-rans: a Bathys Benthic—which Tomlinson loved because of its surf bum mystique—and a Bell & Ross Phantom, a Luminox, a Blancpain Fifty Fathoms and a Traser.

When asked why he'd chosen the Chronofighter, Tomlinson's official response was honest. The Graham was a classic timepiece and the easiest to read at night. The face was articulately luminous, blue on yellow, and because of the way the sapphire crown was shaped the numerals and hands were magnified when viewed from the side—a little like watching fish in a rounded aquarium. And the thumb trigger, of course, made it the perfect choice for a man who often had to time lab procedures.

This was all true, but the actual deal maker was more complex. The Chronofighter had an elegant British swagger, which was very unlike Ford. It was understated and cool—which admittedly was a little bit like the biologist but not enough to tip the scales.

The deciding factor, in truth, was that after all the research Tomlinson had done he had fallen in love with the Chronofighter, too. It wasn't just a watch, it was a serious piece of navigational equipment and ideal for celestial charting.

When the Graham arrived, Tomlinson had opened the box in private and he was hooked. The density of the watch, the weight of the thing on his wrist, its precision tolerances and horological beauty, were too much for him to resist.

So Tomlinson had done a selfish thing. He had kept

Ford's Chronofighter even though it was purchased with
the marina's money. Days later, though, he covered his
tracks by ordering a more subdued version of the same
watch for Doc. Tomlinson had paid for the thing out of
his own checking account so it wasn't exactly stealing,
but it was close enough to require a careful series of ra-
tionalizations to make what he'd done palatable.

A blue watch face with a silver bezel, Tomlinson had
rationalized, would not complement Marion Ford's no-
nonsense approach to life. A Chronofighter Black Seal,
orange on black, was a better fit for a man who eschewed
bright colors and bravado.

It was a lie, of course. Only one of many untruths,
half-truths and bald-faced inventions to which he had
subjected Ford over the years, a fact that Tomlinson now
admitted to himself.

*I took my best pal's watch. I slept with the woman
he's dating. That's low, man. Dying underwater, like the
bottom-feeder I am—it's exactly what I deserve.*

In Tomlinson's brain, a refrain echoed: *I'm a fraud.
A fraud . . . I am a silly, selfish fraud.*

At his very core, Tomlinson believed this was true. So
why wait to die? He was afraid of what came next, but
the case he was building against himself didn't leave an
honorable option.

For an instant, Tomlinson came close to exhaling the
last breath he would ever take. He told himself he should
welcome whatever came next in life's strange journey by
inhaling water, which was the same as inhaling death.

He thought about it. He thought about it intensely,

but he couldn't bring himself to do it. Giving up was not the same as giving in, he realized—a last-ditch tenacity that would not have surprised Ford, but it was like a revelation to Tomlinson.

Truth was, he didn't fear death. What terrified him was the prospect of not living.

As his bloodstream exhausted the last of the air in his lungs, Tomlinson thought frantically, *Screw the next incarnation! I'm not ready to leave—not yet.*

He had just bought a new watch, for chrissake!

Instead of inhaling water, Tomlinson decided to continue holding his breath as long as he could and wait for death to take him. He dreaded the panic that was to come. He feared the loss of control, the frenzy. He feared the escalating terror and even the broken fingernails. He was terrified of the whole sad endgame, but that's the way it would undoubtedly be.

Jesus Christ, what a miserable way to go—like some bat-blind catfish. I'm a bottom-feeder who's finally paying for his sins.

That gave Tomlinson pause. How could the Buddha, the Serene Prince, have his fingers in this ugly business? Universal consciousness had played a role? This was hard for Tomlinson to accept.

It's a shitty trick to pull on anyone, I don't care who's behind it!

Yes, it was. At least three times in previous years, Tomlinson believed that he had died only to be reborn to some unfathomable purpose that he had yet to divine. But those deaths had been as swift as a lightning strike.

ZAP, and that was all she wrote. None of this having to consciously decide the moment of one's own departure bullshit.

There was no avoiding it, though. This was the hand he had been dealt. If he drank down the last of the kid's air, Tomlinson would enter eternity as he had lived—as a fraud, a selfish fraud. He was determined not to let that happen.

If I don't want to die like a fraud, I have to start living like the person I pretend to be . . .

There was no getting around the truth in that, either. Tomlinson knew now exactly what was required of him.

All right, then, he decided, *I'll do it.*

He put one hand on the cave wall to steady himself. He tried to ignore a growing, glowing esophageal burn as his blood cells absorbed the last of his body's oxygen. Experimenting, he exhaled a few bubbles and told himself to relax, but the burning only got worse.

Tomlinson could hear Will Chaser still using his knife to chop at the ceiling of the snow globe. The rhythm increased until it matched the throbbing in Tomlinson's ears, yet fragments of thought continued to form slowly, even peacefully, in his brain. They were veiled arguments against death, he realized, presenting themselves for inspection.

If I die, who'll look after my boat? Ford? Ford hates sailboats—he'd never admit it, but it's true.

An image of *No Más* floated behind Tomlinson's eyes, the sailboat riding low in the water because the bilge pumps had burned themselves dry . . . or possibly because the batteries had gone dead from neglect. Next, he saw his boat at some sterile modern marina, all tin and plastic, his beloved home a vandalized wreck awaiting auction.

It was another rationalization—he knew it even as the images formed and reformed—yet the images were convincing because the prospect of abandoning *No Más*, of allowing the boat to suffer that degree of humiliation, was too much to bear.

Before he realized that his hands were moving, Tomlinson had grabbed the backup octopus hose of his regulator and jammed the mouthpiece between his teeth. After two deep breaths, he settled back a little and began to relax. Dark thoughts about his sailboat were replaced by the reality of what the boy was doing. The sound of Will using the knife, hacking at the ceiling, dominated the darkness. Will was fixated on the tangle of tree roots that pierced the chamber's roof—incontrovertible proof that sweet winter air was only a few feet above them.

Tomlinson told himself, *One more breath. That's all I'll take. One more and I'm done. I'll leave the rest for the kid. He'll need it soon.*

Three breaths later, Tomlinson had to remind himself that the pony canister Will was using had to be almost empty. The same was true of his own tank. Reluctantly, Tomlinson felt around until he found the gauge panel on his BC and then experienced a perverse sense of relief because the pressure gauge was unreadable without a flashlight to shine on the thing.

Even so, he knew that the needle had to be close to

zero. It was Will's air, not his, Tomlinson told himself. Just because he had lived his life as a fraud didn't mean that he must go out that way.

Enough, he thought. *I'm done.*

Done breathing, and this time he meant it.

Tomlinson removed the regulator from his mouth. He waited for several seconds, testing his own resolve, then allowed himself to smile because now he was sure he was doing the right thing. There was no going back. He had lived a big, wild thunder squall of a life—lots of wind and energy and lightning—but the kid was only sixteen. With a few extra minutes, there was no telling what might happen. The boy could still be saved. Dig through those roots before their main tank ran out and Will Chaser might find a little pocket of air.

It wasn't likely, but it was possible. It was also possible that Ford might yet appear, even though many minutes had passed since they'd heard the sound of the jet dredge.

As the boy continued to chop away, Tomlinson's attention returned to his watch. How long could he hold his breath? He still didn't know. He watched the sweep hand closely.

Only forty-three seconds, it turned out.

Tomlinson was still smiling as he exhaled the last of his air. He hesitated before turning his face skyward. He opened his mouth . . . and then he inhaled deeply.

Nearby, in the darkness, as Tomlinson gagged and began to convulse, Will Chaser stopped digging long enough to yell through his mouthpiece, "Eeee atttt? Oook! Iyyyy eeee 'ight!"

Will was telling Tomlinson, *See that? Look! I see daylight!*

When Tomlinson invited the inevitable by inhaling water, his body's involuntary response systems kicked in and saved him from drowning—temporarily.

A message in the form of a reflex arc skipped his brain and flowed directly through the spinal cord, sealing his epiglottis tight and causing him to choke. When he choked, though, his lungs spasmed, which caused him to inhale yet more water.

Tomlinson's last thought before he blacked out wasn't serene, but it wasn't as bad as he had feared. An old voice came to him as if snaking down a tunnel. It spoke the same words he had used to comfort himself the first time he had eaten peyote and then proceeded to embark on a hellishly bad journey—a ball tester of a trip—that had been gifted to him by the Cactus Flower God.

I've gotta ride this ugly snake 'til she's winded. This bullshit can't go on forever . . .

The message dimmed, then vanished as Tomlinson's brain went black.

What seemed like hours later but in fact was only seconds later, Tomlinson regained consciousness. He was aware of a globe of gray light above him. It wasn't the

late-afternoon sky he was seeing. He was looking up into
yet another rock chamber.

Water sloshed at ear level, his mask was gone and his
face was pressed tight into what felt like muck. It was a
viscous substance that had an odor unlike anything he
had ever smelled before.

Will Chaser was holding him, Tomlinson realized, the
boy's fist wrapped in his ponytail. Will had Tomlinson's
face pressed hard against the ceiling of the snow globe
so tight that Tomlinson couldn't turn his head. He
could shift his eyes, though, but when he did he saw
nothing.

Where had his face mask gone? Where was the boy's
pony canister?

Tomlinson tried to speak but gagged, then he vomited. When he vomited, he thrust his hands out and broke
Will's grip. An instant later, he was underwater and floating, encased in darkness again.

Where the hell am I?

Tomlinson felt the boy's hand pull him up by the
collar of his wet suit. Will found Tomlinson's ponytail
once more and thrust his face tight against the ceiling,
where, Tomlinson was slow to realize, there was a small
hole that exited above water level.

It was a breathing hole! Will had chopped his way
through the roots. The kid had found a way to survive!

Tomlinson coughed until his lungs were clear enough
and finally took a good long breath. The breath filled his
lungs but the air tasted horrible.

Tomlinson spoke without a regulator in his mouth for

the first time since they had entered the lake. "Goddamn, man," he muttered. "It smells like something crawled in here and died. What *stinks*?"

He turned his head. Will was beside him, but his head was submerged. Tomlinson could see the boy's left hand next to his ear. Will's fingers were wrapped in tree roots, anchoring them close to the roof of the snow globe.

Every few seconds, air bubbles exploded around Tomlinson's nose. It took a moment for his brain to translate the data—the emergency canister was empty and now the boy was using the last of the air in Tomlinson's tank to save them both.

Tomlinson reached out and used his fingers, digging, to make the hole around his mouth and nose wider, but the ceiling was an amalgam of roots, rock and muck. Bare hands wouldn't do the job, and the hole was too small for two people to breathe from at the same time.

He thought, *If I ever do another dive, I'm carrying a knife! I'm a dunce!*

Tomlinson felt around until he found a good handhold, then ducked underwater as he pulled Will toward the hole, hoping that the kid understood. It took some pulling and pushing, but Will finally got the message. They would share the breathing space, and the last of the air, so that Will could continue using the knife to widen the hole.

Over the next few minutes, they developed a workable system. Tomlinson would take several breaths of the foul air, then it was Will's turn. While Will was at the hole, Tomlinson waited in darkness, eyes closed, body relaxed, listening to the kid's methodical digging. They rarely used the tank now—only when Will got tired or when Tomlinson felt the need to cleanse the stink from his lungs. He was getting into the challenge of holding his breath, sometimes glancing at the firefly dots of his watch and counting off the seconds as if they were a mantra.

Think of this as meditation. Only difference is, this is the real deal. I have to breathe through my belly and focus on the hara center. Do it right and I can extract air from the water—it's there to use! So what if the Serene Prince tried to screw me? The Buddha has been laughing at fools for a thousand years.

Once into Tomlinson's mind came the image of Will swinging the knife too hard, the stainless blade ricocheting off a rock, and he felt a welling terror. What would happen if the boy dropped the knife?

Lose the knife and they were goners. They would never escape from this hellish place with its unholy odor. They would be doomed to share the breathing hole—like two incompetent Arctic seals—until hypothermia or insanity put their reins into God's hands.

Negative vibes, man. I gotta stop thinking this vicious crap. Find a positive wavelength, that's what I have to do. I must allow the good vibes to multiply.

After half an hour of digging, and sharing the airhole, Tomlinson nudged Will away long enough to shout out several calls for help. It wasn't the first time that he and the boy had tried, and he didn't expect results. That's when a better idea came into Tomlinson's mind. He thrust two fingers into his mouth and tortured his own eardrums by blowing a rhythmic series of piercing notes.

Shave-and-a-haircut . . . two bits.

Three times Tomlinson whistled for help, but then he felt a structural tremor in the limestone beneath them and thought, *Oh, no . . . not this bullshit again.*

That was the end of that—for a while, anyway. It was better to dig their way to safety, Tomlinson decided, than to risk another catastrophe.

As Will continued to dig, Tomlinson made an effort to move his consciousness on to a brighter plane of thought. One of the basic exercises in Vipassana meditation was to perceive air flowing through the body as if the veins and capillaries were a river. Considering the situation, how much more positive could he get?

When the river moves—watch it! When the river stops—feel it!

Tomlinson's focus shifted to an imaginary breathing port in his belly. His eyes monitored the sweep hand on his watch, timing himself. Every ninety seconds or so, he would take a breath or two from the octopus hose and then return to his meditation while Will hacked away.

Because of the watch, Tomlinson was able to mark to the second when it happened. They had been using the tank sparingly, but this time when he placed the regulator in his mouth and attempted to inhale he got nothing. There wasn't enough pressure inside the thing to open the demand lever in his mouthpiece.

Beside him, he felt Will's body jolt—the boy had attempted to grab a breath from the primary hose and his regulator had gone dead at the same instant.

It was almost sunset, 5:45 p.m.

They were out of air.

EIGHTEEN

ONE HOUR AFTER SUNSET, AT 7:12 P.M., KING said to me, "Well, Jock-o, the ball's in your corner now. Come back with a big fat sack of coins and we'll say *adios* to you and Grandpa and be on our merry way. But if it turns out you've been lying"—King laughed as if he was sure I *had* been lying—"you can't blame us for being seriously pissed off. Understand what I'm saying?"

He hurled a net bag at me. They had cut me loose, and because the truck was running, lights on, I was able to duck before the bag hit me in the face.

I had resumed the tactic of ignoring King, and was speaking only to Perry. As I Velcroed a spare bottle to a harness, then added a clip-on weight, I said to him, "You can push all you want, but I still need someone in the water to help me with the jet dredge."

Perry replied, "That's something we'll have to talk about." Sending a private signal to me, possibly. Since King would be the one going in the water, maybe he didn't want to discuss it in front of his partner. I took it as a good sign.

"When?" I asked.

"Later. But I want some proof this time."

I said, "Okay—but keep him away from that dredge until I need him. Keep him away from all my gear, in fact."

King claimed he had repaired the hose. He hadn't, of course, so I had made the dredge marginally workable by screwing a radiator clamp tight at the end of the hose to constrict water flow. It would cut through sand, but it wouldn't move rock.

Perry was irritable and tired of making decisions. "You don't say much, but, when you do, it's always trouble."

I told him, "Blame your partner, not me."

King snapped, "I didn't break that hose and you know it. Stop blaming other people for your own screw-ups. That's a sign of immaturity, Jock-o."

The man was maddening. I let him see that I wasn't listening, but he continued to talk, anyway.

"How about this? How about you do what we tell you to do and keep your mouth shut? What's so hard about that? I think you've been around ol' Perry long enough to know he's got quite a temper on him when things don't go our way. Dredge or no dredge, you'd better come back with more coins, Jock-o. If you don't,

Grandpa will end up with a knife in his ribs—and you're next on the menu."

I was sitting at the edge of the lake doing a final check of my gear. Everything had to be as solid as I could make it for this dive and I didn't have much to work with. There were only two tanks of air left, counting the bottle I would use, and one extra regulator. An important additional piece of equipment was a fishing reel I had found in the back of Arlis's truck. It was an old Penn grouper reel, loaded with a couple hundred yards of monofilament that would be useful if I needed to put down a lay line. Old fishing line was a poor substitute for a thousand yards of nylon cord on a Jasper reel, but it would have to do.

The two cons didn't know it, of course, but I wasn't going into the lake to fetch coins. I was going down into that damn drainpipe-sized cave again to search for Tomlinson and Will.

I hadn't imagined hearing Tomlinson's shrill whistle. Maybe the boy was still alive, too. They had somehow managed to find an air bell or a breathing space above the water table. It had to be one of the two, and now they were trapped beneath the limestone awaiting rescue.

I went over and over it in my mind, arguing the likelihood. In all my reading, I could remember only a few rare mentions of air bells. Those were in caves formed during the Pleistocene before the water table fell and then rose again—but I had never heard of an air bell in Florida. Limestone was too porous to maintain the watertight seal an air pocket requires, but it was *possible*.

More likely, though, they had dug their way close enough to the surface to breathe through a hole or some type of vent yet were unable to break free for some reason.

A disturbing fact nagged at me, though. The whistling sound hadn't come from beneath the lake. It had seemed to originate in the swamp far beyond the shoreline. But sound plays tricks when filtered through water or when reverberating through limestone. It was also possible that Tomlinson and the kid had followed a karst vein beyond the perimeter of the lake. Even so, I would have to start where they had started—underwater, in that damn tunnel.

It wouldn't have been an easy operation even with a chopper standing by and a fully manned rescue team. Alone, the difficulties were too many to list. Finding Will and Tomlinson wouldn't be easy, but, if I did, that's when the real work would begin. With only one extra tank and regulator, we would have to somehow buddy-breathe through the tunnel, then back to the surface. I couldn't picture how that was possible in a conduit so narrow, but if I found them we would have to manage.

All I knew for certain was that they were alive and I had to hurry. A true air bell—a pocket of air trapped in a rock chamber beneath the water's surface—would keep them alive for only a short amount of time. Because of that, it was pointless to dwell on the obstacles. I had an objective. I would move toward it. Sometimes, circumstances demand that you step off the high board and deal with water issues while en route to your destination.

Sometimes, difficulties that can't be controlled become tolerable only when viewed as assets.

Looking at it that way, I had a lot going for me.

I was alone—it meant I didn't have a partner to worry about. The fact that there was a single spare tank meant that I didn't have to lug a lot of extra equipment. The tunnel was claustrophobic, it was potentially deadly, but if Will and Tomlinson had made it then chances were good that I could find my way through the maze, too.

King and Perry? I told myself that they were additional motivation. I was tired, my nerves were raw and I was scared—but not of the animal we'd heard banging around in the brush. I was afraid that if I failed underwater, I'd miss the opportunity to deal with King and Perry one-on-one when I returned to the surface.

With that kind of motivation, failure wasn't an option.

As I stood to collect the last of my gear, Perry asked me, "What do you think that hissing noise was? Seriously." He was pacing between the truck and the shoreline, the rifle cradled beneath his arm as if he were hunting pheasants. The man's eyes never stopped moving, and he rammed the words together, talking faster than he had an hour earlier. If he was using drugs, I guessed it was some type of amphetamine. I also guessed that he had amped up recently.

I said, "What's it matter? You've got a gun, and you can always hide in the truck."

The man nodded, oblivious to the veiled slight.

I knelt to secure the octopus hose on the spare regulator. As I did, King moved close enough to grab my night vision mask, then backed away a safe distance before inspecting it. "How do you turn this gizmo on?"

"Put it down," I snapped.

He had the mask pressed against his face as he felt around for the switch. "This is a pretty fancy piece of equipment for a nerd like you to be carrying. How much this thing set you back?"

I was walking toward King, intending to take it away from him, when he found the monocular's switch. After a pause, he said, "Goddamn, Perry, you gotta take a look through this thing! It's like daylight, all of a sudden . . . And you can see about ten times as many stars!"

The man began turning in a circle, looking at the sky, then he stopped and aimed the monocular into the shadows of the swamp. After a moment, he said, "Holy shit! There's something out there!" He paused. "What the hell are *those* things?"

I stared into the darkness as Perry said, "What do you see? Is it that animal we heard? Damn it, let me look, it's my turn!"

They sounded like two kids squabbling over a toy.

In my bag, I had a palm-sized flashlight, an ASP Triad, ultrabright. I switched it on, then listened to King complain, "Dumb-ass, now you scared them!" as Perry whispered, "Jesus Christ, I see them. There must be three or four. What are they?"

Across the lake, staring back at me, were three sets of orange eyes bright as coals. I thought they were small crocodiles at first. As I watched, the animals turned and crashed through the brush toward the swamp. They were reptilian, low to the ground, like crocs, but their movements were snakelike. All three possessed a dense, four-legged musculature, yet they moved over the ground as if swimming on their bellies. As they ran, they held their heads erect like cobras.

In an amphetamine rush, Perry said to me, "They're too small to make that crashing sound we heard. Don't you think? Unless, maybe, they were all running around together. Hey—*Ford*! What do you think they are? Like, little alligators or something?"

With the flashlight, I tracked the animals into the brush before I switched it off. "I think they're Nile monitor lizards," I told him. "They're all about the same size, four or five feet long—so they're probably from the same hatch."

"Hatch?"

I said, "Monitors lay eggs."

King said, "You *think* they're monitor lizards? What the hell's that mean?"

I stared at him without answering as Perry said, "*Monitor lizards?* I never even heard of 'em."

I replied, "Pet-store people started importing monitors from Africa fifteen or twenty years ago and they sold a lot of them cheap. Some escaped, they bred, now they're all over Florida. In some counties, there's a bounty on them."

"No shit! So they're dangerous? If they pay a bounty, they've gotta be dangerous. Maybe there's a bigger one around. Do they hiss?"

No doubt about it, Perry was speeding his brains out and his tongue had to work fast to keep up. I told him, "They kill small dogs, they eat bird's eggs. They eat rodents, too—so you better stay on your toes."

Perry said, "Rodents, huh?" Then he said, "*Hey!* What's that supposed to mean?"

King was laughing. I didn't reply.

"Fucking pet stores," Perry muttered, sounding nervous. "You gotta be shitting me. Are they poisonous? Like snakes? They remind me of snakes, the way they move."

I wasn't in the mood to engage in conversation with Perry. I was still staring at King. "Turn off the monocular and give me my dive mask. I'm not going to ask again."

King said, "Or you'll do what?" He was still laughing as he pretended to use the monocular to focus on me. "You got a gun or knife hidden somewhere? You're all talk, Jock-a-mo. If I don't give you the mask, you'll do what?"

"Quit screwing around!" Perry yelled. "I'm tired of your shit! Give him his goddamn mask!"

I had taken two steps toward King when he held out a palm, stopping me, then said, "Sure, Jock-o, you can have your mask. Here." He lobbed it high over my head.

I could hear him laughing as I hurried to retrieve the mask from the lake before it sank.

For more than an hour, Arlis Futch had not spoken a word, but now he called from the shadows, "Ford! You watch yourself when you go into that lake. You hear me?"

I was in knee-deep water, wearing my BC, bottle strapped on, my night vision mask tilted up on my forehead and my hands full of spare gear. There was something unusual about the old man's voice, a quality that was menacing, serious and real. It caused even Perry, who had been jabbering nonstop, to go silent.

I called back, "How're you feeling, Arlis?"

He coughed—returning to his role as a sick old man, maybe—and said, "Those scum ought to at least let you carry a knife. You got your knife?"

No, Perry had my knife. It was still stuck in his belt. I couldn't tell if Arlis was actually warning me about something dangerous in the water or if it was a ploy designed to rearm me.

King hollered at him, "Shut up and mind your own business, Gramps. What you'd better be worried about is your boyfriend coming back with more of those Cuban pesos."

I called to Arlis, "I'll be fine, don't worry," before saying to Perry, "We have a deal, right?" Intentionally, I said it loud enough for King to hear.

King said, "What the hell's that supposed to mean?"

What it meant was that he had left Perry and me alone long enough to discuss the jet dredge. I had asked Perry what it would take to convince him that they stood to profit by helping me. More coins is what Perry wanted. Give him proof, he had told me, and he would force King back into the water to handle the hose.

Playing it off, Perry said to me, "Sure, sure, whatever you say. Just do your part."

As I backed into the water, my fins feeling for balance on the slick rocks, I heard King asking, "What's he talking about? What deal? Did you two cook up something behind my back?"

I rinsed my mask, fitted it onto my face and flipped the switch on the night vision monocular, the lens of which was hinged tightly against the faceplate.

"Give me ten minutes," I said, looking at Perry. "I'll keep my part of the bargain."

That really galled King. He was still interrogating Perry as I lay back, allowing the buoyancy of water to float me, and began to kick toward the middle of the lake.

I was carrying one oversized LED spotlight and two smaller lights clipped to my BC, but I didn't need them to see now. My right eye is dominant, but I preferred to wear the night vision monocular over my left. When I closed my right, it was like looking through a magic green tube. The night bloomed bright with details. I could see Arlis sitting up, watching me from the distance. The cypress trees above him were isolated and set apart from the starry skyline, their leaves iridescent and waxy.

When I turned my head, the swamp gloom was illuminated, and I could see that two of the monitor lizards had returned. The animals were perched on the high bank among cattails, tongues flicking, probing air molecules for a scent of prey or the warning scent of predators. Their eyes no longer glowed. Through the monocular, their reptilian eyes appeared as opaque as the eyes of a snake that was shedding its skin.

In reality, I was not looking through the monocular. I was seeing an amplified electronic image on a phosphor screen. The device collected a broad spectrum of light, intensified it, then reassembled real-time images that produced the illusion that it was high noon as if viewed through a Heineken bottle, not a windy, starry February night.

Underwater, the monocular would be even more effective once I activated the built-in infrared light. The infrared was invisible to anyone or anything not equipped with night vision, and the unit was waterproof to a hundred feet.

As I swam toward the marker buoy, I gave some thought to the Nile monitor lizards that were still watching me from shore. The monitor is a foul-tempered pet and a prolific breeder that has, over the years, caused too many impulse buyers to dump their purchases along the sides of the road rather than risk their cats or dogs being killed and eaten. Monitors are superb swimmers, they can scramble up trees, they nest in unseen burrows and they will eat just about anything that moves—or doesn't move fast enough.

The Nile monitor is a relentless diurnal predator that hunts in packs when necessary—and there is no shortage of prey in the suburbs of the Sunshine State. On its native continent, monitors are hunted for food by crocs and by humans. In Florida, though, where filet of lizard tail isn't on the menu, the animal has been allowed to ascend to the position of an alpha predator. That's why it has multiplied so rapidly throughout the state.

The lizards didn't cause me any uneasiness, though. They were the size of bulldogs, although twice as heavy. Even if there had been a dozen of them, I doubted if they would have risked attacking a full-grown man. Had I been in Indonesia, though, not the pasturelands of Florida, my reaction would have been much different.

I had spent time in Indonesia and so I knew from experience.

On the islands surrounding Pulau Komodo, there lives a close relative of the animals that were now watching me. There, as in Florida, the monitors have no natural predators, so they have evolved to a massive size—"island gigantism," the phenomenon is called. They grow to eleven feet long, three hundred pounds, and their attacks on man are well documented. The animal's tail is as lethal as its bite.

Their hunting technique is also well documented. Indonesian monitors use their tails to knock their prey to the ground, then inflict one or more tearing bites. Then they wait patiently. When the wounded victim is immobile—it doesn't have to be dead—the monitor begins to feed.

For more than a century, biologists believed that carrion-borne bacteria in the lizard's mouth is what caused paralysis in victims, man and animal alike. It is now known, however, that the monitor lizards of Komodo are indeed venomous. At least one very fine Australian scientist is now assembling evidence that most, if not all, monitors are equipped with poison glands.

They are an ancient species articulately equipped for survival.

I had seen monitors on islands near Sumatra that were the size of rottweilers, not lapdogs, that, with their viper tongues, wind-scented primates as quickly as carrion. One time, on the island of Gili Motang, on the Suva Sea, an Australian friend and I had found the claw and tail prints of a big monitor on a beach beneath coconut palms not far from the lagoon where we had anchored our boat.

The two of us spent the afternoon tracking the animal through dense Indonesian rain forest. A couple hours before sunset, my friend and I were both exhausted and frustrated—outsmarted by a reptile?—and so we returned to the lagoon and our little ridged hull inflatable.

We hadn't lost the monitor lizard, it turned out. She was in the shadows waiting on us. It was one of the big females, probably a couple hundred pounds. She was ten feet tall, standing on her hind legs in a thicket of traveler's palms as if begging for a treat.

It was a rare encounter. Her tongue had probed the air experimentally like a snake, tasting the flavor of us in advance of attacking. She'd been shadowing us the whole time, we guessed later, anticipating our moves. Why she didn't press her attack as we backed away toward our boat and then escaped by sea, we didn't know.

Days later, an Indonesian naturalist, who was as knowledgeable as she was beautiful, suggested it was because some Komodo monitors are nocturnal hunters, either by predilection or genetic coding, so the animal was waiting for nightfall to attack.

If the naturalist was right, sunlight had saved us, not our quick feet.

King's voice interrupted my thoughts, chiding me from the shoreline. "Hurry back, now—you hear, Jock-a-mo! Bring your new boyfriend something real pretty, okay? Perry's waiting!"

Because I suspected he would do it, I had my hands up, shielding my eyes, when he tried to blind me with one of my own flashlights. A second later, a chunk of rock the size of a baseball landed in the water nearby. By the time I'd made it to my marker buoy, the man had lobbed three more rocks at me. I'm not often tempted to reply with a middle finger, but I was tempted now.

Instead, I turned away from the rocks and the blinding light and used night vision to have a last look toward the swamp. The third monitor lizard had returned to the bank—a presence I found reassuring instead of disturbing. If three small lizards were in attendance, it suggested that a very large gator or croc was nowhere in the area.

I tested my regulator, then checked my new watch, a Graham Chronofighter. My pals at the marina had given it to me as a present—Tomlinson's idea, as I knew. It had a big round face that was luminous with orange numerals. The watch read *7:22 p.m.*

I twisted the bezel, marking the time of my descent,

and then I deflated my BC. I submerged, feetfirst, using the buoy line to feel my way downward.

The water was clear again. Details of my fins and my hands were bright through the monocular. Soon, when I could distinguish the bottom, I turned and began to kick slowly downward, hearing the crackle of fast-twitch muscle fiber as fish spooked ahead of me. Sand appeared a luminous blue and fossilized oysters were black—a dinosaur-era tableau that created a nagging worry in the back of my brain. I wasn't sure why. It had something to do with those three monitor lizards, flicking their tongues, wind-profiling me, before I had submerged.

It took a minute to formulate the details, but it finally came to me. The results were unsettling: Nile monitor lizards are diurnal, unlike their monster-sized cousins in Indonesia. They hunt at sunrise and they hunt at sunset, but they spend their days and nights underground.

What were the three lizards doing outside their dens watching me long after sunset? Why were Nile monitors hunting at night?

NINETEEN

NEAR THE ENTRANCE INTO THE KARST TUNNEL, as I reached for the mammoth tusk to steady myself, I stopped and listened, aware that something large had entered the water somewhere above me.

It wasn't close and it wasn't loud, but the object had weight. The awareness came to me as a feeling, not a linear observation. Water, displaced by mass, exerts an expanding wave of pressure. I sensed the subtle force before the vibration registered in my ears.

My first thought was that Perry had forced King into the lake to help me with the jet dredge.

But, no . . . it wasn't King. I had heard only the percussion of entry, no amateurish thrashing and splashing. It wasn't King and it certainly wasn't Perry.

It was something else—something not human, I felt sure. An inanimate object possibly. It could have been a boulder or a chunk of tree trunk. I pictured King throwing something big into the water, another attempt to irritate me. In him, humor took the form of harassment when violence wasn't an option.

Maybe so, but he hadn't thrown a chunk of wood. Wood floats. Whatever had breached the surface now continued to move. I could hear it, descending rapidly down the lake's incline. It made a scraping, clanking noise that was impossible to identify.

I wedged the extra gear close to the marker buoy's line, grabbed my underwater spotlight and looked up, paying attention. If it wasn't a joke, I needed to know what was coming toward me.

Through my naked eye, the lake's surface was a lucid obsidian disk. It was vaguely luminous and star speckled. Through the green eye of the monocular, though, stars glittered brightly against an emerald sky. I could see the silhouette of the marker buoy above and the silver thread of rope that anchored it.

I had done a full turn before I finally saw what was making the noise. It was large and dark and symmetrical. It appeared to be descending at an angle, following the slope of the lake bottom, coming fast in my direction.

I closed my right eye and touched my fingers to the outer ring of the monocular, trying to focus on the object as it drew closer. It wasn't easy to track, because the thing was gaining speed as it descended. Automatically,

I began sculling backward in retreat—an instinctive response that was silly. I was running away, even though I didn't know what was coming at me.

For a moment, I believed my first guess was right: I thought it was a chunk of rock pushed into the water by King because it was like watching something tumble downhill. The thing wobbled and bounced and kicked up sand, snaking its way toward me like a drunken skier on a vertical slope.

In my right hand, I had the big underwater light. I didn't think I would need it because of the night vision system, but I used the spotlight now, swimming on my back so I could maintain visual contact. As the thing rumbled closer, I kicked harder—but then it abruptly slowed, then stopped. I watched it wobble and spin, and then it fell onto its side, kicking up another explosion of sand.

I stopped swimming and righted myself. I painted the object with light until I was sure of what I was seeing. I was breathing hard, I realized. Arlis Futch's warning had spooked me, which now caused me to feel stupid. I had overreacted to a threat that didn't exist.

I swam over and took a closer look. Near the mammoth tusk, where I had left my extra gear, lay the steel wheel from the shredded truck tire. It was thirty pounds of metal, minus the rubber.

King had done it, of course. He had pried the thing free of the tire, then rolled it into the lake to scare me. I had been wrong about the rock, but my instincts had been right about King.

Some people feed on the destruction of others. They are emotional scavengers, and their feeding assumes aspects of frenzy even when it ensures their own doom. But King would never find out that he had succeeded in scaring me. The man had sealed his fate when he'd sabotaged my attempt to help Tomlinson and Will.

I switched off the spotlight and secured it to a D ring on my BC. Because I'd had to use the light, I gave my eyes a minute to adjust before using the monocular again.

As I waited, I found myself glancing over one shoulder, then the other, studying the vacuous emptiness of an underwater lake basin at night. King's joke had jolted my system with adrenaline. Now I felt a lingering buzz of paranoia.

Was something out there? Something that could see me without being seen? It is an ancient fear, the wellspring of all monsters and religions.

My intuition whispered, *Yes, something's out there*. It was a feeling I had, a premonition of danger. Perry had seen something big in the water, his reaction was proof. The strange undertone in Arlis's voice when he'd warned me was additional proof and even more compelling.

Intellectually, though, I knew that premonitions are nonsense. Intuition and lottery numbers are memorable only if they pay off, but both are fast forgotten when they fail to produce.

I don't buy either one.

I went back to work.

———

I couldn't find the opening to the karst vent. It made no sense. What the hell had happened during the last two hours? The mammoth tusk was where I had left it, close to the vertical crater, and the line to the marker buoy was still hanging straight. Nearby, the bottom looked unchanged, but the opening to the tunnel had vanished.

Impossible. Has there been another landslide?

I considered switching off the night vision monocular and using the spotlight again. But visibility wasn't the problem, I decided. More likely, I was disoriented—everything on the water, and underwater, looks different at night—so I gave myself a couple of minutes to get my bearings.

I positioned myself at the edge of the drop-off. I faced the remains of the limestone ledge and reconstructed the bottom in my memory.

Finally, I figured out what had happened. Sand and shell from the top of the crater had funneled down and covered the entrance.

I swam to the approximate area and began digging with my hands. For every scoop of sand I removed, it was replaced by double the amount. I found a sliver of oyster shell and began probing until I found an area where I could bury my arm up to the shoulder without hitting rock. If it wasn't the exact location of the tunnel entrance, it had to be close, so I marked the spot with another inflatable buoy.

For several more minutes I attempted to dig but finally gave up.

Damn it!

Now I really did need the sand dredge, which meant I would have to depend on King once again—if Perry could talk the man into getting into the water.

Before moving on, I decided to try to signal Tomlinson and Will. I had been reluctant for a simple reason: I feared they were no longer alive to answer.

Using one of my smaller flashlights, I leaned over the spare tank and banged out *Shave-and-a-haircut . . . two bits.* I did it several times, then switched off my night vision and settled myself in silence, listening.

I didn't expect an immediate response, but I got one.

The signal I received was faint, very faint, and as surprising as it was galvanizing. I heard a series of eight bell notes repeated several times.

It was Morse code for "fine business." Everything was okay. Tomlinson, at least, was still alive. Suddenly, I was no longer tired.

There was no mistaking the distinctive pattern, but where was it coming from? The signal seemed to seep out of the rocks around me instead of from a specific location or direction. If Will and Tomlinson had escaped into the karst vein, how far could they have traveled?

I pulled the spare bottle closer to the marker, wincing as I imagined myself reentering that black hole, with its lichen gloom and shadows. I rapped on the tank, then pressed the side of my head into the sand and listened.

When Tomlinson responded, the metallic clanking was slightly louder.

Yes. They were somewhere in the karst passageway, which they had followed for a long distance, judging from the sound. Their air had to have run out more than an hour ago, so I'd been right. They had found an air bell or a breathing hole.

I attempted to parrot Tomlinson's "fine business" message—maybe it would buoy his spirits. Next, I muled the rest of the gear and placed it near the marker as my brain worked out the details.

I needed the sand dredge, but I couldn't surface right away. Part of my deal with Perry was that I would present him with proof there was more to salvage—and a reason to make King help me with the hose.

Finding more coins would take time, but that's what I had to do. I wished now that I had grabbed a few extras when I'd had the chance and hidden them for later.

Carrying the spotlight but not using it, I began swimming slowly along the drop-off searching the bottom. I had seen several coins lying in the sand and I was confident I could find at least a few. Question was, would it be more effective using the monocular to search or the spotlight?

I tested both, then decided the light was better. Maybe it would cause the coins to glitter in the distance.

I switched off the monocular. Using oyster shells, I marked off the beginnings of a grid, trying to swim a straight line as I counted off the number of times I kicked with my right fin. Ten strokes would equal about twenty yards—a big search area at night, but I was counting on luck to help me.

I gave myself a time limit. One coin or a dozen—however many I found—I would surface after ten minutes. I would give the coins to Perry, who would then order King back in the lake so he could help me with the hose.

It seemed like a workable plan: Find a few coins, then swim straight back to that damn hole and blast it clear with the dredge. But I had ignored a fundamental reality when it comes to diving: It is never, ever easy to find something underwater even when you supposedly know where it is.

Seven minutes later, when I was about to give up, still empty-handed, I stumbled onto a vein-rich pocket of gold. It was in a little basin of oyster shells and sand where largemouth bass had fanned out a nest. The spot produced a dozen Cuban coins. I found five in a heap, the others scattered nearby.

As I kicked toward the surface, I stashed six of the coins in a mesh pocket inside my wet suit just in case I needed them for later.

TWENTY

BY 6:20 P.M., IN THE LAST ANGLING RAYS OF
daylight, Will had hacked away enough roots and stone
with his knife for Tomlinson to pull his face up to the
airhole, look into the small chamber above them and say,
"You know why the place stinks so bad? Something lives
here."

"What?"

"An animal lives in here," Tomlinson repeated. "Something big. And it's definitely not a vegetarian. At least the
place is above water level, but, *whew,* what a stench."

The airhole was finally large enough for them both to
breathe at the same time, but only if they pressed their
heads together in a way that reminded Will of two desperate carp he'd once seen trapped in a puddle at the

bottom of a drying lake bed, north of the Rez and south of Oklahoma City.

To talk, he and Tomlinson had to pull themselves close to the roof of the cave and turn mouth to ear, then ear to mouth, the air pocket was that small.

"Let me look," Will said. To get leverage with the knife, he'd had to submerge and extend his arm, so he had spent most of the last hour bobbing up and down and hadn't checked what lay beyond the airhole for a while.

Tomlinson said, "There's a bunch of bones and crap. So maybe it's an alligator den. Or coyotes, could be. Jesus, I've never smelled anything so foul in my life. On the bright side, brother William, we're almost out! Can you picture the look on Doc's face when we come strolling back to the truck? I bet he's called in the cavalry by now. Helicopters, cops—you name it. I'm surprised we can't hear all the racket they must be making."

"It took me an hour to get the hole as wide as it is," Will replied. "It's all roots and rock. It'll take another hour, maybe two, to make it wide enough to crawl through."

"Are you getting tired?"

"Naw. I'm just telling you. I think you ought to try whistling again. It's really loud—I want to learn how to do that."

Tomlinson said, "Maybe . . . Once or twice, but that's all. We're close enough to being out now, I don't want to risk another cave-in."

"Oh yeah, play it safe," Will said. "I guess that's smart."

Tomlinson said, "Yeah, man. There's no rush now." After thinking about it, though, he added, "The only thing I'm worried about is Doc and Arlis. They're probably freaking out, looking for us—and I wouldn't want Doc to do anything risky. Like trying to search one of those damn tunnels we crawled through."

"Then you'd better do it," Will said, meaning Tomlinson should try to signal. "A couple of times at least."

Tomlinson touched two fingers to his tongue, produced several shrill notes, alert for the sound of collapsing limestone. When it didn't happen, he settled back, his face showing a private, weary smile. He felt as good as he'd ever felt, coming so close to dying, now to be looking up into the late-winter sunlight. It was a giddy sensation, almost like he'd gulped a couple of sunset rums. It made him talkative.

"I bet your hands are blistered, huh? I'll do the rest of the digging, I don't care if it takes five hours. I don't care about the smell, either. Man, what a beautiful sight to see!"

Will expected Tomlinson to move, but instead the man kept his face to the hole and continued talking. "Oh, wow! You won't believe this one! On the far wall, I can see a petroglyph—you know, a cave drawing. But it's not really a drawing. It's more like someone carved a picture into the rock. It sort of resembles a cow standing on two legs—no, a buffalo. Maybe you can figure it out."

Will was getting impatient. "Unless I see it, I can't figure out anything."

Tomlinson didn't take the hint. "When de Soto landed in Florida back in the fifteen hundreds, he mentioned a buffalo in his ship's log. But some people don't believe it's true." There was a pause. "This is definitely an animal den of some type. Gators and crocs don't nest underground, so now I'm thinking coyotes for sure—the population's making a comeback in Florida."

Will gave the hippie a push—the man was a talker, which Will found irritating. He said, "If I want a history lesson, I'll read a book. Move your bony ass so I can see." He locked both hands in the tree roots and fitted his face into the hole.

Above them was another rock chamber, smaller than the chamber they were in, but at least it wasn't filled with water. Will didn't own a watch, but he saw that it was late, close to sunset, because the chamber had an opening of some type that faced west. He couldn't see the opening, but he knew it was there because a tube of dusty light angled into the space, showing the far limestone wall of the cave, where there were rough etchings cut into the rock. The petroglyph Tomlinson had mentioned resembled the silhouette of a man with horns. It didn't look like any buffalo Will had ever seen and he'd seen more buffalo than most people, having worked on ranches and ridden rodeo all over the Panhandle State.

The drawings were lichen covered—very old, no

doubt about that—and they had the random scrawled look of graffiti.

"Do you see the petroglyph?"

Will responded, "Hold your horses. Give me time for my eyes to adjust." It was strange after all that time in darkness to see daylight.

"There's something very weird and powerful about this journey we're on, man. Feel it, Will-Joseph? Which tells me there's something powerful about *you*. Your ancestors are keeping close tabs on your whereabouts for some reason. I think I'm just along for the ride."

Will turned his face away from the hole. "How am I supposed to think with you talking all the time?"

Tomlinson kept right on talking, anyway. "Maybe you don't know it yet, but I'm convinced you're on a very special mission, man. The real deal. I think you're what we Buddhists call a *Tulku*. You've got all the qualities—the whole transcendent-spirit thing going on. Do you know what I mean?"

Will replied, "I don't think that thing's a buffalo. It's a drawing of a guy wearing horns, that's all. Another hour or so, I can dig enough, we'll be out of here. Maybe archaeologists will want to come back and take a look."

Tomlinson said, "What I'm saying is, people like you don't dissolve at death. That's what I meant by calling you a *Tulku*. I'm not bragging, but I'm the same way. It's the way we're born. People like *us* don't dissolve at death—I might as well put the cards on the table after all the kimchee we've just been through, huh?"

That struck Will as a compliment. He didn't respond, but he listened more carefully.

"From one incarnation to another, *Tulkus* add layers of consciousness every trip around the horn—*skandhas*, we call them. I sensed it in you the first day we met. And I bet you sensed it in me, too. Am I right? Man, I can walk into a concert hall, even if the place is jammed, and spot one of us from twenty rows away. It's a sort of glow. Like an aura, only with less glow but more light. You know what I'm talking about?"

Will was thinking, *Colors, that's what he means when he says "glow."*

He didn't say it, but Will had experienced it many times, seeing certain people who glowed—even in a crowded space—just as Tomlinson had said. It was something he had never discussed with anyone, and now wasn't the time to start. Will said, "There's a root here, one really big, pain-in-the-ass root. If I cut out a chunk big enough, maybe I can wiggle through."

"If that's what your instincts tell you, it'll happen," Tomlinson said. "From here on out, I'm following your lead. We're riding a very heavy spiritual wave and it's pulling both of us along like a tractor beam. The tip-off was swimming into the cave with the pottery and the spear points. Now the petroglyphs! This whole trip has been a weird, wild gift, dude, and I'm honored to be sharing the journey. We're being allowed to see things that other people don't even know exist."

Will was tempted to say, *What do you mean "we,"*

white man? like the old joke he'd once heard, but he didn't want to encourage the hippie to keep talking.

"That's an ancient space you're looking at," Tomlinson told him.

Will replied, "It's not the only thing getting old," and concentrated on what he was seeing.

The cavern above them was about the size of a horse stall, but it had a low ceiling that angled downward, narrowing just as the band of sunlight narrowed. Joining the ceiling to the floor were more tree roots that at first Will thought were stalactites or stalagmites. The roots were clustered as tightly in some spots as the bars on a jailhouse door. At the center of the chamber, roots had been ripped away by something, though, to form a clearing where there were bones and the scattered remains of animals.

Will was at eye level with what looked like a chunk of cow skull. It was some variety of Brahma, judging from the lone remaining horn—the other horn had been chewed to the nub—and the skull wasn't very old because there was still a flap of hide attached to the forehead.

Will thought, *What kind of animal eats the horns off a bull? Jesus, even coyotes don't bother eating horns.*

He wondered about that for a moment, then let his eyes move around the room. He saw more cattle bones, a couple of pig jaws—those pointed tusks were familiar—and what might have been a primitive nest hollowed out in the muck. Will guessed it was a nest because of the rubbery-looking egg casings that lay scattered around the thing. The eggs were big, about half the size of an ostrich's.

He lowered himself enough to turn his mouth close to Tomlinson's ear. "You see those egg casings? Something just hatched in here. Not recent, but not so long ago, either."

"Yeah," Tomlinson said, "that's why I thought a gator at first, but—"

"Coyotes don't lay eggs," Will interrupted. "Not back in Oklahoma, anyway. Not in Minnesota, either, but maybe they're different in Florida."

Seeing the ray of sunlight had affected Will, too. The light moved through his eyes, through his body, replacing the desperation and the fear he had felt with fresh energy. Even Tomlinson's constant talking wasn't so irritating now. The sunlight had refired his sense of humor, too, and Will was struck by the oddness of being so close to death one moment and, the next moment, cracking a smart-ass remark about coyotes laying eggs.

It was like there were two people inside him, one who focused on nothing but survival when it was required but otherwise lay dormant, while the second person— William Joseph Chaser—talked and laughed, living life as if danger and darkness didn't exist, so it was sort of like living behind a mask.

Will lowered himself from the hole and checked the knife scabbard on his BC, which had become a habit. They weren't out yet but soon would be—as long as he still had the knife and the blade didn't break.

Tomlinson sounded cheerful when he replied, "Minnesota, huh?"

Will didn't respond, but it caused him to think about a nice lady named Ruth Gutterson and her pisser of a husband, Otto, who had been on the pro wrestling circuit when he was younger, so almost everyone called him by his ring name, which was "Bull Gutter." The Guttersons had a house in Minneapolis, and Will had lived with the couple for a year. They were nice people who would've adopted him by now if it weren't for the damn court system. But they would—even though he turned eighteen in only a couple of years.

"I sometimes forget you lived up north," Tomlinson said to him, which caused Will to realize that the man was being conversational for a reason. For the first time in hours, it was safe for them to take a little rest. Maybe it was a smart thing to do. His hands were blistered and his right bicep had begun to cramp.

Will dropped back, letting the water support his weight, and listened to Tomlinson add, "It's because you're such a western sort of kid. All rodeo and attitude Did you miss it—rodeo—when you were living in Minnesota?"

Will didn't like being called a kid, but he ignored it. "Sometimes," he said.

"The Land of a Thousand Lakes. Or is it Ten Thousand? You say there are coyotes in Minnesota? I knew there were wolves."

Will allowed himself to smile as he replied, "Everything that grows fur—or can buy fur—lives up there.

That includes a ton of Lutherans. A lot of pretty blondes, though, too."

"Lutherans," Tomlinson replied, chuckling.

Will said, "You wouldn't believe how good-looking the girls are."

The hippie seemed to get the joke because he laughed, but then Will wasn't so sure when Tomlinson said, "*Prairie Home Companion*, man. I love that show. Garrison Keillor."

Will said, "Garrison who?" becoming impatient again, and so he let his attention return to the cave overhead. He pulled himself up, took another look, then lay back and let his BC float him as his brain sorted out impressions.

The space, he now realized, gave him a bad feeling. It wasn't just because of the bones or the petroglyphs or the stench. Truth was, the place smelled bad but not that bad. It was sort of musty, like old roadkill, but it didn't strike Will as being foul like Tomlinson kept saying. Maybe Tomlinson was confusing atmosphere with odor. In Will's experience, people often perceived such things differently than he.

The boy reached his hand through the airhole, touched his fingers to the sandy muck above, then sniffed his fingers.

Darkness, that's what the muck communicated. Darkness was what Tomlinson was smelling, not the stench of bones, although that odor was there, too. The space had the scent of blackness, like peering over a cliff into an abyss.

Will allowed his mind to probe the area and soon the gloom that he sensed was replaced by a brighter odor. The odor was waxy green, like jungle suspended in a cloud of gray. It reminded him of a leaf flickering on the screen of an old black-and-white TV.

Gradually, the sensation changed, but the odors of the changing colors didn't flood into Will's mind. They flowed through a crevice of his brain like a creature with scales—something hunting.

"People with synesthesia sometimes experience exaggerated impressions of the world around them," an Oklahoma shrink had once told him. "It can be exhausting dealing with so much outside stimuli. It can cause panic attacks—even paranoia."

Paranoia, Will thought. *Like now?*

He hoped he was wrong about what he was feeling and decided to bounce it off Tomlinson. The man was a flake, no doubt about that, but he was also smart, and he possessed the ability to perceive things normal people could not. Tomlinson had been right when he'd guessed that Will had sensed his abilities. He'd known about Tomlinson since the first time they had been alone together, talking.

Will said, "There's something about those egg casings that gives me the creeps."

Tomlinson said, "There's no reason why they should," then spent a minute talking about the nesting habits of gators and crocs, still sounding cheerful, but then he became suddenly quiet. After several seconds, he said, "Sorry, I missed the implications. The whole heavy vibe went sailing right over my head. You're serious, aren't you?"

Will said, "It's a feeling I have."

"A *premonition*, you mean?"

"Just a feeling. A bad feeling."

Tomlinson gave it some thought—maybe with his eyes closed, Will couldn't be sure, there wasn't enough light to see detail. The man seemed to understand because after several seconds he said, "A predator lives up there. A killer. That's what you're feeling. And you're right—that's what I've been smelling. It's not an actual scent. It's death that I smell."

Will said, "That cow skull's pretty fresh. Whatever it is, I think she'll find her way back here. Soon, I think." In Will's mind, the animal that lived here was female— definitely female—and she lived alone.

Tomlinson asked him, "Because this is where she hatched her eggs?"

"Not exactly."

"It makes sense that whatever lives in the cave is bound to return to the nest—tonight, tomorrow or next week—is that what you mean?" There was enough room for Tomlinson to twist a strand of his ponytail, then begin to chew on it, his long fingers showing that he was nervous.

Will decided to come right out and say it. "No. I mean I think she's coming back today. Sometime after dark, maybe, but soon. It could be that she knows we're here. It could be that she's on her way now."

Tomlinson went silent, and into Will's mind came the

image of a snake—a huge snake—its belly wider than a man's chest.

Will said, "Doc told me there's a big population of escaped pythons in Florida. Last night, before I went to bed, I checked the Internet. Less than a week ago, state biologists caught a ball python that was eighteen feet long. Did you read about that? It was near Miami, I think."

Tomlinson whispered, "Snakes. Sometimes you've got to ride the snake," his voice sounding far away.

Will said, "It was living under someone's house. They got suspicious because the neighborhood dogs kept disappearing. The snake was close to four hundred pounds. There was a picture."

Tomlinson's voice returned to normal as he said, "I saw the photo. That's exactly what I was thinking about. A really big boa or python. The egg casings, the bones. It all fits."

Will said, "I don't think it's a snake."

"*No?*"

"I'd be surprised."

"Then what?"

Will said, "I can't say for sure. But I have a strong feeling that thing's headed in this direction. It's sunset now, so maybe we have some time. But she's on her way back. Probably soon she'll be here."

Tomlinson sighed, and whispered, "*Shit.*"

Will said, "Yeah. After going through all this crap. But maybe I'm wrong."

After several seconds, Tomlinson said, "A snake, huh?"

"It's not a snake," Will said again.

Tomlinson replied softly, "I know, I know. Metaphorically, I'm saying, it's always a snake."

Will listened.

Tomlinson said, "Sometimes the bastard assumes different forms. Cops, crazy women, right-wing loonies. Don't get me started." He looked at his watch. Will could see the green numerals of the face glowing as Tomlinson added, "We've got to get out of here."

Will replied, "What do you think I've been saying?"

"The sun sets in exactly five minutes. I don't like the idea of having a meat eater poking her head in here hungry for flesh."

Will pulled his knife from the scabbard. "I wish you would have brought one. Doc kept telling you."

Tomlinson said, "Don't remind me."

Will said, "No point talking about it," then tried to nudge Tomlinson away to give himself some room. "I'm going to work on this main root. Maybe if I just cut it in the middle, we can bend it down—"

Tomlinson interrupted. "My turn to dig. You rest for a while."

Too late. Will was already sawing at the root.

TWENTY-ONE

IN WAIST-DEEP WATER, AS I WADED ASHORE carrying a fistful of Cuban pesos, I realized that Arlis Futch had escaped. I had switched off the flashlight and was using night vision so I could see what King and Perry couldn't.

Maybe they hadn't noticed yet.

The two cons were near the truck, about thirty yards from the grassy area where I had spread the blanket for the old man. The truck was no longer running—they probably wanted to conserve fuel—and its headlights were off, which made it easier for me to decipher details in what was now a starry-bright February night.

The blanket was visible beyond the truck. So were the water bottles I'd left and the folded towel he'd been using as a pillow. But there was no sign of Arlis.

As I continued wading toward shore, I scanned the tree line. There was nothing to see but cypress and palmettos. Unless King and Perry had allowed Arlis to get back inside the truck—which was unlikely—the man was gone.

I decided to say nothing and see how it played out.

As I drew closer, I wouldn't have been surprised if the cons had started yelling at me, accusing me of helping Arlis escape. Or they might try a different finesse if they had already killed him. If they were feeling guilty, they might accuse me of helping Arlis get away and then pretend like they didn't care one way or another about the old man. *He'd wandered off in the swamp? So what?*

They did neither, which told me they didn't know that the man was gone. It also told me that Arlis hadn't been gone for long. Even though it was dark, the blanket where he'd been lying was in plain sight.

King and Perry had other things on their mind, I discovered.

"We heard that animal again," Perry called to me as I dropped my fins on the ground. "Just a few minutes ago. That hissing, crashing sound."

The mysterious beast was back. I wondered if Arlis had used the distraction to cover his escape.

I said, "Get the dredge ready, I'm going back in. I don't have time to deal with your paranoia."

"Not until you tell us what's out there. It's somewhere on the other side of the lake." Perry was sitting on the hood of the truck, I realized. King was standing on a running board, driver's side. Whatever they had heard had scared them enough to seek elevation.

Perry said, "For a while, it was crashing around in the trees. Then we heard that hissing noise again. It's big—I'm serious! The size of a car, maybe. How big do the snakes get around here?"

I said, "I already told you, it's probably a wild pig. Or it could be cows that got loose—or a gator. You're like a couple of children, for chrissake. Come here—I've got something to show you."

The truck was dangerously close to the empty blanket. I wanted to lure them away from the thing before they noticed that Arlis was gone.

I watched Perry slide off the fender of the truck. He took a look around as he shouldered the rifle, then walked toward me but reluctantly. King followed for the first few steps, but then hurried to get into the lead, probably because he realized how that might look to me.

"Perry's scared of his own shadow," King called, sounding nervous. "Goddamn, though, whatever's out there, man, he's right. It's got some big shoulders on it. Let me take a look through that night vision thing-amabob you're wearing. Maybe I can see what it is."

I turned my back to him, switched off the monocular, and tilted the mask up on my forehead. "I trust you about as far as you can throw me. I've had enough of your idiotic stunts."

Behind him, Perry said, "I told him not to do it—push that hunk of junk into the lake. Jesus, what a waste of time. He's a punk, dude. Nothing I can do about that."

"What the hell's wrong with you two?" King laughed. "You don't have a sense of humor? Shit, it was a joke, man!" Lowering his voice, having fun with it, he said to me, "Did I scare you, Jock-o? That wheel made a hell of a splash when it went in the water."

I said, "Wheel? I don't know what you're talking about."

"Bullshit, you're lying. It must have scared the hell out of you."

I said, "I've already got plenty of reasons not to trust you. I was talking about busting the hose when you jerked it out of my hands." I gave it a few beats before adding, "Take a look at what I found. Maybe you'll understand how stupid it was busting that dredge."

I was pretending to study the coins—six of them—but was paying close attention to King as he approached. Because King and Perry didn't know that Arlis was gone, they didn't realize that they had lost their leverage. It would be better to deal with them now. Now was better because if I waited and if I was lucky enough to get Will and Tomlinson back to shore alive, my options would be fewer. With the boy and Tomlinson watching, I would have to call in the police and leave the fate of the two cons up to the court system.

Yes, now was the time to act. Using the dredge without help wouldn't be easy, but I could manage.

"What are you looking at? Shine the light so we can see." It was King's voice. His pace had slowed, but he was still coming toward me.

I held out the coins. "Here. Take them. Shine the

light yourself." I looked at him long enough to confirm that he was carrying the pistol. Perry, with the rifle, was trailing several steps behind.

When I saw that, I felt a mild surge of optimism. I knew where their weapons were. I knew the distance that separated the two men and it was ideal—close enough for me to strip the pistol from King and get off a quick shot while ducking under the barrel of the Winchester.

First, though, I had to get my hands on the cheap little automatic, which meant I had to lure King within a step or two. That was key. Get him within lunging distance, I might be able to manufacture an opening, then take both men down.

The risk was obvious. It included more than just risking my own life. If I made a move now but failed, Tomlinson and Will would probably never see daylight again. They would die in the air bell—or wherever the hell they were stuck—awaiting help that would never arrive.

The timing had to be perfect and the setup convincing.

How to do it?

That's what I had to decide.

My mind went to work sorting through options. What I decided was, stick with the coins. King was greedy, he was desperate and he was already in a subtle power struggle with Perry. The combination made them both vulnerable.

I had been playing one against the other, so I de-

cided to ignore Perry for a change and give King my full
attention by offering him the coins. When he reached
for them, I would drop all six into the sand as if by accident. King's eyes would follow the coins to the ground
and he would probably lower the gun in sync because
that's the way hand-eye coordination works.

It was all the opening I would need.

Once I got my hands on the pistol, I would snap off
a shot at Perry, maybe two. After that, King wouldn't be
hard to fight off, would he?

I considered the man's bony frame, his nervous eva-
sions when confronted.

No, King wouldn't be a problem.

Work it right, I could deal with him immediately.
Or . . . I could tie him, gag him and drag him off into
the bushes for later. Tomlinson and the boy would never
know he was there. They knew nothing about King or
Perry.

I liked the idea. It would buy me some time. After-
ward, if I found them, I could send Will and Tomlinson off in the truck to look for Arlis, telling them I
would wait by the lake for the cops. It would provide
me the opportunity I'd been longing for—an opportunity to be alone with King. I had become fixated on that
scenario.

King said to me, "I'm not carrying a flashlight, so
toss me your night vision dealy. I won't hurt it. I'm serious, man. I want to see what was making that noise on
the other side of the lake."

I said, "Was it close?"

"No, I don't think so—way back there in the swamp, maybe, but coming this way. Hard to tell, though. It wasn't like what we heard earlier."

I turned my head, pretending to concentrate, but there was nothing to hear but insects and frogs trilling and wind moving through the trees. Even if I had heard something, I wouldn't have been concerned. The most dangerous animals on earth were right in front of me, not roaming the swamp.

Still looking at the coins, I removed the mask from my forehead and said, "Sounds to me like you're the one who's scared, not Perry."

Perry said, "Hear that? The man's not dumb."

I placed the mask on the ground next to me, adding, "This kind of equipment is hard to come by. You can use it, but if you break it we're all screwed. I won't find any more of these."

I thrust out my hand again and used a flashlight to show them what I was holding. The coins became mirrors in the light. I could feel their golden reflection on my face.

"I'll be goddamned," Perry whispered. "He was telling the truth."

The two men stopped to look for a moment, then continued walking, separating as they approached me— five yards, then ten yards apart—and I felt my optimism fade. About five paces away, they both halted as they continued to stare at the coins. They were careful, always careful—as sly and wary as stray dogs.

I said, "Do you want to try the mask or don't you?" I touched it with my bare foot, then ignored the thing.

King stared at me and nodded. Because it was so dark, I couldn't see his face clearly enough to read his expression. He said, "For now, I'm happy seeing what I'm seeing. Put the flashlight on them again—how many you get?"

I said, "Count them yourself. Most of them look to be in mint condition. You supposedly know all about rare coins"—I turned to face him—"how much do you think they're worth?"

As I took a step toward King, Perry snapped, "Don't give the damn things to him. I'll take them."

I said, "He's the expert, not you. So why not?"

"Don't tell me you believe his bullshit."

I replied, "You don't trust your partner and you don't trust me. How are we going to get anything done?"

Holding the rifle at his side, Perry started toward me, saying, "We sure as hell can't trust him—that's one fact I know for sure."

I said, "If you say so," hoping he would keep coming. Stripping the rifle from Perry, then killing King with a quick shot, would be more difficult, but I had to work with any opening they offered me.

I dropped down on one knee to make myself appear smaller and less of a threat. Using the flashlight, I focused my eyes close to the coins, then extended my arm. "Here. They're yours. There're more where these came from. The surprising thing to me is how heavy they are. Feel."

Perry almost fell for it, but something stopped him—his street instincts, probably—and he caught himself when he was still a safe distance away. He pointed the rifle at my chest. "I don't think I will," he said.

I let him see that I was mildly offended. "Jesus, now what's the problem?"

He motioned with the rifle. "Put the coins in the mask. Then move over there where we can watch you."

King began chuckling as if he'd known all along what I was trying to do.

When I didn't move immediately, Perry raised his voice, still using the Winchester to point. "Move closer to the water! Keep walking until I tell you to stop. Then sit down on your butt and don't budge. Hear me? I don't want you trying nothing stupid." A second later, he said, "You're awful damn slow for a man in a hurry."

When I was sitting on a wedge of limestone, at the edge of the lake, the two men converged on my mask, grabbing at the coins like starving men snatching food. Perry took a fistful, and King, after giving him a look, took the two remaining coins.

"Damn, if he wasn't telling the truth," Perry said again. "Take a look at these things! You still think it was stupid that we stuck around?"

From his knees, King turned his head toward me. "Only six? That's all you found?"

I said, "Get the generator started, we have to go back into the water if you want more. I need someone on the hose—but no more of your games."

"How many more are down there, you think?"

"Enough," I said, "and we're wasting time."

King said, "I don't see why someone has to paddle around on the surface messing with the hose. I'll freeze my balls off—you've got a wet suit, it's easy for you."

I said, "There're a couple of jackets in the truck. Wear a jacket, it'll be almost as good as a wet suit." In my mind, I was picturing King in the lake weighted down by sodden clothes. It would be easier to pull him under if he was wearing a jacket.

King said, "Screw the jacket and screw you. We can watch the hose and the generator from here." He had picked up my mask and was fiddling with the switch on the night vision monocular.

I thought, *Uh-oh.*

From the corner of my eye, I gauged the distance to the blanket where Arlis had been tied. The blanket was hidden by shadows, but King would be able to see it if he used the monocular. I realized I'd been stupid to use the thing as bait.

Perry said to King, "What's the big deal? The water wasn't a problem a couple hours ago. It's no different now that it's dark. Swim out and help the man."

King laughed until he started coughing. "You swim out there if it's so easy! Take the fins, they're yours."

"I don't think so."

"*Why?*"

"Because you're the expert lifeguard–scuba diver," Perry shot back. "What'd you tell me, we can sell these coins for about two grand apiece? We've got ten now, that's only twenty grand. Plus what we took from the farm. Fifty thousand? That's not enough to get us out of the country and buy a place in Mexico. You're the genius, you figure it out."

It was the first time they had referred to robbing a farm, and I now knew for certain they had killed the five people near Winter Haven, three children included. I could picture Perry pulling the trigger, maybe using the knife, too, while King urged him on.

I was watching King and trying to think of a way to distract him as he held the mask to his face. He had finally found the switch.

"This thing's amazing," he said softly. He was framing the mask with both hands, staring across the lake.

"See anything?" Perry asked. He sounded like he didn't much care now, one way or another, his confidence coming back. "The professor's probably right—what we heard was probably just a wild cow or something."

I got to my feet, hoping for a reaction. "When are you two going to stop wasting time? There's enough gold down there, we can all retire. Toss me the mask and let's get to work."

As I stepped toward them, Perry yelled, "Hold it, Jock-a-mo!" which caused King to chuckle as he began a slow pan of the lake's perimeter, his body pivoting toward the truck.

"Goddamn it," I said, looking at Perry, "you know what this guy's like. He'll break the lens and pretend it's an accident. Who's in charge here? You? Or him?"

Perry was stuffing the coins into his pocket as he said,

"Give him his mask back, King, before you break it." He sounded like an irritable father speaking to a child.

King ignored him and began to give us a play-by-play of what he was seeing. "Those lizard-looking bastards have run off somewhere, I guess. I don't see 'em, anyway—maybe that thing we heard scared 'em. There's a couple of birds sitting in that tall tree . . . Hawks, you think? Other than that, it's like we're the only living things for miles. Everything else just sorta disappeared."

King's feet were moving now as he pivoted toward the truck and the empty blanket. I started toward him again, saying to Perry, "Maybe you're willing to let this idiot screw us out of the gold but I'm not."

Perry hollered, "Goddamn it, Ford, you stay right where you are." He looked at his partner. "*King!* Give him his goddamn nightscope thing back before I"—the man swung the rifle toward King—"before I shoot you. I'll do it, you smart-assed bastard. I swear I will."

It was too late. King was facing the truck now. I watched him lean forward to focus as if he couldn't quite believe what he was seeing. "Jesus Christ," he whispered.

The tone of his voice caused Perry to lower the rifle. "What do you see? What's out there?"

"He's gone," King said, his voice rising.

"What?"

"The old man—*Grandpa*—he's gone!"

"Gone where?" Perry was fumbling in his pocket, and a couple of coins went flying as he pulled out a flashlight.

He painted the trees with light, searching, until he found the truck. Next, he found the empty blanket.

"Shit!" Perry yelled, and he began running. "I'll check the truck—you watch this asshole."

King waited until Perry had the truck door open, the dome light on, before saying to me in a surprisingly calm voice, "You knew the old man was gone the whole time, didn't you? You helped him. Maybe cut him loose when you knelt down to give him that water or left a knife or something for him. Which is it?"

I said, "What's it matter? We don't need Captain Futch to salvage the gold. He's an old man. Let him live."

"Let him hike out to the road and flag down help, that's what you mean."

"If I wanted the police involved," I said, "I would have waved in that chopper. Remember?"

"Perry's dumb enough to fall for that routine but I'm not. You're setting us up somehow. Don't think I don't know it."

I said, "All I want is my share of the gold. Perry understands that. If he's dumb, then you're dumber."

I ducked reflexively when King hurled the mask at me but recovered in time to snatch it out of the air with one hand before it sailed over my head.

"You met your match when you met me," King said, his voice still low, keeping the conversation between us.

"Did I?"

"You think you're so smart but you're not. All my life, I've hated you superior-acting dweebs. You, with your know-it-all attitude. But I can guarantee you one thing—if anyone leaves this shithole with a bunch of them coins it'll be me, not you—and not Perry, neither. It'll be me all by my lonesome." He let me hear his smile as he added, "Why share these pretty little things when I can have them all?"

"How do you think Perry will react when I tell him what you're planning?"

"He won't believe you. Go ahead and try. He's dumb as a damn post and he takes orders from me, not you."

From the truck, Perry was now calling to King, "We've got to find the old bastard before he gets to the road. That mouthy old fool, he won't get a third chance with me!"

His voice still low, King said to me, "Perry's about to decide that it's best if we tie your sorry ass up while we go looking, want to bet?" Then he hollered to Perry, "What should we do with numbnuts here?"

"Bring him along, we'll take the truck."

King's patient chuckle was infuriating. He yelled, "And risk both of them getting away? Okay, if that's what you want."

"No! Leave him there. That sack of tie wraps is somewhere near that little bag of his. Put the pistol to his head and use them. Hurry up, goddamn it!"

King grinned. "See? What did I tell you?"

I said, "If you tie me up, you can kiss the gold goodbye." I was watching Perry as he used the flashlight to look under the truck, then search the bushes beyond the stand of cypress.

"Oh, you're going back into that lake," King said. "And you're gonna bring us a bunch more of these coins. Want to bet on something else? Yours truly is not going back into that goddamn water. Not tonight, not ever. Want to know how I'm so sure?"

I stood my ground as he pointed the pistol at me and stepped closer. He said, "Get down on your belly. You know the drill. Hands behind your back. Watch and learn, Jock-o, watch and learn. I'm about to suffer a debilitating injury."

Confused, I said, "What?"

Before I had a chance to move, King pulled the trigger twice. I dropped to the ground automatically even as my brain registered what was obvious: The man had intentionally shot high. The little pistol made a sound like wood smacking wood, the gunshots still echoing through the swamp, as King yelled to Perry, "Shit, this asshole just tried to jump me! Are you happy now?"

"*What?*"

King repeated the lie.

"How the hell did that happen?" Perry was jogging toward us, using the flashlight to find King, then me.

King began limping, shaking his head as if in pain, but was still aiming the gun at me as he pretended to test his right leg. "Your girlfriend just tried to body-block me—that son of a bitch is *heavy*. I knocked him down, but he twisted the hell out of my knee. Goddamn it, Perry, thanks to you I can barely walk."

I said, "He's faking. Take a look and see if there's any swelling—" But Perry cut me off, screaming, "Shut your goddamn mouth or I'll shoot you myself!"

King suddenly became the peacemaker. "Take it easy, Per, not so quick. I don't think he'll try it again. And we want that gold, right?"

"Jesus," Perry said, "I'm getting sick of this whole business. Maybe you were right. Maybe we should just take what we got and get the hell out of here."

King cut in, "No, man, I was wrong. *You* were right. We make Jock-o here fetch us some more coins, then we leave." He paused. "Later, if you decide to carve a piece out of Mr. Smart-ass's hide, I won't object. For now, though, let's stick with your plan. But I don't think it's smart for me to try and tie up this moose without help. Take my pistol and keep the rifle on him. What do you think?"

A few minutes later, after I was tied, hands and ankles, Perry stormed off alone in the truck to search for Arlis. King waited until the truck lights were pointed away from the lake before he sidled up to me, paused and spit. I felt his spittle hot on my face. As I turned away, he kicked me hard in the ribs.

"Didn't I tell you he was dumb as a rock?" King said, drawing his foot back to kick me again. "I hate to say I told you so, but—" He stopped in midsentence for some reason and didn't follow through with his leg.

I couldn't figure it out. I had twisted myself into a ball, trying to get my knees up into a fetal position, and lay there with muscles tensed until I realized that King was listening to something . . . or maybe looking at something across the lake.

"Do you see that?" he said, his tone serious.

I made a croaking noise when I tried to reply—he'd kicked me so hard that my diaphragm muscle was spasming. It took me a couple of tries to say, "If you kick me again, I'll kill you."

King was walking toward the pile of gear where he'd left the night vision mask, then pressed it to his face.

"It's gone," he said after several seconds. "It was right there, I saw it, but I don't see it now."

I gasped, "What are you talking about?"

His voice low, he replied, "I just saw something crawl out of the bushes and slide down into the water. It swam like a snake, but bigger. I mean *a lot* bigger." He was silent for several seconds before adding, "The fucking thing was huge, man, the size of a damn canoe. It's gone now, but I can still see the water moving. How big do alligators get?"

Because I was tied, with my face pressed hard against the ground, I couldn't see anything but King's silhouette and a horizon of trees and stars beyond. I said, "Did you hear what I just told you? If you kick me again, you'd better never untie me because I'll kill you."

King took another look through the mask, then did a slow circle as if whatever he had seen might sneak up and grab him from behind. He said softly, "If you go into that lake, Jock-a-mo, I don't think you'll ever get the chance." He turned, and then he threw the mask at me again.

I couldn't move. An edge of the monocular clipped my forehead, drawing blood.

TWENTY-TWO

ARLIS FUTCH, WHO HAD SURVIVED TWO MILD strokes in recent months but had not told anyone including his closest friends, thought he might be suffering yet another aneurysm—the final nail in the coffin, perhaps—because he could hear voices calling to him and they seemed to be coming from beneath the ground.

He stopped and listened, his hands on his thighs, breathing heavily. His heart was pounding so loud in his ears that he thought he might still be hallucinating, when, once again, a voice called to him. But the words were difficult to decipher. "Doc . . . hey! We are . . . Arlis? Can . . . hear me? Down here!"

The voice was faint, softer than cypress leaves rustling in the wind. The words seemed to float out of the marsh, up through Futch's feet, then into his head.

Was it Tomlinson's voice?

That couldn't be. Tomlinson and the boy were dead. Arlis feared that maybe Ford was dead now, too, after hearing two gunshots just minutes before. The voices couldn't be real, which meant they were coming from inside his skull, not from the woods around him.

Arlis had brought along the only equipment close enough to grab before escaping into the swamp—the tire iron the two killers had used to fix the truck and a flashlight that Ford had slipped him when he'd left the bottles of water. Arlis dropped the iron on the ground, leaned his weight against a tree and checked the far shadows. He could see the lights of his truck angling through the tree canopy, but it didn't sound as if the truck was getting any closer.

That was good. The two Yankee killers didn't have the sense, apparently, to get out of the truck and try to track him on foot. Which meant they didn't have a chance in hell of finding him—not a man who'd grown up in the Everglades and knew good places to hide, like the shadowed dome of a cypress head ringed by water—a natural moat that would spook most men but not him.

Arlis turned and confirmed that an island of cypress trees lay just beyond. The grove was encircled by water that was thick with lilies, the water so black that starlight floated on the surface like shards of ice. If he needed it, the island was handy.

That gave him a good feeling. The cathedral shape of a cypress head always did. It caused him to picture the cool, open space within, moss hanging from orchid-weighted trees, and usually there was a pond with white lilies, and monster bass sometimes, too. He had felt that way about cypress heads since he was a boy.

Arlis stood, but his legs were shaky, so he used the tree again for support. For the last ten minutes, he had been hiking as fast as he could manage through the backcountry, angling toward the asphalt road that by his calculations was due west on the other side of the swamp, less than two miles away as the crow flies.

The road would have been farther if he'd taken the trail they'd hacked through the palmettos and myrtle. Three miles or more. So this was better, cutting cross-country over wet ground. The killers wouldn't follow him because they didn't know their way around a swamp, and they would probably be afraid to get out of the truck, anyway.

Candy-livered city boys.

That's what they were. Snot-nosed punks who believed that carrying a gun made them men. He had heard Perry and King whining about the big gator that had been crashing around, hissing in the distance. True, the animal had made noises Arlis had never heard a gator make before, but what else could it be? The damn thing had been several hundred yards away, way back in the woods, but it had scared the two killers so bad they'd about pissed their jeans hurrying to climb up on the truck—as if a few feet might save them if a full grown she-male gator came sniffing around.

Yankee spawn.

In the western sky, the same planets that Arlis had used many times to guide himself while fishing far offshore—

Venus, Jupiter and Saturn—formed a curving line toward the horizon as white and bright as channel markers. He was headed in the right direction, there was no doubt about that. Question was, would the damaged blood vessels in his brain handle more strain?

Arlis coughed and touched fingertips to the side of his neck. His jugular vein was throbbing like a snare drum and the resonant pressure inside his skull was beginning to produce the first warning signs of a killer headache. He had suffered headaches often enough in recent weeks to recognize the signs. His head had been hurting, anyway, because of the beating that scum killer Perry had given him, but the pain coming into his head now was different. It was a sharp, accelerating pain, as if glass splinters were circulating through his bloodstream.

One more stroke, the doctor had told Arlis, and he'd spend the rest of his life in a bed with tubes stuck up him front and rear so that he wouldn't mess himself. Like a vegetable, in other words, or some wounded animal, unable to speak or fend for himself.

A box in a cemetery was a better option, as far as he was concerned. But not now, not yet. Not before he had found help and returned to rescue Ford. It didn't matter if Ford was dead or alive, Arlis felt honor bound to come back for the man. Just as he was honor bound to do his best later to help recover the bodies of the other two, Tomlinson and the boy.

It was his trip. The least he could do was return and help clean up the mess he had caused.

Arlis touched two fingers to his neck again, checking his pulse, and he thought, *I'll rest here for a while. Not long. It's better than my brain exploding before I find help. I can't screw this up. Not again.*

In his lifetime, Arlis had failed one hell of a lot more often than he had succeeded. Maybe it was that way with most men, he didn't know—but he doubted that was true. He had owned too many businesses that had gone bust. He had led too many fishing or hunting or salvage expeditions that had gone south for one reason or another. Never in his life, though, had he experienced so much tragedy in the short space of a day—and it was nobody's fault but his own.

I'm a Jonah, he thought. *I've always been bad luck. And things ain't gonna change now that I'm near the end.*

The truth of that thought flooded Arlis with weariness. A lifetime of failure was bad enough—but to take the lives of two, maybe three, trusting men with him, as he himself approached his last days, was almost too much to handle.

Quit flogging yourself, take a breather, Arlis told himself. Dying now, with no one around, would only make this nightmare of a day even worse.

As his breathing slowed, yet another hallucination moved through the saw grass, into his ears, because he heard a sudden shrill whistle and then a man's voice calling again, the jumbled words telling him, "Hey, we're over . . . Lost our . . . *Hello?* We need lights . . . Bones . . . something *big*. Shovel and a rope . . . !"

Arlis replied before he could catch himself. "Who's there? Where are you?" He spoke softly and then turned his head to listen.

There was no answer.

Arlis felt like a fool. He had suspected it, but now he knew for certain. He was imagining the voices. It had happened to him before, and he felt a descending helplessness, like a prisoner in his own damaged skull.

The first time a blood vessel had burst in Arlis's brain, something similar had happened. He'd been out fishing for trout in his little green Beck boat, dragging lures on bamboo poles, when he'd felt a searing electric pain inside his head.

Next thing Arlis remembered, he was belly down on the deck of the boat—the boat running free, idling in a tight circle—as a woman's voice spoke to him, calling, "Arlis Futch, you old fool. Wake up! Wake up before you kill your boat and yourself on some damn oyster bar!"

That had been a hallucination, no question, because the voice he had heard was the voice of a woman who had been dead for several years. A pretty woman Arlis had once loved named Hannah Smith.

Hannah had fished for a living, as good as any man and better than most, and she'd had fine, heavy breasts and a good laugh. That woman had loved him, too, at least a little, even though she was young enough and pretty enough to have just about any man she wanted. But Hannah Smith had too much heart and body hunger to settle for just one man.

Hannah had loved men. She didn't bother pretending it wasn't true when she was alive, so Arlis didn't bother to pretend after she was dead.

There was nothing wrong with that, Arlis had told himself when he and Hannah were alone together. He had forgiven her long ago—not that Hannah had asked for forgiveness—and he had forgiven most of the men, too, which included Marion Ford, who, Hannah didn't mind saying, was maybe the man she had loved best of all.

Well . . . Arlis had *almost* forgiven Ford. Sharing Hannah's bed was one thing, but for a man to win her love was another. Arlis still sometimes felt the narrowing constriction of fear and focus that was jealousy, if he let his mind linger on the subject. But that wasn't often—and it would be far less now if Ford actually was dead.

Maybe he was. The gunshots Arlis had heard sounded solitary and irrevocable, like an execution.

Chances were, King and Perry had killed the man.

It would come as no surprise, if true. Ford was a good enough man by most ways of measuring, but he had always struck Arlis as being too bookish to be a dependable partner in a down-and-dirty fight. Ford had been okay in a tussle or two around the docks—Arlis had witnessed it—but Doc was an educated man, better with words and numbers than his fists. A smart-talking biologist would be no match for two low-life murderers who were desperate and on the run.

Marion Ford is dead. Arlis whispered the words to see

how it felt to say them. If it was true, he would soon have to get used to saying it because almost everyone on the islands knew Doc Ford and liked him.

The words felt worse than he could have imagined because the next thought that came into Arlis's mind was *Doc's dead, and I ran away and left him there to die alone!*

Arlis could admit that he had failed many times over the years, but he had never before abandoned a friend in a tight spot. True, Ford had insisted that he escape if he had the chance—no mistaking the signals the man had given him, nor the words Doc had spoken.

Even so, to run away and allow a partner to be shot to death was a sorry damn thing to do, and Arlis felt the weariness in him begin to change to anger. Running away like a coward wasn't how he wanted to be remembered, if anyone remembered him at all—which was unlikely—but he himself knew it. And God, of course, knew it, too.

The more he thought about it, the madder he got.

By God, I'll make it out of here, and nothing's going to stop me, Arlis thought. *I'll bring the law back to nail those Yankee punks and maybe get in a few shots of my own.*

That was *exactly* what he would do.

Arlis began to feel a little better now that he was angry instead of sad and tired. He wasn't running away. He was creating some distance so he could come back and take his revenge. This time, though, he would be carrying a revolver, not his old Winchester. If the cops got sloppy, if they didn't search him, he would pull the thing and shoot down King and Perry both—maybe put a round in Perry's belly first before finishing him off.

Arlis Futch knew he didn't have long to live, anyway. A year at most, the doctors had told him.

If he got lucky and shot the two killers, the cops would lock him in jail and probably charge *him* with murder.

As Arlis leaned against the tree, his heart calming, he thought, *So what?*

Arlis picked up the tire iron. He saw that the truck was returning to the lake—the bastards had given up their search pretty damn fast, which was fine with him.

His mind lingered on the fantasy of Perry crawling around on the ground, possibly crying for mercy after being gut-shot, but then he told himself, *Focus on what you're doing before you screw this up, too.*

Arlis decided that it was best to pace himself now. He would get to the asphalt road as quick as he could, but he wouldn't push so hard that his head would explode. Maybe it was true that he'd lived a life of failure, but he by God wasn't going to die a failure!

He pushed away from the cypress tree. After checking the whereabouts of the truck, he pulled the little light from his pocket and surveyed the route ahead. He found the moat at the edge of the cypress head where lilies floated thick and was surprised that he didn't see the red reflection of at least one pair of gator eyes.

Very damn strange, he thought. *There should be at least a few small gators around.*

He had never visited a Florida lake at night in his life where he hadn't seen at least a couple of gators—not this close to the Everglades, anyway.

Next, he painted the flashlight beyond a clump of saw grass to a high area where there were myrtle trees growing, Spanish bayonet plants and cactus and white stopper trees, too. He knew there were stoppers because he could smell their skunky odor, which was a good smell to him, a boyhood smell from his years camping.

Arlis explored with the flashlight, trying to pick out the best path to take. The high area was peaked with a hill. The hill was oddly shaped, like one of the old shell mounds that were common back on the Gulf Coast. The mounds had been built a couple thousand years ago, he had read, and had once been sided with horse conchs and whelks like four-sided pyramids.

The hill couldn't be an Indian mound, though. It was rock, not shell. Big chunks of limestone poked out of the brush where bayonet plants bristled with their needle spikes, the hillside too thick and rocky for a common man to bother climbing. It wasn't high by Colorado standards—a state Arlis had once visited—but the hill was tall and sharp against the black sky, a chunk of high elevation for Florida.

From the looks of what lay ahead, the best way to bypass the hill was by angling to the south. Arlis didn't like the idea at first. The route would take him uncomfortably close to the lake, but at least he would be able to keep the cypress head in view, which appeared to adjoin the limestone rise at the foot of the hill.

Arlis switched off the light, gave his eyes time to adjust and then began hiking southwest as his brain considered the hill's unusual contour.

I wonder if that's part of the property I bought. A chunk of high land like that would be a good place for a cabin someday.

Prior to buying the land, Arlis hadn't walked the entire ten acres. The owner—a young weekend rancher who had inherited the property—said it wasn't necessary, so why not leave the bushwhacking to the surveyors?

The owner was afraid of going near the lake, that was the problem. The man never came right out and said it plain, but he was.

That fact had struck Arlis as rather humorous. There wasn't an animal in Florida dangerous enough to spook him off his own land and that included a couple of fourteen-foot gators that he had killed personally. He had used the Winchester to shoot one of the monsters behind the eye and he'd caught the other by using a whole chicken on a hook that he'd made himself out of a tarpon gaff.

Up until today, Arlis had believed that buying the acreage—mostly sight unseen—had been maybe the smartest thing he had ever done. He had believed it from the start. Because of the owner's spineless attitude about the lake, Arlis didn't feel bad at all about not telling the man he had found the two gold coins and a busted propeller that he was now convinced had come from Batista's plane.

Doc had returned from the lake with yet another golden peso, hadn't he? That was proof enough.

At least I was right about the plane, Arlis reminded himself. *For fifty-some years, men looked for the thing, but it took me to find it.*

Mixed with his fresh anger, thinking about Batista's plane brought back some of his confidence. It caused him to feel stronger, too, and he decided to pick up the pace a little, not bothering to move quietly through the brush. What did it matter? He could no longer see the lights of his truck, which told him the murderers were busy doing something else.

Perry and King had given up and he was free. It was a mistake the bastards would pay for. Perry, especially.

Because Arlis was feeling more like his old self as he plowed through the brush, he was surprised when he began to hear voices again. He knew it was another damn hallucination, but it sure did sound like Tomlinson calling to him.

"Hey! Don't you . . . we're down here! Follow my . . . Hey! Go get help!"

The same jumbled words, but the voice was fainter now that Arlis was abreast of the limestone mound. Hearing the voice stopped him, though, he couldn't help himself. He stood there listening to the buzz of cicadas and mosquitoes whining near his ear and then he heard a noise that wasn't a man's voice and probably wasn't a hallucination.

Arlis turned and looked in the direction of the lake. It wasn't a comfortable thing to do because one of his eyes was almost swollen shut. After a few seconds, though, he understood the source of the noise.

Something was following him.

It was an animal, not a man—Arlis had spent enough time in the woods to know the difference. The noise came from behind him, a steady, plodding sound of bushes being crushed by the weight of something dragging its body along the ground on four paws. It was the sound a bull gator would make pushing through saw grass.

Seconds after Arlis stopped, the animal stopped.

It's gotta be a gator, he thought. What else could it be?

The man took several experimental steps and he heard the animal begin to move again. He stopped. A moment later, the animal stopped.

Arlis stood there thinking about that, then decided, *Nope, that's no gator. Can't be a croc, either, not this far inland.*

It was because of the way the animal was behaving. In all his years of hunting the swamps, Arlis had never come across a gator that was smart enough to match its own movements to the movement of its prey. When a gator got on the scent, it kept right on coming, even if you had a rifle handy and fired off a few rounds. A gator was about as sensitive as a bulldozer when it was on a feed.

Arlis took another few steps and he heard the animal

begin to move again. Arlis stopped and again the animal stopped.

No, it wasn't a gator. This thing was behaving more like a big cat. A panther, maybe.

Arlis felt a chilly, liquid sensation radiate through his lower spine. He'd never been afraid of panthers in his life. He'd had no reason to be. Back in the days when the Everglades was mostly free-range, wide open and wild, it was a fine place to hunt. People weren't scared of animals. Animals were scared of people—and for good reason.

But Florida had changed in recent years and the Everglades had changed, too—along with the creatures that lived in the swamps.

Gators weren't afraid of people anymore. They didn't need to be, not since the state decided to put them under legal protection. Arlis had heard the same was true of panthers. Less than a year ago, he had talked to some hunters who'd had to shoot a panther that had been shadowing them near their camp off Fortymile Bend. It was hard for Arlis to believe, but the men weren't drunks or braggarts and swore it was true. They'd had no choice, they said, because the damn thing just wouldn't leave them alone. It was a big hungry male.

Behind Arlis, the field of saw grass and scattered trees darkened as a cloud sailed beneath the stars. He gripped the tire iron in his right hand and found the flashlight with his left. With the light, he probed the bushes. Thirty yards behind him, he spotted a thicket of wax myrtle trees that were leaning at an odd angle.

The animal was hunkered down there, he realized. It was something heavy, built low to the ground.

The worst thing he could do was attempt to run away. It was better to take the offensive in these situations—be the attacker man or beast—so Arlis began walking toward the thicket, walking faster and faster, as he waved the light ahead of him like a torch.

He yelled, "Hey! Get out of here!" as he might to an aggressive dog, and it worked. The myrtle trees began to thrash as the animal retreated.

"I'll be damned," Arlis whispered as he stopped to watch. It wasn't one animal, it was three—three lizard-looking creatures, maybe forty pounds each.

Man, they were *fast*.

Iguanas, Arlis thought. They were pet-store animals that had escaped—the port of Boca Grande was loaded with the things. Arlis wasn't related to the famous Lee County Futches, but he knew the story. The iguanas had come over on boats from Central America, the pets of bored cargo captains.

As Arlis watched, the lizards disappeared into the shadows, but then they reappeared a minute later in the far distance. He could see three pairs of orange eyes watching him and he sensed that the lizards were no longer afraid. He felt that radiating chill in his lower spine again.

They're pack hunters, he thought. *They're stalking me.*

But these lizards were too small to attack a man . . . weren't they?

To his left, he heard something else moving and

he spun around to look. It was a familiar sound: the subtle slosh of mud and waves as something big entered the water.

He swung the flashlight toward the cypress head, with its natural moat, and Arlis saw another set of glowing eyes. The eyes were the same bright color—orange. This animal was huge, though. Its eyes were spaced more than a foot apart, which told Arlis that the animal was at least thirteen feet long—the formula used by alligator hunters was a simple one.

The eyes stared back into the light, fixated, for an instant, then vanished in a swirl of silver froth before Arlis could get a good look.

Was it another iguana?

No, he thought. It couldn't have been an iguana. The ugly little bastards didn't grow that big. A croc had orange eyes, but this was too far inland, Arlis reminded himself, for it to be a saltwater croc. And this animal seemed to be spooked by bright light, which was unlike most crocs or gators in his experience.

Because of what Ford had told him—and other hunters, too—Arlis knew that many strange and exotic animals had escaped into the Glades—particularly after hurricanes. He himself had seen photos of a python that had busted open and died after killing and swallowing a six-foot gator. That damn snake had to have weighed three hundred pounds!

Did the orange eyes belong to a python? Arlis couldn't remember ever seeing a snake's eyes glow at night, but maybe some did. Or it could be an anaconda—

those things lived in the water, he had read, and they grew to be thirty feet long.

Arlis tried to picture an anaconda with a head so big that its eyes were a foot apart, and the image settled it in his brain.

My God, he thought. *It's a big-ass damn snake!*

Stunned, Arlis began walking fast toward the limestone mound, seeking higher ground, without even thinking about it. As he hurried, he barked, "Get away, stay away from me!" hoping the tactic would work again.

From a black opening in the rocks, a voice too clear to be a hallucination shouted a faint reply. "Arlis? Arlis, are you up there?"

The old man felt dizzy—so many strange things were happening all at once. He stuttered, "Yeah, sure! I'm here!"

The voice came from beneath rocks and brush, Arlis realized, at the base of the mound. The voice said, "It's us—me and Will-Joseph. Come closer, keep walking. I thought you'd gone off and left us!"

Arlis, beginning to recover, said in a loud voice, "Leaving a partner ain't something I would do!" which was now true. He would never again go off and leave a friend.

He hadn't been hallucinating, which was a relief, and now Arlis felt better about himself than he had in a long time.

It was Tomlinson's voice. There was no doubt about that now.

Tomlinson was alive—maybe the boy, too.

TWENTY-THREE

THE NIGHT WAS COOL, NOT COLD, BUT PERRY had used a towel to wick gasoline out of the generator and built a deadwood fire at the edge of the lake while he bickered with King about who was going into the water to help me with the jet dredge.

They were both afraid, although King was better at hiding it. And he had the fake leg injury to use as an excuse.

"Don't blame me, blame yourself for trusting Jock-a-mo," he had told Perry more than once. "I'd handle the hose if I could—hell, I've done it! But I can't, so it's up to you."

They had left me facedown at the edge of the lake, hands and ankles tie-wrapped again, while they collected wood. It didn't take long because they were in a hurry now that there was a chance that Arlis would hike to the dirt road and flag down help. They decided it would take the old man at least two hours to make it to the road, then another half hour to get to the highway, which left them with some time to help with the salvage work before they had to get in the truck and try to intercept him.

"We can give it an hour, but not a minute more," Perry had finally agreed—one of the few things that he and King hadn't argued about since Arlis had escaped.

I wasn't so sure. Arlis was too smart to follow the trail we had cut. There was too much risk of King and Perry catching him, plus it would be shorter to hike cross-country, through swamp that was too soft for the truck.

Arlis Futch and I had had our differences over the years—the most serious having to do with a woman the old guy had had a crush on—but I didn't doubt his courage or his skills as an Everglades hunter.

When the fire was going, the cons finally cut me loose, then tossed me the remains of an open MRE. I hadn't eaten anything but the crackers they'd given me, so I ripped open a foil pouch and had vegetarian chili as the men continued bickering. I would need the energy before the night was done.

King and Perry were a painful pair to watch. If some scientist had melded prison genetics with random bad luck, the two could have served as a template. Back-dropped by flames and sparks that soared starward, the men resembled absurd rodents, their silhouettes becoming more animated and their voices louder as they squabbled, until Perry finally said, "Okay, okay! I'll get in the goddamn inner tube. But I know damn well you're faking!"

"I wish that was true," King replied, sounding suddenly pleased. "I can barely walk 'cause of that son of a bitch, which is all your fault and you know it."

"Oh . . . bullshit," Perry yelled. "But don't think the cut's gonna still be fifty-fifty because it's not. The cut has to be sixty-forty if I'm doin' extra work. What do you think about that, smart-ass?"

Unperturbed, King said, "Perry, you drive one hell of a hard bargain! I guess I got no choice, now, do I?" He didn't bother to hide the sarcasm, and there was a smile in his tone when he turned toward me and lied, "We're discussing our part of the take—not yours, of course."

I didn't bother answering. I was watching Perry, who had begun pacing. With the rifle angled over his shoulder, he resembled a toy soldier now. Maybe the man had run out of amphetamines or possibly he had recently swallowed a few more, because his voice was quivering when he spun toward King and screamed, "You always get your way, don't you, you son of a bitch? Well, at least I won't screw up the job like you did. But you've got to agree to one more thing before I do it. And you're not gonna weasel out of this one."

"I'd do anything I could to help you, you know that," King replied. "Just name it."

"If I go in that goddamn water, I get sixty percent, which we already agreed on, plus you're going stand right there by the generator ready to haul me back to shore if I say the word. You promise?" He was talking about using the power cord as a towline.

King said, "Afraid something's gonna swim up and bite you on the ass, Perry?"

"I mean it! Unless you promise, I ain't going in that goddamn lake. If I say the word, you'd better by God haul me in quick."

King had been limping unconvincingly—it was his way of teasing Perry with the truth—but now that he'd won the argument he stood on two straight legs and said, "You know you can trust me, old buddy. When have I ever let you down?"

I crumpled the aluminum pack and tossed it next to my gear. "Let's go," I said. "You two have wasted enough time."

All I cared about was getting back to the tunnel and finding Will Chaser and Tomlinson. I no longer had Arlis to worry about, which was freeing. When I was out of bottom time, whether I had found Tomlinson and the kid or not, I would surface quietly and then drown the man on the inner tube—Perry, apparently. If King tried to shoot me, I would submerge and crawl out on the other side of the lake. After that, I would play it by instinct.

I buckled on my BC, checked my regulator, then picked up the night vision mask. I noticed that Perry was unbuckling his trousers. He wasn't in a hurry, but he was going through with it, which surprised me.

"Leave your clothes on," I told him. "The water will seem cold at first, but your clothes will add some insulation. You'll warm up faster. Hey—there's a jacket in the truck. You should wear it."

"A jacket?" Perry asked.

I said, "It's mine. You're welcome to use it."

"You're serious."

I was tempted to say, *Dead serious,* but instead I told him, "You'll need the insulation."

"Like dressing for cold weather, huh?" Perry said. "I never heard of that working in water." As I looked at him, I was struck by his expression. Illuminated by the fire, the man's face was pale, his eyes wide. He resembled a frightened child. Maybe the children he had murdered had exhibited similar reactions.

I said, "We're in this together, right?" as I carried my fins and the extra gear into the water.

Nearby, King was starting the generator.

King had the rifle now, I noticed. The man had been right about Perry.

Perry wasn't very smart.

Fifteen feet was only three strong strokes with my fins, but the world beneath the surface was so different that I might have traveled the distance between the earth and the moon. My vision narrowed, and isolation stripped away the filters from my senses. Hearing became a survival tool.

Because of that, I froze momentarily when I heard what by now was a familiar sound: the distant thump and slap of something big breaching the water's surface.

I had been arranging my gear next to the lake bottom's most recognizable feature—the prehistoric tusk, near where the buoy was tied. My head swiveled as I searched for the source.

It was King again, I decided. He had probably found something else to push into the lake. Another one of his adolescent jokes, and I thought, *It will be his last.*

But what had he used? There weren't any more handy truck wheels, so maybe he'd rolled a chunk of limestone into the lake. If the rock was big enough and if it hit me, it could mean the end of my search—possibly the end of me.

I spun toward shore. Through the green lens of the monocular, I focused on the jagged incline where the wheel had appeared but saw nothing. Next, I checked the surface fifteen feet above. I could see the silhouette of the inner tube, Perry's legs dangling over the side, the contour of his fins gray against the emerald, star-speckled sky. I could picture the man shivering with fear and cold as he waited to play out the hose when I signaled him by giving a tug.

Perry wasn't much of a swimmer, so he had seated himself in the big rubber doughnut like a kid at a water park and paddled out using the spare fins. For the last several minutes, he had been floating above me motion-less, too scared to move.

Perry hadn't caused the noise I'd heard, that was for sure. It was something else.

I considered using the underwater spotlight to check the area. The monocular was effective for a radius of about fifteen feet, but it would take the light's thousand lumens of white LED to pierce the darkness of the lake basin.

Using the spotlight, though, was a bad idea, I decided. I could see nothing tumbling down the incline toward me, and a flashlight would only screw up my night vision—yet I still felt uneasy.

I told myself to ignore the lingering paranoia I'd experienced earlier. Even so, my nagging inner voice repeated the same ancient questions: Was something out there, watching? Maybe a predator had sensed my vibrations, my body heat. Was something swimming my way?

I remembered the fear in King's voice when he'd said, *I just saw something go in the water. It was fucking huge, man!*

His fear was real. He had seen something—but it was also true that King and Perry were easily frightened by the sounds of a Florida swamp at night. To King, a five-foot alligator would appear huge—or a monitor lizard.

I clipped the light to my BC and turned my attention to the jury-rigged jet dredge. The brass nozzle was gone, as well as the trigger, so I could no longer control the flow of water.

That was Perry's job.

After taking a last look around, I signaled the man by tugging three times on the hose. Above me, I watched the inner tube rock as Perry stirred—and then I saw something that convinced me that King was still taunting us with his absurd tricks. I saw a spinning bright light appear in the sky—a meteorite, I thought at first.

But the light tumbled downward, then slapped the water next to the inner tube, creating a shower of sparks.

King had pulled a chunk of burning wood from the fire, I realized, and thrown it at Perry.

Idiot.

The man reminded me of a spoiled child who got nastier and nastier if he wasn't the center of attention. I imagined the two cons shouting at each other, exchanging threats—wasting time again—so I repeated my signal to Perry by jerking on the hose.

A moment later, Perry recovered enough to provide me a descending coil of slack. Soon, he opened the flow valve, and the hose jolted in my hand, writhing like a snake. I waited until I had the thing under control, then swam to the mound of sand that now covered the mouth of the karst vent.

King. I had never met anyone I had disliked so intensely, so quickly. For now, the best way to deal with the man was to ignore him.

I focused on my work.

The dredge had lost a lot of its pressure, but the jet was still powerful enough to peel away layers of soft bottom as I searched for the tunnel. Around me, as I probed with the hose, sand and silt exploded, forming a cloud as dense as smoke. Visibility dropped from excellent to zero. Soon, I had to work by feel.

With my left hand, I found what I hoped was the upper lip of the tunnel. I used my weight to burrow downward, the hiss of water meshing with the bell-sound exhaust of my own regulator as I excavated.

Because I was operating blindly, my fingers became adept at identifying chunks of limestone or fossilized shell. I removed the debris mechanically, tossing it aside. Five times, though, my fingers also found the slick, dense weight of coins. They were unexpected, but finding them provided me no pleasure. I slipped them one by one into the pocket of my BC. Before I surfaced, I would hide them with the others that were still in the mesh pocket inside my wet suit.

I kept an eye on the time—not an easy thing to do, but I could see the orange numerals if I held my watch against the faceplate of my mask. I had clicked the trigger of the Chronofighter just before submerging, so I knew exactly how many minutes had passed.

It took me five minutes of digging to confirm that I had indeed found the karst opening. Ten minutes later, the opening was only slightly wider than my shoulders, but that was good enough. I tugged on the hose again, a series of two sharp pulls, which was Perry's signal to close the valve.

He didn't respond immediately, and I thought, *Now what?*

After several more attempts, though, I felt a couple of tentative tugs in reply. Moments later, the hose went limp. I pushed the coils aside. Because visibility was so bad, I kept my left arm anchored to the tunnel's entrance and waited for the siphoning current to clear the water.

It was strange to kneel there, underwater, anchored

to a rock, my visual world reduced to a random swirl of sand granules that banged against my faceplate. Above me, below me and on every side, there was a void of sensory data that caused a dizzying interchange between my eyes and brain as they struggled to extract form from the murk.

I had switched off the monocular soon after starting the jet dredge—there was nothing to see, so why waste the battery? Now, though, I clicked the switch downward, which powered the monocular but not the built-in infrared light. The darkness that encircled me was transformed into a boiling green cauldron of silt.

My arm still anchored in the tunnel, I did a slow three-sixty. Soon, I could see my watch if I held it a foot from my face, which told me visibility was improving. A minute later, I could see the vague outline of my own fins.

I looked toward the surface and told myself to relax until the water had cleared. As it did, I expected to see the familiar silhouette of the inner tube and Perry's dangling fins. Instead, I saw something that startled me. It was an animated darkness, the size of a small plane, off to my right. The thing was fast moving—and its shape and its behavior impossible to assess.

I pulled my body close to the tunnel opening and watched as the thing drew nearer. It was an animal, I realized, an elongated crocodilian shadow snaking toward me and gaining speed. I decided it was an alligator—maybe the gator that King had seen entering the water earlier. It could be nothing else.

I was fumbling for the oversized spotlight to use as a shield when suddenly the animal slowed and turned. I couldn't make out details. I could see only its massive silhouette. The shape was visible for a few seconds, but then it melted into the gloom.

I was so surprised that I had stopped breathing. I drew three fast breaths as my brain replayed what had just happened. The animal had been descending, moving from my right to my left like a shark banking downward for an attack. Then it had disappeared. Why—and *where*?

I stood, with my fins on the bottom, and gave it a few seconds, then I leaned over the tunnel's opening, straining to see.

Nothing.

I did another careful three-sixty, silt swirling before my eyes, and I soon began to wonder if I had imagined the damn thing. I've seen monster alligators in my life, but none the size of the thing that had just buzzed me. And the shape didn't seem quite right, either.

So . . . perhaps I had been wrong. Maybe a plane had swooped in low, throwing a shadow, as it checked on the lakeside fire. Or possibly I'd seen a school of baitfish, moving past me in a dense cloud. In zero visibility, the human brain will scan randomly like a frozen computer, attempting to impose form on chaos.

I comforted myself with similar reassuring explanations, but I didn't believe any of them. I had seen something. It was an animal. A reptile of some type or possibly an oversized alligator gar—a freshwater fish that grows to three hundred pounds. The thing had been descending toward me, swimming fast, but then it had veered away.

Why?

Once again, I recalled the fear in King's voice when he'd said that he'd just seen something huge slide into the water. That suggested that it was a gator, not a fish. A big gator was a threat I had to take seriously.

It's a popular fallacy that infrared light can pierce fog, smoke and silt, but it's not true. Even so, I touched my fingers to the monocular and switched on the infrared. Maybe the invisible beam of light would extend my range of visibility.

Seconds later, as I continued scanning, I felt a shock wave of pressure behind me. It was as if a torpedo had shot past me. The wave caused me to duck and pull my body hard against the rock ledge. I don't know why my first instinct was to switch off the infrared light but that's what I did. It was an atavistic response; a limbic impulse to extinguish the campfire, to draw the limbs into a fetal position and then retreat into a dark place to hide.

My heart was pounding but my hand unaccountably sure as I unsnapped the spotlight and found the switch. The beam was blinding. Stupidly, I hadn't first switched off my night vision system, so the intensifier tube automatically flared before shutting down to protect the precision optics as well as my own eyes.

I extended the big flashlight and moved it around. Underwater, a thousand-lumen LED projects a beam that is as dense as a shaft of glowing marble. Maybe the light saved me . . . Or maybe there was, in fact, nothing from which to be saved. I was partially blinded, as I probed the darkness, so I couldn't be certain of what I was seeing. For the briefest instant, though, I *thought* I saw a massive reptilian head in profile and a single glowing orange eye. The animal materialized on the far black rim of visibility and then hesitated, as if deciding whether or not to turn and face me.

It did not turn. Instead, it seemed to shrink as it descended into deeper water toward the bottom. And then it vanished.

I didn't know what I'd just seen, but I was sure it wasn't an alligator. So what was it?

Slowly, like a drunk approaching a mountain ledge, I moved away from the cave opening. I took a couple of strokes with my fins and then poked my head over the drop-off. The flashlight drilled a brilliant white conduit downward into the depths. I painted the beam over the bottom but was still alert to movement behind me.

It took a while for my eyes to adapt. Through a haze of silt, I identified an elongated darkness, which I knew was the fuselage of the plane. Then . . . I saw something that was too animated and well defined to be imaginary. I saw the fanning pendulum of what appeared to be a reptilian tail as the creature nosed itself into a limestone hole. The tail was miniaturized by distance, but I knew it had to be big—longer than a man.

Pushing the light ahead of me, I started downward to get a closer look. But then stopped myself.

Don't press your luck, Ford. Leave it alone.

As I watched, I tried to convince myself that I was watching an oversized gator, but I knew it wasn't true. More than anything else, it looked like the tail of a Nile monitor lizard—but that couldn't be. Monitors didn't grow to be thirteen feet long, and the animal I was watching had to be at least that big.

I extended the light downward as if using the beam to pin the creature to the bottom. As I did, a chilling memory flashed into my mind, and I pictured myself on the island of Gili Motang, in the Suva Sea, where my friend and I had been tracked by a reptile of a similar size.

A Komodo monitor? In Florida?

Even as I thought the word *Impossible,* I knew that I was wrong again. Florida was the perfect habitat for the world's largest venomous lizard.

"Something lives in that lake that kills cows," the land's previous owner had told Arlis. I had smiled when I'd heard the story—me, a skeptic by nature and also by profession.

Yes, it *was* possible . . . possible that I was now watching an Indonesian monitor. In the remote pasturelands of central Florida, a Komodo-sized lizard wouldn't just survive, it would thrive. An animal with its habits could live unnoticed for years, feeding by night and sleeping underground by day. With miles of tree cover and lakes connected by karst vents and tunnels, the topography was ideally suited to support just such a creature. On the islands of Indonesia, the giant monitors are more often obligate scavengers, reliant on the success of their pack.

In Florida, though, there was no competition. Even an immature Komodo would soon ascend to the top of the food chain as an alpha predator.

My mind shifted to the three lizards that I had believed were Nile monitors. I had been surprised to see diurnal animals hunting well after sunset. I didn't want to believe it, but I no longer doubted my eyes or the evidence—evidence that suggested that at least one adult Komodo lived in this area and it had reproduced.

That's why the young lizards were out feeding at night.

Maybe the spotlight had saved me when the animal swooped in close. True or not, I gripped the light tighter as I watched the monitor's tail stir the water twice more, then vanish into the hole. Another karst vent, most likely.

I glanced over my shoulder at the tunnel I was about to enter. I compared it with the location and the apparent angle of the hole into which the giant lizard had disappeared. If the hole beneath me was indeed a karst vent, the two tunnels ran roughly parallel. Even though they were separated by forty feet of limestone and sand, it was likely that they intersected at some distant place, perhaps far from the rim of the lake.

I couldn't let myself dwell on it.

I had to find Will and Tomlinson—before the Komodo monitor found them.

TWENTY-FOUR

AS ARLIS FUTCH HUNTED AMONG THE BUSHES, he called to Tomlinson and Will Chaser, "You can quit making so much noise now—my God, you could raise the dead! I've got a good fix on where you are."

Looking over his shoulder every few seconds, Arlis had used the tire iron to hack his way up the western side of the mound. When he had cleared enough cactus and bayonet plants, he tracked Tomlinson's voice and the steady echo of the boy treading water until he found an opening in the rocks.

The hole wasn't wide enough to crawl through, but it was large enough to poke the flashlight in and have a look. As he did, Arlis told them again, whispering, "Quiet down! I'm here, stop making so much racket. Do you see my light?"

They were close enough to the lake that the two convicts might be able to hear them—sound carried over water—which was risky enough. And Arlis sure as hell didn't want that snake he'd seen, the monster with the orange eyes, to come cruising around. He wanted to concentrate on what he was seeing and not have to worry about someone or something sneaking up behind him.

Lying on his belly, he pushed the flashlight into the hole, then pressed his face close enough to see. Below was a bone-strewn animal den. It was a small cave, with tree roots hanging down. Near the far eastern wall, the floor of the chamber angled into a pool of water. When the flashlight hit the pool just right, the water was tannin red but clear.

Judging from the bones and the egg casings and the stink, Arlis guessed that the pool was somehow connected to the cypress head where he'd seen the massive reptile, and he thought, *Dear God Aw'mighty, this is where the thing lives. It's a by God snake den!*

Near the center of the chamber, a karst vent creased the southern wall. There was a hole in the limestone floor there, water visible beneath. Tomlinson's face floated within the hole, as if someone had taken his picture and placed it in a rock frame. His face was covered with mud, and he held up a hand to shield the light from his eyes until Arlis swung the light away.

Arlis called, "How the hell did you get down there? Where's the boy, is he with you?"

Instead of answering, Tomlinson was already asking

questions. "Where's Doc? We heard him using the sand dredge. He signaled us a couple of times, but then he stopped. Is he with you?"

Arlis felt the pain in his head sharpen and he winced before saying, "Doc's fine, don't worry about him. Where's the boy?"

Tomlinson's face disappeared and Will Chaser's face suddenly filled the little opening. The teen was grinning, but he sounded irritable when he said, "I've been digging at this hole for more than an hour! We've got nothing but one knife, and both our lights went out." The boy's grin widened. "Man! Never thought I'd say this, but it sure is good to see a bossy old redneck."

Arlis laughed, feeling ridiculously close to tears. "I've got a tire iron—watch your eyes, and I'll try to dig my way through."

Will shouted, "No! You need a shovel and maybe a pickax. These goddamn roots are hard as iron."

The boy had a mouth on him, and Arlis knew that he would soon be asking for Ford's opinion. "I'll do it my way, if you don't mind," he told Will Chaser. "Move aside or this bossy old redneck won't rescue your mouthy young ass."

Arlis thought for a moment and then said again, "And keep your voices down. This cave's got an echo to it."

The lake was on the other side of the swamp, less than a hundred yards away, and the punk killers might hear them. But he was also still thinking of that snake.

If the thing had hatched eggs in the cave, it would be back.

"Why? What's the problem with making a little noise?" the boy asked, sounding more suspicious than respectful.

Still whispering, Arlis said, "Just do it."

Because of the bayonet plants—they were as sharp and hard as darts—Arlis was bleeding from puncture wounds on his arms and hands when he lowered himself into the cave. The space was less than five feet high, ceiling to floor, but it was wide and long, counting the pool of water at the far end of the chamber.

Arlis kept his eye on the pool, thinking, *That's how the snake comes and goes. These little lakes are all connected.*

It wasn't unusual in Florida for lakes to be connected by underground rivers or karst tunnels, as the man was aware. A good example was a sinkhole called Deep Lake, which wasn't far from Copeland, off Highway 27, on the way to Everglades City. Every spring, ocean-going tarpon appeared in that little lake, rolling on the surface. By fall, they were gone—the fish had followed a tunnel or underground river back to the Gulf of Mexico, twenty-some miles away, to spawn. Arlis had witnessed it with his own eyes long ago when he was a boy, although it was the rare Yankee fisherman who actually believed the story.

Arlis stood there for a second, his mind playing tug-of-war with his courage. He thought, *Crawling into this hole might be the stupidest thing I've ever done. And sure as hell the most dangerous.*

Then he thought, *What's it matter? I ain't never going to run away again. And I'm gonna die soon, anyway.*

The man took a big breath, then ducked headfirst into the cave and began to shimmy his way through a curtain of tree roots. The floor was greasy slick with mud and moss, and there was no avoiding the bones, which rolled and levered beneath his feet. Twice, his boots nearly went out from under him, so he got down on his hands and knees and crawled in the muck. Crawling was easier here—no wonder the snake had chosen it as a good place to hatch its young.

As Arlis worked his way closer, Tomlinson and the boy took turns watching him. The hole was big enough to provide them both air, but just barely. The boy didn't say much, but Tomlinson was even more hyperactive than usual, and he talked nonstop when it was his turn to push his face into the hole.

Arlis had noticed that reaction before in men who had come close to dying, and a thought came into his head. *First time since I met Tomlinson that he's ever behaved like a normal human being.*

Tomlinson yammered away until the light must have hit Arlis's face just right, which caused the hippie to pause, and then he said in a soft voice, "My God, Arlis, what happened to your face?"

Arlis hadn't thought about what he must look like, but he knew that his left eye was almost swollen shut and the skin of his jaw was puffy tight with bruising and blood. It was embarrassing, in a way—Arlis had never been beaten so badly by another man, and he hated to lie about it but did. "I took a spill back there on the rocks. Probably because I'm not used to roaming around the woods at night clean sober, but here I am. So don't worry about it."

Still concerned, Tomlinson said, "Man . . . you need a doctor." But then he sensed the old man's embarrassment and recovered by adding, "I'll buy us a twelve-pack on the way home. It's important to stay hydrated down here in the tropics—a few beers will make us both feel better."

Arlis was having trouble getting through the roots. Every few feet, he had to stop and whack at them with the tire iron before proceeding. During the pauses, Tomlinson continued to talk away, telling Arlis about the series of underwater landslides that had buried them and how they'd ended up here, several hundred feet from the lake. Of course, the hippie also repeatedly asked questions about Ford, which Arlis found disconcerting. He didn't mind exaggerating a story—that's the way stories were meant to be told—but he had seldom told so many outright lies in the space of only a few minutes.

To get Tomlinson off the subject, Arlis said, "Once you're out of here, you can ask Doc your own self how he's doin'. But right now, let's focus on the best way to get this job done." He shined the flashlight toward the eastern wall.

"There's a pool of water there. See it?"

Tomlinson squeezed his face tighter against the rock hole before saying, "Not from this angle. Is it under the petroglyphs? I can only see part of the floor from here."

Arlis said, "Petro-what?" but then realized the man was speaking of the cave drawings on the wall. There was a bizarre-looking stick figure of a man with horns and what might have been a sun and a moon, plus a lot of other scratching.

Arlis had no interest in archaeology, but the stone drawings gave him an uneasy sensation in his belly. It was bad enough to be crawling around in a snake den where there were bones and chewed-on cow skulls, but the witchy-looking images gave him the feeling that the cave would be a dark place no matter how many flashlights a man brought along. The Indian mounds along the Gulf Coast all had this same heavy feel to them, full of shadows and weight, even at high noon.

"Jesus Christ," Arlis said, "I mighta known a man like you would end up in a weird place like this."

"Don't blame me," Tomlinson replied. "Will gets all the credit for this one. He's on a journey, man. Will's a shaman, he doesn't even know it. His ancestors have something big planned for the kid, which I can explain later if you want. That's why we ended up here."

Arlis heard the kid say something sharp to Tomlinson about kicking his ass, but Arlis put an end to it by raising his voice, saying, "There's a water hole there, that's what I'm trying to tell you. An opening in the limestone wide enough for you to crawl out. Shut up long enough for me to make my point, if you don't mind."

Tomlinson shot back, "I'm only trying to help. Shallow-up, Arlis."

Squeezing his way between two roots, only a few yards from the hole now, Arlis replied, "We don't have time for you to help. Just be quiet and listen to what I'm saying! There's a bigger opening in the floor of this dungeon. It's right over there, no more than ten or twelve feet from where you are. I'm thinking the crevice you followed might be linked to this hole I'm looking at. Are you with me so far?"

Tomlinson said, "Sorry . . . I get excited. This has been God's own hell broth of a day, man. We've been time-traveling, Arlis, our asses on the line the whole time. It has been one continual monkey-fuck after another, but—"

"Quiet until I finish!" Arlis told him. "I can chop away at those roots, dig your hole wider and get you out. But all I got is this tire iron. It might be a lot easier for you to swim underwater to the next hole and climb out on your own."

Tomlinson sounded dubious, saying, "I don't know, man. I've had just about enough of swimming around in the dark."

"At least take a look! I'll shine the light on the water hole. Maybe you'll be able to see it if you stick your heads under." Arlis motioned with the flashlight toward the pool, its water blackish red in the light.

As his head turned to look, though, Arlis's breath caught. The surface of the pool had been flat, glassy and still, when he'd first entered the cave. But now the water had begun to vibrate for some reason. The surface showed expanding, concentric rings that lapped against the rock perimeter. The waves sailed outward, as if the hole was connected to a distant sea.

God Aw'mighty, it's that damn snake, Arlis thought. *She's left the cypress moat and now she's swimming home to her den.*

Tomlinson interrupted his thoughts, saying, "Hey— what's wrong? What do you see over there?"

Arlis replied, "Jesus-frogs, you ask more questions than a schoolteacher. I'm trying to find a quicker way for us to get out of here, that's all. Why are you being so pigheaded about it?"

"The openings aren't connected," Tomlinson replied, sounding sure of himself. "The chamber we're in is only a little bit bigger than the one you're in. We searched the ceiling before our lights went out."

Arlis looked away from the water hole long enough to see Tomlinson blinking at him like a turtle, as Tomlinson continued, "Will was lucky to find this hole—he saved our lives. It wasn't even big enough to grab more than a quick breath until he dug it out with his knife."

Arlis said, "Are you sure?" and was surprised that his voice wasn't shaking. His eyes were locked on the pool again and he was as scared as he'd ever been in his life, which was a strange thing to admit at his age. But there was nothing to be gained by lying to himself. In his brain, he could picture the snake, with its burning orange eyes, swimming through the tunnel, getting closer and closer, while they wasted time talking.

Arlis added, "I'm in sort of a hurry to get out of here. Did I mention that? And if there's a faster way to do it—"

"Do you think we're enjoying ourselves?" Tomlinson laughed. "The smell's about to kill us."

Arlis said, "Well, at least let me try it," but he was thinking, *That's not the only thing down here that can kill us.*

A minute later, Will Chaser's face appeared. Arlis realized the kid had moved Tomlinson out of the way and thought, *Good. The boy ain't as fond of conversation as the hippie.*

"Go ahead and shine the light," the teen told Arlis. "We didn't have time to look the place over good—he's wrong about that. Could be there is another opening. If you think it would be faster, we might as well check. Our lights ran out of juice, so how would we know?"

Arlis replied, "Okay, okay. I'm glad one of you has some brains." He focused the light on the little pool, and he also got a good grip on the tire iron, as he said, "I'm all set. Stick your head under and tell me what you see."

Will Chaser said, "Now?"

"Hell yes, now. What are you waiting for?"

The kid sounded miffed when he answered, "Jesus Christ, that's not going to tell us anything. Crawl over there and stick the light down in the hole. Aim it in our direction. That's the only way we're gonna see anything."

Arlis could feel the pressure in his head building, the blood moving through his damaged brain like sand-spurs, but the boy was right, and he said, "Hold your horses, that's what I was planning to do, anyway. God-damn, you are one bossy kid."

He put the flashlight in his teeth, grimacing at the sulfuric taste of mud, and crawled toward the pool. A chunk of cow skull was in his path, as well as more bones and tree roots, and he had to use the iron to clear a path.

Behind him, he heard Tomlinson saying, "Why don't you leave the crowbar with us? I can start digging while you and Will experiment."

Before he could think, Arlis snapped, "You can kiss my ass in the county square if you think I'm doing this with-out a weapon," and immediately regretted the sharpness of his tone. Tomlinson and the boy had been through enough without giving them cause to suspect they weren't as safe as they thought they were—which they weren't, not by a long shot.

Tomlinson said, "A weapon? Why would you need to use a crowbar as a weapon?" He paused, thinking about it, then said, "Hey, man, there's something you haven't told us. Arlis? *Arlis?* What's wrong? Did something happen to Doc?" After another pause, he added, "What *really* happened to your face?"

Arlis was at the edge of the limestone pool now, where water was lapping from side to side, splashing up over the rim like water in a bowl that was being tilted back and forth. Something was definitely down there causing the water to move. He didn't want to risk making more noise, but he had to answer Tomlinson, so he did, saying, "This is a tire iron, not a crowbar, you cottonheaded hippie. You being a damn sailor, I reckon that's reason enough for you not to know the difference."

Slowly, Arlis leaned his head over the pool. He could see his own reflection in the black water. His skin was caked with blood from the beating Perry had given him and it was like seeing the face of a stranger. A tired old man stared up at him, a man who was shrunken by age and fear, and it caused Arlis to feel a jolt of sadness that was soon displaced by annoyance, and he thought, *Screw it. I'd rather die here from a snakebite than die in a bed with tubes up me,* and he plunged the flashlight down into the pool until water was up to his shoulder.

After a couple of seconds, he yelled, "See anything?" as he aimed the light toward the breathing hole. He forced himself to reach deep, and Arlis knew in that instant what it would be like to stick his arm into boiling water and hold it there.

After several seconds, he heard a sputtering sound and then Will Chaser's voice say, "Are you sure the light's on? Move the damn thing around. I didn't see anything."

"It's on, by God," Arlis hollered. "But if you didn't see anything, then there must be nothing to see. So I guess maybe Tomlinson was right, this is a waste of time." He began to pull his arm out of the water.

"No, stay where you are!" the boy ordered. "I'll try again. Could be the limestone's thick there. Can you reach any deeper? Give me thirty seconds or so and I'll try to work my way closer."

Arlis said, "Well, hurry up—while I'm still young!" trying to make a joke, but his voice broke.

He heard another splash and he knew the teenager was underwater again, so he began to wave the light back and forth. To get the light even deeper, he used his boots to feel around until he felt a tree root and hooked an ankle around it. Slowly, he inched his body forward into the pool until his ear was suspended over the surface. The water felt cool against the side of his damaged face and he could taste sulfur and iron on his lips.

Arlis hadn't looked down into the water since he'd seen his own reflection, but he decided to look now. And what he saw caused him to almost drop the flashlight.

The water was black and clear. The pool was deep enough to show bands of light piercing the darkness forty feet below, where there were boulders and more bones. Moving from beneath one of the boulders, Arlis saw a head appear, then a thick reptilian body.

Frozen, that's how Arlis felt seeing something so strange, and he continued to watch as if hypnotized.

The animal turned and began swimming upward, and Arlis could now see two pale orange coals, which he knew were the eyes of the reptile. The eyes weren't bright because he wasn't pointing the light directly at the thing, but the animal was there, ascending toward the surface, swimming snakelike, the orange eyes sway-

RANDY WAYNE WHITE

ing back and forth, the snake's eyes getting bigger because the animal was gaining speed, coming fast toward the surface.

Arlis thought, *God Aw'mighty! I gotta move!* and he did. As he struggled to pull his body away from the hole, he focused the light directly downward and saw, full-on, a massive reptilian head swimming toward him that was unlike any snake he had ever seen. The damn thing looked like the head of a dinosaur, its grim mouth sealed tight against the force of water, its eyes two luminous balls that flared into explosions of gold as if detonated by the flashlight.

Arlis rolled away from the hole, yelling, "Sweet Jesus, where's the boy? Is he still underwater?" He had to feel around for the tire iron because he couldn't take his eyes off the pool, where the surface was bubbling like a cauldron now—the animal was releasing air as it swam, Arlis realized.

Behind him, Tomlinson was yelling, "What's wrong? What did you see?" as Arlis tried to get to his knees, but his boot was still wedged in the roots. He had the iron in his right fist, the flashlight in his left, and he finally had to put both on the ground to use his hands to pull his foot free of the boot.

He yelled again, "Where's the boy?" and was relieved to hear Will Chaser's voice answer, "How am I supposed to see the goddamn light if you're sitting on your ass tying your shoes? Let me know when you're ready, 'cause I'm not gonna waste my time—"

Arlis didn't hear the rest because the head of an animal bigger than any gator he had ever killed burst through the surface of the pool, throwing a wave of water that soaked him. The animal bobbed under briefly, then appeared to slow itself when it resurfaced, its head turning like a robot's as Arlis tried to scooch himself backward, but tree roots blocked his retreat.

When the animal saw Arlis, its mouth hinged open wide. A yard-long ribbon of tongue squirted toward him, flinging saliva as the animal made a raspy hiss that filled the room with a clouding stench of carrion. Its teeth were jagged rows of brown, its mouth frothy with something that looked as black as blood.

Will Chaser saw the reptile, too, because he was suddenly yelling, "Get out of here, Arlis! Run for it!" but Arlis couldn't move because of the roots and also because his body felt frozen, like in some slow-motion nightmare, as he watched the reptile's head lean toward him, its goat-bright pupils constricting even though the flashlight lay in the mud pointed toward the wall.

Arlis was trying to thread his body through the roots as he screamed at the thing, "Get out of here! Git!" which had worked temporarily with the three little lizards that had been tracking him, but this one didn't budge.

Arlis watched the reptile draw its head back like a cobra while its claws found the lip of the water hole. Slowly, the animal pulled its shoulders up onto the floor of the cave. Its yellow tongue slapped the air, feeling for heat, the tongue snapping closer and closer, until the pointed forks were near enough to flick at Arlis's bare ankle.

Arlis yanked one foot away, then another. He had managed to bull his upper body through the tangle of roots and now he had the fingers of his left hand in the muck, trying to drag himself out of the reptile's range, while he stabbed at the cave floor with the flashlight, trying to anchor the thing for leverage.

Will Chaser had stopped yelling. His voice became calm but intense as he called, "Arlis, listen to me. Use the light. Shine the light! Shine it right in the goddamn thing's eyes!"

Something about the steadiness of the kid's voice snapped Arlis out of his panic. Never once had he taken his eyes off the reptile. The animal was still pulling itself from the pool—the thing had to be *thirteen feet long*—its claws making a sound on limestone so metallic that the stink of sulfur and carrion filled the room like sparks.

Tomlinson was now saying, "Hey—what's happening? Let me see!" as Will ordered in a louder voice, "Arlis—the flashlight. Use it!"

Arlis lifted the flashlight from the mud and swung it toward the animal, the bright beam panning along the cave wall, first showing roots, then the petroglyphs. The stick figure with horns appeared buckskin yellow behind the black bulk of the reptile, which had drawn its head back again, snakelike, its dull eyes beginning to glow orange as the light panned closer.

Tomlinson's voice said, "Mother of God! What *is* that thing?" as Will continued calling directions, saying, "Right in its goddamn eyes! But turn it off first. Hear me? Arlis—kill the light first!"

Arlis's thumb explored the body of the flashlight, trying to find the switch. He understood what the kid was saying. Shock the animal with the light. It made so much sense that Arlis was surprised that he didn't think of it himself because it might have worked if he had done it in time but he didn't. He was just switching off the light when the animal struck, its head spearing forward so fast that the blur of movement continued to fill Arlis's eyes even as darkness swamped the cave. He felt a thudding impact on his right calf that was like getting hit with an ax.

"Shit!" he screamed. "It got me!"

The cave echoed as Tomlinson hollered, "Arlis, are you okay?" and Will was yelling, "Turn it on! Turn the goddamn light on, Arlis!"

Arlis's thumb punched the switch, and the flashlight drilled a silver beam through the blackness, a beam so intense that all he could see for an instant were the twin orange stars of the reptile's eyes, its face separated from his own only by the space of a few tree roots.

The animal hissed, flinging slobber, as it lurched backward. Arlis leaned toward the thing, jabbing at it with the flashlight, as he drew his legs under him and got to his knees. A chunk of flesh was gone from his calf, he noticed, the wound so fresh that it hadn't yet started to bleed.

For several seconds, the lizard held its ground, striking once at Arlis—or the flashlight—but it was disoriented by the light, or temporarily blinded, because its teeth came away with only a chunk of root, which it flung away with a slash of its head, before continuing to slide backward into the water.

There was a swirl, then bubbles. The reptile submerged.

In shock, Arlis sat back in the mud, breathing heavily, as he continued to aim the light at the pool. Behind him, he heard Tomlinson's voice, slow with wonder, say, "A fucking *dragon,* man. I knew it—I *knew* this day was coming."

Arlis muttered, *"What?"* as Tomlinson continued to talk, saying, "Those bastards have been tracking me for years."

TWENTY-FIVE

FOR FIFTEEN MINUTES, I SNAKED AND SHIM-
mied my way through the darkness of the karst tunnel
but gave up when I came to a dead-end chamber, where
I found Will's swim fins hanging motionless from the
rock ceiling.

Seeing the fins gave me an emotional boost at first.
The boy and Tomlinson had been here, I was on the
right path. But my optimism soon faded. There had
once been an exit vent—that was obvious—but the unstable limestone had shifted, or collapsed, and I couldn't
find the opening they had used.

I tried signaling—there was no response—so I
searched and probed and dug carefully with my hands,
but after another ten minutes I knew it was suicide to
continue looking. My air was low. I had already broken

the rule of thirds. And dying wasn't going to help my friends. I would have to surface and return later with help.

I was as disappointed as I was desperate, but I also took perverse pleasure in the knowledge that first I would have to deal with the two convicts. There was nothing to hold me back now. The sooner they were out of the way, the sooner I could call in a rescue team and press ahead with the search.

Perry was too scared to risk swimming back to shore alone, which meant he was still somewhere above me floating on the inner tube. I knew how I would work it. I would surprise him from behind and then go after King. Somewhere in their clothing, or hidden nearby, I would find our cell phones and the VHF. Get rid of the killers and help would soon be on its way.

I turned and worked my way out of the chamber, pushing my BC rig and the spare bottle ahead of me. It was slow going. I couldn't hurry. Even though I had not passed any intersecting vents, I maintained contact with the monofilament lay line that was attached to the Penn reel, wrapping it inch by inch over my right wrist as I retraced my path, until I sensed the opening ahead of me.

As I exited free into the blackness of the lake basin, I activated the night vision monocular and took my time searching the space above me and below me. As I searched, a Tomlinson superstition came into my mind. *Thoughts are energy. They sculpt reality from the noosphere. Focus on a dream—or a fear—and it will happen.*

What I didn't want to happen was to see the Komodo

monitor waiting for me as I exited. But the axiom forced me into its own unavoidable paradox. Attempting to blank the creature from my mind only made the image stronger. Call the monster and the monster will appear, the axiom suggested.

The monster did appear, although the coincidence proved nothing. Even so, the timing left me with the unsettling possibility that my fear had summoned a nightmare.

Before exiting the tunnel, I took my time searching even though I didn't have much air left. Finally, though, I abandoned the quasi-safety of the limestone hole and did a slow three-sixty as I swam upward. My fins worked slowly, propelling me at an angle that would allow me to approach Perry from behind and surprise him.

The man was still above me, curled up in the inner tube, as I had hoped. I could see the silhouettes of the tube and his swim fins, although his feet weren't in the water. That's how bright the winter sky appeared as seen through night vision. It was all backdropped by stars, plus a pulsing illumination that I knew was firelight. It told me that King was staying busy collecting wood even though he had promised Perry to stand guard by the generator in case Perry called for help.

That was good news for me, bad news for the two killers.

The water clarity was flawless, but the green eye of the monocular had its limits. I wanted to be certain that the Komodo monitor wasn't lurking somewhere out there in the darkness at the edge of visibility, and I had only two options. I could use the spotlight, which might alert Perry, or I could flip on the little infrared light that was built into the system.

I chose the invisible infrared . . . and that's when I saw the monitor. It was hanging on the surface, over deep water, at the northern rim of the lake, forty yards away. The thing's body drifted, motionless, pitched downward at an eighty-degree angle, its head above water, facing the inner tube. It suggested to me that the animal had recently surfaced for air and that it had spotted Perry.

Now the monitor was waiting . . . watching . . . observing the habits of its prey before leveling off for an attack. Perry, who had been terrified of the lake from the start and who was probably now numb with cold and fear, wouldn't see or hear the lizard approaching until it was too late.

To me, it was exquisite irony. A killer who had stabbed or shot children, who flaunted his manhood with a dragon tattoo, was about to be attacked and possibly killed by a species that had existed unchanged for fifty million years.

I stopped kicking toward the surface when I saw the lizard. I decided it was safer if I remained on the bottom, where I could watch events unfold, so I purged my BC and began to descend fins first, still focused on the creature.

Maybe it heard the bubbles from my exhaust valve—that was the first explanation that came to mind, anyway—because the thing pivoted instantly and thrust its head beneath the surface and began searching the bottom.

I remained motionless as I descended, watching the distant reflection of the monitor's eyes. Most reptiles don't have great eyesight, particularly at night. They can detect movement, but inanimate objects—even if warm-blooded—are invisible to them, which is why snakes and lizards rely on their tongues when hunting.

I inhaled enough air to stop my descent, then held my breath. I could see the monitor's tongue working, stabbing the water for information. A popular rural legend is that snakes and alligators can't attack underwater, but it's a myth. Reptiles have a palatal valve that prevents water from breaching their throats when they open their mouths underwater. They can attack, they can bite, they can feed.

Could the monitor taste my heat beneath the surface? I didn't know.

The animal's head panned briefly, but then suddenly speared deeper in my direction. Short paws sculled the water as it straightened itself and then began to sink. I watched its putty-colored eyes appear to brighten as they focused. And then its body pivoted parallel to the bottom. Until then, it had more closely resembled a floating tree trunk, but now it came alive.

Not once had the monitor taken its eyes off me.

It began swimming in my direction, slowly at first, undulating like a dinosaur-sized snake, and that's when I knew for certain—motionless or not, it could see me.

I turned and kicked hard toward the bottom. Would the monitor pursue? I risked a quick glance over my shoulder and confirmed that the lizard was coming fast now, closing the distance at a terrifying rate.

I had been carrying the extra air bottle and the fishing reel. I dropped both and then struggled to unclip the spotlight from a D ring on my vest as I swam toward the ivory tusk ten feet below. It marked the opening into the karst vent—my only hope of escaping the creature. It wouldn't provide me much protection, though, and I couldn't hide there for long because I was almost out of air.

Kicking as hard as I could, I flew past the tusk and threw one hand out in time to snag the lip of the tunnel from above. My momentum swung me around as I struggled with the spotlight. As I turned, I saw through the green lens that the animal was only twenty yards away. Its head was streamlined, extended flat, as it knifed through the water, coming at me with the weight and speed of a torpedo.

My fins were too wide to slip cleanly into the vent. With my left hand, I yanked off one, then the other, as I finally freed the spotlight. I jammed my feet into the hole and used the light to pole myself backward until my body was encased by limestone like some oversized lobster hiding from an attacker. Then I waited . . . waited in a green and eerie darkness . . . with the spotlight in my right hand ready to fend off the monitor if it tried to follow me into the cave.

I didn't have to wait long. My clumsy entrance had stirred up a cloud of silt and, seconds later, the monitor's head appeared as a gray, elongated shape at the tunnel's entrance, only a few feet from my face mask. I heard its claws scrabbling for purchase on the rocks, and then it pushed its head deeper into the hole. Just as I was about to turn on the spotlight, though, it suddenly retreated. The bulk of its body covered the entrance for a few moments and then it disappeared.

I lay motionless on my belly, trying to slow my breathing. Several seconds later, the monitor was back again, the silhouette of its head a sullen black wedge at the edge of visibility. It seemed to be waiting for me to come out.

The animal appeared to be in no hurry now. It knew where I was, that was obvious. But how? The spotlight was off, so there was no way for it to see me. A reptile's eyesight isn't good at night, even on land. How had the thing tracked me so exactingly underwater? I wondered if it had somehow followed my bubble trail, but rejected the possibility. If it was tracking my bubbles, the animal would now be searching around on the surface. It made no sense.

It was when I reached to readjust the monocular's focus that I finally made the connection. The infrared light was still on. It gave me pause and I began to search for linkage. Had I been using infrared when the animal buzzed me earlier?

I couldn't remember for certain . . . But now I *did* recall that some animals can see infrared light. Infrared light is heat. It can be read through a variety of sensory organs. Bees can see infrared, some fish can process both infrared and ultraviolet light—and certain reptiles not only see infrared, they can sense it through their tongues, as well.

Immediately, I switched off the infrared. Fearing that the monocular was producing some kind of electronic signature, I switched it off, too, then lay there in a blackness so absolute that ocular connectors to my brain created sparks and swirls behind my eyes that were uncomfortably bright. I blinked, trying to mitigate the reaction, as I calculated the chances that shutting down the night vision system actually would make a difference.

It did make a difference—but the monitor didn't respond as I had hoped. Within seconds of switching off the infrared, I heard a frenzied digging—claws on limestone—and then I heard the clatter of falling rocks only a few feet from my face mask. Maybe the animal feared it had lost me because it was now clawing its way into the hole.

I retreated a few feet deeper, throwing my left hand over my head for protection from rocks as I extended my right arm so I could use the spotlight as a shield. The spotlight was my only weapon now and I knew I had to time it right. Hit the switch too soon and the monitor's eyes would have time to adjust. If I waited, though, waited until the animal was only a few feet away, its dilated pupils would allow a thousand lumens of blinding light to pierce its optic nerve. If I blinded the thing, maybe it would retreat to the surface and decide that Perry was an easier target.

The clawing sounds grew louder and more frenzied, and I realized that the vent wasn't wide enough for the monitor to wedge its body through. Like a hyena in pursuit of a rodent, it was trying to dig me out of my hole. I decided to risk activating my night vision—but not the infrared. I was now convinced infrared was an invitation to be attacked.

When the monocular was on, I saw the monitor's head through a veil of silt. Its viper tongue probed the darkness, flicking at limestone only inches from my right hand, as its front claws continued to tractor its body closer.

Startled that the animal was only a yard away, I lurched backward, which caused it to lift its head, alerted by my sudden movement. Through a green haze, I could see the monitor's opaque eyes—they were the color of lead, like two indifferent ball bearings—and I could also see that its vertical pupils were dilated wide in the darkness as it attempted to decipher details.

I jabbed the spotlight forward, closed my eyes and hit the switch. The explosion of light was so bright that it pierced my own eyelids. I felt a suctioning void of water pressure as the monitor lunged backward, and then rocks and sand began to rain down on me as it bucked its body free of the hole.

I waited for several seconds, eyes closed, waving the spotlight like a flamethrower. Carefully, then, I switch off my night vision and opened my eyes.

Even in the searing brightness of the light, all I could see was silt. Visibility might have been better had I switched off the spotlight, but I wasn't going to risk that. Instead, I allowed several seconds to pass and then crawled to the opening, thrusting the spotlight ahead of me like a spear.

At the mouth of the tunnel, I stopped. I found my fins and put them on as I swiveled my head, expecting the monitor to attack at any moment. Visibility in the lake basin was fair, and I used the light to search the area as far away as the drop-off. Just because I couldn't see the monitor, though, didn't mean that it had abandoned its pursuit.

I switched off the spotlight and activated my night vision. Instantly, visibility improved. Perry was still above me on the inner tube less than thirty feet away. It seemed incredible that he was unaware of what had just taken place, but water is the relentless keeper of its own secrets.

I continued to search, rechecking the lip of the drop-off, then scanning the lake's surface. Stars were bright. I could still see the bouncing lucency of the beach fire. If the monitor hadn't surfaced, it was somewhere nearby—perhaps behind me, or below me in deeper water, waiting for me, its prey, to reappear.

I checked the orange numerals of my watch. It was 8:07 p.m. I had been underwater for forty-three minutes and my tank was nearly empty. Alligators can stay under for up to two hours and perhaps the same was true of monitor lizards. I couldn't sit there and wait for the thing to surface. I had only a few minutes of air left, so I had to do something and I had to do it fast.

Die on the bottom of an ancient lake or risk dying on the surface in the jaws of a prehistoric lizard?

I forced myself to settle back against the rocks and think about it. There had to be a better option.

TWENTY-SIX

IT WAS 7:58 P.M., ACCORDING TO TOMLINSON'S new watch, when he and Will and Arlis stopped at the rim of the cypress head, still hidden by trees but close enough to the lake to see King. They watched the man toss a limb onto the fire and then yell toward the water, "Quit your complaining! You stay right there until your new boyfriend surfaces. This was all your idea, so just shut up and do what you're told."

The little Honda generator was running, but not loud, and from the darkness they heard a man reply, "Shit, he's been down there for almost an hour! I'm damn near frozen to death, King! *King*? Goddamn it, pull me in, dude—I'm serious!"

The men continued bickering as Arlis whispered,

"Those are the two killers—sounds like I was wrong about those gunshots. They haven't killed Doc yet. By God, that's good news!"

Will spoke, saying, "Yeah, but they will—we've got to do something," his voice soft compared to the sapwood fire crackling and the cicada roar that echoed through the darkness of cypress trees and starlight. Then he said, "You think you'll be okay if we sit you down against a tree? How's your leg?"

Arlis's leg had been bleeding since he was bitten—not fast but steady—even though Tomlinson had done something smart right away, which might have saved the man's life. He had stripped off his wet suit and cut off one of the sleeves. Then he'd helped Arlis slip his foot through the neoprene tube and slide it tight over his calf, which had slowed the bleeding. But the bleeding wouldn't stop.

When Tomlinson guessed it was because there was something in the reptile's saliva that prevented coagulation, Arlis had said, "Maybe that's what's causing me to feel so sick, too. A by God giant lizard! A Florida boy like me, I would've never guessed this would happen in a million years."

"Don't blame yourself," Tomlinson had replied. "Blame me. I've been dodging dragons for years—those *bastards*. You just happened to get in the way."

That had struck Will as funny and he'd laughed for the first time since they'd arrived at the lake. And his opinion of Tomlinson climbed another notch. The man had an easy, gentle way of dealing with people, always making himself the butt of his own jokes, pretending to be weirder than he really was—something Will understood but, he guessed, not many other people did.

Arlis was badly hurt—not just from the lizard—and he was sick, but that didn't cause the old fisherman to be any less stubborn or full of fight. He had used the tire iron to chop away at the roots, making the hole wider, until he got too dizzy and then finally sat down in the mud and the stink of old bones. It had taken Will and Tomlinson twenty minutes to finish the job.

When Will had finally muscled himself through the hole and was safely above water for the first time in hours, Tomlinson had shouted, "We did it!" sounding surprised and happy even though they were all thinking the same thing: *Hurry up and get out of there before that damn giant reptile returns.*

Every step of the way, their mood improved, until they were safely down the mound, and Arlis decided it was time to tell them about the killers and about the gunshots that might have killed Doc Ford. Tomlinson and Will had Arlis slung between them, acting as crutches, so the man could move along on his one good leg, but they stopped when they heard that, and Tomlinson said to Will, "That can't be. I would know it if Doc was dead. I think Arlis is wrong."

Whispering, Arlis had replied, "How would you know? You've been underwater the whole time."

"It's a feeling I've got," Tomlinson said. "We've got to find him."

"By God, I hope you're right. But I'm not wrong about those killers. Unless they skedaddled while we were down in that snake pit, they're still at the lake. I would have seen truck lights. Or maybe you've got a feeling about that, too?"

Lowering his voice, Tomlinson asked, "The lake's just through those trees, right? I'm all turned around. It seemed like we came a hell of a lot farther than we did."

"It's close," Arlis said. "Why do you think I keep telling you to keep your voices down? Those fools got my Winchester and a little bitty pistol and they'd just as soon shoot us as look at us. So this is where we part ways. You and the boy head west, cut straight through the swamp to the road. You're a sailor, you've spent your life following stars, so I reckon you can find your way out. I'm gonna rest here for a few minutes, then I'm going back for Doc. I just wish I didn't feel so sick and dopey. I think that lizard by God poisoned me. It's like there's acid in my veins."

Will had felt free and full of energy until then, happy to be alive. It was good to be outside, with plenty of air to breathe, walking on his own two feet instead of treading water. But the quality of the old man's voice was upsetting. Arlis's whole body was shaking and his skin felt fragile like wet paper. He was talking brave, but his voice couldn't hide how sick he felt. Arlis was scared and weak, and sometimes his voice cracked, like he might be close to collapsing.

Will had whispered to Tomlinson, "We're not going to let Captain Futch go after those sons of bitches by himself. You go on and head to the road if you want. I'm staying here."

Tomlinson had spent enough time with Ford to recognize rage in a certain type of man's voice—the words assumed a cold, flat rhythm as if they were speaking through the barrel of a gun focused on their target. Will and Ford were the same in many ways—which was probably why they didn't like each other—and he knew now that it was dangerous to let the boy go anywhere near the men who had beaten Arlis and who now threatened Ford. The fact was, though, they needed to get to their cell phones or the truck. Arlis wouldn't last another hour without medical attention.

Tomlinson said, "Maybe if I talk to them, I can win them over."

That struck Will as a contemptible thing to suggest—make peace with men who had beaten a friend so badly—but Arlis settled it, saying, "If you try and talk to them, you'll kill us all. So we're sticking together, if that's what you're thinking. Tomlinson? You stay out of sight when we get there and don't open your mouth."

The lake was close, but it still took them ten minutes to slog their way to the grove of cypress trees. They moved carefully, resting every few yards, but picked up the pace when they heard a rustling noise behind them. Arlis guessed they were being tracked by three monitor lizards and then proved it with a quick blast of his flashlight that showed pairs of orange eyes watching them from the bushes.

Maybe trying to be funny—or maybe not—Tomlinson said, "Jesus Christ, throw a tent over this place and you'd have a circus. Those things look like pit bulls with scales."

"And they're on the hunt, too," Arlis told him. "I don't think they'll risk jumping the three of us. But, God Aw'mighty, I wouldn't want to be a man out here alone. Will?" He looked at the boy. "You got your knife handy, right?"

The teenager said, "Let's keep moving. I think someone built a fire over there. See the light in the trees?"

When they were close enough to see King and hear him arguing with his partner—"Perry," Arlis said the man's name was—Will made his suggestion about letting Arlis rest with his back to a tree while he moved closer to get a better look. But Arlis didn't like the idea, and Tomlinson wouldn't allow it.

"With those dragons on our tail? We're not splitting up, man." Then to Arlis he whispered, "Any idea where they put our cell phones? That's what we need. A phone would be better than the keys to the truck." As he spoke, Tomlinson concentrated on Will, aware of what was in Will's mind, seeing the way Will's eyes were focused, watching the way Will held the knife low, the blade pointed at King, who was throwing another limb on the fire.

Will was peripherally aware of how closely Tomlinson was observing him, which was irritating because it was like static the way it interrupted his concentration. Will was gauging the distance to the generator, where he could see the Winchester rifle braced at an angle, as Arlis whispered to Tomlinson, "Just before I took off, I heard what might have been a phone, only it sounded like hippie music to me. See that backpack next to the generator? It came from there."

The generator was closer to the cypress grove than the truck; and the man, King, was farther down the shoreline, where they could see him plainly in the firelight.

Will was on his knees now and beginning to crawl toward the generator only twenty yards away, feeling Tomlinson's eyes on him as Tomlinson told Arlis, "Jimi Hendrix. 'Purple Haze,' man. That was my phone." And then Tomlinson said, "Will . . . Will, wait!"

Will didn't look back until Tomlinson raised his voice from a whisper to call, "Will! See the light coming from the lake? That's Doc's spotlight from underwater. He must be surfacing."

Will took a deep breath, feeling a cold reddish odor move through his brain, as he heard Tomlinson add, "Don't do anything stupid. *Please*."

What was stupid was to talk so loud that close to the water because it stopped King in his tracks. Will dropped to his belly as King spun toward the sound of Tomlinson's voice and then began walking toward them. He was tall and skinny-looking—a coyote kind of skinny—and he was holding something in his right hand as he approached.

It was the little pistol Arlis had mentioned.

A moment later, King aimed a flashlight at them, and Will could feel the brightness of the light through his skull as he lay facedown and immobile. He opened one eye long enough to see that the man was pointing the pistol at him, too.

Will thought, *He's getting ready to pull the trigger.*

TWENTY-SEVEN

I SWUNG THE SPOTLIGHT FROM THE DROP-OFF to the surface several times, not worried about alerting Perry now. In fact, I wanted him to see it. He had been floating up there in the dark for forty minutes, scared and cold, and like a moth he would be attracted to light. The Komodo monitor hadn't reappeared, but I knew it was somewhere out there in the shadows—just as I also knew that I had only a couple of minutes of air left.

I had decided there were only two workable options: I could sprint for the surface and then try to beat the animal to shore or I could attempt a diversion of some sort and buy myself a little extra time. I chose the second option. I'm a strong swimmer, but even without the drag created by my BC and tank it was unlikely I could outswim a monitor.

I had to jettison my gear. As I stripped off my vest, I reviewed the details of a finesse that I hoped was worth a try. What did I have to lose?

From the pocket of my BC, I took a length of nylon cord that was too long, so I had to double it to make it work. I tied one end to the handle of the spotlight and the other end to my tank harness. Next, I removed enough weight from the vest to hold me fast on the bottom for as long as I needed to stay there. Every few seconds, I interrupted my work to scan the area with the light. Maybe because I was exhausted, or maybe because I was resolute, my hands were as steady as the steady thudding of my own heartbeat. If the monitor caught me before I got to shore, so be it. There was nothing more I could do. Arlis was free at least. The man was hurt, but he was also stubborn, and I knew he would somehow manage to return with help.

When I was ready, I lifted my BC and tank harness and held them out in front of me like a shield, tethered to the rig only by my breathing hose. Using the spotlight, I did one last slow circle, hoping I would see the monitor . . . and I did. It was at the edge of the drop-off, peering over the limestone rim, watching me.

I shined the light directly into the monitor's eyes, but it didn't spook this time. It stared back at me with two blazing orange mirrors that soon began to undulate, cobralike, so I knew the animal was swimming toward me.

It approached slowly at first as if hypnotized by the beam, but then its eyes grew incrementally larger as it gained speed. I held my ground, watching as the monitor closed the distance, coming fast now, thrusting hard with its prehistoric tail, creating a trail of silt explosions as it sought maximum speed, vectoring in for the kill.

I was taking deep breaths, hyperventilating to reduce carbon dioxide in my bloodstream, trying to overoxygenate my lungs for what I hoped happened next. I was working the spotlight with my right hand and I had the vest's emergency inflation cord in my left. Pull the cord and CO_2 cartridges would inflate the BC like a balloon.

I waited for another long second—the monitor was less than fifteen yards from impact, its bulk casting a shadow on the sand the size of a Cessna, its weight alone enough to snap my spine if it hit me.

I closed my eyes and forced myself to wait another second. I took a last deep breath. Simultaneously, then, I spit the regulator from my mouth and ripped the emergency cord downward. There was an explosive hiss that snatched the spotlight and the vest from my hands.

When I felt the rig rocket skyward, I fell back among the rocks, knees against my chest, lead weights on my lap, and I held my breath. I didn't move. I couldn't even allow myself to brace for a collision that I knew would preface my last cognitive thoughts.

There was a rhythmic, crackling silence that I recognized as the flex of muscle fiber as the animal closed on me. My eyes opened. The world was all blackness and shadow, yet I still perceived a deeper, streaming darkness that was the monitor lizard. It soared past me, rocking my body with a shock wave of displaced water. I didn't allow my head to move, but my eyes followed the shadow upward as it arched toward the surface, chasing the spotlight, which was now spinning wildly beneath the vest, casting a bizarre propeller blur of white that pierced the darkness like random lightning.

I waited and watched. Methodically, I removed the lead weights from my lap and then activated the night vision monocular, but not the infrared because *using the infrared was to invite death*. On the surface, I could see a collective, frenzied thrashing that was suggestive of a shark feeding. I didn't pause to observe. I pushed away from the rocks and swam close to the bottom, following the contour of sand and rock for more than a minute, until I couldn't hold my breath any longer, and then I surfaced—less than thirty yards from shore, I guessed.

Sound was suddenly added to the turmoil I had witnessed underwater. I could hear a wild splashing and Perry's voice screaming, "King! Pull me in! My God . . . King! There's something out here. Please! *King!*"

I didn't look back. I put my head down and sprinted for shore, taking long, strong strokes and kicking hard with my fins. I could either deal with King on land or risk the monitor coming after me when it was done with Perry.

It wasn't a difficult choice to make.

TWENTY-EIGHT

WHEN KING HEARD A VOICE WHISPERING IN
the shadows of the cypress grove, he figured it was the old
man. Gramps had been out there wandering around in
the darkness of the swamp, probably lost and scared shitless, and now here he was back again ready to beg for
forgiveness. The old fool would expect a share of the gold,
too, no doubt—and after he and Perry had done most of
the work!

The greedy old ass-wipe.

Thinking that caused King to frown, as he pulled the
little automatic from his pocket and started toward the
tree line that lay beyond the truck and the generator and
outside the yellow perimeter of the fire he had been
tending. He moved slowly because he didn't like the

idea of straying too far from the fire. He had been piling on the wood, building the thing higher and higher, because who knew what kind of animals were roaming around out there in the blackness of stars and wind and trees.

After what they'd heard—that weird hissing noise—and the size of the thing he'd seen slide into the lake? Man, he couldn't wait to get back to a decent-sized city.

What King hoped to see before he walked much farther was the old man stumbling out of the shadows too worn out and hurt to be much trouble now. When that happened, he would . . . do what?

King had to think about it. He felt the weight of the pistol in his hand. The pistol was freshly loaded—five rounds in the clip and one in the chamber—and he liked the feel of it, hard and dense in his fingers, and he enjoyed the power it gave him, remembering the way that smart-ass Ford had almost crapped his pants when King had fired a few rounds—three at least—to scare him.

The first time was the best. Just a few inches to the right and the bullet would have gone into Ford's thigh or pelvis instead of the fender of the pickup truck. King hadn't intended to come so close—cheap little automatics weren't accurate—but that's the way it had happened. Only a few inches, but what a difference it would have made, which caused King to wonder how that would feel actually shooting a man.

It would've made a hell of a big difference, King thought. Especially a superior-acting dude who reminded him of that ass-wipe science teacher who'd flunked him, which was why he'd had to take the fucking eighth grade all over again.

Great, King decided, that's how it would feel to shoot Ford. Maybe it would feel just as good to shoot the mouthy old man. Later, if he had to, he could blame it all on Perry, the born killer.

Why not?

Hanging another murder on Perry would be easy enough if the cops near Orlando had done their work and collected DNA from the body of that girl Perry had stabbed to death after they'd both had some fun with her.

King had played around with the girl, but that's all. It was Perry who had actually *used* her while killing her. Judging from the sounds King heard, Perry probably left enough evidence behind to hang himself.

Perry . . . Perry was a problem. King had been thinking about it as he fed the fire. The man had been dangerous from the start, but now he was crazy, too—*mean* crazy, with an attitude—so maybe it made sense to shoot the old man to sort of get used to what it was like killing a person. Practice made perfect, after all. The part King couldn't figure out, though, was how could he blame Perry for seven murders if the cops found Perry dead with a bullet in him?

The key to it all, of course, was to end up in Mexico with enough money not to get caught.

As King neared the pickup truck, he stopped and took a flashlight from his pocket—the bright little light he had stolen from Ford's bag. He touched the switch, pointed the beam at the base of the tree line and began panning slowly, seeing a miniature forest of ferns and those weird-looking cypress roots poking out of the ground . . . And then he saw something that made no sense and he took a couple of steps closer. Lying in weeds near a cypress tree was what looked sort of like the body of a man lying flat, facedown—a young man, maybe, but not the old man—which surprised King and caused him to raise the pistol fast, ready to fire.

That's when he heard a voice behind him screaming, "King! Help me! *Kinnnggggggg!*"

King spun toward the lake. It had to be Perry, but it didn't sound like his voice because the screaming was so wild and shrill, and now King could hear frenzied splashing, too.

He took another quick look at the tree line, where the man's body lay—if it was a body—immobile in the bright beam of the flashlight. It had to be the old man, he decided. Yeah, that's who it had to be—Gramps . . . probably almost dead after having groaned for help, which would have explained the whispering he had heard.

King thought, *Good!* as he turned and began running toward the lake. The frantic splashing was louder, and now Perry was screaming, "There's something after me! King! Pull me in . . . *King?* For God's sake, help me!"

King was wondering if maybe Ford was trying to drown the whacko son of a bitch, which caused him to relax a little, and he felt even better.

Now King was thinking, *I hope he does it.*

King had the flashlight on when he got to the shoreline, but the beach fire was bright enough that it cast a
flickering, shadowed glow midway across the lake, where
he could see the inner tube looking silver in the misty
light. The tube was rolling, as if in heavy surf, even
though the lake was black and still beneath the stars. But
it wasn't until King froze the scene with his flashlight
that he saw what was happening.

It was such a bizarre mix of images that it took a
moment for King to separate them in his brain. Perry
was on his knees atop the coil of hose, leaning his chest
over the inner tube and paddling wildly with his hands,
as he continued to scream for help. Floating on the
other side of the inner tube was what looked like a log
floating high in the water. The log was as long as a tree,
but it had a tail that was fanning the water into a froth,
which caused the log to hammer against the inner tube
over and over as Perry paddled, trying to get back to
shore.

At first, King thought that an alligator, maybe, was
trying to crawl up onto the log, but then as he moved
the light he realized that he was wrong. It wasn't a log
he was seeing and it wasn't an alligator. It was a huge
reptile of some type, with a snake-shaped head and
glowing orange eyes. The thing resembled the monitor
lizards he'd seen earlier, only this animal was about
twenty times bigger.

King thought, *Jesus Christ, that's the thing I saw crawl into the lake,* and he began to back away, still watching, because he couldn't take his eyes off what was happening now.

He watched the creature's head lift high above the water as its paws tried to find traction on the inner tube, but the tube squirted away when it tried to lift itself close enough to get to Perry. It swam after the inner tube, its tail stirring a smooth wake, and then the same thing happened. This time, Perry stopped clawing at the water long enough to squint into the beam of the flashlight and holler, "King, shoot the fucking thing, goddamn it! *Shoot!*"

King had the pistol in his hand, but now he slipped it into his pocket as he watched the creature pursue the inner tube. It reminded him of something he'd seen at a beach on Lake Michigan, a Labrador retriever swimming after a beach ball that was too big to get into its mouth.

King cupped one hand to his lips and yelled, "Get out and swim for it!" hoping his partner would because that would mean the end of him and the end of one more pain-in-the-ass problem.

As he watched, King began to relax again, and he realized that he was smiling. It was sort of fun, as long as that big slimy bastard didn't come after him, and it only got better when the animal tried something different, this time swimming so fast that its body skated halfway up onto the inner tube, where King could see Perry crouched low, with his hands up, palms out, eyes white and wide in the beam of the flashlight, as he moaned, "Help me, King . . . *please*."

The creature lifted its head high and paused for a moment, as if surprised that Perry's body was right there beneath its claws, and then the glowing eyes blurred as it struck at Perry's leg three times, so fast that King began walking backward again, as he whispered, "Jesus Christ Aw'mighty."

Perry was sobbing now, calling, "It bit me! Pull me in, King! The fuckin' thing just bit me!"

King thought he should say something—give Perry a taste of his own medicine, maybe, by yelling, *Whatever*—but he didn't because he realized that he'd been so focused on Perry, he hadn't noticed something important happening nearby.

There was a man in the water not far from where the inner tube had been anchored. He was swimming fast in the darkness, using long, clean strokes, headed for the shoreline near the pickup truck.

It was Ford. The ass-wipe wasn't wearing all his heavy scuba gear, either, which suggested that he was trying to sneak off on his own—probably carrying a bunch more gold coins somewhere on him, too.

King pulled the pistol from his pocket and started running. He didn't like Ford—hell, he despised the man—but Perry had been right when he'd said there was something quiet and scary about the professor-looking dude. King didn't want to have to face the man, not just the two of them, alone on dry land.

As King sprinted along the shore, there was something else he realized, judging from the direction Ford was headed. He had to beat Ford to the generator, where his idiot partner, Perry, had left the Winchester unattended.

TWENTY-NINE

WHEN I REACHED SHALLOW WATER, I ROLLED onto my back and continued kicking fast over the bottom toward shore, wanting to avoid the slippery limestone and muck beneath me. Through the night vision, I could see what was happening forty yards away.

The Komodo monitor was trying to climb onto the inner tube and get to Perry, who hadn't stopped screaming for help since I'd surfaced. Underwater, the lizard had appeared big. On the surface, though, with its tail slashing and the breadth of its back visible in the glow of the beach fire, it was massive.

Perry was still alive. I was surprised. But Komodos feed differently than most animals, as I knew, striking and then waiting for their venom to do its work.

I could also see my BC vest, spotlight attached, drifting shoreward in the wake of all that splashing, and I could see King, too, sprinting toward me, the pistol in one hand, my flashlight in the other. The angle wasn't good, and I knew it was going to be close. I was thinking about changing directions and swimming to the other side of the lake, but I remembered that King had left the Winchester leaning against the generator out in plain sight.

Was it still there? I swung my head to look and there it was, standing lean and western-looking against the Honda generator, with two rounds left in the chamber. And the pickup truck was parked nearby.

I was closer to the rifle than King was, but I was at least thirty yards away. And I was still in the water. I abandoned the idea of changing directions and decided to risk a footrace. Three times, King had fired the little pistol at me. Cheap pocket guns are notoriously inaccurate, and he had only three rounds left—unless the man had been smart enough to reload, which was unlikely.

King was sloppy. If I could get to my feet before he was close enough to open fire or if he started shooting too soon, his sloppiness would get him killed.

When my butt banged bottom, I swung my legs under me and yanked off my fins, hearing King yell, "Get your hands up, Jock-o! Don't move a goddamn muscle!"

I glanced at him as I stood, feeling moss-coated rocks beneath my feet, and I yelled in reply, "Help your partner. Fire a few rounds, maybe you'll scare off the lizard."

It was possible King heard me, but maybe he didn't because Perry was shrieking for help now, his words interrupted only by his own wild sobbing and the depth-charge implosions of the monitor's tail hitting water. I guessed that the monitor had begun to feed.

"Stay right where you are! I don't want to shoot you but I will, goddamn it!"

It was the first time King had said he *didn't* want to shoot me, which told me the opposite was true—this time, he meant to do it. I pulled my face mask down around my neck before throwing my hands up because now he was blinding me with the flashlight. King mistook the gesture for surrender and he immediately slowed to a walk. When he did, I dropped my hands and took off running toward the Winchester, kicking water, knees high, but it was tough to keep my balance because of the moss.

WHAP!

King fired. The slug threw a geyser up a few feet in front of me, where the water was only ankle-deep, but I kept running, trying to juke a zigzag pattern, which would have been a smart tactical move on land but not in the shallows of a lake, all limestone and marl. Only a couple of yards from shore, my ankle snagged the lip of a rock and I stumbled, almost regained my footing, but then hit a slippery patch, and I crashed, shoulder first, into the water, hitting hard.

When I raised my head, I heard King fire again—*WHAP!* The slug skipped off the water so close to my face that I wondered for an instant if I'd been hit, and I knew that King was lying again when he yelled, "That's the last time I fire a warning shot, Jock-o! Stay right where you are, goddamn it!"

It wasn't a warning shot. The man wanted to kill me, but he had missed. And now he had only one round left—unless I was wrong about him reloading.

By the time I got to my feet and had stumbled another few yards, King was on me. He stood staring at me, the pistol aimed at my chest, too close to miss this time. He was breathing heavily, but he was grinning.

He said, "I thought we were partners, but now I get the feeling you're trying to avoid me. We still got ourselves some trust issues, don't we, Jock-o?"

He spoke in a normal voice that sounded inexplicably loud until I realized that, behind me, the lake had gone silent. I glanced over my shoulder. The inner tube was there, drifting shoreward, beneath a massive swirl that was animated by stars. There was no sign of Perry, so I knew that the lizard had taken him under.

I said, "Perry would agree about the trust issues."

Glancing at the lake, King said, "Perry's an idiot. Or . . . he *was* an idiot," trying to sound tough, but he was shocked enough by what had just happened to add in a voice that suggested awe, "Jesus Christ, you ever seen anything like that in your life? Perry was right there, but now he's fucking *gone*, man. What the hell is that thing? It's not an alligator. What is it?"

I said, "It could have been you instead of Perry."

"No way, Jock-o. Some people are born to be snack food, but I'm not one of 'em. Perry lived what we'd call an unhealthy lifestyle. Maybe it made him tasty. But if that slimy son of a bitch had messed with me? We'd be roasting the damn thing's tail over that fire right now."

I didn't trust myself to respond.

King motioned with the gun, his eyes nervous as they swung from me to the inner tube. "Move your ass out of there. Lock your hands behind your head and walk toward the fire. There's something I'm just dying to see."

I did it as I calculated my next move, not listening to King, who continued talking to mitigate his nervousness, telling me, "I tried to help ol' Per, I really did. But there's only so much a man can do. He's a murderer, you know. A couple days ago, Perry got drunked up and murdered five people. I tried to stop him because a couple were just kids—he stabbed them to death and then the asshole *bragged* about it. And I'm pretty sure he raped the girl. Or maybe you already figured that out, you being such a genius."

King added the last part so bitterly that I believed he might shoot me in the back, so I said quickly, "I loaded two sacks with coins when I was down there. I found a couple of gold bars, too. I left them in the shallows, though, until we had a chance to discuss it. Just because Perry's dead—or dying—that doesn't mean our deal's off."

"Sure you did . . . sure," King said, letting me talk. I got the impression that, if it wasn't for the monitor lizard, he would have shot me where I stood, still ankle-deep in water, but he didn't want to risk searching my body until he was a safe distance from the lake.

Maybe I was right because when we were close enough to feel the fire's heat, King said, "Okay. Take off that wet suit. Let's see what you really found." As he spoke, he used the flashlight to search along the base of the cypress grove as if expecting to see something, but then he stuffed the light in his pocket and gave me his full attention. "Don't be shy," he added. "There's no one around but just us guys."

The coins were in a mesh pocket, near my left arm-pit, inside the neoprene. He would have to turn the wet suit inside out to find them, which might give me the opening I needed, but I didn't want to appear too eager.

I said, "There's no need to search me, I'll tell you right now what I've got. I've got about a dozen coins on me, but there are three, maybe four, hundred more lying out there in bags. Why not do something smart for once in your life, King? Stop acting like a hard-ass. All we have to do is wait for that monitor lizard to clear out. You take your bag of coins, take the truck, too. You'll leave here a rich man."

"A monitor lizard," he said. "That's what that thing is? Like those three little bastards we saw earlier. Only the giant economy-sized version."

"When the cops show up," I said, "I'll blame everything on Perry. Think about it. Why would I want the cops to find you? If they find you, they'll find out what I took out of that lake."

King tilted his head back to smile. "Now, isn't that sweet of you, making me such a fair offer." His smile vanished as he pointed the pistol at me. "I'm not going to say it again. Strip off that goddamn wet suit!"

I reached behind my back to find the zipper lanyard as King continued walking, making a slow circle, until he was on the other side of the fire, safely away from the water's edge. The positioning provided me with a couple of options—neither of them good—but I would have to choose one soon because the man had made up his mind now. That was apparent. He was going to shoot me. Even with the prescription face mask hanging around my neck, I could read King's intent in his twitching mannerisms and his nervous smile as he watched me peel the wet suit down around my ankles.

When I stepped free of the thing, he clicked his tongue and said, "My, my, my . . . Why, look at you, Jock-a-mo! You'd have been real popular back in the joint. I bet you're a regular lady-killer."

I said, "That's something else we don't have in common. Do you want to search this thing or not? Here it is."

King motioned with the gun. "Kick it over here. I want that fancy night vision thing, too. Take it off."

I had been hoping he'd give me a reason to get a hand on my face mask. It was the size and shape of a brick, and the monocular added enough weight to cause serious damage if I got a chance to rifle the thing at his face. As I was removing the mask, though, King told me, "Hold it. Don't move," his voice sounding strange enough to cause me to stop what I was doing.

He was looking toward the lake. When I turned, I understood.

In the oscillating light of the fire, I could see the Komodo monitor. It was gliding along the rim of the lake, tail ruddering smoothly, as it swam toward the marshy juncture where pastureland became swamp. Perry was in the lizard's jaws. His body was hanging limp, his eyes open wide and dead, staring up at the stars.

Behind me I heard King whisper, "Look at the size of that goddamn thing," and then I heard *WHAP!*

It took a microsecond for me to understand that King had just fired at the lizard—fired his last round. I was so shocked that I dropped low even as I saw the slug punch a silver furrow in the water that missed the monitor by yards. How the lizard reacted, I didn't know or care. I was already turning toward King, my arm drawn back, and I threw the mask so hard that he didn't have time to flinch before it glanced off his forehead.

He stumbled backward and fired off another round as I charged toward him, which was even more unexpected because the pistol should have been empty, and I thought, *Wrong again, Ford*. He had reloaded.

But it was too late to stop what was happening. I dodged past the fire as King got to one knee, his hand coming up fast, aiming the pistol at my chest, his mouth contorted as if to say something, but then I went airborne, diving toward him, and he fired again. The impact of the bullet that might have hit me, and the impact of me crashing into King were too closely spaced to know if I had been shot, but my hands and brain were still working as I tumbled clear of the gun, then used an elbow to knock the man's jaw crooked and send him sprawling on his back.

I rolled to my feet, took a step toward him, hesitated—which was a mistake—and then stopped. Because I'd hesitated, I now had no choice. King's mouth was bleeding but not badly. He looked dazed, but I had failed to knock him unconscious and he was still holding the pistol. He had fired five times since I had surfaced. If he had reloaded a full six rounds, he still had one round left. And now he was so close that it was unlikely he would miss again.

"You motherfucker," he croaked, holding his broken jaw with his left hand. "You don't feel so goddamn smart now, do you?"

No, I did not. I felt ridiculous and vulnerable, standing there in shorts, knowing that I had failed once again, and that I was about to be shot by a loser like King—shot for the first time, because I could see no blood when I glanced down at my belly. King was using a small-caliber pistol, though, and it would take more than one round to stop me unless he put a bullet through my head.

It was another one of those moments—perhaps my last. King would pull the trigger and drop me or within seconds I would have my hands on him and that would be the end of him. Either way, I wasn't going to stop now.

I took a step toward him, saying, "Go ahead. But you'd better hit me in the heart," and I watched him scoot backward on his butt.

I took another step, as King extended his arm, and I watched him squint one eye closed to fire. But before I could dive for him and before he could pull the trigger, we both heard a rustling noise in the shadows that caused us to pause. King's eyes swiveled, I turned. We watched a person I recognized step into the circle of firelight. He was sighting down the barrel of the Winchester rifle, taking careful aim at King.

"I don't want to kill you," he told King. "But I will."

THIRTY

WHEN KING SWUNG THE LIGHT AWAY FROM Will Chaser and they heard a man screaming for help somewhere out there on the lake, Tomlinson said to Arlis Futch, not bothering to whisper, "That's not Doc. That's not Doc's voice."

Arlis, who was using a cypress stave for support because he felt so sick, took a moment to listen before he replied, "How can you be so sure? It doesn't even sound human to me."

After another moment, though, Arlis's voice brightened, as he added, "Know who I think that is? I think it's that bastard Perry. That skinny Yankee scum rifle-whipped me—and his partner *kicked* me when I was down. What do you think? Maybe that dragon's got him?"

Using the walking stick, Arlis limped out of the shadows and peered toward the lake, before he said softly, "My God Aw'mighty. That devil's finally getting his due."

Tomlinson didn't allow himself to look. He was focused on Will, watching the teenager while his brain translated the boy's behavior into patterns of thought and motive. Will was on his knees now, the knife in his right hand, his eyes following King as he jogged toward the lake and away from the generator, where the Winchester rifle was braced at an angle—maybe loaded, maybe not.

Tomlinson didn't know anything about guns, but he could see the boy's head swiveling, gauging the distance, and he knew what was in the boy's mind because Tomlinson could feel rage emanating from Will's body, a rage that appeared as a red aura, the most potent and dangerous shade in the auric spectrum. Tomlinson had witnessed the phenomenon before, but only rarely—and usually in his friend, Doc Ford.

Tomlinson called to the boy, "Will! Stay here with Arlis. I'm going to try and find Doc."

The boy was crawling toward the generator now but paused long enough to say over his shoulder, "Instead of spying on me, you should open your eyes. Doc's right out there, swimming for shore."

As Tomlinson moved, trying to see, he heard a gunshot . . . then another . . . and then Tomlinson could see Doc, with his hands up, marching toward the beach fire with one of the convicts behind him pointing

something at his back. It was a pistol, Tomlinson
guessed, although he wasn't close enough to see. But
then his senses sharpened when, abruptly, the screaming
coming from the lake stopped, and Tomlinson thought,
*That must be King. He's got a gun and he's going to
kill Doc.*

Tomlinson knew he had to do something, but more
than Doc's life was at stake. In a way, Will Chaser's life
was on the line, too. It had been gutsy for the boy to
lie so still while King painted him with the flashlight—it
was, in fact, a chilling display of nerve and self-control
that few people possessed. Tomlinson didn't doubt
Will's courage, but he feared what might happen if Will
got his hands on that gun. In Tomlinson's mind, the boy
was teetering between two worlds—the worlds of darkness and light. Will's ancestors hadn't gifted them with
a tour of the ancient underworld just to turn the boy
into a stone-cold killer . . . or had they?

The possibility was disturbing to consider, and it gave
Tomlinson pause.

There had been violence done in the lizard's den—
and death, too—violence and darkness that dated back
centuries. The aura was there, among the bones and pottery and flint-sharp spear points. And there was no mistaking the scent of death.

It was a realization that made Tomlinson decide to do
something he seldom had the nerve to do. He knew he
had to intercede. He didn't often jump in the path of
karma, but sometimes God helped those who helped

themselves, and this might be one of those times because the kimchee was really about to hit the fan.

Will saved my ass at least twice, Tomlinson thought.
It's about time I save his.

He stood. His eyes were still on Will as he turned to
Arlis and said, "Stay here with the boy. I'm going after
Doc."

Arlis replied, "I hope you grab that Winchester instead of your cell phone," but Tomlinson didn't hear
him because he was already running, sprinting hard, trying to beat Will to the generator because he was up and
running now, too.

Using the cypress stave to hop toward the campfire,
Arlis Futch was thinking, *I hope the boy's got that rifle, not
Tomlinson. Tomlinson will get us all killed. We'd all be
better off if my finger was on that trigger.*

Arlis could see the shadows of the hippie and the boy
creeping up behind the pickup truck, getting closer to
the fire, but he couldn't make out details. He could no
longer see Ford and King, either. The truck blocked his
view.

Fifteen yards from the truck, Arlis had to stop for a
moment to rest. He didn't want to do it, but he had to
because he felt like he might pass out unless he got some
air, and the throbbing headache had started beating
again in his temples. It was the ground-glass pain, which
told him his brain might explode if he kept going. Worse

was the burning sensation in his veins, circulating through his body, making him sick and sleepy. It was poison, Arlis knew, from the lizard, which was a piss-poor way for a Florida boy to die after all the years he had spent hunting the Everglades.

Arlis thought, *I've got to get my hands on that by God Winchester before I fall out.*

He had started hopping toward the truck again when he heard *WHAP!*, a gunshot. Then he could hear the wild sounds of men fighting—a distinctive, out-of-control yelling, plus the *smack* of flesh hitting flesh. It was familiar to Arlis, having witnessed many fights around the docks, and he had been in a few himself. He began to hobble faster, thinking, *Doc's probably not much of a fighter, but King's a coward so who knows?*

As Arlis drew closer to the truck, though, he could see that Doc had done okay. King was sitting flat on his ass, with his mouth bleeding, and his face looked crooked like maybe his jaw was busted. Doc hadn't done a complete job of it, though, because King was still holding that little bitty pistol of his and it was pointing at Doc's chest.

Arlis started to call out a warning but then caught himself because he saw Tomlinson and Will Chaser step out of the shadows and into the firelight, and their intentions were plain. They had done a good job of sneaking up, but now instead of just shooting that son of a bitch King when they had the chance they were going to confront him.

As the two moved closer to the fire, Arlis understood why.

He was thinking, *God Aw'mighty, we're in trouble now.*

It was Tomlinson who had the Winchester.

As the hippie leveled the rifle at King, Arlis Futch hurried to catch up before Tomlinson did something stupid or before the hippie's nerve failed them all.

THIRTY-ONE

WHEN TOMLINSON STEPPED CLOSE ENOUGH to the fire for both of us to see him, I hoped that King didn't recognize the uncertainty in my friend's voice when he said, "I don't want to kill you. But I will."

It was a shock to see Tomlinson after so many hours—and I was relieved, of course—but he wasn't the man I would have chosen to come walking out of the shadows with a gun. Tomlinson was *Tomlinson*. He was the life-long advocate of passive resistance, the prophet of peace, love, harmony and goodwill toward men. There was no doubt that Tomlinson didn't want to kill King. But did he even have the nerve to pull the trigger? And if he did, what were the chances that he also had the resolve to fire a second time if he missed? As far as I knew, Tomlinson had never fired a weapon in his life, yet he stood there somberly with the Winchester pressed against his left cheek as if he meant to do it.

I took a step back from King, who was still pointing the pistol at me, and I said, "Let's all calm down now. This doesn't have to happen. King? Toss the pistol away. Your partner's dead, but that doesn't mean you have to die, too."

I had observed panic in King's face when Tomlinson first appeared, but now I saw the convict's brain working as he studied him. Tomlinson's long hair was sticky with mud, a sleeve from his wet suit was missing. He looked pale and shaky in the firelight, about as unimposing as a scarecrow with a toy rifle. King's reaction was no surprise, nor was the finesse he attempted next.

Looking from me to Tomlinson, King said, "I think we've got ourselves a misunderstanding. I got no intentions of shooting Dr. Ford. You're wrong about that. This business isn't as serious as you think—it doesn't have to be, anyway."

I was thinking, *Pull the trigger . . . Pull the damn trigger,* hoping for once that it was true that Tomlinson could read my thoughts. If he engaged King in conversation, I knew what King would probably do. He would use it as an opening to put his last round into Tomlinson and then race me for the rifle.

Tomlinson didn't pick up on my message, though, because he answered King, saying, "I'm glad to hear that. Lose that gun, brother, and we'll talk. Talking's always better. This killing-each-other bullshit is wrong, man, really *wrong*." There was a pleading quality in his tone that boosted King's confidence.

Now I was thinking, *Don't let him do it!* as King swung the pistol toward Tomlinson and then showed him a crooked smile with his broken jaw, which added a painful articulateness to his speech. "No . . . *you* put the rifle down first. You seem like a reasonable sort of dude. Personally, man, I hate violence. In fact, toss that rifle into the bushes, just to be safe. I'll do the same—*I promise*. Then you can work it out with the King."

Tomlinson sounded confused, asking, "The King?"

"Me," King told him. "I bet you're an Elvis fan, too. Aren't you, now? Admit it."

Tomlinson lost his concentration and lifted his cheek away from the rifle stock long enough to say, "Sure, man—'the King,' I get it. We've got that in common. So why are you still pointing that gun at me?"

King said it again, "You toss the rifle away first—and hurry up before my finger slips." He motioned with the pistol toward the shadows, telling Tomlinson that's where he should toss the Winchester.

I was aware of movement behind Tomlinson. It was Will Chaser, I realized, who was circling into position behind the convict. King noticed him, too, and appeared startled, saying, "Hey, you—*kid*! Stop right where you are."

His voice flat, Will answered, "I don't think so," and he continued walking until King was unable to see him without taking his eyes off Tomlinson—a risk he couldn't take.

King snapped, "Get back here where I can see you or I'll put a bullet through your sugar daddy's head."

Tomlinson said, *"Hey, now,"* sounding offended, as Will surprised us all by stepping close enough to the fire to flash a knife in the yellow light and saying, "Mister, if you pull that trigger, I'll cut your goddamn throat."

Will's voice was spooky calm. It was a chilling voice to hear, which caused King to glance at the boy again in reassessment, his eyes widening with concern, then a growing panic. He tried to scoot away to reposition himself so he could see Tomlinson and Will both, but the pile of blazing driftwood was behind him and he couldn't get the angle right because Will continued to circle.

"I'm not going to warn you again," King told him, focusing only on Tomlinson now.

From the shadows, Will replied, "Then go ahead and do it, mister. I've never been too fond of hippies, anyway," and he began walking toward King.

Now King had a trapped expression on his face. It was the look of an animal that's been cornered. And as he steadied the gun, getting ready to fire, I took one long step and then dived for the man because I knew there was no more talking. For an instant, King hesitated, trying to decide whether to shoot me or the guy with the rifle, then he leaned toward Tomlinson and fired.

WHAP! WHAP!

My hands found King's throat as my body slammed into his, deafened by two simultaneous gunshots. King was writhing beneath me. But he wasn't fighting back, I realized, and I became aware there was blood on me—blood on my hands and on my chest. As I pinned the man's gun hand to the ground, I understood the source of the blood: A chunk of King's left hand was missing. I saw a bleeding black hole, like a spike had been driven through it.

I slapped the pistol away, not sure it was empty, not sure of anything, in all the noise and confusion, until I turned and saw Tomlinson. My friend's face was pale, but he appeared unhurt, standing there with the rifle at waist level, and he said to me, sounding dazed, "Are you okay, Doc? Did I kill him?"

Will Chaser was hovering over me, a dive knife gripped in his right hand, ready to pile on if I needed help, but I pushed him away to give myself room, saying, "It's okay. Get back," and then I stood, my ears numb to King's cursing. He was rolling on the ground, clutching his disfigured hand and yelling, "You shot me! You shot *the King*, you worthless ass-wipe!"

Tomlinson took a step toward the man, as if wanting to help, and asked me again, "Where did I hit him? Is he going to die?"

Speaking over the noise, I said, "No. He'll be okay. You hit him in the hand. Did you *mean* to?" and then I knelt and picked up the pistol. I popped the clip—the chamber was empty—so I tossed the gun to Will as I skirted the fire and put my hand on Tomlinson's shoulder. His eyes were fixated on King, and I gave him a little shake. "You did good," I told him. "Relax. You won't have to shoot him again. I promise. Give me the rifle."

Tomlinson appeared to be in shock. His fingers were frozen on the weapon, and, as I began to unwrap the Winchester from his hands, he asked me. "Are you sure? Because I *would* do it. I'd pull the trigger again if I had to."

I looked around, seeing Arlis Futch now limping toward us and Will Chaser, too. Staring at Will, I said to Tomlinson, "There's no need for that. You're right. Killing's just wrong, man. Let's get out of here."

My eyes moved to Arlis, who was glaring at King. "Doc?" he said. "That's the Yankee spawn who kicked me like a dog. Why don't you boys walk on back to the truck and find your telephones? I'll stand watch on this snake." The old man's eyes found mine as he added, "Any rounds left in that Winchester?"

From old habit, I had checked the breech immediately. "There's one round left, Arlis," I replied, "but you're not going to use it. What happened to your leg?"

"That by God lizard bit me."

"One of the small ones attacked you?"

"They tried, but it was that big bastard! It took a chunk out but not too bad. I'd be okay to stand watch over this scum. Seriously, Doc. Let me hold that rifle. He *kicked* me, Doc."

It was sickening to hear that the monitor had bitten Arlis after we had dodged so many other near tragedies. I knew that we had to get the man to a hospital, fast.

I said, "I understand how you feel—the guy slapped

me around, too. But we're going to let the police deal with this"—I glanced at Will again—"because that's the way things work."

I was tempted to eject the last remaining cartridge onto the ground, but the Komodo monitor was still in the area, and so were its offspring, possibly watching us right now from the shadows. Night stalkers and meat eaters should never be underestimated. I learned that truth while hiding on the bottom of the lake . . . And I learned something else, too. I learned how monitors responded to infrared light.

It gave me an idea.

To Will I said, "Would you mind getting that for me?" as I pointed to my dive mask, which lay on the far side of the fire.

Tomlinson was helping Arlis hobble toward the truck as Will handed me the heavy mask, with its pointed rail and monocular tube. I bounced the weight of the thing in my hand for a thoughtful moment before I handed Will the Winchester, telling him, "You go with Tomlinson and Arlis, okay? Find our cell phones. Captain Futch needs to be airlifted or he's going to lose that leg. Maybe worse."

I didn't want the kid around to see what I was going to do next. He was smart enough to recognize false compassion for what it was—a lethal bait.

Will Chaser was staring at me, his expression suspicious. "And leave you alone with this asshole? Just the two of you, huh?" With his chin, he gestured toward King, who was sitting up now, trying to flex his wounded hand. The bleeding wasn't too bad, I noted.

I told Will, "Oh, I get it—you want proof I'm not going to kill him." The boy knew things intuitively, he had claimed, which implied that he knew about me.

"I didn't say that," Will replied.

"But that's what you're thinking—but why would I risk something so stupid?" I was inspecting the face mask, which appeared to be undamaged. I switched on the infrared light and confirmed that it still threw its invisible beam straight and true.

"Maybe Tomlinson was right," I added. "Maybe we are a lot alike. How about this? Why don't we *both* help Arlis back to the truck? If he loses that leg, we don't want the rest of him to go with it."

"And leave this guy all alone?" Will said, still unconvinced. With his expression asking *Why are you going so easy on this jerk?*

I replied, "He's not going anywhere. He knows how dangerous it is out here in the sticks." I turned. "Don't you, King?"

The man was on one knee, trying to use his jacket as a bandage, but he stopped long enough to glare at me and say, "Go to hell."

I was thinking, *You'll get there before me,* as I double-checked to make sure the infrared light was on and then lobbed the mask close to King's feet. His surprised expression caused me to smile, as I added, "No hard feelings, partner. When that fire burns down and you get scared? You can always use my night vision to see—*Jock-o.*"

And so would the monitors.

EPILOGUE

ON A BALMY, MOON-BRIGHT NIGHT IN FEBRU-
ary, one week after Arlis Futch was airlifted to the hospital and four days after police finally located King, I was
on the deck outside my lab trying to bracket a camera to
my new telescope when I heard the familiar two-stroke
rattle of Tomlinson's dinghy. I covered the Celestron
with a towel, let the screen door slam behind me and
went inside to fetch a fresh quart of beer.

Tomlinson prefers beer from the bottle. I like mine
over ice—an old habit from years of traveling the tropics. We would compromise: most of the quart for him, a
mug for me. It was Tuesday night, long after sunset, so
there wasn't much doubt he would be thirsty.

Tomlinson had been away. On Friday night—an hour
after police confirmed that they had found King—he

had left aboard *No Más* on the flood, motoring to the mouth of Dinkin's Bay before setting his mainsail, which suggested to me that the man was upset and in a hurry. In a hurry to where, there was no telling.

Who knows where Tomlinson goes? Key West is a favorite, but a four-day trip wouldn't have allowed him much time on Duval Street. And the same was true of Pensacola, another of his favorite haunts. So I had guessed Sarasota—he likes the public anchorage there, possibly because so many pretty girls jog in the park— and he likes Venice Beach, too, for the same reason, and also because there's a nightly drum circle nearby.

It made for interesting speculation among the fishing guides and live-aboards, but no one truly knew. We hadn't heard a word from the man since Friday night, which was not unusual. When Tomlinson leaves, he leaves. There are no phone calls, no postcards saying *Wish you were here*.

"You're not really sailing unless you let go of all the lines," the man is fond of saying.

For me, it had been a productive few days. I had done my version of a Tomlinson escape, which is to say I hadn't left the island, and I had rarely left my lab. I read books I had been meaning to read, I worked out twice a day on my new VersaClimber, then swam to the NO WAKE buoy off West Wind Hotel. I listened to my short-wave radio at night, or I enjoyed the marvels of my new Celestron. And I awoke each morning *alone*.

Because the quarter moon was waxing, I was stuck with neap tides, which aren't good for collecting by hand, so I had spent two evenings and part of a day dragging for specimens in my old twenty-four-foot flat-bottomed trawl boat.

Stenciled neatly on the stern of the craft is the name of my little company, SANIBEL BIOLOGICAL SUPPLY. It is built of cypress planking and duct tape. The trawler is equipped with nets and outriggers, which must be hand-cranked when lowered or raised, but it's a ceremony of which I never tire. No matter how many times I drop the trawls, I still feel a pleasant treasure hunter's anticipation when I pop the strings and dump the nets because a small, secret universe comes spilling out onto the deck. There, alive at my feet, are tunicates, sea horses, cowfish, catfish, pinfish, filefish, eels, shrimp, sea trout and sting-rays—a flopping, throbbing mound of life among the sea grasses and hydroids. As I do the culling, rushing to pre-serve or release each creature, I am reminded that the universe beneath us is wild and alive—*relentlessly* alive—despite the outrages, the small kindnesses, the small wars and the brief, brief lives that stumble on blindly above.

In other words, I did what I wanted to do, when I wanted to do it. In further words, I got a hell of a lot more done because Tomlinson wasn't around to interrupt my lab procedures or lure me away from the instruments of my craft and a solitude of my own choosing.

That doesn't mean I resented his arrival, though, on this soft winter night. It was hours before moonset. Coupling the camera—a Canon 5d—onto the telescope had gone smoothly enough, and I was getting thirsty myself.

The solar system could wait. Tomlinson and I had a lot to talk about.

I was using one foot to push the screen door open, beer in hand, when I felt his dinghy nudge the pilings of my home and then I heard him call, "Hello, the house! Can I come aboard?"

I replied, "Since when did you start asking?"

"I'm changing my ways, Doc, I mean it," he hollered. "This is a whole fresh start for me," and then I heard his bare feet slapping the steps.

I placed the bottle on the little teak table next to the railing, then returned to the galley for a block of Gorgonzola cheese and Colombian hot sauce.

"Again?" I said over my shoulder.

Two quarts of beer and a jar of salsa later, Tomlinson was saying to me, "I don't know why I did it, Doc. It wasn't her fault, it was mine. I got Barbara a little drunk, I followed her home on my bike. She was pissed off for some reason or another . . . Hell, who knows. Will was on the beach, we knew he wouldn't be back, and one thing led to another. Man, oh man, I don't know what gets into me sometimes." He shook his head, his voice shy with remorse, and he looked at his toes as if they held the answer to some inexorable secret.

I said, "What gets into *you* isn't the problem, Tomlinson. There are only about five or six nonnegotiable rules in life and seducing a pal's girlfriend breaks at least three of them."

"Valid point," he nodded.

"We're not debating, we're discussing the women I date. Plural, because this wasn't the first time it happened—no, don't deny it. Just because I never mentioned it doesn't mean I'm unaware. And what kind of example does that set for Will? He's a sharp kid. He doesn't miss much."

Tomlinson lifted his head, concerned. "Do you think he knows?"

The wind gusted, and I got a whiff of patchouli and cannabis as I replied, "If they let him come back to Florida, ask him."

I was speaking of Oklahoma Social Services. Using her political clout, Barbara Hayes had petitioned some board to allow Will to return to Sanibel on a work-study program, with her serving as temporary guardian. His grades were so poor and he'd already missed so much school that it seemed a reasonable proposal. The work would include helping us map the wreckage of Batista's gold plane and possibly—*possibly*—salvaging the manifest—all under the guise of marine science of course. But that now, too, involved politics. Cuba's people had already lost too much of their wealth to thievery, and Arlis's instincts had been right from the start about intervention from attorneys.

That didn't mean we wouldn't be able to dive the lake we were now referring to as Lost River. We would. And if the few coins I had seen were an indicator, Will Chaser's share would be more than enough to pay for college. The rest of us would bank sizable sums as well, even if we had to work it on some kind of shared-percentage deal. But much of the timing depended on Barbara Hayes's jockeying and also on the progress Arlis Futch was making at the hospital. He had lost his leg to what tests determined was the bacterium *Pasteurella multocida,* but the reptile's blood-thinning venom may have in fact prevented Arlis from suffering a fatal stroke during what he himself described as "the by God scariest moment of my life."

For me, information on Barbara's progress wasn't easy to come by. Our relationship had turned frosty, which was not unexpected. Because it's rare, in my experience with Tomlinson, to be in a position of moral superiority, I didn't want to let him off the hook now by confessing that I had been as unfaithful to Barbara as she had been to me. Technically, Tomlinson hadn't done anything wrong because Barbara had every right to do whatever she wanted, considering my own infidelities. I'm a hypocrite, I admit it. But now was not the time to admit it to Tomlinson.

"I feel like hell," he said. "What I did was in my mind the whole time that Will-Joseph and I were trapped down in those vents. My last dying thoughts, I'm saying, which is a very heavy tribute to you. Doc"—he paused to load a wedge of cheese with hot sauce—"Doc, I will never make a cuckold of you again."

I said, *"What?"* even though I knew what the word meant. "You've been hanging out with Brits, I can tell. Where'd you disappear to?"

"I anchored off the shrimp docks at Fort Myers

Beach. It's still Old Florida down there, man. Fisher-man's Wharf, Hansen's Shrimp Packing—a good place for a rum bar, that's what I think. There was a group of British officers on some kind of exchange program at the Coast Guard Station. There were these three young en-signs who'd never been to the States before, so I sort of felt like it was my duty to show them around."

"All female," I said flatly. "Very patriotic of you."

"Your sensory powers just keep getting better and better." Tomlinson smiled, nodding his approval. "But I would've invited them to stay aboard *No Más* even if they weren't. I like Brits, that accent just knocks me out. And they were fun—once they loosened their buttons a little and let their hair down."

I was shaking my head, but the man was oblivious. Or maybe he wasn't, because he quickly changed the subject to the fate of the Komodo monitor and its offspring.

"What's the news from your biologist pals in Talla-hassee?" he asked.

There had been very little news until biologists, sent by the Florida Wildlife Commission and the Florida In-vasive Animal Task Team, had finally confirmed the ex-istence of Komodo monitors living in and around the lake.

They had managed to catch one of the small lizards, but their efforts didn't get serious until police stumbled upon the giant female while combing the area for King. That had happened Friday afternoon, so Tomlinson already knew the details—most of the details, anyway—

because he had been there. But he hadn't heard the latest.

Tomlinson and I had returned to the lake with an archaeologist from the University of Florida—Dr. Bill Walker—to do a preliminary survey of the cave that he and Will had found. By one p.m., the three of us had cut our way to the mound, unaware of what police were dealing with only a quarter mile away.

I had assigned myself the uneasy task of standing watch as Dr. Bill lowered a camera into the cave and then used a special low-light lens and a remote shutter control to snap more than a hundred blind photos.

"I'll let you know if we have anything," he had told us, "when I get back to the house and download them on the computer."

A quick photo survey was the best we could do, under the circumstances. I wasn't going down into that damn cave—or into the lake—until the area was secured, and Tomlinson agreed. We had already done enough research to know that, while Komodos usually reproduce sexually, they can also reproduce asexually through a process called *parthenogenesis*. Unfertilized eggs hatch as an all-male brood, which is evolution's way of guaranteeing that a lone female Komodo can repopulate a remote island in Indonesia . . . or the remote pasturelands of Florida.

Judging from the size of the monitor that attacked me, she could have lived near the lake for a long, long time—more than fifty years, I believed. It wasn't a guess, and I didn't arrive at the figure simply because two generations of ranchers had made the creature into a family legend. Something that Arlis had told me about Fulgencio Batista had put me on the right track. I asked friends in Cuba to do the research, and it was from them I learned that in December of 1958 two fledgling Komodo monitors had vanished from the Havana zoo. My own research confirmed that the animals can live and reproduce for more than seven decades.

At least one of the fledglings had survived a plane crash on a December night long ago. Now there was no telling how many Komodos were stalking the area, and I, for one, didn't relax until we were safely in my truck, headed for Sanibel.

Because Tomlinson had sailed on that Friday evening, though, he had yet to see Dr. Bill's photos. I knew that's why he had come straight to the lab after returning to Dinkin's Bay.

I replied to Tomlinson's question by telling him, "They haven't caught the big female yet, if that's what you're asking. And they haven't killed her, either, although police could have. They decided that a reptile her size might be of interest to science, so they cordoned off the area until biologists figure out a way to trap her. Or use some kind of tranquilizer gun. Personally, I'm glad she's still alive. It should make you happy, too. Maybe that will change your attitude about cops a little."

Tomlinson shrugged, smiled and said, "I've always been against slaying my personal dragons. It's more interesting to get aboard and enjoy the ride. The view's better, too." He sent me a message by holding his quart bottle up to the moon so that I could see that it was empty. I also noticed something else.

"What happened to my watch?" I asked him as I stood. I had more beer in the fridge, and there was a stack of Dr. Bill's photos on the kitchen table, too.

Tomlinson replied, "I gave the Chronofighter to Will, man. I figured I owed him something—the kid saved my life, after all. Besides, I found this really cool surfer dive watch that fits me better. It's called a Bathys—" He stopped in midsentence, finally realizing what I had just said. "What do you mean, *your* watch?"

I stared at the man until he sought refuge in his toes again. "You know about that, too, huh?"

I said, "I may not have a dazzling intellect, but I don't miss much, either."

"*Jesus*, Ford," he whispered, looking up at me. "You're getting a little too good at this. Not that I don't think . . . not that I don't really *believe* . . . you have a first-rate intellect—"

"Forget it," I said, mystified by his reaction. I patted the man's shoulder, went into the galley and returned with two more quarts of beer, plus a single photograph from the stack on the table. I placed a bottle near Tomlinson's elbow but held on to the photo until I had asked, "Back there by the fire, when you shot King, you never answered my question. Did you mean to shoot him in the hand? If you did, that was one hell of a shot. Have you ever fired a rifle before in your life?"

Tomlinson opened his beer and sat back. Then he

took several long gulps, as if working up the courage to say, "That's why I sailed out of here Friday night, Doc. After the police called and told us about King, I just couldn't stand it, being around people I care about—people who see me as something . . . I don't know . . . something special. I'm not, Doc. You know that better than anyone. I'm nothing special. I'm an asshole and I'm a fraud."

I nodded. "Well, you're at least half right—in my opinion, anyway."

Tomlinson looked at me for a moment and managed to chuckle before he turned away. "And I'm a shitty shot, too. I wasn't aiming at King's hand. I wanted to kill the man. I thought I was aiming right at his heart, but I must have flinched or closed my eyes or something because I missed. But I meant to do it. I meant to kill him."

I nodded, and gave it more time than was required to reply, "King fired his last round at you, but you still feel guilty? That doesn't make a hell of a lot of sense, pal."

"You're right," Tomlinson said, missing my point. "Killing another human being never makes any sense. But that's what I did. And that's what happened. I killed King just as sure as if I'd hit him in the heart. When we left him alone by the fire, with his hand bleeding, man . . ." Tomlinson cleared his throat, getting emotional. "It was the same as staking out a wounded lamb. I knew that. And I knew there was a lion in the area."

I leaned and placed the photo on my friend's lap. Then I stood to hit the deck lights so Tomlinson could confirm the details for himself. As I walked away, I said, "When Dr. Bill downloaded the photos and saw what he had, he e-mailed the picture you're holding straight to the police. When they called Friday night? That picture is how they found King. That's how they knew for sure what happened to him."

I added, "But you didn't kill the man, pal. You're looking at the proof. It was his decision to run—not yours."

I watched Tomlinson study the photo, familiar with what he was seeing because I had examined the image so many times. The photo showed a section of a rock room where roots connected ceiling and floor. In the deep, deep shadows of the room, beneath what looked like a cave petroglyph—a stick man with horns—lay a portion of a human skull, the broken jaw grinning up at the wide-angle lens.

Next to the skull was my night vision monocular. The camera's unfiltered photocells had captured something that was invisible to us but not to other predators. The infrared light was still on, throwing a beam that was straight as an arrow and true.

BLACK WIDOW

FROM *NEW YORK TIMES* BESTSELLING AUTHOR

Randy Wayne White

Doc Ford is drawn into a deadly battle when his god-daughter Shay is blackmailed. Someone filmed her at an out-of-control bachelorette party—and they want big money to keep it quiet. When Ford investigates, he finds that the woman responsible is an agent of corruption unlike any Ford has ever encountered before. And she may be the last encounter he ever has.

HUNTER'S MOON
by RANDY WAYNE WHITE

Doc Ford saves a former President of the United States from assassination—and regrets it. Months ago, Kal Wilson's wife was killed in a plane crash. President Wilson is sure it was no accident, and he wants revenge. He needs Doc Ford to spring him loose from the watchful eye of the Secret Service, keep him alive, then get him home. Ford has just been picked for presidential duty—whether he likes it or not.

> "Randy Wayne White takes us places that no other Florida mystery writer can hope to find."
> —Carl Hiaasen

> "Complex and emotionally charged."
> —*Sarasota Herald-Tribune*

> "Brisk, tense, and tightly wrought."
> —*The Miami Herald*

> "The plot is twisted."
> —*St. Petersburg Times*

penguin.com